To honor

Dr. Robert J. Wickenheiser

and his installation in 1977

as President of

Mount Saint Mary's College,

Emmitsburg, Maryland

holdings in the area of English

have been strengthened

through the gift of

Mr. Robert H. Taylor

of Princeton, New Jersey.

SERAPHITA

HONORÉ DE BALZAC

TRANSLATED BY

KATHARINE PRESCOTT WORMELEY

SERAPHITA

WITH AN INTRODUCTION

BY

GEORGE FREDERIC PARSONS

Short S·ory Index Reprint Series

BOOKS FOR LIBRARIES PRESS
A Division of Arno Press, Inc.
New York, New York

First Published 1889
Reprinted 1970

INTERNATIONAL STANDARD BOOK NUMBER:
0-8369-3691-4

LIBRARY OF CONGRESS CATALOG CARD NUMBER:
73-134961

PRINTED IN THE UNITED STATES OF AMERICA

CONTENTS.

INTRODUCTION.

It is highly probable that " Seraphita " cost its author
more than any other of his intellectual offspring. The
evidence of this appears in his correspondence. Writing
to Madame Zulma Carraud in January, 1834, he says,
" Seraphita is a work more severe than any other upon
the writer." What he thought of it may be gathered
from another passage in the same letter, in which he
speaks of it as " a work as much beyond ' Louis Lambert' as ' Louis Lambert' is beyond ' Gaudissart.' "
As he proceeded with it his labor became more intense.
In March, 1835, writing to the Duchesse de Castries,
he says : " The toil upon this work has been crushing
and terrible. I have passed, and must still pass, days
and nights upon it. I compose, decompose, and recom-
pose it." He did not delude himself as to the kind of
reception it was likely to encounter : " In a few days,"
he observes, " all will have been said. Either I shall
have won fame or the Parisians will have failed to
understand me. And inasmuch as, with them, mockery
commonly takes the place of understanding, I can hope
only for a remote and tardy success. Eventually appre-
ciation will come, and at once here and there. For the

rest, I think this book will be a favorite with those souls
that like to lose themselves in the spaces of infinity."

There is a legend to the effect that Balzac first conceived the idea embodied in " Seraphita " while contemplating a beautiful sculptured figure of an angel in the
studio of a friend.   It is possible that he himself may
have made this statement, for he was fond of picturesque
and dramatic incidents, and might easily have ascribed
to a trivial occurrence a significance greater than it was
entitled to.   The true genesis of this, perhaps the most
remarkable and unquestionably the most elevated work
of fiction ever written, is fortunately not doubtful, for
the proofs are in the book itself.   " Seraphita " is the
natural crowning flower of that philosophic exposition
begun in the " Peau de Chagrin," and developed so
much more fully in " Louis Lambert."   The latter work
moreover may be said both to have adumbrated and
necessitated " Seraphita ; " and it is proper to state here
that whoever wishes to grasp the full meaning of this
book must first read " Louis Lambert," which intro-
duces and to a considerable extent explains the present
work.   The profound system embodied in the oracular
fragments which fell from the lips of the rapt young
sage, and were taken down and preserved by the faithful and clear-sighted Pauline contains the interpretation
of the marvellous being Balzac's genius has set in that
most harmonious and appropriate frame of the Northern
skies and snow-covered plains, frozen fiords and black,
ice-clad mountains.   Indeed there is nothing more
striking in this masterpiece than the beauty and ex-

quisite taste of its setting. Theophile Gautier without
exaggeration styles it "one of the most astonishing
productions of modern literature;" and proceeds:
"Never did Balzac approach, in fact almost seize, the
very Ideal of Beauty as in this book: the ascent of the
mountain has in it something ethereal, supernatural,
luminous, which lifts one above the earth. The only
colors employed are the blue of heaven and the pure
white of the snow, with some pearly tints for the
shadows. We know nothing more ravishing than this
opening."

It is all true. Nowhere have Balzac's artistic delicacy and spiritual subtlety been so victoriously employed as in the conception and execution of "Seraphita." There is no change in it from lower to higher
regions. The author launches himself like an eagle
from a cliff, high upon the bosom of the loftier atmosphere, and his powerful wings sustain him to the end at
an elevation which enables the reader to separate himself with facility from the existence of vulgar commonplace, if it does not help him to respire easily in air so
rarefied as to be scarcely adequate to the expansion of
gross and fleshly lungs. To Balzac himself, whose versatility and sympathetic range were almost as broad
and deep as those of Nature, this final flight of his
philosophical and theosophical exposition was painful
and laborious. Like Nature he could compass all forms
of existence, but, like Nature too, he was most at home
in the free working of tangible matter. In the "Com-
édie Humaine" he had however undertaken to picture

and to analyze life as it existed in his period, and to him this meant all life, from the lowest to the highest. Shakspeare is the only other writer who shows the same marvellous breadth of scope ; to whom every state and condition of humanity is sympathetic ; who sees into and apprehends every form of existence ; who can put himself in the place equally of the outcast and the saint, — the soul black with sin and shame, and the soul white with good deeds and noble aspirations. These two, Balzac and Shakspeare, have in common the qualities which most emphatically denote the highest form of genius. Among those qualities the precious endowment of Intuition ranks perhaps the highest. It is this mysterious and magical gift which explains the influence upon the human mind of the few great souls — Specialists, as Louis Lambert styles them — that have appeared at long intervals through the ages and have left their mark upon generations and centuries.

Louis Lambert declares that Jesus Christ was a Specialist, and the interpretation of this is that he possessed the power of striking that chord which vibrates in all hearts, of embodying in words those thoughts whose expression appeals to the largest audience and awakes the deepest and purest emotions. The great Mother of us all, from whom we proceed, in whose bosom we must lie, has the same characteristics, the same fecundity, elasticity, comprehensiveness, and sympathy. Jesus, indeed, came at a time when there was little laughter in the world. Life was very stern and grim when Rome was the mistress of the known habitable globe. It could

hardly have been deemed worth living if measured by
modern gauges. As in the time of Gautama Buddha, five
centuries before, the central problem was the wretchedness of existence. We who, surrounded by the comforts
and luxuries of the nineteenth century, stand perplexed
at the dark and gloomy views which those old races
seem to have held in so matter-of-course a way, fail
sufficiently to realize the actual pressure of misery upon
the great majority of human beings at those periods.
In sad truth, life was to them a painful puzzle. They
were not, like us, chiefly occupied in determining how
best to employ it and derive from it the greatest happiness or usefulness. Most of them were born into conditions escape from which was hopeless and continuance
in which was intolerable. They were helpless and they
suffered. What wonder if they looked bewildered to
the unanswering sky, questioned the dumb face of
Nature, and lost themselves in sombre speculations as
to the why and wherefore of their existence, and the
causes of the seemingly purposeless chain of being. To
them deliverance from incarnation was the first requisite
of a rational gospel ; and this deliverance was offered,
though in different ways, by the two great Teachers
whose wisdom and promises have been respectively the
Light of Asia and of Christendom.

To understand " Seraphita " it is necessary to take a
somewhat wide preliminary survey. We must begin by
fixing in our minds the scheme of evolution which it is
intended to illustrate and to carry to its farthest mundane development, while projecting the vision even

beyond this point, and foreshadowing the outlines of a higher and an incorporeal state of existence. Human destiny, according to this theory, is a painful course of elevation and emancipation ; a working out of what we call Matter into what we call Spirit, — but which really is merely different conditions of one primal substance. There are three worlds : the Material, the Spiritual, and the Divine. These three worlds must be traversed in turn by the souls of men, which in these journeyings must pass through three stages, namely the Instinctive, the Abstractive, and the Specialist. Now the soul is guided on its way and raised gradually by the influence of Love. First, Self-Love stimulates and urges it onward and upward until the clogging stagnation of Savagery is escaped, and progress toward Barbarism and thence to what is now termed Civilization, is secured. Second, the love of others, Altruism, supersedes Self-Love in the most advanced men and women, and then the time is ripe for the establishment of those great religions which in their infancy, when the central doctrine is pure and fresh and full of magnetism, sways peoples and countries so powerfully, and changes the direction of the age. It is Altruism which has produced all the highest and noblest works the human race possesses to-day. It is that which is at the root of Duty, Honor, Faithfulness, Loyalty, Self-Sacrifice. It did not indeed have to be invented anew for modern humanity as the lost arts in many cases have been, for Altruism was never dead. But for long ages it was overlooked by man, for its hiding-place was then in the breast of

Woman, whose tender heart served as the Shechinah — the Sanctuary of exiled Unselfish Love.

Woman practised the long-forgotten virtue while suffering in silence the tyranny to which her constitutional weakness condemned her. From the beginning she has been the chief conservator of this indispensable aid to the higher life. If she has not succeeded in manifesting so strikingly as advanced men the serviceableness of Altruism to material progress, it is because the repression from which she suffered through so protracted a period stunted her intellectual growth, and thus rendered her deficient in the capacity to apply practicall, what she cultivated almost instinctively. On the other hand, her aptitude was greater in the direction of the Divine. There her facility in renunciation assisted her greatly. Her experience in sorrow and self-sacrifice through daily life, her culture in the philosophy of patient endurance, her habit of expending herself upon others, all fitted her in an especial way for ascent towards those lofty heights of emotion, aspiration, and ecstasy, which are as a rule known only by name to men. It is by the Love of God — the Divine Love — that the soul must be guided and supported in its passage through the third sphere, which is called the Divine World ; and to this cult the woman-nature addresses itself with less reluctance and repugnance than the masculine spirit, so deeply attached to material interests, so unaccustomed to what seem the cold abstractions of divinity. As the Abstractive condition prevails more and more it carries with it a scepticism

which to the timid spectator appears to threaten Religion with total extinction; and as the tide of materialism flows ever deeper and wider the cult of the
Supreme, of the Unmanifest, of the Spiritual generally,
is maintained by women almost single-handed. The
French Revolution might have banished Faith from
the soil of France had not the women refused to abandon their altars. Even to-day, in the same country,
the spiritual elements of its civilization are being supplied mainly by the same humble believers in the Over-
Soul. As to the men, materialism has smothered their
higher feelings, and caused them for the time to imagine
that they are or can be content with a world from which
spirituality is excluded.

The function of the Specialist, following Balzac's
theosophy, is to stimulate and develop the higher culture while working out his own enfranchisement. When
the world has proceeded so far upon the path of purely
material evolution as to threaten a fatally one-sided
outcome, one of these advanced souls is incarnated and
lifts the divine standard anew. The very fact of the
close commixture between Spirit and Matter renders it
impossible that the inclination and tendency toward
the loftier mysteries of life should ever be wholly lost,
and when the wave of materialism seems at its height
the reaction is nearest and the spirit of the age is best
prepared for fresh impregnation by the Logos. No
more poetical or striking picture of one of these spiritual transmutations can be found than that which the
late Matthew Arnold embodied in " Obermann once

More." This was the world of "some two thousand years " since :

> " Like ours it looked in outward air,
> Its head was clear and true,
> Sumptuous its clothing, rich its fare,
> No pause its action knew;

> " Stout was its arm, each thew and bone
> Seemed puissant and alive,
> But, ah! its heart, its heart was stone,
> And so it could not thrive!

> " On that hard Pagan world disgust
> And secret loathing fell;
> Deep weariness and sated lust
> Made human life a hell.

> " In his cool hall, with haggard eyes,
> The Roman noble lay;
> He drove abroad, in furious guise,
> Along the Appian way.

> " He made a feast, drank fierce and fast,
> And crowned his hair with flowers;
> No easier nor no quicker passed
> The impracticable hours.

> " The brooding East with awe beheld
> Her impious younger world;
> The Roman tempest swelled and swelled,
> And on her head was hurled.

> " The East bowed low before the blast
> In patient, deep disdain;
> She let the legions thunder past,
> And plunged in thought again.

" So well she mused, a morning broke
  Across her spirit gray;
A conquering, new-born joy awoke
  And filled her life with day.

" ' Poor world,' she cried, ' so deep accurst,
  That runn'st from pole to pole
To seek a draught to slake thy thirst, —
  Go, seek it in thy soul ! '

" She heard it, the victorious West,
  In crown and sword arrayed,
She felt the void which mined her breast,
  She shivered and obeyed.

" She veiled her eagles, snapped her sword,
  And laid her sceptre down;
Her stately purple she abhorred,
  And her imperial crown.

  .   .   .   .

" Lust of the eye and pride of life
  She left it all behind,
And hurried, torn with inward strife,
  The wilderness to find.

" Tears washed the trouble from her face !
  She changed into a child !
'Mid weeds and wrecks she stood, — a place
  Of ruin, — but she smiled! "

The poet intimates that the influences brought by
Christianity are now exhausted, that they have ceased
to operate because faith is dead. Yet he is not without
hope for the future. Human expectation, raised in
modern times to great heights by the promise of the

French Revolution, has indeed been sadly disappointed. Nevertheless,

> " The world's great order dawns in sheen
> After long darkness rude,
> Divinelier imaged, clearer seen,
> With happier zeal pursued."

Despite all premature confidence and too sanguine anticipation, there is warrant for the inspiration which leads men to labor for the attainment of

> " One common wave of thought and joy
> Lifting mankind again ! "

When the Hour arrives the Man will appear. That is the teaching of history and that is the doctrine of the sages. The darkest moments are those which precede the dawn, and it is at what seems the very point of desperation that relief is given. There is indeed nothing occult in this view. It is founded upon observation and experience. The mystery lies in the causes of these opportune and portentous events ; in the evolution of the Avatars who in turn appear to change a world's course and to rekindle the pure flame of Religion and Spirituality. Balzac, however, has not encumbered his subtle and profound study, as an inferior artist would have been apt to do, by showing the Specialist in the discharge of his function of Deliverer. His purpose was to exhibit and analyze, as far as possible, that rare and precious form of existence in which the progress of the spirit toward the Divine has been carried so far as to render continued toleration of earthly

life impossible. Seraphita is the Specialist upon whom
no world-mission has been laid ; a final efflorescence of
long-cultivated spirituality ; the last, most delicate and
fragile link between Mortality and Immortality. In the
androgynous symbolism under which Seraphita is presented, the author has embodied an archaic and profound
doctrine. The male and female qualities and characteristics are so manifestly complementary that human
thought at a comparatively early stage arrived at the
idea of the original union of the sexes in one relatively
perfect and self-sufficient being. In the Divine World,
according to Swedenborg, such a union consummates
the attachment of those souls which during their corporeal life have been in complete sympathy. The Angel
of Love and the Angel of Wisdom combine to form a
single being which possesses both their qualities.

To the theory of spiritual evolution taught by Swedenborg the doctrine of metempsychosis, or as it is more
commonly termed at present, the doctrine of re-incarnation, is necessary. This doctrine may be traced to
a remote antiquity, and while it is still comparatively
unfamiliar to the Western world, it has for ages been
at the very foundation of all Eastern religion and philosophy. The Rev. William R. Alger, in his " Critical
History of the Doctrine of a Future Life," observes
upon this subject : " No other doctrine has exerted so
extensive, controlling, and permanent an influence
upon mankind as that of the metempsychosis, — the
notion that when the soul leaves the body it is born
anew in another body, its rank, character, circum-

stances, and experience in each successive existence depending on its qualities, deeds, and attainments in its preceding lives. Such a theory, well matured, bore unresisted sway through the great Eastern world long before Moses slept in his little ark of bulrushes on the shore of the Egyptian river ; Alexander the Great gazed with amazement on the self-immolation by fire to which it inspired the Gymnosophists ; Cæsar found its tenets propagated among the Gauls beyond the Rubicon ; and at this hour it reigns despotic, as the learned and travelled Professor of Sanscrit at Oxford tells us, ' without any sign of decrepitude or decay, over the Burman, Chinese, Tartar, Tibetan, and Indian nations, including at least six hundred and fifty millions of mankind.' There is abundant evidence to prove that this scheme of thought prevailed at a very early period among the Egyptians, all classes and sects of the Hindus, the Persian disciples of the Magi, and the Druids, and, in a later age, among the Greeks and Romans as represented by Musæus, Pythagoras, Plato, Plotinus, Macrobius, Ovid, and many others. It was generally adopted by the Jews from the time of the Babylonian captivity. Traces of it have been discovered among the ancient Scythians, the African tribes, some of the Pacific Islanders, and various aboriginal nations both of North and of South America."

In fact there is scarcely a division of the human family, advanced at all beyond the stage of savagery, in which either the germs of this theory or the fully developed belief may not be discovered. The form in

which it has been held differs. Thus the Platonists
and Pythagoreans supposed that human souls might
inhabit the bodies of animals, birds, etc. The Mani-
cheans went further, and taught that such spirits might
be reborn in vegetable forms; and some have even
imagined that sin and degradation could condemn human souls to imprisonment in rocks, stones, or the
dust of the field. The Talmudists, the teachers of
Oriental esotericism, and generally speaking the older
and more authoritative exponents of the wisdom-
religion, maintained that human souls transmigrated
through human bodies alone, rising, step by step, to
higher planes. A very convenient collection of opinions
upon re-incarnation has lately been published by Mr.
E. D. Walker, and this work may be commended to
those who desire to realize something of the extent to
which the doctrine has been held both in the past and
the present. By abundant quotations Mr. Walker
shows, not only that it was a cardinal tenet of the
so-called Pagan religions, but that many of the early
Christians — notably Origen — maintained it; while the
array of modern philosophers, poets, men of science, and
theologians who have even in recent times received it is
well calculated to give pause to reflective minds. Such
names as Kant, Schelling, Leibnitz, Schopenhauer,
Bruno, Herder, Lessing, Goethe, Boehme, Fichte, and
others, are found in the list, and even the sceptical
Hume, in his essay on the Immortality of the Soul,
observes: " The metempsychosis is therefore the only
system of this kind that philosophy can hearken to."

Schopenhauer declares that "the belief in metempsychosis presents itself as the natural conviction of man, whenever he reflects at all in an unprejudiced manner. It would really be that which Kant falsely asserts of his three pretended Ideas of the reason, a philosopheme natural to human reason, which proceeds from its forms; and when it is not found it must have been displaced by positive religious doctrines coming from a different source. I have also remarked that it is at once obvious to every one who hears of it for the first time." The same writer observes further: "In Christianity, however, the doctrine of original sin, that is, the doctrine of punishment for the sins of another individual, has taken the place of the transmigration of souls and the expiation in this way of all the sins committed in an earlier life. Both identify, and that with a moral tendency, the existing man with one who has existed before; the transmigration of souls does so directly, original sin indirectly." This venerable doctrine, proceding in an unbroken line from the pre-Vedic period to the present time, and held even now by the larger moiety of the earth's inhabitants, is, as Schopenhauer remarks, a natural belief; for it is that which most rationally and plausibly accounts for the most perplexing mysteries of existence. As developed by the subtle Hindu intellect it is full of attraction and persuasion to unprejudiced minds, and when the so-called law of Karma is applied to it, the resulting scheme may well seem to embrace and explain the most formidable considerations and objections.

Schopenhauer, it is true, raises the objection that in the Buddhist (or Hindu) doctrine of metempsychosis the discontinuousness of memory between re-births practically renders the process palingenesis and not metempsychosis. The German philosopher, however, but imperfectly apprehended the doctrine which he adapted so closely ; for his substitution of the " will to live " for " Karma " is really little more than a change of terminology, his theory of the functions of Will being at bottom a Germanization of the law of Karma. Had he lived to study the later developments of Asiatic philosophy and metaphysics, it cannot be doubted that so open and clear an intelligence would have recognized the force of those deeper implications which round out and give consistency and completeness to the Oriental scheme of thought, and dissipate the surface difficulties of the subject. The advances made recently in Western psychology have contributed to the growth of a better understanding on many points, and among the most suggestive and illuminating studies may be cited those of Ribot on disease of the memory, and on double and other abnormal conditions of personality. The persistence of memory was held to be indispensable to a true metempsychosis by Schopenhauer because he had no conception of the refinements of Hindu speculation, which postulate the deathless principle of man as a congeries of separable parts, to the perishable among which physical recollection belongs. The Hindu posits, however, an undying psychical memory, which is incognizable by the incarnate soul, but which, nevertheless, stores up every event of the numerous transmigrations through which it passes, to bring the whole series into the consciousness of the persistent spirit when it has accomplished all its educational changes, and has attained an elevation which enables it fully to comprehend itself and its evolution.

Science, nay, common experience and observation, throw some light upon this difficult subject. The phenomena of normal sleep serve to show how the persistence of physical life is maintained notwithstanding periodical, frequent, and continuous lapses of consciousness. The rarer phenomena of double personality, so carefully studied by Charcot, Azam, Binet, Ribot, Liégois, and others, emphasize the lessons of every-day experience in this direction. The remarkable cases in which, memory having been lost for considerable periods of time, it has been recovered as suddenly as it had disappeared, point out the lines of reasoning upon which the apparent change of personality may be reconciled with latent persistence and continuation of individuality. And indeed Schopenhauer might have perceived that the action of the Hindu law of Karma would be futile and purposeless if, as he concluded, each re-birth involved, to all practical intents, the creation of a new person. For to what end should the results of acts done in a former life follow and modify the succeeding incarnation if the two existences had no connection? Schopenhauer's misapprehension on this point was indeed far-reaching in its effect; for it led him to postulate a contradiction in terms, — an unconscious

which to the timid spectator appears to threaten Religion with total extinction; and as the tide of materialism flows ever deeper and wider the cult of the
Supreme, of the Unmanifest, of the Spiritual generally,
is maintained by women almost single-handed. The
French Revolution might have banished Faith from
the soil of France had not the women refused to abandon their altars. Even to-day, in the same country,
the spiritual elements of its civilization are being supplied mainly by the same humble believers in the Over-
Soul. As to the men, materialism has smothered their
higher feelings, and caused them for the time to imagine
that they are or can be content with a world from which
spirituality is excluded.

The function of the Specialist, following Balzac's
theosophy, is to stimulate and develop the higher culture while working out his own enfranchisement. When
the world has proceeded so far upon the path of purely
material evolution as to threaten a fatally one-sided
outcome, one of these advanced souls is incarnated and
lifts the divine standard anew. The very fact of the
close commixture between Spirit and Matter renders it
impossible that the inclination and tendency toward
the loftier mysteries of life should ever be wholly lost,
and when the wave of materialism seems at its height
the reaction is nearest and the spirit of the age is best
prepared for fresh impregnation by the Logos. No
more poetical or striking picture of one of these spiritual transmutations can be found than that which the
late Matthew Arnold embodied in " Obermann once

of death and re-birth, and that among these processes was the transmission, across the gap caused by death, of the qualities and tendencies and spiritual attainments belonging to the individual undergoing re-incarnation. In Oriental terminology Swedenborg's embryo Angels were the products of continued operation of good Karma. They represented the best results of human aspiration faithfully maintained until the upward yearning had destroyed the strong attachments to earth and qualified the spirit to breathe the rarefied atmosphere of the Divine World. In this evolutionary process, moreover, the highest examples of human development were reached, and in these a type was attained which exhibited the ideal of humanity as it was or as it might have been immediately after the descent of Spirit into Matter, and before that Fall which in the symbolism of the occultists signifies the victory of Materialism over Spirituality, the beginning of that long course of mundane and gross development which men call civilization, and which has blinded them, by its material gains, to the extent of the divergence of the race from its only permanent and worthy interests.

Seraphita was conceived by Balzac in a moment of supreme insight and inspiration, to embody Swedenborg's noblest ideas. Not that Swedenborg can be regarded as the originator of the theory which he expanded and modified and stamped with his own individuality and his own imperfectly developed spiritual perceptions. For it must be admitted by all candid students of the Seer that his supposed revelations are

often clogged and overlaid with the most palpable
anthropomorphism ; that he derives his notions of celestial phenomena and existences from his personal envi-
ronment with a curious childish simplicity at times ;
that he exhibits in many ways his inadequacy as the
vehicle of supra-mundane communications ; and his in-
ability, partly through physical, partly through intellectual conditions, to transmit with fidelity or even to
observe with accuracy that which was presented to his
internal vision. Indeed it may be said that whoever
wishes to enjoy the beauties which undoubtedly subsist
in his writings must be prepared to submit them to
a certain analytic and refining process. For they may
be likened to the great world-religions, which, issuing
clearly and nobly from their sources, have in time
become discolored and polluted and changed sometimes
into quite unsavory and ignoble streams by the operation upon them, during long periods, of all the gross-
ness, perversity, materialism, selfishness, mendacity,
and iniquity which men bring to the amelioration of
their condition and the improvement of the creeds upon
which they profess to rely for the security of their future
well-being. Not to carry the parallel too far, it should
be distinctly stated that Swedenborg assuredly infused
no elements of evil into his representations and interpre-
tations. He erred solely through temperament, and it
may be surmised that the first period of his life, which
was devoted to study in the physical sciences, strengthened in him that unconscious tendency to materialize
spiritual things which is characteristic of his writings,

and which imparts to much of his description of the
higher spheres so strange and infelicitous an atmosphere
of earthly commonplace.

To penetrate to the heart of his subject it is therefore
necessary to clear away a good deal of obstructive and
non-essential matter. Had the Sage been a poet he
would certainly have written more interestingly, and
it may even be thought perhaps, more accurately, concerning many minor details. But the broad outlines,
the firm framework of his system, remain entirely unaffected by his lack of imagination and grace of fancy ;
and it is upon the body of doctrine itself, and not upon
the narrative powers of the Seer, that his reputation
and the vitality of his teaching must rest. Here there
is no defect of nobility, no sign of narrowness, no sub-
servience to inherited beliefs, no undue elevation of
symbolic or ceremonial hypotheses. From the volu-
minous theological library given out by him during his
life and added to by posthumous publications, may be
obtained a perfectly harmonious, essentially lofty, and
intellectually attractive religious scheme and cosmo-
logical theory, though the latter is less easily cleared
from its impediments than the former. It would not
be possible, even were it desirable, to indicate more
than the outlines of this system here. Balzac himself
has presented all that he thought necessary to the comprehension of " Seraphita," in the following pages, and
it is the purpose of this introduction principally to
supply explanations which he omitted, perhaps because,
coming fresh from mystical and occult studies which had

filled his mind to saturation, he took too much for granted the intellectual preparation of his readers.

One interesting consideration related to the peculiarities of Swedenborg's writings remains to be pointed out, and it has a wide bearing. All who are sufficiently interested in spiritual things to have examined what may be called the literature of revelation, have probably been perplexed and possibly discouraged, by the innumerable contradictions and discrepancies which are apparent in this branch of mysticism. Relations purporting to embody truthful presentations of the unseen universe, and believed by the Seers to be faithful records of true visions, offer, when compared, apparently hopeless and inexplicable divergencies. One consequence of this striking lack of harmony and consistency has naturally been to reinforce scepticism, and to give ground for the facile explanation of all such representations upon the theory of hallucination or disordered imagination. Such as are content with that explanation cannot be expected to make any farther inquiry into the subject; and this is the case with the majority, who regard with concealed or open dissatisfaction any hypothesis which by broadening the area of existence threatens to increase its responsibilities and extend its obligations. On the other hand, there will always be a considerable minority the character of whose minds leads them to explore the unknown, and the dominant influence of whose spiritual elements compels them to accept the possibility of a higher life beyond the grave, and under conditions difficult alike of conception and comprehension. These inquirers are aware that according to analogy the problem referred to is not incapable of solution. Even in purely material life, for example, observation is invariably colored and modified by the personality of the observer. Every court of justice is a perpetual reminder of this. Human evidence concerning the most ordinary matters differs radically according to the character of the witnesses. Six men seeing the same thing will each give a different account of it, and they will rarely be found in agreement even as to essentials. Put six men into new and strange conditions, let them witness something the like of which none of them has ever seen before, and which is in itself seemingly opposed to all their experience, and we must expect still more divergent and irreconcilable reports. In such a case the evidence would be practically of no use in forming a conclusion.

In the researches by which men have sought to obtain knowledge of the supra-mundane the inherent difficulties must necessarily be very much greater. Supposing, for the purpose of the argument, that it is possible for certain peculiarly spiritual persons, by mental and physical discipline and preparation, or by natural aptitude, to penetrate behind the veil of Matter and obtain glimpses into the region of Spirit, it is nevertheless not credible that such persons should, while in the body, be capable either of clearly seeing or correctly repeating what they have seen. For however their spiritual perception may have been strengthened and clarified, it is obvious that its vehicle is ill adapted to the work of observation in so

foreign and unfamiliar a sphere. Between embodied
and disembodied Spirit there is a great gulf fixed. Ul-
timately all Spirit may be identical in substance, but
Spirit mixed with the grosser arrangements of Matter
which constitute material life and phenomena has not,
and cannot be made capable of, perfect insight to a
higher state of existence, or a radically different state.

That this is the case the history of all mystical
visions appears to indicate. It is not that the various
Seers are hallucinated, or that they invent; it is that
the divergences in their reports represent the insuperable influence of their material elements upon their
spiritual perception. This may be tested by harmonics
as well as by discords, indeed. The student of such
subjects knows that remarkable resemblances in outline
occur frequently among the mystical writings of widely
separated races and ages. These resemblances cannot,
in many instances, be accounted for on the theory of
simple borrowing, for the proof is frequently attainable
that borrowing would have been impossible. It would
rather seem that these coincidences point to and emphasize the limitations of human research in this direction. It might be thought that many aspiring minds in
many countries and at various times had obtained a
certain dim insight to these obscure phenomena, — had
grasped, so to speak, some salient points and broad
general outlines; but that this imperfect perception
had marked the utmost verge of their discovery, and
that in every case the attempt to give exact form and
body to the vision had been baffled and defeated by the

intrusion of those material elements which are inseparable from existence under the conditions with which
alone we are acquainted at present. Thus we find that
every so-called supernatural vision reflects, in greater
or less degree, the educational equipment of the Seer,
his habitat, his racial peculiarities, his every-day envi-
ronment, and, almost invariably, the leading tenets of
the religion he knows best, or which he professes.
According to the theory here stated all these local
characteristics are indications of spiritual myopia and
defective enfranchisement from physical memories and
material habits of thought. Nor is there one such vision,
from the highest to the lowest, from the most ancient
to the most modern, which does not bear the same
marks of earthly distortion and adulteration. The
visions of Swedenborg are full of such unconscious in-
terpolations and perversions.

The danger of self-deception in all these spiritual ad-
ventures and experiments is obvious, and there are
other dangers independent of the seeker's volition.
The temptation to receive without much inquiry the
flattering suggestion of a special revelation is of course
in the very front rank of these incidental perils. The
inquirer who ventures without due preparation and
study to cross the boundary which divides the seen
from the unseen is exposed, however, to far more subtle
and insidious foes than the weaknesses and vanities of
his own heart. He may easily drift into a Fool's Paradise wherein illusions of every kind cheat his undisci-
plined senses, and he may return to material existence

qualified to do much more harm than good by dissemi-
nating views which perhaps his personal character invests with a factitious authority. Nevertheless, the
possibility of a certain insight to the phenomena of
other conditions of existence is unaffected by these
considerations, which after all only go to show the
urgent need of caution both in essaying such excursions
into the supra-mundane, and in dealing with the representations subsequently offered concerning discoveries
made in them. It is perhaps scarcely necessary to point
out that the novelist who undertakes such a theme as
that of "Seraphita" must work under unfamiliar conditions. He is not free to give the reins to his imagination. He must be careful to maintain communication
with his base, to use a military figure. He cannot employ machinery wholly unknown to his public, but must
confine his efforts to embellishing and expanding those
popular conceptions of spiritual phenomena reference
to which is readily understood, even though the prevailing ideas may be poor, or grotesque, or gross. In
" Seraphita " Balzac has followed this course with the
success to have been expected from the versatility and
subtlety of his genius. He has produced the most lofty
and beautiful spiritual fiction to be found in literature.

Brief reference has been made already to a striking
peculiarity in the portrait of Seraphita, — the fact,
namely, that to Minna she conveys the impression of
masculinity and to Wilfrid that of womanhood. So
strange a confusion of sex, or perhaps it would be more
exact to say so strange a dualism, certainly required

more explanation than Balzac has seen fit to offer; and
as the ideas involved relate to very ancient and recon-
dite doctrines, it is necessary to treat the subject somewhat fully. Seraphita is intended to typify the nearest
approach to physical and psychical perfection possible
under the limitations of human existence. The whole
narrative of her birth and training indicates this. Her
parents are devout followers of Swedenborg, to whom
they are related. There is much more of mystical
spirituality than of material relations about their union
and married life. In fact, the chief aim and end of both
their lives seems to have been the securing of the proper
conditions for the generation of a being who should be
so pure and so in harmony with celestial things from
her birth as to be capable of accomplishing in one incarnation the transition from the mortal to the divine.
Seraphita as here represented offers curious analogies
with Oriental theosophy. One might say that in Eastern
terminology she was born to Arhatship; and that though
for her, as for all merely human beings, temptation and
trial were unavoidable, her triumph was no less certain
than that which Gotama Buddha attained to as the culmination of his vigil under the Bodhi tree. But the Northern ideal of human perfection embraced some conceptions
which were less congenial to the Oriental intellect. It is
one of the central merits of Christianity that it did much
to recover for Woman the position too long denied her in
the psychical scheme. Buddha indeed went far beyond
his Asiatic predecessors in this direction. He admitted
women to all the spiritual gains open to men, with one

c

exception. No woman could be a Buddha, according
to him, though any woman might elevate herself to
Arhatship. Christianity raised woman to the highest
celestial dignities, and if in process of time superstition
and bigotry warped and travestied the original pure
symbolism and the early doctrines of the creed, much
solid good remained from the mere familiarizing of
men's minds with the higher view of womanly excel-
lences and capacities.

In the esoteric creeds of many peoples, but chiefly
those of European habitat, the place of Woman has for
ages been, not merely among the highest, but literally
the highest. She symbolized the Soul in the beautiful
myth of Psyche. She was the spiritual element in
humanity, lacking union with which mankind must be
chained forever to the material, and waste his energies
in struggles and labors which, even when most suc-
cessful, only carried him farther from the true purpose
of life, and rendered emancipation from carnal conditions more tedious and difficult. Something of this
venerable doctrine may be gathered from the following
citations, which occur in that beautifully written but
mystical work called " The Perfect Way." Speaking of
the " substance of existence," the authors say : " As
Living Substance, God is One. As Life and Substance, God is Twain. HE is the Life, and SHE is
the Substance. And to speak of Her is to speak of
Woman in her supremest mode. She is not ' Nature ; '
Nature is the manifestation of the qualities and properties with which, under suffusion of the Life and Spirits

of God, Substance is endowed. She is not Matter,
but is the potential essence of Matter. She is not
Space, but is the *within* of Space, its fourth and
original dimension, that from which all proceed, the
containing element of Deity, and of which Space is
the manifestation. As original Substance, the substance of all other substance, She underlies that whereof
all things are made; and, like life and mind, is interior, mystical, spiritual, and discernible only when
manifested in operation." The elucidation of the feminine principle is carried much further, and the whole
passage will repay study, for it throws new light upon
the mythologies and occult systems of many ages and
peoples, and tends to exhibit a continuity of thought
and a unity of conception regarding fundamentals,
such as few would suspect who examine these questions hastily or without due preparation. The following passage relates to the concrete question in hand
more directly : " As on the plane physical, man is not
Man, — but only Boy, rude, froward, and solicitous
only to exert and exhibit his strength, — until the time
comes for him to recognize, appreciate, and appropriate Her as the woman ; so on the plane spiritual,
man is not Man, — but only Materialist, having all
the deficiencies, intellectual and moral, the term implies, until the time comes for him to recognize, appreciate, and appropriate Her as the Soul, and counting
Her as his better half, to renounce his own exclusively
centrifugal impulsions, and yield to her centripetal attractions. Doing this with all his heart, he finds that

she makes him in the highest sense, Man.   For, adding
to his intellect Her intuition, she endows him with that
true manhood, the manhood of Mind.   Thus, by Her
aid obtaining cognition of substance, and from the
phenomenal fact ascending to the essential idea, he
weds understanding to knowledge, and attains to cer-
titude of truth, completing thereby the system of his
thought."

In rejecting, as the present age has virtually done, the
soul and her intuition, "man excludes from the system
of his humanity the very idea of woman, and renounces
his proper manhood."   This it is which determines the
wholly materialistic bent of modern physical science,
and the coarse, callous, and corrupt tendencies which,
as the century declines to its close, appear to characterize the prevailing civilization more strongly, and to
emphasize with greater distinctness even the faintest
reactionary movements and impulses.   Balzac, in drawing Seraphita, was wholly true to the best received
occult doctrine in endowing her with duality of sexual
attributes, and the subtlety of his delineation is especially exhibited in the dominance of her womanly side.
For though Minna is apparently misled by the masculine vigor and the self-contained resolution of her
companion, the reader is permitted to see clearly enough
that the impression which Seraphita produces upon
Wilfrid is not only by far the stronger but by far the
most natural; and this impression is that which the
highest type of womanhood can alone create.   But there
is another symbol in this phase of Seraphita's nature.

For it is held that in truth and fact the dualism exaggerated for the sake of effect in her case is inherent in all human beings; that, to quote the same work once more, " whatever the sex of the person, physically, each individual is a dualism, consisting of exterior and interior, manifested personality and essential individuality, body and soul, which are to each other masculine and feminine, man and woman ; he the without, she the within. And all that the woman, on the planes physical and social is to the man, that she is also on the planes intellectual and spiritual. For, as Soul and Intuition of Spirit, she withdraws him, physically and mentally, from dissipation and perdition in the outer and material; and by centralizing and substantializing him redeems and crowns him, — from a phantom converting him into an entity, from a mortal into an immortal, from a man into a god." For, without Love, Force can work only evil. It is the union of these two from which springs true progress, — the progress which overlooks the material and plants discovering feet in the permanent region of the spiritual. Woman is the symbol and the vehicle of the Divine Life. She is the one stable principle of human evolution, — the principle without which man's development would be in the line of decomposition instead of toward a higher vitality; his restless energies would wear themselves away in making the conditions of his existence more and more impossible of endurance. And this is the doctrine of all Hermetic Scriptures, including the Book of Genesis.

It is to be observed that Balzac does not follow

Swedenborg closely here. He goes rather to the sources of esoteric doctrine from which all students of occultism, from the earliest recorded times, have drawn their principles and the guiding outlines of their schemes of thought. It is also deserving of notice that however the personal element may and does alter and not infrequently disguise or pervert the details of such teachings, there is in the general form and character of them a certain harmony and close affinity which indicate community of origin; and as in the genesis of language philologists argue from root likenesses affiliation of several tongues which time has separated widely, with one mother tongue lost perhaps in the mists of antiquity, so from these indications of a common focus of knowledge may be inferred the pre-existence of such a spring and source; and not less rationally may be assumed in it a purity and approximation to absolute truth superior to the representations which have descended through defective vehicles, exposed to all the sophisticating influence of time and ignorance and materialism. Swedenborg was an agent in some respects peculiarly susceptible to these distorting influences. It does not appear that he at any time rose to the height of spiritual perception attained in the thoughts last quoted. Yet he recognized somewhat of the importance of the Womanhead in spiritual existence, and though he did not escape from the narrow and material views of Woman common to his age, he brought from his visions a reflection of the truth too exalted to be understood by his contemporaries.

" Man," he says in one place, " is born an understanding, and woman a love." And speaking again of
marriage he says: " The wife cannot enter into the
proper duties of the man ; nor the man, on the other hand,
into the proper duties of the wife ; because they differ,
as wisdom and its love, or thought and its affection, or
understanding and its will. In the proper duties of
men the understanding, thought, and wisdom act the
chief part ; but in the proper duties of wives the will,
affection, and love act the chief part." He recognizes
also the necessity of harmonious conjunctions between
the two natures to make the perfect man ; but he does
not realize the superior importance, the higher spirituality, of the woman's nature. Here Balzac's knowledge,
intuitive or acquired, surpasses that of the teacher whose
doctrine he has undertaken to illustrate, and in his conception of Seraphita he rises to the level of the loftiest
mystical doctrine to which human faculty has ever
attained.

Goethe, like Balzac, penetrated to the heart of the
great problem in the last scene of the second part of
" Faust." His *Ewig-Weibliche* is the divine element
which Woman both embodies and typifies, and to the
purifying and stimulating emanations from which Man
is indebted for whatever degree of enfranchisement
from the clogging embraces of materialism he is enabled to accomplish. This is the force which *zieht uns
hinan*, which lifts us toward higher spheres and inspires us with nobler aims ; which on the physical plane
keeps before our dull and earth-drawn eyes constant

examples of self-sacrifice, altruism, patience, compassion, and love stronger than death; which is most effective in subduing and extirpating the sordid animal tendencies and inclinations from our nature, and in substituting impulses and aspirations which may give us foothold in the path that leads toward a life better worth living. In the figure of Seraphita we contemplate the final efflorescence of such endeavor, the culminating product of a long chain of incarnations, during which the dominant impulse has been uniformly spiritual, and through which the carnal elements have been gradually subdued until at length they suffice only to give the mortal form coherency, and to supply the physical means of that inevitable agony of temptation which is the price of translation to the Divine, exacted equally from all who bear the conditions of earthly life, under whatever name they may be known. For when the day of Deliverance is about to dawn, the hosts of Mara assemble, or Satan calls his legions together, and the supreme test of the aspirant is undergone. Not for naught did the devisers of the mysteries of Eleusis subject the neophyte to a series of ordeals requiring mental and physical resolution and intrepidity. These ordeals symbolized the difficulties and pains which must be endured by all who seek to pass directly from the natural to the celestial.

When — to employ for a moment the terminology of Schopenhauer — the mortal resolves upon exercising " the denial of the will to live," all the forces of life marshal themselves in battle array against him. The

Temptation, which figures in so many religious, is the
exoteric symbol of this inevitable conflict. Nature,
which knows only the conditioned, revolts in every
fibre against the unconditioned. The Mephistopheles
of the material world, she cannot suffer any of her
children to escape her, and when she perceives that they
are bent upon renunciation she summons her Lemures
to guard all the outlets and prevent the flight of the soul
to higher spheres. Nor is purification, innocence, inherited elevation of spirit, preparedness for the taking
on of more lofty conditions, any defence against these
attacks. On the contrary, the greater the refinement
the greater the sensibility. So the red Indian, bound
to the stake, endures with stolidity torture which
would destroy life in the highly strung nervous system
of a civilized man. When Sir Robert Peel received the
injuries from which he died, so acute was his sensitiveness that he could not tolerate the gentlest surgical
examination, even the pressure of the bandages occa-
sioning him so much pain that it was found necessary
to remove them. It is true that great mental excitement may so completely dominate pain as to render
those injured insensible to it. Thus in battle men
desperately wounded will go on fighting sometimes
until loss of blood causes them to faint. So also strong
spiritual excitement may operate as an anæsthetic, as is
shown in the case of martyrs who, while their bodies
were burning, are reported to have spoken with all the
indications of religious rapture or ecstasy. It is known
that in the hypnotic state complete physical insensi-

bility may be induced, so that needles or knives can be
plunged deep into the tissues without causing the least
sensation. Similar phenomena have been observed in
many phases of the mysterious and Protean conditions called hysterical. Thus the Convulsionnaires of
St. Medard actually found satisfaction in being beaten
with the utmost violence by strong men, and suffered
themselves to be struck with heavy iron bars, experiencing no pain or injury from assaults which were
quite severe enough to have killed persons in the normal
state.

But none of these instances affect the fact that as
a rule sensibility increases with the gradual predomi-
nance of the nervous system, which is one of the most
marked concomitants of civilization. There is indeed
one consideration which at first sight may appear not
to be in accord with this theory. It has long been
observed that women commonly bear pain better than
men ; and it is perhaps generally supposed that the
sensibility of women is greater than that of men. Of
course no conclusion of any value on such a point can
be established in the absence of trustworthy data, and
statistics here are unattainable.   While, however, it
may be admitted, as a deduction from general experience, that women are usually more patient under
pain than men are, it is by no means so certain that
their sensibility is greater than men's, nor should it be
too hastily assumed that it is even equal to the latter.
Reasoning from analogy it might be supposed that the
capacity of women to bear pain would be greater than

that of men, because the performance of their natural
functions requires them to bear more pain, and Nature
always makes provision for special requirements of the
kind. Endurance may be confounded with insensi-
tiveness, moreover, and this renders it more difficult to
arrive at the actual state of the case. Woman has been
disciplined by centuries of servitude and oppression to
a patience which man has not, save in certain subject
races, learned to exhibit. The American Indian, trained
from infancy to conceal his feelings, and especially to
repress all signs of suffering, could face torture with
firmness. The modern city-bred man undoubtedly
dreads the dentist's chair more, and perhaps actually
suffers more in it, than did the savage in the hands
of his enemies. Women, however, without any preparation but that of heredity, endure prolonged and
poignant suffering, and often, if not always, with a
composure which men at least are prone to impute to
inferior sensitiveness. This inferiority, if indeed it
exists, is merely physical, for there can be no doubt
as to the superior spiritual sensibility of women; and
there is room for considerable hesitation regarding the
other branch of the subject.

In regard, however, to the capacity for bearing the
psychical agony inseparable from such struggles as
have to be borne by all who attain to the great Deliverance, the higher resolution must be accorded to the
woman, and this Balzac recognized in drawing the
character of Seraphita. We see her, as the final change
approaches, plunged in the horrors of a supreme con-

flict with all the earthly desires and longings and ambitions.   This pure and nearly perfect creature is indeed
beyond the reach of the gross animal passions and
coarse lusts which sway and control the merely natural
man.   She has been relieved by her resolute and austere
progenitors from those burdens.   But still she is not
exempt from the common destiny.   When Gotama took
his station under the Bodhi tree —

> " He who is the Prince
> Of Darkness, Mara — knowing this was Buddh
> Who should deliver man, and now the hour
> When he should find the Truth and save the worlds —
> Gave unto all his evil powers command.
> Wherefore there trooped from every deepest pit
> The fiends who war with Wisdom and the Light,
> Arati, Trishna, Raga, and their crew
> Of passions, horrors, ignorances, lusts,
> The brood of gloom and dread ; all hating Buddh,
> Seeking to shake his mind : nor knoweth one,
> Not even the wisest, how those fiends of Hell
> Battled that night to keep the truth from Buddh."

Even so the pure Seraphita was assailed ; and if not
perhaps with all the sensual temptations which Mara
deployed under the eyes of the indomitable Tathagata,
with enticements not less powerful, and seductions not
less insidious.   For such is the constitution of human
nature that it is unable to pass even to a state the infinite superiority of which it is fully assured of, without
experiencing reluctance and sadness.

" For who to dumb Forgetfulness a prey,
This pleasing anxious being e'er resigned,
Left the warm precincts of the cheerful day,
Nor cast one longing, ling'ring look behind? "

or, as the poet of " The Light of Asia" puts a like thought :

" Sorrow is
Shadow to life, moving when life doth move;
Not to be laid aside until one lays
Living aside, with all its changing states,
Birth, growth, decay, love, hatred, pleasure, pain,
Being, and doing. How that none strips off
These sad delights and pleasant griefs who lacks
Knowledge to know them snares."

Even the possession of that knowledge cannot avail to
release the mortal from the pain of conflict. He may
triumph over Mara in the end ; he may realize the illu-
siveness of material existence ; he may attain to Nir-
vana the blessed, the peaceful ; but he must win his
way through the hosts of the tempter and prove his
right to the crown by bearing the cross.

In this great ordeal Seraphita finds no help in her sin-
lessness, because her spiritual development has brought
with it not only increase of sensitiveness, but an expansion of the perceptive faculties which enables her to
comprehend to the fullest extent the attractions and
delights of the material opportunities and enjoyments
she is required to renounce. The sacrifice demanded
of her moreover embraces the slaying of Self. It is not
only earthly desires that she must surrender, but all

desires; for the yearning for the Divine, pure as it may seem, is capable of perversion into a disguised form of selfishness. She cannot cease to aspire, for all her nature is attuned heavenward; but she must be prepared for any event, even for the disappointment of her dearest hopes. And that she is so prepared is shown in her reply to the inquiry of one of her companions as to whether, in dying, she expects to enter the Divine sphere at once. "I do not know," she replies. "It may be but one more step in advance;" that is to say, she may not have reached the end of incarnation. But she must suffer temptation none the less for being uncertain of the future. She must demonstrate her fitness for translation independently of any guarantee. The reader is not admitted to the solemn spectacle of the agonized soul's passion; and this is a fresh illustration of the delicacy and subtlety which characterize this masterpiece. It is Seraphita's old servant David who describes the contest between the Celestial and Infernal powers, in exalted and mystical terms appropriate to the theme. The interest and impressiveness of the situation are deepened by the contrasting discord of the sceptical pastor's sarcastic and incredulous comments. To him mistress and servant are alike mad. The excitement of David, which finds vent in the most ultra-Swedenborgian language, only amuses him. It is true that he is unable to explain, even to himself, many of the phenomena which he witnesses, but he fitly represents the natural world in getting rid of insoluble problems by the simple method of denying their existence.

There are crises in the night-long struggle, at which David seems almost to fear that Seraphita will succumb to her tempters; but it is clearly impossible that she should do so, having reached the elevation at which she is arrested in order that she may purge herself of the last earthly ties. The whole episode is full of beauty and suggestiveness, and it is so skilfully executed that no touch of bathos mars its deep spiritual charm.

The scene which follows the Temptation of Seraphita is intended to illustrate at once the clairvoyant and the intellectual powers of this marvellous creature. It is the final manifestation of the masculine elements in her nature, the demonstration of a superiority of knowledge and understanding not less marked than that of her spirituality. Wilfrid, who represents a soul in a state of unstable equilibrium, poised so insecurely that a comparatively feeble impulse may alter its direction upward or downward, is possessed by a strong but wholly carnal passion for the beautiful and mysterious maiden, and he is the vehicle — on the physical plane — of those material powers which are leagued in the endeavor to drag her back to earth. But Seraphita's spirituality is too strong for Wilfrid's materialism. She sees through his design, reads his character, and at once determines that he shall be saved from himself, and by marriage with Minna — the typical union between Understanding and Love — be set in the path of aspiration, and assisted toward the attainment of divine enfranchisement. At the same time Seraphita resolves to open the eyes of the sceptical pastor as far as may be pos-

sible, and to lift him out of his gross and paralyzing
carnality.   To these ends she addresses herself in the
remarkable exposition and arguments which she delivers at a length which would be wearisome but for
the lucidity, force and closeness of the reasoning, and
the profound interest which attaches to the problems
brought under discussion.

This speech is also to be regarded as a vindication of
Intuition, for Seraphita is represented as having been
reared entirely without education after the usual methods, and the pastor Becker naturally insists that she
must be phenomenally ignorant, and quite incapable of
showing a reason for her faith, however fanatical that
faith may be.   His object, therefore, is to test and ex-
pose her want of information, and so to convince Wilfrid, whose infatuation for her vexes him, that she is
merely a self-deluded visionary, who probably inherits a
strong tendency toward mysticism from her Swedenborgian parents.   Seraphita at once perceives the mixed
purposes of her visitors, and loses no time in showing
that she understands the situation.   Then she proceeds
to dissect Becker's mind, to analyze his scepticism, to
state his positions with care and candor, to allow all
his objections and difficulties their full weight, and
finally to retort upon him with a defence and exposition of the spiritual in the universe, which leaves him
amazed and dumb.   In concluding the review of M.
Becker's doubts and the reasonings upon which they
rest, it is to be noted that the feminine element in Seraphita again comes to the front.   The understanding

does not suffice for the elucidation of the spiritual truths which are next to be dealt with. The Woman-Soul is at this point called upon to expound those highest mysteries which are involved in the apprehension of the great scheme of things. The key-note of this second and more elevated branch of Seraphita's discourse is struck in the opening words. "Belief is a gift. To believe is to feel. To believe in God it is necessary to feel God." Is this the language of Mysticism? Seraphita has in her opening remarks dwelt upon the fact — patent beyond serious controversy — that Man unites, or is the point of junction for, two worlds, the Finite and the Infinite. But if this be so how is it possible to explain all his relations in terms of the Finite; how can it be possible to comprehend all his relations without taking account of those which link him with the Infinite? Nevertheless, neither explanation nor comprehension is to be attained so long as the methods and the terminology of the inferior, the conditioned state, are alone employed in the investigation. The situation is precisely that of the men of science who involve themselves and others in hopeless confusion by discussing Spirit in terms of Matter. Neither can Matter be discussed in terms of Spirit. To each world its own terminology, its own methods and instruments of research. The Finite in Man can never apprehend Infinity; but the Infinite in Man may approach realization of that to which it is by unity of nature allied.

Belief, then, or Faith, is the key which alone opens

d

the door of the Infinite, and it does so by lifting the soul above the material plane, and endowing it with perceptive powers which cannot be acquired through any material educational methods. The Understanding can be cultivated to such an extent that it may explain and realize the meaning of the purely phenomenal ; but there the limit of its capacity is reached. It is the agent of material apprehension, perfectly fitted to that end, and supreme judge in its own court. But its jurisdiction ceases where the domain of Faith begins, and the latter must be the guide and interpreter throughout the spiritual regions. The Understanding refuses to believe what it cannot grasp, and the position is perfectly natural and perfectly just. But the Understanding is, after all, only one element in the constitution of Man, and it is the lower power of the two which are given him for guidance. According to the philosophy of Louis Lambert (of which " Seraphita " is the final fruition) the civilization of the world is supported and carried forward in the main, and altogether so far as its material aspects are concerned, by what he terms the Abstractive, — that is, by those who confine themselves to the development of their intellectual faculties, and virtually ignore their spiritual side. There is no height or splendor or glory of material civilization which cannot be thus attained ; but a purely material civilization, however brilliant and outwardly prosperous and flourishing it may appear, must contain the seeds of its own decay and overthrow, as all history teaches by the most pregnant and impressive examples. Unassisted Reason shows the existence of many mysteries beyond the power of Reason to solve; yet Reason persists in rejecting the agencies whereby if at all these mysteries may be explained, — and in so acting renounces the hope of ever penetrating beyond secondary causes and phenomenal appearances. This, according to Seraphita, is the explanation of what is now called Agnosticism.

It may be of interest to see what Swedenborg teaches in this connection. Faith, according to the Swedish sage is " an internal acknowledgment of truth." Faith and truth, he declares, are one, and the angels know nothing of faith, but what men call faith they call truth. But he affirms that " by things known to explore the mysteries of faith is as impossible as for a camel to pass through the eye of a needle, or for a rib to govern the purest fibrils of the chest and heart, — so gross, yea, much more gross, is the sensual and knowing relatively to the spiritual and celestial." And concerning the belief in and acceptance of things not comprehended by the intellect, he says : " Every one may see that a man is governed by the principles he adopts, be they ever so false, and that all his knowledge and reasoning favor his principles ; for innumerable considerations tending to support them readily present themselves to his mind, and thus he is confirmed in falsities. He, therefore, who assumes as a principle that nothing is to be believed until it is seen and understood can never believe ; for spiritual and celestial things are neither seen with the eyes nor grasped by the imagination." And again, he says : " There are

two principles, one of which leads to all folly and madness, the other to all intelligence and wisdom. The
former principle is to deny all things, or to say in one's
heart that he cannot believe them until he is convinced
by what he can comprehend or be sensible of; this
principle is what leads to all folly and madness, and
may be called the negative principle. . . . Those who
think from the negative principle, the more· they take
counsel of matters of reason, of knowledge, and of
philosophy, the more they plunge themselves into darkness, until at length they come to deny all things.
The reason is that from things inferior no one comprehends things superior, that is, things spiritual and celestial, — still less things divine, because they transcend
all understanding ; and besides, everything is then
involved in negatives from the beginning."

The argument of Seraphita is to the same effect.
Finite Reason, she contends, cannot comprehend Infinite purposes and orderings. The measuring instrument
which man seeks to apply to the divine is inadequate.
He might be more modest if he could be made to see
how frequently he fails to comprehend, not solely the
Infinite, but phenomena which lie, so to speak, at his
own door, and upon his own plane of existence. Again,
this sceptical being ventures to deny God because of
His intangibility and invisibility, while at the same
time he gives name and form to abstractions, — as for
instance, Number. It is true that Number is a reality,
but the average man does not comprehend its significance, and the Number which he figures to himself, and

wherewith he amuses himself, is very different from the real Number. The same considerations apply to the abstractive Time and Space, neither of which is more than a name, representing no noumenon, answering to no actual entity, being in fact no more than an invention for the convenience of measuring those human relations which cannot be more truly and exactly estimated, because — and only because — the human mind is so inadequate to the work which it desires and attempts to perform. The human mind as confined and restricted by scepticism, that is ; for when opened by spiritual illumination it is capable of rising to great altitudes, and of apprehending many things in their true and ultimate significance.

The staple objection to the form of argument employed here by Seraphita is the futility of all modes of inquiry which transcend the Reason ; it being assumed that the human mind is incapable of receiving demonstration of truth otherwise than through the operation of the reasoning faculty, which proceeds entirely upon experience, and, where experience ends, ceases to have any *point d'appui.* A very fair example of this line of argument is to be found in Lotze's " Microcosmos." " If," that author observes, " reason is not of itself capable of finding the highest truth, but on the contrary stands in need of a revelation which is either contained in some divine act of historic occurrence, or is continually repeated in men's hearts, still reason must be able to understand the revealed truth at least so far as to recognize in it the satisfying and convincing conclu-

sion of those upward-soaring trains of thought which
reason itself began, led by its own needs, but was not
able to bring to an end. For all religious truth is a
moral good, not a mere object of curiosity. It may
therefore include some mysteries inaccessible to reason,
but will only do so in as far as these are indispensable
in order to combine satisfactorily other and obvious
points of great importance ; the secrecy of any mystery
is in itself no reason for venerating it ; a secrecy that
was permanent and in its nature eternal would only be
a reason for indifference towards anything which should
thus refuse to be brought into connection with mental
needs ; and finally, above all things, to revel in secrets
which are destined to remain secrets is necessarily not
in accord with the notion of a revelation." The
philosopher then proceeds to put these questions : " But
must that which is a secret for cognition be always really
a secret? Does not the nature of faith consist in this,
that it affords a certainty of that which no cognition can
grasp, as well of *what* it is, as *that* it is? And does
not all science itself, when it has finished its inves-
tigations of particulars, come back to grasp, in a faith
of which the certainty is indemonstrable and yet irrefragable, those highest truths on which the evidence
of other knowledge depends? There is certainly a
germ of truth in this rejoinder ; but not the less
clear is the essential difference that separates such
scientific faith from religious faith." It is unnecessary
to follow Lotze's argument further. Enough has been
quoted to illustrate the common error of what Louis

Lambert would have called the abstractive method of
ratiocination.

Seraphita tells Pastor Becker that he and she speak
different languages in discussing these high questions,
and the same may be said of all who take opposite sides
on the question of psychologic capacities and poten-
tialities. The position of Seraphita, who is a Specialist,
should, however, be made clear. All knowledge is relative. There are mysteries which no created being can
ever comprehend. As Seraphita puts it, " To understand God would be to *be* God." Thus also the Asiatic
occultists, who profess to derive their knowledge of the
origin and destiny of the universe from higher intelligences, corresponding in many respects to the angels
of the Christian Church, affirm that neither their exalted correspondents and revelators nor the still higher
beings with whom the latter are in relations, possess
any knowledge of the Supreme Being. Science pre-
tends no farther than to the origination of the universe
by Motion ; the genesis of that Motion lies beyond its
utmost reach of apprehension. But the contention of
Balzac is that a much higher knowledge than is attainable by the Reason is within the grasp of a duly trained
and disciplined Humanity, developed in one direction
through many incarnations, as Seraphita is supposed
to have been, and so purified from the materialism
which in the race at large obstructs perception that to
her strengthened and clarified vision mysteries cease to
be obscure, and the sphere of cognition is indefinitely
enlarged. Of course it is apparent that such a being

cannot argue cn anything like equal terms with such a
gross sceptic as Pastor Becker. In her, intellection
has already come to operate angelically rather than
humanly, and what to her opponent appears paradox
and incomprehensibility is to her demonstrated and
familjar truth. Nowhere is the tension of Balzac's
thought and the resolute maintenance of his imagination upon this elevated plane of imaginative creation
more strikingly exhibited than in this long and subtle
discourse of Seraphita. An inferior artist could not
have borne so severe a test, but would have lapsed into
commonplace before the end was reached. Seraphita,
however, supports her high arguments with perfectly
natural ease throughout. The philosophy of Louis
Lambert will be recognized repeatedly in it. This is
in accordance with the author's general scheme. Seraphita herself is the culmination of the noble body of
thought outlined in " Louis Lambert." In her we see
the consummation of the long process of transformation
and evolution through and by which the mortal puts
on immortality, the merely Human blossoms into the
celestial.

It is also to be observed that though Balzac has
modernized the conception of this marvellous and beautiful process, he is in no way to be regarded as the
inventor of that conception. As to its origin we shall
perhaps seek it in vain, for the deeper we explore the
occult and religious literature of antiquity the more
evidence we find of the archaism of the central belief.
The doctrine of metempsychosis is correlated with that

of perfectibility, while the means by which the latter end may be attained have been so constantly and minutely discussed, tested, and analyzed by Eastern philosophers and psychologists as to furnish forth a complete code, the very terminology of which has bewildered and baffled Western philologists, men of science, and above all, theologians. Nevertheless, a belief in the possibility of realizing in the flesh a much higher knowledge and perception than materialist methods of education are capable of attaining to, has in various ways descended and persisted through all ages to the present time ; and in support of this belief there has been preserved and recorded a certain amount of what, in almost any other case, would generally be accepted as substantive evidence, but in this case is accepted or rejected with little regard to its true evidential value, and for the most part according as the individual to whom it is submitted is dominated by Spiritual or Materialist prepossessions. It is true that in the West the credibility of all such phenomena has been weakened by the fading out of the doctrine of reincarnation ; for apart from that doctrine every approximation to the higher life recorded must savor so much of miracle as to repel philosophic minds and cause consideration of the alleged facts to be refused or abandoned. In Oriental countries, where metempsychosis has never ceased to be accepted, it obviously supplies plausible explanations for many appearances which under other conditions would strongly suggest the supernatural. Among Asiatics, reincarnation is con-

sidered the normal, nay, the inevitable, career, and in
connection with the Law of Karma it affords a faith
which is held by a large proportion of the earth's inhabitants. Thus it is clear that the idea of Seraphita
would be at once understood by a Hindu, who would
see nothing fanciful or extravagant in the personification, which he would probably classify in his own mind
as that of a female Rishi. Swedenborg, whether con-
sciously or unconsciously, derived many of his beliefs
as to other states of existence, it is not necessary to
say from the Eastern sages, but at all events from the
same sources which were open to those sages. He
altered some of these Oriental ideas strangely, beyond
a question, and clothed them with material garments
such as would have bewildered the Indian philosophers,
whose theories were of the soul, without the alloy of
earth which modern civilization has, naturally perhaps,
given to them. In some respects Seraphita is more
Oriental than Swedenborgian; but in truth Balzac has
put many occult principles together in fashioning this
unique creature, and in the end he has, perhaps wisely,
borrowed freely the imagery and the color as well as the
general conceptions which characterize what are called
the ecstatic visions of the Christian saints, especially
the mystics of comparatively modern times.

The occult doctrine of Number is touched upon in
Seraphita's discourse. As the subject has already been
considered at some length in the Introduction to " Louis
Lambert," and as Balzac makes his meaning comparatively clear, perhaps it is not necessary to reopen that

question; to a full understanding of which, moreover, some knowledge of the Kabbala is requisite. It may, however, be as well to point out that Balzac does not follow Pythagoras in materializing Number; the entities to which he refers are purely spiritual and mystical. But there is in this remarkable discourse of Seraphita a view of the straight line and the circle which it is necessary to examine carefully, for at first sight it appears to be in hopeless contradiction with all occult teaching. Having shown that the circle and the curve govern created forms, Seraphita proceeds thus: "Who shall decide between rectilinear and curvilinear geometry? between the theory of the straight line and that of the curve? If in His vast work, the mysterious Artificer, who knows how to reach his ends miraculously fast, never employs a straight line except to cut off an angle and so obtain a curve, neither does man himself always rely upon it. The bullet which he aims direct proceeds by a curve, and when you wish to strike a certain point in space, you impel your bombshell along its cruel parabola. None of your men of science have drawn from this fact the simple deduction that the Curve is the law of the material worlds, and the Straight line that of the spiritual worlds; one is the theory of finite creations, the other the theory of the infinite. Man, who alone in this world has a knowledge of the Infinite, can alone know the straight line; he alone has the sense of verticality placed in a special organ. A fondness for the creations of the curve would seem to be in certain men an indication of the impurity of their nature still con-

joined to the material substances which engender us;
and the love of great souls for the straight line seems to
show in them an intuition of heaven."

This doctrine is clearly not derived from Swedenborg, whose central theory of Correspondences is funda-
mentally in conflict with it. According to the Swedish
seer everything material is a type and representation of
something spiritual.   Swedenborg's philosophical hypothesis of vortices, moreover, has nothing in common
with this intimation of the superior spirituality of the
line.   That the circle is the most perfect of all figures
is never doubted by the author of the vortical theory.
Professor Winchell has condensed this theory conven-
iently, and from him a few sentences may be quoted:
"The first cause is the infinite or unlimited. This
gives existence to the first finite or limited. That
which produces a limit is analogous to motion. The
limit produced is a point, the essence of which is motion; but being without parts, this essence is not actual motion but only a conatus to it. From this first
proceed extension, space, figure, and succession, or time.
As in geometry a point generates a line, a line a surface, and a surface a solid, so here the conatus of the
point tends towards lines, surfaces, and solids.   In
other words, the universe is contained *in ovo* in the first
natural point. The motion toward which the conatus
tends is circular, *since the circle is the most perfect of
all figures, and tendency to motion impressed by the
Infinite must be tendency to the most perfect figure.*"
And again: "The most perfect figure of the motion

above described must be the perpetually circular. . . .
It must necessarily be of a spiral figure, which is the
most perfect of all figures," — and much more reasoning
to the same effect. And in this view of the circle Swedenborg does but follow the most ancient of occult doctrines,
as may readily be perceived. The most venerable cosmo-
gonic symbol is the point in the circle, — the point representing the creating Logos, the Breath of the Absolute
imparting Motion to Matter; the circle typifying the unlimited, the Infinite, which includes and controls all created things. Again, the Spirit of Life and Immortality
have from the earliest times been symbolized by the
circle. The whole Kabbala proceeds upon the theory
of circles, which is the formulating principle of the doctrine of Emanations. In all hermetic scriptures the
same teaching will be found. The circle was the symbol of the most spiritual views. Thus Proclus says:
" Before producing the material worlds which move in
a circle, the Creative Power produced the *invisible*
Circles." The Golden Egg of Brahma is another illustration of the universality of this doctrine. In fact, as
is observed in " The Secret Doctrine," " In the secret
doctrine the concealed unity — whether representing
Parahrahmam, or the ' Great Extreme ' of Confucius,
or the Deity concealed by Phta, the Eternal light, or
again, the Jewish En-Soph — is always found to be symbolized by a circle, or the 'nought' (absolute *No —
Thing* and Nothing, because it is *infinite* and the
All); while the God-manifested (by its works) is referred to as the *diameter of that circle.* The symbol-

ism of the underlying idea is thus made evident; the right line passing through the centre of a circle has, in the geometrical sense, length, but neither breadth nor thickness; it is an imaginary and feminine symbol, crossing eternity and made to rest on the plane of existence *of the phenomenal world.* It is dimensional, whereas its circle is dimensionless, or, to use an algebraical term, it is the dimension of an equation."

The doctrine of Correspondences, which requires that everything material must be patterned upon something spiritual is indeed not original with Swedenborg. We find it already formulated in the *Timæus* of Plato. Timæus there says : "Which of the patterns had the artificer in view when he made the world, the pattern which is unchangeable, or that which is created? If the world be indeed fair and the artificer good, then, as is plain, he must have looked to that which is eternal. . . . Every one will see that he must have looked to the eternal, for the world is the fairest of creations and he is the best of causes." And again Timæus says : "And he gave to the world figure which was suitable and also natural. But to the animal which was to comprehend all animals, that figure was suitable which comprehends within itself all other figures. Whereupon also he made the world in the form of a globe, round as from a lathe, in every direction equally distant from the centre to the extremes, the most perfect and the most like itself of all figures ; for he considered that the like is infinitely fairer than the unlike." To the same effect may be cited Schopenhauer, who ob-

serves : " Throughout and everywhere the true symbol
of nature is the circle, because it is the scheme or type
of recurrence. This is, in fact, the most universal form
in nature, which it carries out in everything, from the
course of the stars down to the death and the genesis
of organized beings, and by which alone, in the ceaseless
stream of time, and its contents, a permanent existence, *i. e.*, a nature, becomes possible." Is not the
curve too emblematic of all that to the human mind appears pure and beautiful and spiritual? What is it that
appeals to the eye as beauty in regarding a landscape?
A level plain upon which the sole relief of form occurs
in straight trees, produces not only a passing impression of dreary monotony but affects the temperaments
of all who inhabit it, as the character of the steppe-
dweller everywhere demonstrates. So too in architecture. Its primitive forms, ere the arch was discovered,
were harsh and almost repulsive. This may be seen in
the earliest Egyptian architecture. The whole system
was elevated by the introduction of the arch, and by
the adoption of the curves of Nature in the lotus capital and the bulb-form pillar. Mentally eliminate the
curves from the noblest architectural monuments, such
as the Taj Mahal, and their charm is destroyed. Compare Shah Jehan's superb construction with the Parthe-
non, and it will be seen at once that while in the latter
it is mainly the sense of symmetry which is impressed,
the former awakens emotions of a far higher character,
for it suggests a beauty scarcely of earth ; it is in the
perfect grace and exquisite harmony of its lines, in unity

with Nature's noblest mood, and might well be the
creation of these Devas with which the mythology of
Hindustan peoples the unseen universe.   No poet can
fail to perceive and take delight in the beauties of the
curve as exhibited in Nature; and the poetical vision
has never been more subtly or sweetly expressed than
by Emerson: —

> " For Nature beats in perfect tune,
>   And rounds with rhyme her every rune,
>   Whether she work in land or sea,
>   Or hide underground her alchemy.
>   Thou canst not wave thy staff in air,
>   Or dip thy paddle in the lake,
>   But it carves the bow of beauty there,
>   And the ripples in rhymes the oar forsake."

So fond is Nature of the curve that it underlies all her
work and gives to it the deepest charm and attraction.
The straight line she does not greatly affect, nay, she
takes a mischievous pleasure, apparently, in baffling
man's efforts to establish it.   Even her blindest forces
resist its manifestations as by some law.   " Thou canst
not wave thy staff in air," but it " carves the bow of
beauty there."   The resistance of the tenuous atmosphere thwarts the downright, rectilinear impulse, and
forces the staff into the curves which symbolize the
perfection of form.

But Seraphita affirms that the curve is really the
inferior symbol; that it belongs to and expresses the
Finite; whereas the straight line pertains to the Infinite.   How shall this paradox be explained?   To the
merely mortal understanding, nay, to that understand-

ing when raised to its highest power, the circle and the
curve are and have ever been the symbols of the loftiest conceptions, the keys to the profoundest systems
of thought. No doubt the line may be regarded mathematically as the sign of infinite extension, but it surely
has little connection with Idealism, with Poetry, with
Imagination, or Beauty, or Religion. With Duty it assuredly has clear and close affiliations, however, and
that fact may well give us pause ; for to comprehend
Duty thoroughly is indeed to penetrate into arcana
which, if such vision be possible to the finite, extend to
the very threshold of infinity. There is nothing which
so synthesizes and embraces Matter and Spirit as this
same apprehension of Duty ; and keeping fast hold of
that idea we may perhaps be able to throw a little light
upon Seraphita's meaning in the difficult passage under
consideration. The ideal here concerned is indeed too
little reverenced in these days. Yet it is as true as ever
that " the path of duty is the way to glory," and that

> " He that, ever following her commands,
>   On with toil of heart and knees and hands,
>   Thro' the long gorge to the far light has won
>   His path upward, and prevail'd,
>   Shall find the toppling crags of Duty scaled
>   Are close upon the shining table-lands
>   To which our God himself is moon and sun."

For " Duty, lov'd of Love " is the highest test of human
aspiration, the surest measure of human progress, and
it may well be that the straight line which is associated
with and symbolizes it is in the final analysis an intima-

e

tion and a belonging of that supreme existence whose
remoteness and majesty transcend conditioned thought,
and on this plane can only be dimly perceived as the
Something which metaphysical analysis feels compelled
to postulate in partial explanation of the Knowable.

The Logos, the Point within the Circle, was not, as
often mistakenly supposed, held by the students of the
archaic doctrine to be the Supreme or Absolute. It
was really but the symbol of the Manifested, — that of
which the human mind can in some way take cogni-
zance. The old theogonies avoid the perplexities and
contradictions so strongly presented by Seraphita when
examining the doubts which assail the sceptical Pastor,
by postulating a First Cause beyond the actual Artificer
of the Universe. So Porphyry (cited by Taylor) says :
" To that God who is above all things, neither external
speech ought to be addressed, nor yet that which is
inward." Thus Proclus speaks of the highest principle
as " more ineffable than all silence, and more occult
than all essence," and as being " concealed amidst the
intelligible gods." This is the Ain-Soph of the Kabbala,
— the name given it there being almost synonymous
in meaning with the Unknowable of modern Agnosticism, though the latter professes to find the Logos
equally inscrutable. Now it is conceivable that while
the circle is, as Seraphita says, the symbol of the
Created, the line may be that of the Uncreated, that is
to say, the Infinite. The fact that to us who exist on
this earthly plane the circle presents the most perfect
figure does not appear a really serious obstacle to the

reception of this view; for the circle might very well
be the most perfect figure as related to Matter in all
its modifications, or even as related to the lower spiritual spheres into which alone it may be supposed that
incarnated spirit is capable of penetrating; and yet it
might not be adapted to that highest form of existence
which is altogether above and beyond human apprehension. Either this is the interpretation to be put
upon Seraphita's statement concerning the relations
and symbolism of the line and the circle, or it must be
concluded that Balzac has fallen into an error so gross
that it is incredible it should have been committed by
a student of occultism in every other particular so
firmly grounded.

There is indeed no theory advanced in either of the
philosophical romances of Balzac which cannot be traced
to authorities and co-ordinated with some accepted doctrine. He never delivers himself over recklessly to his
fancy in these works, and the smallest suggestion has
a significance of its own. In the present instance he
certainly appears to traverse even widely adopted esoteric teachings, but the more reasonable assumption
must be that this contradiction is only apparent and not
fundamental. It moreover evidently encloses a bold
conception, and one which is calculated to exalt the
character and convey a lofty idea of the powers and
perceptions of Seraphita. Never does she tower more
majestically over her interlocutors and companions
than when she is delivering herself of this magnificent
thought; and nowhere are the capabilities and poten-

tialities of humanity more strikingly and comprehen-
sively suggested than in the intimation that man
contains within himself an element which links him
not alone with the highest heavens, but with that inscrutable, eternal power which transcends our conception of the celestial as much as that surpasses our
material experience. The thought involved is indeed
most noble. It is that the destiny of man connects
him with an existence independent of and superior to
all the changes which Matter can undergo; with an
existence indissoluble by the termination either of
Material or Spiritual universes; with an existence
unaffected by *pralayas* and *manvantaras*, and which
will bear him scathless through every catastrophe and
cataclysm to which the formed and the formless worlds
are said by Eastern occultism to be alike subject. The
vista thus opened to the imagination is stupendous
beyond question, but it may be explored boldly or
timidly as the reader's inclinations and mental and
spiritual tendencies determine.

The strictures of Seraphita upon the half-truths and
fallacies of physical science may be studied profitably
in connection with that critical work of Judge Stallo,
"The Concepts and Theories of Modern Physics,"
which is cited in the Introduction to Louis Lambert.
But the real uncertainty of many alleged scientific
certainties is perhaps best shown in the mercilessly
destructive criticism which rival men of science practise
upon one another's theories and doctrines. The reference to " the greatest man among you " — who is said by

Seraphita, with rhetorical exaggeration, to have "died in despair" because toward the close of his life he realized the inadequacy of his favorite hypothesis to account for the universe — of course applies to Sir Isaac Newton, whose essay at interpretation of the Apocalypse caused his brother scientists to shrug their shoulders and lament the breaking down of that superb mind. Nor is it at all incredible that Newton should have been drawn to his Scriptural studies by recognition of the need for some such initiating and sustaining force in the universe as the old doctrine of the Logos supplies. It is certain, as has been pointed out before, that he was by no means so self-confident as his followers, and that in particular he entertained serious doubts as to the sufficiency of his theory of gravitation, — doubts, be it said, which modern research and scientific progress have strengthened instead of diminishing. Indeed, Seraphita might have reinforced her argument with many more instances of scientific mistakes and insufficient explanations. There are to-day few even of the theories commonly regarded as most firmly established which do not present difficulties hitherto insoluble, and which are not cautiously held by men of truly open minds as at the best provisional, — convenient working hypotheses, but not to be safely made the ground of definitive conclusions.

At the close of Seraphita's harangue her auditors withdraw, confounded; but the impression produced upon their minds rapidly fades, and the next morning the Pastor is once more prepared to find, in the pages

of his favorite Wier, a clue to the mysterious knowledge and argumentative powers of the young girl,
whom he would fain regard as insane or under " possession." As Balzac cites Wier on several occasions
in this book, and as he is an author probably not
known to the generality of readers, it may be well to
give some account of his writings, the more particularly as there is some special significance in the reference to his once celebrated work on witchcraft. John
Wier was a learned physician of Cleves, who was the
first to publish a protest against the wild witchcraft
panic that in the sixteenth and many preceding centuries, caused a frightful slaughter of deluded and innocent victims throughout Europe. Wier's book, entitled
" De Præstigiis Dæmonum," would not in the present
day be regarded as anything but a grossly superstitious
work. The author was indeed no less credulous than
his contemporaries. He believed with them that the
atmosphere swarmed with evil spirits, that a personal
devil went around like a roaring lion, destroying souls,
that all manner of miraculous events were continually
occurring. In fact, he accepted all the evidence upon
which Sprenger, Bodin, and the whole school of the Inquisition, founded their theories of witchcraft ; but he
interpreted the alleged phenomena differently, and more
in accord with the scientific spirit. His explanation
was that many of the so-called witches were lunatics,
and that the majority of those said to be bewitched,
together with many accused of sorcery, were simply
possessed by the devil. The latter, he argued, had no

need to act indirectly through witches, when he could
delude his victims directly, and he disposed of the
witch theory by asserting that Satan put it into the
heads of the possessed to denounce old women as
witches, in order that as much mischief and suffering
as possible might be caused. Wier was a humane
man, — a rare phenomenon in his time, — and the tortures and burnings occurring everywhere revolted him.
He was careful to declare his opinion that all real
witches deserved the most severe punishment; but
he was plainly doubtful whether there were any real
witches.

Conservative and credulous as his book appears now,
it created intense indignation among the believers in
witchcraft, who were not merely the majority of men
then living, but, which seems far stranger, the majority
of the educated and (relatively) intelligent class. In
proof of this, the fact may be cited that Wier's book
was answered by John Bodin, in an equally remarkable
work entitled " De la Démonomanie des Sorciers."
Bodin attacked Wier with ferocity, upholding the authority of the indorsers of witchcraft and denouncing
the kindly doctor of Cleves as little better than an atheist and a heretic. Now Bodin, as Lecky observes
in his " History of Rationalism," was " esteemed by
many of his contemporaries the ablest man who had
then arisen in France, and the verdict has been but
little qualified by later writers. Amid all the distrac-
tions of a dissipated and intriguing court, and all the
labors of a judicial position, he had amassed an amount

of learning so vast and so various as to place him in
the very first rank of the scholars of his nation.   He
has also the far higher merit of being one of the chief
founders of political philosophy and political history,
and of having anticipated on these subjects many of
the conclusions of our own day." Yet there is no
superstition, no legend, no absurd and preposterous
invention, no wild and grotesque imagination, too difficult to be received and digested by this philosopher
and sage.   He relies absolutely upon authority.   He
never questions traditions.   He never reasons upon
matters of fact.   He never exhibits for a single moment
a tendency toward scientific investigation, comparison, and inference.   He abuses Wier in the old-fash-
ioned dogmatic, theological manner.   He calls his book
a " tissue of horrible blasphemies."   He declares that
it cannot be read " without righteous anger."   Wier
has " armed himself against God ; " he has done his
best to disseminate witchcraft, to support the kingdom
of Satan, and so forth through many pages.   Yet Wier
had truly not advanced very far before his age.   He
held to most of the old barbarous doctrines, and among
them to that of the superior innate frailty and deprav-
ity of women.   He, in common with many others,
had asked himself why so large a proportion of alleged
witches were women ; and he, in common with many
others, explained the fact by asserting that they were
so prone to evil that Satan found them an easy prey.
Perhaps it was especially because of Wier's chapter
upon the weaknesses and wickedness of women that

Balzac chose this author as the favorite authority of
Pastor Becker.

In the twenty-seventh chapter of his sixth book he
cites a long array of classical writers in support of the
contention that women have always been specially ad-
dicted to the employment of poison as an agent of re-
venge or passion. In the sixth chapter of his third
book he observes: " Le diable ennemi fin, ruzé et
cauteleux, induit volontiers le sexe feminin, lequel est
inconstant à raison de sa complexion, de legere croy-
ance, malicieux, impatient, melancolique pour ne pou-
voir commander à ses afections ; et principalement les
vieilles, débiles, stupides et d'esprit chancelant." This
is why that Old Serpent addressed himself rather to
Eve than to Adam ; and this is why he so easily
seduced Eve. The holy Saint Peter also has denomi-
nated them " weak vessels," and Saint Chrysostom has
remarked, in his homily upon Matthew, that the female
sex is imprudent and ductile, easily influenced and
swayed, either from good to evil or from evil to good.
He ventures into the difficult region of etymology in
search of further proof, and discovers one in the deri-
vation of the Latin *mulier* from *mollier* or *molli*, " which
signifies softness." It may be conjectured that when
·Pastor Becker sought in the treatise of John Wier con-
firmation of his theory regarding Seraphita's inspiration,
he had in mind the worthy doctor's views concerning
women, and their special fitness as vehicles of diaboli-
cal influences. Pastor Becker refers, as a case in point,
to the history of a young Italian girl who, at the age of

twelve, spoke forty-two languages, ancient and modern. Wier has a story of a Saxon woman, unable to read or write, who "being possessed by the devil" spoke in Latin and Greek, and prophesied concerning future events, — all of which came to pass. He also tells of an idiotic Italian woman who, being under the same infernal influence, and asked which was Virgil's finest verse, replied suddenly —

"Discite justitiam moniti et non temnere Divos."

It is an interesting point in these old ideas that the mediæval notions about women rested upon observation of the essential differences between the masculine and feminine natures ; but external observation alone. To quote Lecky's admirable analysis of mediæval persecution again : "The question why the immense majority of those who were accused of sorcery should be women early attracted attention ; and it was generally answered, not by the sensibility of their nervous constitution, and by their consequent liability to religious monomania and epidemics, but by the inherent wickedness of the sex. There was no subject on which the old writers expatiated with more indignant eloquence, or with more copious illustration," — of which we have just given an example in John Wier. Another instance of the horrible perversion of ideas which characterized those dark ages may be found in the interpretation given to the superior constancy of women in facing torture. The contemporary explanation of this was that the Devil provided all witches with means

of withstanding the torment; and the inevitable corol-
lary of such reasoning was a stimulation of ingenuity
in devising and applying more searching and cruel
tortures to women. There can be no question that
had Seraphita lived in the time of Wier and Bodin the
former would have considered her a demoniac, and the
latter would have denounced her as a witch, the only
fit destiny of whom was the stake; and it may be that
Balzac intended to hint at the contrast between med
iæval and modern thought in introducing, in John Wier,
the most signal, but at the same time narrow and feeble,
illustration of sixteenth century liberalism.

The sixth chapter of " Seraphita " is chiefly occupied
with the beautiful and noble discourse in which the
dying mystic unfolds to her companions the secret of
" the Path." Up to this time Wilfrid, who represents
the Abstractive type, has failed to understand Seraphita.
Earthly ambitions still burn fiercely in his breast.
He cherishes what seem to him high thoughts of conquest. He would go to Central Asia and plot against
the British supremacy in India. He would head such
a formidable irruption of Asiatic tribes as Genghis
Khan organized. He thinks that the prospect of sovereignty, of Oriental luxury and splendor, will tempt
Seraphita, and he lays before her his far-reaching
schemes and invites her to share his glory. But Seraphita smiles. There is for her no temptation in such
offers. As she says, beings more powerful than Wilfrid
have already sought to dazzle her with far greater gifts.
Minna approaches with a more dangerous because a

purer and higher petition. She offers nothing but herself as a vicarious sufferer. Love raises her above the
sphere of the Abstractive. Already the divine is shining through her envelope of flesh. Already the tender
loyal heart has found the entrance to the Path by
which alone the celestial sphere can be attained. Then
the prophetic vision of Seraphita recognizes in these
two the elements of Force and Love which, when purified by the discipline of patient suffering, will unite to
constitute the relatively perfect Angelic entity. This
is the meaning of the exclamation she utters in gazing
upon Wilfrid and Minna before she begins her final
address to them.

That address may be regarded as in some sense a
recapitulation of all the doctrines indicated and shad-
owed forth in the preceding parts of the story. Once
more, and now with large insistence, the doctrine of re-
incarnation is dwelt upon, and referred to as the necessary and sole explanation of human evolution. Balzac
here treats it more in detail than he has done elsewhere,
although it is the basis of Seraphita's history, and
makes intelligible the whole structure of her existence
and theosophy. Seraphita traces existence from the
Instinctive sphere upward. The lower life is occupied,
she says, with exploitation of the purely material. It is
there that the inevitable lust of possession has to be
worked out. It is there that men toil and struggle to
amass earthly treasures, and, having succeeded, slowly
realize the uselessness of such riches. Matter must be
exhausted before Spirit assumes control, and it may

happen that many existences are required to expend the craving for impermanent possessions. As a rule men indulge their lowest desires to satiety, and it is only when disgust overcomes them, when the emptiness of all mundane enjoyments is demonstrated by prolonged experiment, that they begin to seek a more excellent way. The long period of education is protracted still further by relapses and excesses. "A lifetime is often no more than sufficient to acquire virtues which balance the vices of the preceding existence." At length suffering brings love, and love self-sacrifice, and that aspiration, and aspiration, prayer; which is the direct bond of union between the finite and the infinite. It is indeed no new lesson. The directions for gaining the strait and narrow path have been vouchsafed to the sons of men in countless forms and ways, and with characteristic perseverance and malign ingenuity they have nullified their opportunities again and again by quarrelling over the phraseology and disputing the authority of the guide-books, while ignoring the significance of the essential harmony which subsists between all the rules laid down for the attainment of ultimate felicity and emancipation from evil. Yet the recognition of the superior attractions of the Divine can never be for all alike. For the souls still chained to Matter in the Instinctive sphere, for the majority even of the Abstractives, the allurements of the impermanent world must continue to be insuperable. It is only the minority who possess the courage to endure what follows every sincere movement of separation from the Material. The

latter, though in one sense but a condition of Spirit, is
in its lower forms hostile to Spirit, and it resents its
renunciation by the few who elect to enter the Path.
Instinctive Man not only deliberately prefers his inferiority, but regards with positive enmity all who evince a
desire to ascend in the scale of existence. This enmity
is in part automatic and literally instinctive, and resembles the resistance which an air-breathing creature offers
to immersion in the water. Instinctive Man cannot
breathe nor live in the rarified atmosphere of the Divine, and feeling this he fights with all his strength
against every attempt to raise him to that uninhabitable
sphere. The Path once chosen, therefore, the pilgrim
must make his account with persecution and scorn and
ill-feeling. The world will not let him go at all will-
ingly, and if he tear himself away will surely follow
him with its sharp displeasure.

These two, however, — Wilfrid and Minna, — were,
as Seraphita knows, prepared by previous incarnations
to take the step which should separate them from the
world ; and her final task is the application of the stimu-
lus which shall determine them in entering upon their
new and arduous career. As he listens to the se-
raphic eloquence of the mysterious being he has in vain
tried to entangle in the meshes of an earthly love, Wilfrid feels his carnal impulses dying, and a purer, loftier
aspiration takes their place. For the first time he
begins to comprehend who and what Seraphita is. For
the first time he is made to perceive the delusive character of his dreams of earthly glory and magnificence.

For the first time, also, he looks upon the human girl beside him with a feeling of respect and sympathy, and is drawn toward her by the attraction of a common yearning after the higher life. Then the work of Seraphita on the plane of humanity is finished, and in a final burst of rapture and adoration her spirit breaks the last fragile bonds uniting it to the body, and she rises into the celestial spheres to receive judgment, reward, whatever is awaiting her. The final chapter, entitled "The Assumption" by Balzac, is an exquisitely imagined vision. Wilfrid and Minna, kneeling by the body of Seraphita, are rapt into the heavens. For a time their spirits are permitted to leave their shells and traverse the lower fields of space, whence they are enabled to witness the splendor and majesty of their late companion's divine initiation. There is no need to follow or interpret this closing scene. It is only necessary to say that it fitly concludes a marvellous work; that notwithstanding the unavoidable employment of some conventional forms, the elevation, nobility, solemnity, and beauty of the whole picture render it a literary masterpiece, scarcely equalled and not surpassed by the most glowing conceptions of the greatest mystical poets.

So ends Balzac's philosophical trilogy. The human imagination, stretched to the utmost in sustaining these last and loftiest creations, can proceed no farther. The author has traced the evolution of the spirit from the natural to the divine world. Beyond the threshold of the latter it is not given to incarnated souls to penetrate save in vision, but the path which leads upward has been indicated with equal skill and subtlety, and some intimation has been given of the glories which attend translation to the celestial sphere. As a literary experiment " Seraphita " stands alone. It is bold, — some may think even to rashness, — but its beauty and spirituality must be admitted, and it crowns a difficult and laborious enterprise finely, harmoniously, and majestically.

GEORGE FREDERIC PARSONS.

SERAPHITA.

SERAPHITUS.

As the eye glances over a map of the coasts of
Norway, can the imagination fail to marvel at their
fantastic indentations and serrated edges, like a granite lace, against which the surges of the North Sea
roar incessantly? Who has not dreamed of the majestic sights ever to be seen on those beachless shores,
of that multitude of creeks and inlets and little bays, no
two of them alike, yet all trackless abysses? We may
almost fancy that Nature took pleasure in recording by
ineffaceable hieroglyphics the symbol of Norwegian life,
bestowing on these coasts the conformation of a fish's
spine, fishery being the staple commerce of the country,
and well-nigh the only means of living of the hardy
men who cling like tufts of lichen to the arid cliffs.
Here, through fourteen degrees of longitude, barely
seven hundred thousand souls maintain existence.
Thanks to perils devoid of glory, to year-long snows
which clothe the Norway peaks and guard them from
profaning foot of traveller, these sublime beauties are

virgin still ; they will be seen to harmonize with human phenomena, also virgin — at least to poetry — which here took place, the history of which it is our purpose to relate.

If one of these inlets, mere fissures to the eyes of the eider-ducks, is wide enough for the sea not to freeze between the prison-walls of rock against which it surges, the country-people call the little bay a *fiord*, — a word which geographers of every nation have adopted into their respective languages. Though a certain resemblance exists among all these fiords, each has its own characteristics. The sea has everywhere forced its way as through a breach, yet the rocks about each fissure are diversely rent, and their tumultuous precipices defy the rules of geometric law. Here the scarp is dentelled like a saw ; there the narrow ledges barely allow the snow to lodge or the noble crests of the Northern pines to spread themselves ; farther on, some convulsion of Nature may have rounded a coquettish curve into a lovely valley flanked in rising terraces with black-plumed pines. Truly we are tempted to call this land the Switzerland of Ocean.

Midway between Trondhjem and Christiansand lies an inlet called the Ström-fiord. If the Ström-fiord is not the loveliest of these rocky landscapes, it has the merit of displaying the terrestrial grandeurs of Norway, and of enshrining the scenes of a history that is indeed celestial.

The general outline of the Ström-fiord seems at first sight to be that of a funnel washed out by the sea.

The passage which the waves have forced present to
the eye an image of the eternal struggle between old
Ocean and the granite rock, — two creations of equal
power, one through inertia, the other by ceaseless motion. Reefs of fantastic shape run out on either side,
and bar the way of ships and forbid their entrance.
The intrepid sons of Norway cross these reefs on foot,
springing from rock to rock, undismayed at the abyss —
a hundred fathoms deep and only six feet wide — which
yawns beneath them. Here a tottering block of gneiss
falling athwart two rocks gives an uncertain footway;
there the hunters or the fishermen, carrying their loads,
have flung the stems of fir-trees in guise of bridges,
to join the projecting reefs, around and beneath which
the surges roar incessantly. This dangerous entrance
to the little bay bears obliquely to the right with a
serpentine movement, and there encounters a mountain rising some twenty-five hundred feet above sea-
level, the base of which is a vertical palisade of solid
rock more than a mile and a half long, the inflexible
granite nowhere yielding to clefts or undulations until
it reaches a height of two hundred feet above the
water. Rushing violently in, the sea is driven back
with equal violence by the inert force of the mountain
to the opposite shore, gently curved by the spent force
of the retreating waves.

The fiord is closed at the upper end by a vast gneiss
formation crowned with forests, down which a river
plunges in cascades, becomes a torrent when the snows
are melting, spreads into a sheet of waters, and then

falls with a roar into the bay, —vomiting as it does so
the hoary pines and the aged larches washed down
from the forests and scarce seen amid the foam. These
trees plunge headlong into the fiord and reappear after
a time on the surface, clinging together and forming
islets which float ashore on the beaches, where the
inhabitants of a village on the left bank of the Ström-
fiord gather them up, split, broken (though sometimes
whole), and always stripped of bark and branches.
The mountain which receives at its base the assaults
of Ocean, and at its summit the buffeting of the wild
North wind, is called the Falberg. Its crest, wrapped
at all seasons in a mantle of snow and ice, is the
sharpest peak of Norway; its proximity to the pole
produces, at the height of eighteen hundred feet, a
degree of cold equal to that of the highest mountains
of the globe. The summit of this rocky mass, rising
sheer from the fiord on one side, slopes gradually
downward to the east, where it joins the declivities of
the Sieg and forms a series of terraced valleys, the
chilly temperature of which allows no growth but that
of shrubs and stunted trees.

The upper end of the fiord, where the waters enter it
as they come down from the forest, is called the Siegdahlen, — a word which may be held to mean " the shedding of the Sieg," — the river itself receiving that name.
The curving shore opposite to the face of the Falberg
is the valley of Jarvis, — a smiling scene overlooked by
hills clothed with firs, birch-trees, and larches, mingled
with a few oaks and beeches, the richest coloring of all

the varied tapestries which Nature in these northern regions spreads upon the surface of her rugged rocks. The eye can readily mark the line where the soil, warmed by the rays of the sun, bears cultivation and shows the native growth of the Norwegian flora. Here the expanse of the fiord is broad enough to allow the sea, dashed back by the Falberg, to spend its expiring force in gentle murmurs upon the lower slope of these hills, — a shore bordered with finest sand, strewn with mica and sparkling pebbles, porphyry, and marbles of a thousand tints, brought from Sweden by the river floods, together with ocean waifs, shells, and flowers of the sea driven in by tempests, whether of the Pole or Tropics.

At the foot of the hills of Jarvis lies a village of some two hundred wooden houses, where an isolated population lives like a swarm of bees in a forest, without increasing or diminishing; vegetating happily, while wringing their means of living from the breast of a stern Nature. The almost unknown existence of the little hamlet is readily accounted for. Few of its inhabitants were bold enough to risk their lives among the reefs to reach the deep-sea fishing, — the staple industry of Norwegians on the least dangerous portions of their coast. The fish of the fiord were numerous enough to suffice, in part at least, for the sustenance of the inhabitants; the valley pastures provided milk and butter; a certain amount of fruitful, well-tilled soil yielded rye and hemp and vegetables, which necessity taught the people to protect against the severity of the cold and the fleeting but terrible heat of the sun with the shrewd ability which Norwegians display in the two-fold struggle. The difficulty of communication with the outer world, either by land where the roads are impassable, or by sea where none but tiny boats can thread their way through the maritime defiles that guard the entrance to the bay, hinder these people from growing rich by the sale of their timber. It would cost enormous sums to either blast a channel out to sea or construct a way to the interior. The roads from Christiana to Trondhjem all turn toward the Ström-fiord, and cross the Sieg by a bridge some score of miles above its fall into the bay. The country to the north, between Jarvis and Trondhjem, is covered with impenetrable forests, while to the south the Falberg is nearly as much separated from Christiana by inaccessible precipices. The village of Jarvis might perhaps have communicated with the interior of Norway and Sweden by the river Sieg; but to do this and to be thus brought into contact with civilization, the Ström-fiord needed the presence of a man of genius. Such a man did actually appear there, — a poet, a Swede of great religious fervor, who died admiring, even reverencing this region as one of the noblest works of the Creator.

Minds endowed by study with an inward sight, and whose quick perceptions bring before the soul, as though painted on a canvas, the contrasting scenery of this universe, will now apprehend the general features of the Ström-fiord. They alone, perhaps, can thread their way through the tortuous channels of the

reef, or flee with the battling waves to the everlasting
rebuff of the Falberg whose white peaks mingle with
the vaporous clouds of the pearl-gray sky, or watch
with delight the curving sheet of waters, or hear the
rushing of the Sieg as it hangs for an instant in long
fillets and then falls over a picturesque abatis of noble
trees toppled confusedly together, sometimes upright,
sometimes half-sunken beneath the rocks. It may be
that such minds alone can dwell upon the smiling
scenes nestling among the lower hills of Jarvis; where
the luscious Northern vegetables spring up in families,
in myriads, where the white birches bend, graceful as
maidens, where colonnades of beeches rear their boles
mossy with the growths of centuries, where shades
of green contrast, and white clouds float amid the
blackness of the distant pines, and tracts of many-
tinted crimson and purple shrubs are shaded end-
lessly; in short, where blend all colors, all perfumes
of a flora whose wonders are still ignored. Widen
the boundaries of this limited amphitheatre, spring
upward to the clouds, lose yourself among the rocks
where the seals are lying and even then your thought
cannot compass the wealth of beauty nor the poetry
of this Norwegian coast. Can your thought be as
vast as the ocean that bounds it? as weird as the
fantastic forms drawn by these forests, these clouds,
these shadows, these changeful lights?

Do you see above the meadows on that lowest slope
which undulates around the higher hills of Jarvis two
or three hundred houses roofed with "nœver," a sort

of thatch made of birch-bark, — frail houses, long and low, looking like silk-worms on a mulberry-leaf tossed hither by the winds? Above these humble, peaceful dwellings stands the church, built with a simplicity in keeping with the poverty of the villagers. A grave-yard surrounds the chancel, and a little farther on you see the parsonage. Higher up, on a projection of the mountain is a dwelling-house, the only one of stone; for which reason the inhabitants of the village call it " the Swedish Castle." In fact, a wealthy Swede settled in Jarvis about thirty years before this history begins, and did his best to ameliorate its condition. This little house, certainly not a castle, built with the intention of leading the inhabitants to build others like it, was noticeable for its solidity and for the wall that inclosed it, a rare thing in Norway where, notwithstanding the abundance of stone, wood alone is used for all fences, even those of fields. This Swedish house, thus protected against the climate, stood on rising ground in the centre of an immense courtyard. The windows were sheltered by those projecting pent-house roofs supported by squared trunks of trees which give so patriarchal an air to Northern dwellings. From beneath them the eye could see the savage nudity of the Falberg, or compare the infinitude of the open sea with the tiny drop of water in the foaming fiord; the ear could hear the flowing of the Sieg, whose white sheet far away looked motionless as it fell into its granite cup edged for miles around with glaciers, — in short, from this

vantage ground the whole landscape whereon our simple
yet superhuman drama was about to be enacted could
be seen and noted.

The winter of 1799–1800 was one of the most severe
ever known to Europeans. The Norwegian sea was
frozen in all the fiords, where, as a usual thing, the
violence of the surf kept the ice from forming. A
wind, whose effects were like those of the Spanish
levanter, swept the ice of the Ström-fiord, driving
the snow to the upper end of the gulf. Seldom indeed could the people of Jarvis see the mirror of
frozen waters reflecting the colors of the sky; a wondrous sight in the bosom of these mountains when all
other aspects of nature are levelled beneath successive sheets of snow, and crests and valleys are alike
mere folds of the vast mantle flung by winter across
a landscape at once so mournfully dazzling and so
monotonous. The falling volume of the Sieg, suddenly frozen, formed an immense arcade beneath which
the inhabitants might have crossed under shelter from
the blast had any dared to risk themselves inland.
But the dangers of every step away from their own
surroundings kept even the boldest hunters in their
homes, afraid lest the narrow paths along the precipices, the clefts and fissures among the rocks, might
be unrecognizable beneath the snow.

Thus it was that no human creature gave life to
the white desert where Boreas reigned, his voice alone
resounding at distant intervals. The sky, nearly always gray, gave tones of polished steel to the ice of

the fiord. Perchance some ancient eider-duck crossed
the expanse, trusting to the warm down beneath which
dream, in other lands, the luxurious rich, little knowing
of the dangers through which their luxury has come
to them. Like the Bedouin of the desert who darts
alone across the sands of Africa, the bird is neither
seen nor heard; the torpid atmosphere, deprived of
its electrical conditions, echoes neither the whirr of
its wings nor its joyous notes. Besides, what human
eye was strong enough to bear the glitter of those
pinnacles adorned with sparkling crystals, or the sharp
reflections of the snow, iridescent on the summits in
the rays of a pallid sun which infrequently appeared,
like a dying man seeking to make known that he still
lives. Often, when the flocks of gray clouds, driven
in squadrons athwart the mountains and among the
tree-tops, hid the sky with their triple veils Earth,
lacking the celestial lights, lit herself by herself.

Here, then, we meet the majesty of Cold, seated
eternally at the pole in that regal silence which is the
attribute of all absolute monarchy. Every extreme
principle carries with it an appearance of negation and
the symptoms of death; for is not life the struggle
of two forces? Here in this Northern nature nothing
lived. One sole power — the unproductive power of ice
— reigned unchallenged. The roar of the open sea no
longer reached the deaf, dumb inlet, where during one
short season of the year Nature made haste to produce
the slender harvests necessary for the food of the patient people. A few tall pine-trees lifted their black

pyramids garlanded with snow, and the form of their long branches and depending shoots completed the mourning garments of those solemn heights.

Each household gathered in its chimney-corner, in houses carefully closed from the outer air, and well supplied with biscuit, melted butter, dried fish, and other provisions laid in for the seven-months winter. The very smoke of these dwellings was hardly seen, half-hidden as they were beneath the snow, against the weight of which they were protected by long planks reaching from the roof and fastened at some distance to solid blocks on the ground, forming a covered way around each building.

During these terrible winter months the women spun and dyed the woollen stuffs and the linen fabrics with which they clothed their families, while the men read, or fell into those endless meditations which have given birth to so many profound theories, to the mystic dreams of the North, to its beliefs, to its studies (so full and so complete in one science, at least, sounded as with a plummet), to its manners and its morals, half-monastic, which force the soul to react and feed upon itself and make the Norwegian peasant a being apart among the peoples of Europe.

Such was the condition of the Ström-fiord in the first year of the nineteenth century and about the middle of the month of May.

On a morning when the sun burst forth upon this landscape, lighting the fires of the ephemeral diamonds produced by crystallizations of the snow and ice, two

beings crossed the fiord and flew along the base of
the Falberg, rising thence from ledge to ledge toward
the summit. What were they? human creatures, or
two arrows? They might have been taken for eider-
ducks sailing in consort before the wind. Not the
boldest hunter nor the most superstitious fisherman
would have attributed to human beings the power to
move safely along the slender lines traced beneath the
snow by the granite ledges, where yet this couple glided
with the terrifying dexterity of somnambulists who, forgetting their own weight and the dangers of the slightest deviation, hurry along a ridge-pole and keep their
equilibrium by the power of some mysterious force.

"Stop me, Seraphitus," said a pale young girl, "and
let me breathe. I look at you, you only, while scaling
these walls of the gulf; otherwise, what would become
of me? I am such a feeble creature. Do I tire you?"

"No," said the being on whose arm she leaned.
"But let us go on, Minna; the place where we are is
not firm enough to stand on."

Once more the snow creaked sharply beneath the long
boards fastened to their feet, and soon they reached the
upper terrace of the first ledge, clearly defined upon the
flank of the precipice. The person whom Minna had
addressed as Seraphitus threw his weight upon his right
heel, arresting the plank — six and a half feet long and
narrow as the foot of a child — which was fastened to
his boot by a double thong of leather. This plank, two
inches thick, was covered with reindeer skin, which
bristled against the snow when the foot was raised, and

served to stop the wearer. Seraphitus drew in his left
foot, furnished with another " skee," which was only
two feet long, turned swiftly where he stood, caught his
timid companion in his arms, lifted her in spite of the
long boards upon her feet, and placed her on a projecting rock from which he brushed the snow with his
pelisse.

" You are safe there, Minna; you can tremble at
your ease."

"We are a third of the way up the Ice-Cap," she
said, looking at the peak to which she gave the popular
name by which it is known in Norway ; " I can hardly
believe it."

Too much out of breath to say more, she smiled at
Seraphitus, who, without answering, laid his hand upon
her heart and listened to its sounding throbs, rapid as
those of a frightened bird.

" It often beats as fast when I run," she said.

Seraphitus inclined his head with a gesture that was
neither coldness nor indifference, and yet, despite the
grace which made the movement almost tender, it none
the less bespoke a certain negation, which in a woman
would have seemed an exquisite coquetry. Seraphitus
clasped the young girl in his arms. Minna accepted the
caress as an answer to her words, continuing to gaze at
him. As he raised his head, and threw back with impatient gesture the golden masses of his hair to free his
brow, he saw an expression of joy in the eyes of his
companion.

" Yes, Minna," he said in a voice whose paternal

accents were charming from the lips of a being who
was still adolescent, "Keep your eyes on me; do not
look below you."

" Why not?" she asked.

" You wish to know why? then look!"

Minna glanced quickly at her feet and cried out
suddenly like a child who sees a tiger. The awful sensation of abysses seized her; one glance sufficed to
communicate its contagion. The fiord, eager for food,
bewildered her with its loud voice ringing in her ears,
interposing between herself and life as though to de-
vour her more surely. From the crown of her head
to her feet and along her spine an icy shudder ran;
then suddenly intolerable heat suffused her nerves,
beat in her veins and overpowered her extremities
with electric shocks like those of the torpedo. Too
feeble to resist, she felt herself drawn by a mysterious
power to the depths below, wherein she fancied that she
saw some monster belching its venom, a monster whose
magnetic eyes were charming her, whose open jaws
appeared to craunch their prey before they seized it.

" I die, my Seraphitus, loving none but thee," she
said, making a mechanical movement to fling herself
into the abyss.

Seraphitus breathed softly on her forehead and eyes.
Suddenly, like a traveller relaxed after a bath, Minna
forgot these keen emotions, already dissipated by that
caressing breath which penetrated her body and filled
it with balsamic essences as quickly as the breath itself
had crossed the air.

" Who art thou?" she said, with a feeling of gentle terror. "Ah, but I know! thou art my life. How canst thou look into that gulf and not die?" she added presently.

Seraphitus left her clinging to the granite rock and placed himself at the edge of the narrow platform on which they stood, whence his eyes plunged to the depths of the fiord, defying its dazzling invitation. His body did not tremble, his brow was white and calm as that of a marble statue, — an abyss facing an abyss.

" Seraphitus! dost thou not love me? come back!" she cried. "Thy danger renews my terror. Who art thou to have such superhuman power at thy age?" she asked as she felt his arms inclosing her once more.

" But, Minna," answered Seraphitus, " you look fearlessly at greater spaces far than that."

Then with raised finger, this strange being pointed upward to the blue dome, which parting clouds left clear above their heads, where stars could be seen in open day by virtue of atmospheric laws as yet unstudied.

" But what a difference!" she answered smiling.

" You are right," he said; " we are born to stretch upward to the skies. Our native land, like the face of a mother, cannot terrify her children."

His voice vibrated through the being of his companion, who made no reply.

" Come! let us go on," he said.

The pair darted forward along the narrow paths traced back and forth upon the mountain, skimming

from terrace to terrace, from line to line, with the
rapidity of a barb, that bird of the desert. Presently
they reached an open space, carpeted with turf and
moss and flowers, where no foot had ever trod.

"Oh, the pretty sæter!" cried Minna, giving to
the upland meadow its Norwegian name. "But how
comes it here, at such a height?"

"Vegetation ceases here, it is true," said Seraphitus.
"These few plants and flowers are due to that shelter-
ing rock which protects the meadow from the polar
winds. Put that tuft in your bosom, Minna," he
added, gathering a flower, — "that balmy creation
which no eye has ever seen; keep the solitary matchless flower in memory of this one matchless morning of
your life. You will find no other guide to lead you
again to this sæter."

So saying, he gave her the hybrid plant his falcon eye
had seen amid the tufts of gentian acaulis and saxifrages, — a marvel, brought to bloom by the breath of
angels. With girlish eagerness Minna seized the tufted
plant of transparent green, vivid as emerald, which was
formed of little leaves rolled trumpet-wise, brown at the
smaller end but changing tint by tint to their delicately
notched edges, which were green. These leaves were so
tightly pressed together that they seemed to blend and
form a mat or cluster of rosettes. Here and there from
this green ground rose pure white stars edged with a
line of gold, and from their throats came crimson anthers
but no pistils. A fragrance, blended of roses and of
orange-blossoms, yet ethereal and fugitive, gave some-

thing as it were celestial to that mysterious flower, which Seraphitus sadly contemplated, as though it uttered plaintive thoughts which he alone could understand. But to Minna this mysterious phenomenon seemed a mere caprice of nature giving to stone the freshness, softness, and perfume of plants.

"Why do you call it matchless? can it not reproduce itself? she asked, looking at Seraphitus, who colored and turned away.

"Let us sit down," he said presently; "look below you, Minna. See! At this height you will have no fear. The abyss is so far beneath us that we no longer have a sense of its depths; it acquires the perspective uniformity of ocean, the vagueness of clouds, the soft coloring of the sky. See, the ice of the fiord is a turquoise, the dark pine forests are mere threads of brown; for us all abysses should be thus adorned."

Seraphitus said the words with that fervor of tone and gesture seen and known only by those who have ascended the highest mountains of the globe, — a fervor so involuntarily acquired that the haughtiest of men is forced to regard his guide as a brother, forgetting his own superior station till he descends to the valleys and the abodes of his kind. Seraphitus unfastened the skees from Minna's feet, kneeling before her. The girl did not notice him, so absorbed was she in the marvellous view now offered of her native land, whose rocky outlines could here be seen at a glance. She felt, with deep emotion, the solemn permanence of those frozen summits, to which words could give no adequate utterance.

" We have not come here by human power alone,"
she said, clasping her hands.   " But perhaps I dream."

" You think that facts the causes of which you cannot perceive are supernatural," replied her companion.

" Your replies," she said, " always bear the stamp
of some deep thought.   When I am near you I understand all things without an effort.   Ah, I am free!"

" If so, you will not need your skees," he answered.

" Oh!" she said; " I who would fain unfasten yours
and kiss your feet!"

" Keep such words for Wilfrid," said Seraphitus,
gently.

" Wilfrid!" cried Minna angrily; then, softening as
she glanced at her companion's face and trying, but in
vain, to take his hand, she added, " You are never
angry, never; you are so hopelessly perfect in all
things."

" From which you conclude that I am unfeeling."

Minna was startled at this lucid interpretation of her
thought.

" You prove to me, at any rate, that we understand
each other," she said, with the grace of a loving
woman.

Seraphitus softly shook his head and looked sadly
and gently at her.

" You, who know all things," said Minna, " tell me
why it is that the timidity I felt below is over now
that I have mounted higher.   Why do I dare to look
at you for the first time face to face, while lower down
I scarcely dared to give a furtive glance?"

" Perhaps because we are withdrawn from the petti-
ness of earth," he answered, unfastening his pelisse.

" Never, never have I seen you so beautiful ! " cried
Minna, sitting down on a mossy rock and losing herself
in contemplation of the being who had now guided
her to a part of the peak hitherto supposed to be
inaccessible.

Never, in truth, had Seraphitus shone with so bright
a radiance, — the only word that can render the illumination of his face and the aspect of his whole person.
Was this splendor due to the lustre which the pure air
of mountains and the reflections of the snow give to the
complexion? Was it produced by the inward impulse
which excites the body at the instant when exertion is
arrested? Did it come from the sudden contrast between the glory of the sun and the darkness of the
clouds, from whose shadow the charming couple had
just emerged? Perhaps to all these causes we may add
the effect of a phenomenon, one of the noblest which
human nature has to offer. If some able physiologist
had studied this being (who, judging by the pride on
his brow and the lightning in his eyes seemed a youth
of about seventeen year of age), and if the student
had sought for the springs of that beaming life beneath
the whitest skin that ever the North bestowed upon her
offspring, he would undoubtedly have believed either in
some phosphoric fluid of the nerves shining beneath the
cuticle, or in the constant presence of an inward lumi
nary, whose rays issued through the being of Seraphitus
like a light through an alabaster vase. Soft and slen-

der as were his hands, ungloved to remove his companion's snow-shoes, they seemed possessed of a strength
equal to that which the Creator gave to the diaphanous
tentacles of the crab. The fire darting from his vivid
glance seemed to struggle with the beams of the sun,
not to take but to give them light. His body, slim and
delicate as that of a woman, gave evidence of one of
those natures which are feeble apparently, but whose
strength equals their will, rendering them at times
powerful. Of medium height, Seraphitus appeared to
grow in stature as he turned fully round and seemed
about to spring upward. His hair, curled by a fairy's
hand and waving to the breeze, increased the illusion
produced by this aerial attitude ; yet his bearing, wholly
without conscious effort, was the result far more of a
moral phenomenon than of a corporal habit.

Minna's imagination seconded this illusion, under the
dominion of which all persons would assuredly have
fallen, — an illusion which gave to Seraphitus the appearance of a vision dreamed of in happy sleep. No
known type conveys an image of that form so majestically male to Minna, but which to the eyes of a man
would have eclipsed in womanly grace the fairest of
Raphael's creations. That painter of heaven has ever
put a tranquil joy, a loving sweetness, into the lines of
his angelic conceptions ; but what soul, unless it contemplated Seraphitus himself, could have conceived
the ineffable emotions imprinted on his face ? Who
would have divined, even in the dreams of artists,
where all things become possible, the shadow cast by

some mysterious awe upon that brow, shining with intellect, which seemed to question Heaven and to pity Earth? The head hovered awhile disdainfully, as some majestic bird whose cries reverberate on the atmosphere, then bowed itself resignedly, like the turtledove uttering soft notes of tenderness in the depths of the silent woods. His complexion was of marvellous whiteness, which brought out vividly the coral lips, the brown eyebrows, and the silken lashes, the only colors that trenched upon the paleness of that face, whose perfect regularity did not detract from the grandeur of the sentiments expressed in it; nay, thought and emotion were reflected there, without hindrance or violence, with the majestic and natural gravity which we delight in attributing to superior beings. That face of purest marble expressed in all things strength and peace.

Minna rose to take the hand of Seraphitus, hoping thus to draw him to her, and to lay on that seductive brow a kiss given more from admiration than from love; but a glance at the young man's eyes, which pierced her as a ray of sunlight penetrates a prism, paralyzed the young girl. She felt, but without comprehending, a gulf between them; then she turned away her head and wept. Suddenly a strong hand seized her by the waist and a soft voice said to her: "Come!" She obeyed, resting her head, suddenly revived, upon the heart of her companion, who, regulating his step to hers with gentle and attentive conformity, led her to a spot whence they could see the radiant glories of the polar Nature.

"Before I look, before I listen to you, tell me, Seraphitus, why you repulse me. Have I displeased you? and how? tell me! I want nothing for myself; I would that all my earthly goods were yours, for the riches of my heart are yours already. I would that light came to my eyes only through your eyes just as my thought is born of your thought. I should not then fear to offend you, for I should give you back the echoes of your soul, the words of your heart, day by day, — as we render to God the meditations with which his spirit nourishes our minds. I would be thine alone."

"Minna, a constant desire is that which shapes our future. Hope on! But if you would be pure in heart mingle the idea of the All-Powerful with your affections here below; then you will love all creatures, and your heart will rise to heights indeed."

"I will do all you tell me," she answered, lifting her eyes to his with a timid movement.

"I cannot be your companion," said Seraphitus sadly.

He seemed to repress some thoughts, then stretched his arms towards Christiana, just visible like a speck on the horizon and said : —

"Look!"

"We are very small," she said.

"Yes, but we become great through feeling and through intellect," answered Seraphitus. "With us, and us alone, Minna, begins the knowledge of things ; the little that we learn of the laws of the visible world enables us to apprehend the immensity of the worlds invisible. I know not if the time has come to speak thus to you, but I would, ah, I would communicate to you the flame of my hopes! Perhaps we may one day be together in the world where Love never dies."

"Why not here and now?" she said, murmuring.

"Nothing is stable here," he said, disdainfully. "The passing joys of earthly love are gleams which reveal to certain souls the coming of joys more durable; just as the discovery of a single law of nature leads certain privileged beings to a conception of the system of the universe. Our fleeting happiness here below is the forerunning proof of another and a perfect happiness, just as the earth, a fragment of the world, attests the universe. We cannot measure the vast orbit of the Divine thought of which we are but an atom as small as God is great; but we can feel its vastness, we can kneel, adore, and wait. Men ever mislead themselves in science by not perceiving that all things on their globe are related and co-ordinated to the general evolution, to a constant movement and production which bring with them, necessarily, both advancement and an End. Man himself is not a finished creation; if he were, God would not Be."

"How is it that in thy short life thou hast found the time to learn so many things?" said the young girl.

"I remember," he replied.

"Thou art nobler than all else I see."

"We are the noblest of God's great works. Has He

not given us the faculty of reflecting on Nature; of gathering it within us by thought; of making it a footstool and stepping-stone from and by which to rise to Him? We love according to the greater or the lesser portion of heaven our souls contain. But do not be unjust, Minna; behold the magnificence spread before you. Ocean expands at your feet like a carpet; the mountains resemble amphitheatres; heaven's ether is above them like the arching folds of a stage curtain. Here we may breathe the thoughts of God, as it were like a perfume. See! the angry billows which engulf the ships laden with men seem to us, where we are, mere bubbles; and if we raise our eyes and look above, all there is blue. Behold that diadem of stars! Here the tints of earthly impressions disappear; standing on this nature rarefied by space do you not feel within you something deeper far than mind, grander than enthusiasm, of greater energy than will? Are you not conscious of emotions whose interpretation is no longer in us? Do you not feel your pinions? Let us pray."

Seraphitus knelt down and crossed his hands upon his breast, while Minna fell, weeping, on her knees. Thus they remained for a time, while the azure dome above their heads grew larger and strong rays of light enveloped them without their knowledge.

"Why dost thou not weep when I weep?" said Minna, in a broken voice.

"They who are all spirit do not weep," replied Seraphitus rising; "Why should I weep? I see no longer human wretchedness. Here, Good appears in all its majesty. There, beneath us, I hear the supplications and the wailings of that harp of sorrows which vibrates in the hands of captive souls. Here, I listen to the choir of harps harmonious. There, below, is hope, the glorious inception of faith ; but here is faith — it reigns, hope realized ! "

" You will never love me ; I am too imperfect ; you disdain me," said the young girl.

" Minna, the violet hidden at the feet of the oak whispers to itself : ' The sun does not love me ; he comes not.' The sun says : ' If my rays shine upon her she will perish, poor flower.' Friend of the flower, he sends his beams through the oak leaves, he veils, he tempers them, and thus they color the petals of his beloved. I have not veils enough, I fear lest you see me too closely ; you would tremble if you knew me better. Listen : I have no taste for earthly fruits. Your joys, I know them all too well, and, like the sated emperors of pagan Rome, I have reached disgust of all things ; I have received the gift of vision. Leave me ! abandon me !" he murmured, sorrowfully.

Seraphitus turned and seated himself on a projecting rock, dropping his head upon his breast.

" Why do you drive me to despair ? " said Minna.

" Go, go ! " cried Seraphitus, " I have nothing that you want of me. Your love is too earthly for my love. Why do you not love Wilfrid ? Wilfrid is a man, tested by passions ; he would clasp you in his vigorous arms and make you feel a hand both broad and strong. His

hair is black, his eyes are full of human thoughts, his heart pours lava in every word he utters; he could kill you with caresses. Let him be your beloved, your husband! Yes, thine be Wilfrid!"

Minna wept aloud.

"Dare you say that you do not love him?" he went on, in a voice which pierced her like a dagger.

"Have mercy, have mercy, my Seraphitus!"

"Love him, poor child of Earth to which thy destiny has indissolubly bound thee," said the strange being, beckoning Minna by a gesture, and forcing her to the edge of the sæter, whence he pointed downward to a scene that might well inspire a young girl full of enthusiasm with the fancy that she stood above this earth.

"I longed for a companion to the kingdom of Light; I wished to show you that morsel of mud, I find you bound to it. Farewell. Remain on earth; enjoy through the senses; obey your nature; turn pale with pallid men; blush with women; sport with children; pray with the guilty; raise your eyes to heaven when sorrows overtake you; tremble, hope, throb in all your pulses; you will have a companion; you can laugh and weep, and give and receive. I, — I am an exile, far from heaven; a monster, far from earth. I live of myself and by myself. I feel by the spirit; I breathe through my brow; I see by thought; I die of impatience and of longing. No one here below can fulfil my desires or calm my griefs. I have forgotten how to weep. I am alone. I resign myself, and I wait."

Seraphitus looked at the flowery mound on which he
had seated Minna; then he turned and faced the
frowning heights, whose pinnacles were wrapped in
clouds; to them he cast, unspoken, the remainder of
his thoughts.

"Minna, do you hear those delightful strains?" he
said after a pause, with the voice of a dove, for the
eagle's cry was hushed; "it is like the music of those
Eolian harps your poets hang in forests and on the
mountains. Do you see the shadowy figures passing
among the clouds, the wingèd feet of those who are
making ready the gifts of heaven? They bring refresh-
ment to the soul; the skies are about to open and shed
the flowers of spring upon the earth. See, a gleam is
darting from the pole. Let us fly, let us fly! It is
time we go!"

In a moment their skees were refastened, and the
pair descended the Falberg by the steep slopes which
join the mountain to the valleys of the Sieg. Miraculous perception guided their course, or, to speak more
properly, their flight. When fissures covered with
snow intercepted them, Seraphitus caught Minna in
his arms and darted with rapid motion, lightly as a
bird, over the crumbling causeways of the abyss.
Sometimes, while propelling his companion, he deviated to the right or left to avoid a precipice, a tree, a
projecting rock, which he seemed to see beneath the
snow, as an old sailor, familiar with the ocean, discerns
the hidden reefs by the color, the trend, or the eddying
of the water. When they reached the paths of the

Siegdahlen, where they could fearlessly follow a straight line to regain the ice of the fiord, Seraphitus stopped Minna.

"You have nothing to say to me?" he asked.

"I thought you would rather think alone," she answered respectfully.

"Let us hasten, Minette; it is almost night," he said.

Minna quivered as she heard the voice, now so changed, of her guide, — a pure voice, like that of a young girl, which dissolved the fantastic dream through which she had been passing. Seraphitus seemed to be laying aside his male force and the too keen intellect that flamed from his eyes. Presently the charming pair glided across the fiord and reached the snow-field which divides the shore from the first range of houses; then, hurrying forward as daylight faded, they sprang up the hill toward the parsonage, as though they were mounting the steps of a great staircase.

"My father must be anxious," said Minna.

"No," answered Seraphitus.

As he spoke the couple reached the porch of the humble dwelling where Monsieur Becker, the pastor of Jarvis, sat reading while awaiting his daughter for the evening meal.

"Dear Monsieur Becker," said Seraphitus, "I have brought Minna back to you safe and sound."

"Thank you, mademoiselle," said the old man, laying his spectacles on his book; "you must be very tired."

" Oh, no," said Minna, and as she spoke she felt the soft breath of her companion on her brow.

" Dear heart, will you come day after to-morrow evening and take tea with me? "

" Gladly, dear."

" Monsieur Becker, you will bring her, will you not? "

" Yes, mademoiselle."

Seraphitus inclined his head with a pretty gesture, and bowed to the old pastor as he left the house. A few moments later he reached the great courtyard of the Swedish villa. An old servant, over eighty years of age, appeared in the portico bearing a lantern. Seraphitus slipped off his snow-shoes with the graceful dexterity of a woman, then darting into the salon he fell exhausted and motionless on a wide divan covered with furs.

" What will you take? " asked the old man, lighting the immensely tall wax-candles that are used in Norway.

" Nothing, David, I am too weary."

Seraphitus unfastened his pelisse lined with sable, threw it over him, and fell asleep. The old servant stood for several minutes gazing with loving eyes at the singular being before him, whose sex it would have been difficult for any one at that moment to determine. Wrapped as he was in a formless garment, which resembled equally a woman's robe and a man's mantle, it was impossible not to fancy that the slender feet which hung at the side of the couch were those of a woman, and equally impossible not to note how the forehead and the outlines of the head gave evidence of power brought to its highest pitch.

" She suffers, and she will not tell me," thought th old man. " She is dying, like a flower wilted by t! burning sun."

And the old man wept.

II.

SERAPHITA.

LATER in the evening David re-entered the salon.

" I know who it is you have come to announce," said Seraphita in a sleepy voice. " Wilfrid may enter."

Hearing these words a man suddenly presented himself, crossed the room and sat down beside her.

" My dear Seraphita, are you ill?" he said. " You look paler than usual."

She turned slowly towards him, tossing back her hair like a pretty woman whose aching head leaves her no strength even for complaint.

" I was foolish enough to cross the fiord with Minna," she said. " We ascended the Falberg."

" Do you mean to kill yourself?" he said with a lover's terror.

" No, my good Wilfrid; I took the greatest care of your Minna."

Wilfrid struck his hand violently on a table, rose hastily, and made several steps towards the door with an exclamation full of pain; then he returned and seemed about to remonstrate.

" Why this disturbance if you think me ill?" she said.

" Forgive me, have mercy ! " he cried, kneeling beside her. " Speak to me harshly if you will; exact all that the cruel fancies of a woman lead you to imagine I least can bear; but oh, my beloved, do not doubt my love. You take Minna like an axe to hew me down. Have mercy ! "

" Why do you say these things, my friend, when you know that they are useless? " she replied, with a look which grew in the end so soft that Wilfrid ceased to behold her eyes, but saw in their place a fluid light, the shimmer of which was like the last vibrations of an Italian song.

" Ah ! no man dies of anguish ! " he murmured.

" You are suffering? " she said in a voice whose intonations produced upon his heart the same effect as that of her look. " Would I could help you ! "

" Love me as I love you."

" Poor Minna ! " she replied.

" Why am I unarmed ! " exclaimed Wilfrid, violently.

" You are out of temper," said Seraphita, smiling. " Come, have I not spoken to you like those Parisian women whose loves you tell of ? "

Wilfrid sat down, crossed his arms, and looked gloomily at Seraphita. " I forgive you," he said; " for you know not what you do."

" You mistake," she replied; " every woman from the days of Eve does good and evil knowingly."

" I believe it ; " he said.

" I am sure of it, Wilfrid. Our instinct is precisely that which makes us perfect. What you men learn, we feel."

" Why, then, do you not feel how much I love you?"

" Because you do not love me."

" Good God ! "

" If you did, would you complain of your own sufferings ? "

" You are terrible to-night, Seraphita. You are a demon."

" No, but I am gifted with the faculty of comprehending, and it is awful. Wilfrid, sorrow is a lamp which illumines life."

" Why did you ascend the Falberg ? "

" Minna will tell you. I am too weary to talk. You must talk to me, — you who know so much, who have learned all things and forgotten nothing ; you who have passed through every social test. Talk to me, amuse me, I am listening."

"What can I tell you that you do not know? Besides, the request is ironical. You allow yourself no intercourse with social life ; you trample on its conventions, its laws, its customs, sentiments, and sciences ; you reduce them all to the proportions such things take when viewed by you beyond this universe."

" Therefore you see, my friend, that I am not a woman. You do wrong to love me. What! am I to leave the ethereal regions of my pretended strength, make myself humbly small, cringe like the hapless females of all species, that you may lift me up? and then, when I, helpless and broken, ask you for help, when I need your arm, you will repulse me ! No, we can never come to terms."

3

" You are more maliciously unkind to-night than I have ever known you."

" Unkind ! " she said, with a look which seemed to blend all feelings into one celestial emotion, " no, I am ill, I suffer, that is all. Leave me, my friend ; it is your manly right. We women should ever please you, entertain you, be gay in your presence and have no whims save those that amuse you. Come, what shall I do for you, friend ? Shall I sing, shall I dance, though weariness deprives me of the use of voice and limbs ? — Ah ! gentlemen, be we on our deathbeds, we yet must smile to please you ; you call that, methinks, your right. Poor women ! I pity them. Tell me, you who abandon them when they grow old, is it because they have neither hearts nor souls ? Wilfred, I am a hundred years old ; leave me ! leave me ! go to Minna ! "

" Oh, my eternal love ! "

" Do you know the meaning of eternity ? Be silent, Wilfrid. You desire me, but you do not love me. Tell me, do I not seem to you like those coquettish Parisian women ? "

" Certainly I no longer find you the pure celestial maiden I first saw in the church of Jarvis."

At these words Seraphita passed her hands across her brow, and when she removed them Wilfrid was amazed at the saintly expression that overspread her face.

" You are right, my friend," she said ; " I do wrong whenever I set my feet upon your earth."

" Oh, Seraphita, be my star! stay where you can ever bless me with that clear light!"

As he spoke, he stretched forth his hand to take that of the young girl, but she withdrew it, neither disdainfully nor in anger. Wilfrid rose abruptly and walked to the window that she might not see the tears that rose to his eyes.

" Why do you weep?" she said. " You are not a child, Wilfrid. Come back to me. I wish it. You are annoyed if I show just displeasure. You see that I am fatigued and ill, yet you force me to think and speak, and listen to persuasions and ideas that weary me. If you had any real perception of my nature, you would have made some music, you would have lulled my feelings — but no, you love me for yourself and not for myself."

The storm which convulsed the young man's heart calmed down at these words. He slowly approached her, letting his eyes take in the seductive creature who lay exhausted before him, her head resting in her hand and her elbow on the couch.

" You think that I do not love you," she resumed. " You are mistaken. Listen to me, Wilfrid. You are beginning to know much; you have suffered much. Let me explain your thoughts to you. You wished to take my hand just now;" she rose to a sitting posture, and her graceful motions seemed to emit light. " When a young girl allows her hand to be taken it is as though she made a promise, is it not? and ought she not to fulfil it? You well know that I cannot be yours.

Two sentiments divide and inspire the love of all the women of the earth. Either they devote themselves to suffering, degraded, and criminal beings whom they desire to console, uplift, redeem; or they give themselves to superior men, sublime and strong, whom they adore and seek to comprehend, and by whom they are often annihilated. You have been degraded, though now you are purified by the fires of repentance, and to-day you are once more noble; but I know myself too feeble to be your equal, and too religious to bow before any power but that On High. I may refer thus to your life, my friend, for we are in the North, among the clouds, where all things are abstractions."

"You stab me, Seraphita, when you speak like this. It wounds me to hear you apply the dreadful knowledge with which you strip from all things human the properties that time and space and form have given them, and consider them mathematically in the abstract, as geometry treats substances from which it extracts solidity."

"Well, I will respect your wishes, Wilfrid. Let the subject drop. Tell me what you think of this bearskin rug which my poor David has spread out."

"It is very handsome."

"Did you ever see me wear this *doucha greka?*"

She pointed to a pelisse made of cashmere and lined with the skin of the black fox, — the name she gave it signifying "warm to the soul."

"Do you believe that any sovereign has a fur that can equal it?" she asked.

" It is worthy of her who wears it."

" And whom you think beautiful? "

" Human words do not apply to her. Heart to heart is the only language I can use."

" Wilfred, you are kind to soothe my griefs with such sweet words — which you have said to others."

" Farewell ! "

" Stay. I love both you and Minna, believe me. To me you two are as one being. United thus you can be my brother or, if you will, my sister. Marry her ; let me see you both happy before I leave this world of trial and of pain. My God ! the simplest of women obtain what they ask of a lover ; they whisper ' Hush ! ' and he is silent ; ' Die ' and he dies ; ' Love me afar ' and he stays at a distance, like courtiers before a king ! All I desire is to see you happy, and you refuse me ! Am I then powerless? — Wilfred, listen, come nearer to me. Yes, I should grieve to see you marry Minna but — when I am here no longer, then — promise me to marry her ; heaven destined you for each other."

" I listen to you with fascination, Seraphita. Your words are incomprehensible, but they charm me. What is it you mean to say? "

" You are right ; I forget to be foolish, — to be the poor creature whose weaknesses gratify you. I torment you, Wilfrid. You came to these Northern lands for rest, you, worn-out by the impetuous struggle of genius unrecognized, you, weary with the patient toils of science, you, who well-nigh dyed your hands in crime and wore the fetters of human justice — "

Wilfred dropped speechless on the carpet. Seraphita breathed softly on his forehead, and in a moment he fell asleep at her feet.

"Sleep! rest!" she said, rising.

She passed her hands over Wilfrid's brow; then the following sentences escaped her lips, one by one, — all different in tone and accent, but all melodious, full of a Goodness that seemed to emanate from her head in vaporous waves, like the gleams the goddess chastely lays upon Endymion sleeping.

"I cannot show myself such as I am to thee, dear Wilfrid, — to thee who art strong.

"The hour is come; the hour when the effulgent lights of the future cast their reflections backward on the soul; the hour when the soul awakes into freedom.

"Now am I permitted to tell thee how I love thee. Dost thou not see the nature of my love, a love without self-interest; a sentiment full of thee, thee only; a love which follows thee into the future to light that future for thee — for it is the one True Light. Canst thou now conceive with what ardor I would have thee leave this life which weighs thee down, and behold thee nearer than thou art to that world where Love is never-failing? Can it be aught but suffering to love for one life only? Hast thou not felt a thirst for the eternal love? Dost thou not feel the bliss to which a creature rises when, with twin-soul, it loves the Being who betrays not love, Him before whom we kneel in adoration?

"Would I had wings to cover thee, Wilfred; power to give thee strength to enter now into that world where all the purest joys of purest earthly attachments are but shadows in the Light that shines, unceasing, to illumine and rejoice all hearts.

"Forgive a friendly soul for showing thee the picture of thy sins, in the charitable hope of soothing the sharp pangs of thy remorse. Listen to the pardoning choir; refresh thy soul in the dawn now rising for thee beyond the night of death. Yes, thy life, thy true life is there!

"May my words now reach thee clothed in the glorious forms of dreams; may they deck themselves with images glowing and radiant as they hover round you. Rise, rise, to the height where men can see themselves distinctly, pressed together though they be like grains of sand upon a sea-shore. Humanity rolls out like a many-colored ribbon. See the diverse shades of that flower of the celestial gardens. Behold the beings who lack intelligence, those who begin to receive it, those who have passed through trials, those who love, those who follow wisdom and aspire to the regions of Light!

"Canst thou comprehend, through this thought made visible, the destiny of humanity? — whence it came, whither it goeth? Continue steadfast in the Path. Reaching the end of thy journey thou shalt hear the clarions of omnipotence sounding the cries of victory in chords of which a single one would shake the earth, but which are lost in the spaces of a world that hath neither east nor west.

"Canst thou comprehend, my poor beloved Tried-one,

that unless the torpor and the veils of sleep had wrapped
thee, such sights would rend and bear away thy mind
as the whirlwinds rend and carry into space the feeble
sails, depriving thee forever of thy reason? Dost thou
understand that the Soul itself, raised to its utmost
power can scarcely endure in dreams the burning communications of the Spirit?

"Speed thy way through the luminous spheres; behold,
admire, hasten! Flying thus thou canst pause or advance without weariness. Like other men, thou wouldst
fain be plunged forever in these spheres of light and
perfume where now thou art, free of thy swooning body,
and where thy thought alone has utterance. Fly! enjoy
for a fleeting moment the wings thou shalt surely win
when Love has grown so perfect in thee that thou hast
no senses left; when thy whole being is all mind, all
love. The higher thy flight the less canst thou see the
abysses. There are none in heaven. Look at the
friend who speaks to thee; she who holds thee above
this earth in which are all abysses. Look, behold,
contemplate me yet a moment longer, for never again
wilt thou see me, save imperfectly as the pale twilight
of this world may show me to thee."

Seraphita stood erect, her head with floating hair
inclining gently forward, in that aerial attitude which
great painters give to messengers from heaven; the
folds of her raiment fell with the same unspeakable grace
which holds an artist — the man who translates all things
into sentiment — before the exquisite well-known lines
of Polyhymnia's veil. Then she stretched forth her

hand. Wilfrid rose. When he looked at Seraphita she was lying on the bear's-skin, her head resting on her hand, her face calm, her eyes brilliant. Wilfrid gazed at her silently ; but his face betrayed a deferential fear in its almost timid expression.

" Yes, dear," he said at last, as though he were answering some question ; " we are separated by worlds. I resign myself; I can only adore you. But what will become of me, poor and alone ! "

" Wilfrid, you have Minna."

He shook his head.

" Do not be so disdainful : woman understands all things through love ; what she does not understand she feels ; what she does not feel she sees ; when she neither sees, nor feels, nor understands, this angel of earth divines to protect you, and hides her protection beneath the grace of love."

" Seraphita, am I worthy to belong to a woman ? "

" Ah, now," she said, smiling, " you are suddenly very modest; is it a snare ? A woman is always so touched to see her weakness glorified. Well, come and take tea with me the day after to-morrow evening ; good Monsieur Becker will be here, and Minna, the purest and most artless creature I have known on earth. Leave me now, my friend ; I need to make long prayers and expiate my sins."

" You, can you commit sin ? "

" Poor friend ! if we abuse our power, is not that the sin of pride ? I have been very proud to-day. Now leave me, till to-morrow."

" Till to-morrow," said Wilfrid faintly, casting a long glance at the being of whom he desired to carry with him an ineffaceable memory.

Though he wished to go far away, he was held, as it were, outside the house for some moments, watching the light which shone from all the windows of the Swedish dwelling.

"What is the matter with me?" he asked himself. "No, she is not a mere creature, but a whole creation. Of her world, even through veils and clouds, I have caught echoes like the memory of sufferings healed, like the dazzling vertigo of dreams in which we hear the plaints of generations mingling with the harmonies of some higher sphere where all is Light and all is Love. Am I awake? Do I still sleep? Are these the eyes before which the luminous space retreated further and further indefinitely while the eyes followed it? The night is cold, yet my head is fire. I will go to the parsonage. With the pastor and his daughter I shall recover the balance of my mind."

But still he did not leave the spot whence his eyes could plunge into Seraphita's salon. The mysterious creature seemed to him the radiating centre of a luminous circle which formed an atmosphere about her wider than that of other beings; whoever entered it felt the compelling influence of, as it were, a vortex of dazzling light and all consuming thoughts. Forced to struggle against this inexplicable power, Wilfrid only prevailed after strong efforts; but when he reached and passed the inclosing wall of the courtyard, he regained his freedom of will, walked rapidly towards the parsonage, and was soon beneath the high wooden arch which formed a sort of peristyle to Monsieur Becker's dwelling. He opened the first door, against which the wind had driven the snow, and knocked on the inner one, saying : —

" Will you let me spend the evening with you, Monsieur Becker? "

" Yes," cried two voices, mingling their intonations.

Entering the parlor, Wilfrid returned by degrees to real life. He bowed affectionately to Minna, shook hands with Monsieur Becker, and looked about at the picture of a home which calmed the convulsions of his physical nature, in which a phenomenon was taking place analogous to that which sometimes seizes upon men who have given themselves up to protracted contemplations. If some strong thought bears upward on phantasmal wing a man of learning or a poet, isolates him from the external circumstances which environ him here below, and leads him forward through illimitable regions where vast arrays of facts become abstractions, where the greatest works of Nature are but images, then woe betide him if a sudden noise strikes sharply on his senses and calls his errant soul back to its prison-house of flesh and bones. The shock of the reunion of these two powers, body and mind, — one of which partakes of the unseen qualities of a thunderbolt, while the other shares with sentient nature that soft resistant force which defies destruction, — this shock, this struggle, or, rather let us say, this painful

meeting and co-mingling, gives rise to frightful suffer·
ings. The body receives back the flame that consumes
it ; the flame has once more grasped its prey. This
fusion, however, does not take place without convulsions, explosions, tortures ; analogous and visible signs
of which may be seen in chemistry, when two antagonistic substances which science has united separate.

For the last few days whenever Wilfrid entered Seraphita's presence his body seemed to fall away from him
into nothingness. With a single glance this strange
being led him in spirit through the spheres where meditation leads the learned man, prayer the pious heart,
where vision transports the artist, and sleep the souls of
men, — each and all have their own path to the Height,
their own guide to reach it, their own individual sufferings in the dire return. In that sphere alone all veils
are rent away, and the revelation, the awful flaming
certainty of an unknown world, of which the soul brings
back mere fragments to this lower sphere, stands revealed. To Wilfrid one hour passed with Seraphita
was like the sought-for dreams of Theriakis, in which
each knot of nerves becomes the centre of a radiating
delight. But he left her bruised and wearied as some
young girl endeavoring to keep step with a giant.

The cold air, with its stinging flagellations, had begun
to still the nervous tremors which followed the reunion
of his two natures, so powerfully disunited for a time ;
he was drawn towards the parsonage, then towards
Minna, by the sight of the every-day home life for which
he thirsted as the wandering European thirsts for his

native land when nostalgia seizes him amid the fairy
scenes of Orient that have seduced his senses. More
weary than he had ever yet been, Wilfrid dropped into
a chair and looked about him for a time, like a man who
awakes from sleep. Monsieur Becker and his daughter
accustomed, perhaps, to the apparent eccentricity of
their guest, continued the employments in which they
were engaged.

The parlor was ornamented with a collection of the
shells and insects of Norway. These curiosities, admirably arranged on a background of the yellow pine
which panelled the room, formed, as it were, a rich tapestry to which the fumes of tobacco had imparted a
mellow tone. At the further end of the room, opposite
to the door, was an immense wrought-iron stove, carefully polished by the serving-woman till it shone like
burnished steel. Seated in a large tapestried armchair
near the stove, before a table, with his feet in a species
of muff, Monsieur Becker was reading a folio volume
which was propped against a pile of other books as on
a desk. At his left stood a jug of beer and a glass, at
his right burned a smoky lamp fed by some species of
fish-oil. The pastor seemed about sixty years of age.
His face belonged to a type often painted by Rembrandt;
the same small bright eyes, set in wrinkles and surmounted by thick gray eyebrows; the same white hair
escaping in snowy flakes from a black velvet cap; the
same broad, bald brow, and a contour of face which
the ample chin made almost square; and lastly, the
same calm tranquillity, which, to an observer, denoted

the possession of some inward power, be it the supremacy bestowed by money, or the magisterial influence of the burgomaster, or the consciousness of art, or the cubic force of blissful ignorance. This fine old man, whose stout body proclaimed his vigorous health, was wrapped in a dressing-gown of rough gray cloth plainly bound. Between his lips was a meerschaum pipe, from which, at regular intervals, he blew the smoke, following with abstracted vision its fantastic wreathings, — his mind employed, no doubt, in assimilating through some meditative process the thoughts of the author whose works he was studying.

On the other side of the stove and near a door which communicated with the kitchen Minna was indistinctly visible in the haze of the good man's smoke, to which she was apparently accustomed. Beside her on a little table were the implements of household work, a pile of napkins, and another of socks waiting to be mended, also a lamp like that which shone on the white page of the book in which the pastor was absorbed. Her fresh young face, with its delicate outline, expressed an infinite purity which harmonized with the candor of the white brow and the clear blue eyes. She sat erect, turning slightly toward the lamp for better light, unconsciously showing as she did so the beauty of her waist and bust. She was already dressed for the night in a long robe of white cotton; a cambric cap, without other ornament than a frill of the same, confined her hair. Though evidently plunged in some inward meditation, she counted without a mistake the threads of her napkins or the meshes of her socks. Sitting thus, she presented the most complete image, the truest type, of the woman destined for terrestrial labor, whose glance may pierce the clouds of the sanctuary while her thought, humble and charitable, keeps her ever on the level of man.

Wilfrid had flung himself into a chair between the two tables and was contemplating with a species of intoxication this picture full of harmony, to which the clouds of smoke did no despite. The single window which lighted the parlor during the fine weather was now carefully closed. An old tapestry, used for a curtain and fastened to a stick, hung before it in heavy folds. Nothing in the room was picturesque, nothing brilliant; everything denoted rigorous simplicity, true heartiness, the ease of unconventional nature, and the habits of a domestic life which knew neither cares nor troubles. Many a dwelling is like a dream, the sparkle of passing pleasure seems to hide some ruin beneath the cold smile of luxury; but this parlor, sublime in reality, harmonious in tone, diffused the patriarchal ideas of a full and self-contained existence. The silence was unbroken save by the movements of the servant in the kitchen engaged in preparing the supper, and by the sizzling of the dried fish which she was frying in salt butter according to the custom of the country.

" Will you smoke a pipe? " said the pastor, seizing a moment when he thought that Wilfrid might listen to him.

" Thank you, no, dear Monsieur Becker," replied the visitor.

" You seem to suffer more to-day than usual," said Minna, struck by the feeble tones of the stranger's voice.

" I am always so when I leave the château."

Minna quivered.

" A strange being lives there, Monsieur Becker," he continued after a pause. " For the six months that I have been in this village I have never yet dared to question you about her, and even now I do violence to my feelings in speaking of her. I began by keenly regretting that my journey in this country was arrested by the winter weather and that I was forced to remain here. But during the last two months chains have been forged and riveted which bind me irrevocably to Jarvis, till now I fear to end my days here. You know how I first met Seraphita, what impression her look and voice made upon me, and how at last I was admitted to her home where she receives no one. From the very first day I have longed to ask you the history of this mysterious being. On that day began, for me, a series of enchantments."

" Enchantments! " cried the pastor shaking the ashes of his pipe into an earthen-ware dish full of sand, " are there enchantments in these days? "

" You, who are carefully studying at this moment that volume of the ' Incantations ' of Jean Wier, will surely understand the explanation of my sensations if I try to give it to you," replied Wilfrid. " If we study Nature attentively in its great evolutions as in its minutest works, we cannot fail to recognize the pos-

sibility of enchantment — giving to that word its exact
significance. Man does not create forces ; he employs
the only force that exists and which includes all others
namely Motion, the breath incomprehensible of the
sovereign Maker of the universe. Species are too
distinctly separated for the human hand to mingle
them. The only miracle of which man is capable
is done through the conjunction of two antagonistic
substances. Gunpowder for instance is germane to a
thunderbolt. As to calling forth a creation, and a
sudden one, all creation demands time, and time
neither recedes nor advances at the word of command.
So, in the world without us, plastic nature obeys
laws the order and exercise of which cannot be in-
terfered with by the hand of man. But after fulfilling, as it were, the function of Matter, it would be
unreasonable not to recognize within us the existence
of a gigantic power, the effects of which are so in-
commensurable that the known generations of men
have never yet been able to classify them. I do not
speak of man's faculty of abstraction, of constraining
Nature to confine itself within the Word, — a gigantic
act on which the common mind reflects as little as it
does on the nature of Motion, but which, nevertheless,
has led the Indian theosophists to explain creation by
a word to which they give an inverse power. The
smallest atom of their subsistence, namely, the grain
of rice, from which a creation issues and in which alternately creation again is held, presented to their
minds so perfect an image of the creative word, and

of the abstractive word, that to them it was easy to apply the same system to the creation of worlds. The majority of men content themselves with the grain of rice sown in the first chapter of all the Geneses. Saint John, when he said the Word was God only complicated the difficulty. But the fructification, germination, and efflorescence of our ideas is of little consequence if we compare that property, shared by many men, with the wholly individual faculty of communicating to that property, by some mysterious concentration, forces that are more or less active, of carrying it up to a third, a ninth, or a twenty-seventh power, of making it thus fasten upon the masses and obtain magical results by condensing the processes of nature.

"What I mean by enchantments," continued Wilfrid after a moment's pause, "are those stupendous actions taking place between two membranes in the tissue of the brain. We find in the unexplorable nature of the Spiritual World certain beings armed with these wondrous faculties, comparable only to the terrible power of certain gases in the physical world, beings who combine with other beings, penetrate them as active agents, and produce upon them witchcrafts, charms, against which these helpless slaves are wholly defenceless; they are, in fact, enchanted, brought under subjection, reduced to a condition of dreadful vassalage. Such mysterious beings overpower others with the sceptre and the glory of a superior nature, — acting upon them at times like the torpedo which electrifies or paralyzes the fisherman, at other times like a dose of phosphorus which stimulates life and accelerates its propulsion; or again, like opium, which puts to sleep corporeal nature, disengages the spirit from every bond, enables it to float above the world and shows this earth to the spiritual eye as through a prism, extracting from it the food most needed; or, yet again, like catalepsy, which deadens all faculties for the sake of one only vision. Miracles, enchantments, incantations, witchcrafts, spells, and charms, in short, all those acts improperly termed supernatural, are only possible and can only be explained by the despotism with which some spirit compels us to feel the effects of a mysterious optic which increases, or diminishes, or exalts creation, moves within us as it pleases, deforms or embellishes all things to our eyes, tears us from heaven, or drags us to hell, — two terms by which men agree to express the two extremes of joy and misery.

" These phenomena are within us, not without us," Wilfrid went on. " The being whom we call Seraphita seems to me one of those rare and terrible spirits to whom power is given to bind men, to crush nature, to enter into participation of the occult power of God. The course of her enchantments over me began on that first day, when silence as to her was imposed upon me against my will. Each time that I have wished to question you it seemed as though I were about to reveal a secret of which I ought to be the incorruptible guardian. Whenever I have tried to speak, a burning seal has been laid upon my lips, and I myself have become the involuntary minister of these mysteries. You see me here to-night, for the hundredth time, bruised, defeated, broken, after leaving the hallucinating sphere which surrounds that young girl, so gentle, so fragile to both of you, but to me the cruellest of magicians! Yes, to me she is like a sorcerer holding in her right hand the invisible wand that moves the globe, and in her left the thunderbolt that rends asunder all things at her will. No longer can I look upon her brow; the light of it is insupportable. I skirt the borders of the abyss of madness too closely to be longer silent. I must speak. I seize this moment, when courage comes to me, to resist the power which drags me onward without inquiring whether or not I have the force to follow. Who is she? Did you know her young? What of her birth? Had she father and mother, or was she born of the conjunction of ice and sun? She burns and yet she freezes; she shows herself and then withdraws; she attracts me and repulses me; she brings me life, she gives me death; I love her and yet I hate her! I cannot live thus; let me be wholly in heaven or in hell!"

Holding his refilled pipe in one hand, and in the other the cover which he forgot to replace, Monsieur Becker listened to Wilfrid with a mysterious expression on his face, looking occasionally at his daughter, who seemed to understand the man's language as in harmony with the strange being who inspired it. Wilfrid was splendid to behold at this moment, — like Hamlet listening to the ghost of his father as it rises for him alone in the midst of the living.

" This is certainly the language of a man in love,"
said the good pastor, innocently.

" In love ! " cried Wilfrid, " yes, to common minds.
But, dear Monsieur Becker, no words can express the
frenzy which draws me to the feet of that unearthly
being."

" Then you do love her? " said Minna, in a tone of
reproach.

" Mademoiselle, I feel such extraordinary agitation
when I see her, and such deep sadness when I see her
no more, that in any other man what I feel would be
called love. But that sentiment draws those who feel
it ardently together, whereas between her and me a
great gulf lies, whose icy coldness penetrates my very
being in her presence ; though the feeling dies away
when I see her no longer. I leave her in despair ; I
return to her with ardor, — like men of science who
seek a secret from Nature only to be baffled, or like the
painter who would fain put life upon his canvas and
strives with all the resources of his art in the vain
attempt."

" Monsieur, all that you say is true," replied the
young girl, artlessly.

" How can you know, Minna? " asked the old pastor.

" Ah ! my father, had you been with us this morning
on the summit of the Falberg, had you seen him praying, you would not ask me that question. You would
say, like Monsieur Wilfrid, when he saw his Seraphita
for the first time in our temple, ' It is the Spirit of
Prayer.'"

These words were followed by a moment's silence.

"Ah, truly!" said Wilfrid, "she has nothing in common with the creatures who grovel upon this earth."

"On the Falberg!" said the old pastor, "how could you get there?"

"I do not know," replied Minna; "the way is like a dream to me, of which no more than a memory remains. Perhaps I should hardly believe that I had been there were it not for this tangible proof."

She drew the flower from her bosom and showed it to them. All three gazed at the pretty saxifrage, which was still fresh, and now shone in the light of the two lamps like a third luminary.

"This is indeed supernatural," said the old man, astounded at the sight of a flower blooming in winter.

"A mystery!" cried Wilfrid, intoxicated with its perfume.

"The flower makes me giddy," said Minna; "I fancy I still hear that voice, — the music of thought; that I still see the light of that look, which is Love."

"I implore you, my dear Monsieur Becker, tell me the history of Seraphita, — enigmatical human flower, — whose image is before us in this mysterious bloom."

"My dear friend," said the old man, emitting a puff of smoke, "to explain the birth of that being it is absolutely necessary that I disperse the clouds which envelop the most obscure of Christian doctrines. It is not easy to make myself clear when speaking of that incomprehensible revelation, — the last effulgence of faith that has shone upon our lump of mud. Do you know Swedenborg?"

" By name only, — of him, of his books and his religion I know nothing."

" Then I must relate to you the whole chronicle of Swedenborg."

III.

SERAPHITA-SERAPHITUS.

AFTER a pause, during which the pastor seemed to be gathering his recollections, he continued in the following words : —

" Emanuel Swedenborg was born at Upsala in Sweden, in the month of January, 1688, according to various authors, — in 1689, according to his epitaph. His father was Bishop of Skara. Swedenborg lived eighty-five years ; his death occurred in London, March 29, 1772. I use that term to convey the idea of a simple change of state. According to his disciples, Swedenborg was seen at Jarvis and in Paris after that date. Allow me, my dear Monsieur Wilfrid," said Monsieur Becker, making a gesture to prevent all interruption, " I relate these facts without either affirming or denying them. Listen ; afterwards you can think and say what you like. I will inform you when I judge, criticise, and discuss these doctrines, so as to keep clearly in view my own intellectual neutrality between HIM and Reason.

" The life of Swedenborg was divided into two parts," continued the pastor. " From 1688 to 1745 Baron Emanuel Swedenborg appeared in the world as a man of vast learning, esteemed and cherished for his virtues, always irreproachable and constantly useful. While fulfilling high public functions in Sweden, he published, between 1709 and 1740, several important works on mineralogy, physics, mathematics, and astronomy, which enlightened the world of learning. He originated a method of building docks suitable for the reception of large vessels, and he wrote many treatises on various important questions, such as the rise of tides, the theory of the magnet and its qualities, the motion and position of the earth and planets, and, while Assessor in the Royal College of Mines, on the proper system of working salt mines. He discovered means to construct canal-locks or sluices ; and he also discovered and applied the simplest methods of extracting ore and of working metals. In fact he studied no science without advancing it. In youth he learned Hebrew, Greek, and Latin, also the oriental languages, with which he became so familiar that many distinguished scholars consulted him, and he was able to decipher the vestiges of the oldest known books of Scripture, namely : ' The Wars of ·Jehovah ' and ' The Enunciations,' spoken of by Moses (Numbers xxi. 14, 15, 27–30), also by Joshua, Jeremiah, and Samuel, — ' The Wars of Jehovah ' being the historical part and ' The Enunciations ' the prophetical part of the Mosaical Books anterior to Genesis. Swedenborg even affirms that ' the Book of Jasher,' the Book of the Righteous, mentioned by Joshua, was in existence in Eastern Tartary, together with the doctrine of Correspondences. A Frenchman has lately, so they tell me, justified these statements of Swedenborg, by the discovery at Bagdad of several portions of the Bible hitherto unknown in Europe. During the widespread discussion on animal magnetism which took its rise in Paris, and in which most men of Western science took an active part about the year 1785, Monsieur le Marquis de Thomé vindicated the memory of Swedenborg by calling attention to certain assertions made by the Commission appointed by the King of France to investigate the subject. These gentlemen declared that no theory of magnetism existed, whereas Swedenborg had studied and promulged it ever since the year 1720. Monsieur de Thomé seized this opportunity to show the reason why so many men of science relegated Swedenborg to oblivion while they delved into his treasure-house and took his facts to aid their work. 'Some of the most illustrious of these men,' said Monsieur de Thomé, alluding to the 'Theory of the Earth' by Buffon, 'have had the meanness to wear the plumage of the noble bird and refuse him all acknowledgment;' and he proved, by masterly quotations drawn from the encyclopædic works of Swedenborg, that the great prophet had anticipated by over a century the slow march of human science. It suffices to read his philosophical and mineralogical works to be convinced of this. In one passage he is seen as the precursor of modern chemistry by the announcement that the productions of organized nature are decomposable and resolve into two simple principles; also that water, air, and fire are *not elements.* In another, he goes in a few words to the heart of magnetic mysteries and deprives Mesmer of the honors of a first knowledge of them.

" There," said Monsieur Becker, pointing to a long
shelf against the wall between the stove and the window
on which were ranged books of all sizes, " behold him !
here are seventeen works from his pen, of which one,
his ' Philosophical and Mineralogical Works,' published
in 1734, is in three folio volumes. These productions,
which prove the incontestable knowledge of Swedenborg, were given to me by Monsieur Seraphitus, his
cousin and the father of Seraphita.

" In 1740," continued Monsieur Becker, after a slight
pause, " Swedenborg fell into a state of absolute silence,
from which he emerged to bid farewell to all his earthly
occupations ; after which his thoughts turned exclusively to the Spiritual Life. He received the first com-
mands of heaven in 1745, and he thus relates the nature
of the vocation to which he was called : One evening,
in London, after dining with a great appetite, a thick
white mist seemed to fill his room. When the vapor
dispersed a creature in human form rose from one
corner of the apartment, and said in a stern tone, ' Do
not eat so much.' He refrained. The next night the
same man returned, radiant in light, and said to him,
' I am sent of God, who has chosen you to explain to
men the meaning of his Word and his Creation. I will
tell you what to write.' The vision lasted but a few
moments. The ANGEL was clothed in purple. During
that night the eyes of his *inner man* were opened, and
he was forced to look into the heavens, into the world
of spirits, and into hell, — three separate spheres ; where
he encountered persons of his acquaintance who had

departed from their human form, some long since, others lately. Thenceforth Swedenborg lived wholly in the spiritual life, remaining in this world only as the messenger of God. His mission was ridiculed by the incredulous, but his conduct was plainly that of a being superior to humanity. In the first place, though limited in means to the bare necessaries of life, he gave away enormous sums, and publicly, in several cities, restored the fortunes of great commercial houses when they were on the brink of failure. No one ever appealed to his generosity who was not immediately satisfied. A sceptical Englishman, determined to know the truth, followed him to Paris, and relates that there his doors stood always open. One day a servant complained of this apparent negligence, which laid him open to suspicion of thefts that might be committed by others. 'He need feel no anxiety,' said Swedenborg, smiling. ' But I do not wonder at his fear ; he cannot see the guardian who protects my door.' In fact, no matter in what country he made his abode he never closed his doors, and nothing was ever stolen from him. At Gottenburg — a town situated some sixty miles from Stockholm — he announced, eight days before the news arrived by courier, the conflagration which ravaged Stockholm, and the exact time at which it took place. The Queen of Sweden wrote to her brother, the King, at Berlin, that one of her ladies-in-waiting, who was ordered by the courts to pay a sum of money which she was certain her husband had paid before his death, went to Swedenborg and begged him to ask her husband where she could find proof of the payment. The following day Swedenborg, having done as the lady requested, pointed out the place where the receipt would be found. He also begged the deceased to appear to his wife, and the latter saw her husband in a dream, wrapped in a dressing-gown which he wore just before his death ; and he showed her the paper in the place indicated by Swedenborg, where it had been securely put away. At another time, embarking from London in a vessel commanded by Captain Dixon, he overheard a lady asking if there were plenty of provisions on board. ' We do not want a great quantity,' he said ; ' in eight days and two hours we shall reach Stockholm,' — which actually happened. This peculiar state of vision as to the things of earth — into which Swedenborg could put himself at will, and which astonished those about him — was, nevertheless, but a feeble representative of his faculty of looking into heaven.

" Not the least remarkable of his published visions is that in which he relates his journeys through the Astral Regions ; his descriptions cannot fail to astonish the reader, partly through the crudity of their details. A man whose scientific eminence is incontestable, and who united in his own person powers of conception, will, and imagination, would surely have invented better if he had invented at all. The fantastic literature of the East offers nothing that can give an idea of this astounding work, full of the essence of poetry, if it is permissible to compare a work of faith with one of oriental fancy. The transportation of Swedenborg by the Angel who served as guide to his first journey is told with a sublimity which exceeds, by the distance which God has placed betwixt the earth and sun, the great epics of Klopstock, Milton, Tasso, and Dante. This description, which serves in fact as an introduction to his work on the Astral Regions, has never been published; it is among the oral traditions left by Swedenborg to the three disciples who were nearest to his heart. Monsieur Silverichm has written them down. Monsieur Seraphitus endeavored more than once to talk to me about them; but the recollection of his cousin's words was so burning a memory that he always stopped short at the first sentence and became lost in a revery from which I could not rouse him."

The old pastor sighed as he continued : "The baron told me that the argument by which the Angel proved to Swedenborg that these bodies are not made to wander through space puts all human science out of sight beneath the grandeur of a divine logic. According to the Seer, the inhabitants of Jupiter will not cultivate the sciences, which they call darkness ; those of Mercury abhor the expression of ideas by speech, which seems to them too material, — their language is ocular; those of Saturn are continually tempted by evil spirits; those of the Moon are as small as six-year-old children, their voices issue from the abdomen, on which they crawl; those of Venus are gigantic in height, but stupid, and live by robbery, — although a part of this latter planet is inhabited by beings of great sweetness, who live in the love of Good.

In short, he describes the customs and morals of all the peoples attached to the different globes, and explains the general meaning of their existence as related to the universe in terms so precise, giving explanations which agree so well with their visible evolutions in the system of the world, that some day, perhaps, scientific men will come to drink of these living waters.

" Here," said Monsieur Becker, taking down a book and opening it at a mark, " here are the words with which he ended this work : —

" ' If any man doubts that I was transported through a vast number of Astral Regions, let him recall my observation of the distances in that other life, namely, that they exist only in relation to the external state of man ; now, being transformed within like unto the Angelic Spirits of those Astral Spheres, I was able to understand them.'

" The circumstances to which we of this canton owe the presence among us of Baron Seraphitus, the beloved cousin of Swedenborg, enabled me to know all the events of the extraordinary life of that prophet. He has lately been accused of imposture in certain quarters of Europe, and the public prints reported the following fact based on a letter written by the Chevalier Baylon. Swedenborg, they said, informed by certain senators of a secret correspondence of the late Queen of Sweden with her brother, the Prince of Prussia, revealed his knowledge of the secrets contained in that correspondence to the Queen, making her believe he had obtained this knowledge by super-

natural means. A man worthy of all confidence,
Monsieur Charles-Léonhard de Stahlhammer, captain
in the Royal guard and knight of the Sword, answered
the calumny with a convincing letter."

The pastor opened a drawer of his table and looked
through a number of papers until he found a gazette
which he held out to Wilfrid, asking him to read aloud
the following letter : —

STOCKHOLM, May 18, 1788.

I HAVE read with amazement a letter which purports to
relate the interview of the famous Swedenborg with Queen
Louisa-Ulrika. The circumstances therein stated are wholly
false; and I hope the writer will excuse me for showing him
by the following faithful narration, which can be proved by
the testimony of many distinguished persons then present
and still living, how completely he has been deceived.

In 1758, shortly after the death of the Prince of Prussia
Swedenborg came to court, where he was in the habit of
attending regularly. He had scarcely entered the queen's
presence before she said to him : " Well, Mr. Assessor, have
you seen my brother ? " Swedenborg answered no, and
the queen rejoined : " If you do see him, greet him for me."
In saying this she meant no more than a pleasant jest, and
had no thought whatever of asking him for information
about her brother. Eight days later (not twenty-four as
stated, nor was the audience a private one), Swedenborg
again came to court, but so early that the queen had not left
her apartment called the White Room, where she was con-
versing with her maids-of-honor and other ladies attached to
the court. Swedenborg did not wait until she came forth,
but entered the said room and whispered something in her
ear. The queen, overcome with amazement, was taken ill,

and it was some time before she recovered herself. When she did so she said to those about her : " Only God and my brother knew the thing that he has just spoken of." She admitted that it related to her last correspondence with the prince on a subject which was known to them alone. I cannot explain how Swedenborg came to know the contents of that letter, but I can affirm on my honor, that neither Count H—— (as the writer of the article states) nor any other person intercepted, or read, the queen's letters. The senate allowed her to write to her brother in perfect security, considering the correspondence as of no interest to the State. It is evident that the author of the said article is ignorant of the character of Count H——. This honored gentleman, who has done many important services to his country, unites the qualities of a noble heart to gifts of mind, and his great age has not yet weakened these precious possessions. During his whole administration he added the weight of scrupulous integrity to his enlightened policy and openly declared himself the enemy of all secret intrigues and underhand dealings, which he regarded as unworthy means to attain an end. Neither did the writer of that article understand the Assessor Swedenborg. The only weakness of that essentially honest man was a belief in the apparition of spirits; but I knew him for many years, and I can affirm that he was as fully convinced that he met and talked with spirits as I am that I am writing at this moment. As a citizen and as a friend his integrity was absolute ; he abhorred deception and led the most exemplary of lives. The version which the Chevalier Baylon gave of these facts is, therefore, entirely without justification; the visit stated to have been made to Swedenborg in the night-time by Count H—— and Count T—— is hereby contradicted. In conclusion, the writer of the letter may rest assured that I am not a follower of Swedenborg. The love of truth alone impels me to give this faithful account of a fact which has been so often stated with details that are entirely false. I certify to the truth of what I have written by adding my signature.

CHARLES–LÉONHARD DE STAHLHAMMER.

" The proofs which Swedenborg gave of his mission to the royal families of Sweden and Prussia were no doubt the foundation of the belief in his doctrines which is prevalent at the two courts," said Monsieur Becker, putting the gazette into the drawer. " However," he continued, " I shall not tell you all the facts of his visible and material life ; indeed his habits prevented them from being fully known. He lived a hidden life ; not seeking either riches or fame. He was even noted for a sort of repugnance to making proselytes ; he opened his mind to few persons, and never showed his external powers of second-sight to any who were not eminent in faith, wisdom, and love. He could recognize at a glance the state of the soul of every person who approached him, and those whom he desired to reach with his inward language he converted into Seers. After the year 1745, his disciples never saw him do a single thing from any human motive. One man alone, a Swedish priest, named Mathesius, set afloat a story that he went mad in London in 1744. But a eulogium on Swedenborg prepared with minute care as to all the known events of his life, was pronounced after his death in 1772 on behalf of the Royal Academy of Sciences in the Hall of the Nobles at Stockholm, by Monsieur Sandels, counsellor of the Board of Mines. A declaration made before the Lord Mayor of London gives the details of his last illness and death, in which he received the ministrations of Monsieur Ferelius a Swedish priest of the highest standing, and pastor of the Swedish Church in London, Mathesius being his assistant. All persons present attested that so far from denying the value of his writings Swedenborg firmly asserted their truth. 'In one hundred years,' Monsieur Ferelius quotes him as saying, 'my doctrine will guide the *Church.*' He predicted the day and hour of his death. On that day, Sunday, March 29, 1772, hearing the clock strike, he asked what time it was. 'Five o'clock' was the answer. 'It is well,' he answered; 'thank you, God bless you.' Ten minutes later he tranquilly departed, breathing a gentle sigh. Simplicity, moderation, and solitude were the features of his life. When he had finished writing any of his books he sailed either for London or for Holland, where he published them, and never spoke of them again. He published in this way twenty-seven different treatises, all written, he said, from the dictation of Angels. Be it true or false, few men have been strong enough to endure the flames of oral illumination.

"There they all are," said Monsieur Becker, pointing to a second shelf on which were some sixty volumes. "The treatises on which the Divine Spirit casts its most vivid gleams are seven in number, namely : ' Heaven and Hell ; ' ' Angelic Wisdom concerning the Divine Love and the Divine Wisdom ; ' ' Angelic Wisdom concerning the Divine Providence ; ' ' The Apocalypse Revealed ; ' ' Conjugial Love and its Chaste Delights; ' 'The True Christian Religion ; ' and ' An Exposition of the Internal Sense.' Swedenborg's explanation of the Apocalypse begins with these words," said Monsieur Becker, taking down and opening the volume nearest to him: " ' Herein I have written nothing of mine own ; I speak as I am bidden by the Lord. who said, through the same angel, to John: " Thou shalt not seal the sayings of this Prophecy." ' (Revelation xxii. 10.)

" My dear Monsieur Wilfrid," said the old man, looking at his guest, " I often tremble in every limb as I read, during the long winter evenings the awe-inspiring works in which this man declares with per-fect artlessness the wonders that are revealed to him. ' I have seen,' he says, ' Heaven and the Angels. The spiritual man sees his spiritual fellows far better than the terrestrial man sees the men of earth. In describing the wonders of heaven and beneath the heav-ens I obey the Lord's command. Others have the right to believe me or not as they choose. I cannot put them into the state in which God has put me ; it is not in my power to enable them to converse with Angels, nor to work miracles within their understanding ; they alone can be the instrument of their rise to angelic inter-course. It is now twenty-eight years since I have lived in the Spiritual world with angels, and on earth with men ; for it pleased God to open the eyes of my Spirit as he did that of Paul, and of Daniel and Elisha.'

" And yet," continued the pastor, thoughtfully, " cer-tain persons have had visions of the spiritual world

through the complete detachment which somnambulism
produces between their external form and their inner
being. 'In this state,' says Swedenborg in his treatise on Angelic Wisdom (No. 257) 'Man may rise
into the region of celestial light because, his corporeal
senses being abolished, the influence of heaven acts
without hindrance on his inner man.' Many persons
who do not doubt that Swedenborg received celestial
revelations think that his writings are not all the result
of divine inspiration. Others insist on absolute adher-
ence to him ; while admitting his many obscurities, they
believe that the imperfection of earthly language prevented the prophet from clearly revealing those spiritual
visions whose clouds disperse to the eyes of those whom
faith regenerates ; for, to use the words of his greatest
disciple, ' Flesh is but an external propagation.' To
poets and to writers his presentation of the marvellous
is amazing ; to Seers it is simply reality. To some
Christians his descriptions have seemed scandalous.
Certain critics have ridiculed the celestial substance of
his temples, his golden palaces, his splendid cities where
angels disport themselves ; they laugh at his groves of
miraculous trees, his gardens where the flowers speak
and the air is white, and the mystical stones, the sard,
carbuncle, chrysolite, chrysoprase, jacinth, chalcedony,
beryl, the Urim and Thummim, are endowed with motion, express celestial truths, and reply by variations
of light to questions put to them ('True Christian Religion,' 219). Many noble souls will not admit his spiritual worlds where colors are heard in delightful concert,

where language flames and flashes, where the Word is
writ in pointed spiral letters ('True Christian Religion,'
278). Even in the North some writers have laughed at
the gates of pearl, and the diamonds which stud the
floors and walls of his New Jerusalem, where the most
ordinary utensils are made of the rarest substances of
the globe. 'But,' say his disciples, 'because such things
are sparsely scattered on this earth does it follow that
they are not abundant in other worlds? On earth they
are terrestrial substances, whereas in heaven they assume
celestial forms and are in keeping with angels.' In this
connection Swedenborg has used the very words of Jesus
Christ, who said, 'If I have told you earthly things
and ye believe not, how shall ye believe if I tell you of
heavenly things?'

" Monsieur," continued the pastor, with an emphatic
gesture, " I have read the whole of Swedenborg's works ;
and I say it with pride, because I have done it and
yet have retained my reason. In reading him men
either miss his meaning or become Seers like him.
Though I have evaded both extremes, I have often experienced unheard-of delights, deep emotions, inward
joys, which alone can reveal to us the plenitude of
truth, — the evidence of celestial Light. All things
here below seem small indeed when the soul is lost in
the perusal of these Treatises. It is impossible not to
be amazed when we think that in the short space of
thirty years this man wrote and published, on the
truths of the Spiritual World, twenty-five quarto volumes, composed in Latin, of which the shortest has

five hundred pages, all of them printed in small type.
He left, they say, twenty others in London, bequeathed
to his nephew, Monsieur Silverichm, formerly almoner
to the King of Sweden. Certainly a man who, between
the ages of twenty and sixty, had already exhausted
himself in publishing a series of encyclopædical works,
must have received supernatural assistance in composing these later stupendous treatises, at an age, too,
when human vigor is on the wane. You will find in
these writings thousands of propositions, all numbered,
none of which have been refuted. Throughout we see
method and precision; the presence of the Spirit issuing and flowing down from a single fact, — the existence of angels. His ' True Christian Religion,' which
sums up his whole doctrine and is vigorous with light,
was conceived and written at the age of eighty-three.
In fact, his amazing vigor and omniscience are not
denied by any of his critics, not even by his enemies.

" Nevertheless," said Monsieur Becker, slowly,
" though I have drunk deep in this torrent of divine
light, God has not opened the eyes of my inner being,
and I judge these writings by the reason of an unregenerated man. I have often felt that the *inspired*
Swedenborg must have misunderstood the Angels. I
have laughed over certain visions which, according to
his disciples, I ought to have believed with veneration.
I have failed to imagine the spiral writing of the
Angels or their golden belts, on which the gold is of
great or lesser thickness. If, for example, this statement, ' Some angels are solitary,' affected me power-

fully for a time, I was, on reflection, unable to reconcile this solitude with their marriages. I have not understood why the Virgin Mary should continue to wear blue satin garments in heaven. I have even dared to ask myself why those gigantic demons, Enakim and Hephilim, came so frequently to fight the cherubim on the apocalyptic plains of Armageddon; and I cannot explain to my own mind how Satans can argue with Angels. Monsieur le Baron Seraphitus assured me that these details concerned only the angels who live on earth in human form. The visions of the prophet are often blurred with grotesque figures. One of his spiritual tales, or 'Memorable relations,' as he called them, begins thus : ' I see the spirits assembling, they have hats upon their heads.' In another of these Memorabilia he receives from heaven a bit of paper, on which he saw, he says, the hieroglyphics of the primitive peoples, which were composed of curved lines traced from the finger-rings that are worn in heaven. However, perhaps I am wrong; possibly the material absurdities with which his works are strewn have spiritual significations. Otherwise, how shall we account for the growing influence of his religion? His church numbers to-day more than seven hundred thousand believers, — as many in the United States of America as in England, where there are seven thousand Swedenborgians in the city of Manchester alone. Many men of high rank in knowledge and in social position in Germany, in Prussia, and in the Northern kingdoms have publicly adopted the beliefs of Swedenborg ; which, I may remark, are more comforting than those of all other Christian communions. I wish I had the power to explain to you clearly in succinct language the leading points of the doctrine on which Swedenborg founded his church ; but I fear such a summary, made from recollection, would be necessarily defective. I shall, therefore, allow myself to speak only of those ' Arcana' which concern the birth of Seraphita."

Here Monsieur Becker paused, as though composing his mind to gather up his ideas. Presently he continued, as follows : —

" After establishing mathematically that man lives eternally in spheres of either a lower or a higher grade, Swedenborg applies the term ' Spiritual Angels' to beings who in this world are prepared for heaven, where they become angels. According to him, God has not created angels ; none exist who have not been men upon the earth. The earth is the nursery-ground of heaven. The Angels are therefore not Angels as such (' Angelic Wisdom,' 57), they are transformed through their close conjunction with God ; which conjunction God never refuses, because the essence of God is not negative, but incessantly active. The spiritual angels pass through three natures of love, because man is only regenerated through successive stages (' True Religion'). First, the LOVE OF SELF: the supreme expression of this love is human genius, whose works are worshipped. Next, LOVE OF LIFE : this love produces prophets, — great men whom the world accepts as guides and proclaims to be divine. Lastly, LOVE

OF HEAVEN, and this creates the Spiritual Angel. These angels are, so to speak, the flowers of humanity, which culminates in them and works for that culmination. They must possess either the love of heaven or the wisdom of heaven, but always Love before Wisdom.

"Thus the first transformation of the natural man is into Love. To reach this first degree, his previous existences must have passed through Hope and Charity, which prepare him for Faith and Prayer. The ideas acquired by the exercise of these virtues are transmitted to each of the human envelopes within which are hidden the metamorphoses of the INNER BEING; for nothing is separate, each existence is necessary to the other existences. Hope cannot advance without Charity, nor Faith without Prayer; they are the four fronts of a solid square. 'One virtue missing,' he said, 'and the Spiritual Angel is like a broken pearl.' Each of these existences is therefore a circle in which revolves the celestial riches of the inner being. The perfection of the Spiritual Angels comes from this mysterious progression in which nothing is lost of the high qualities that are successively acquired to attain each glorious incarnation; for at each transformation they cast away unconsciously the flesh and its errors. When the man lives in Love he has shed all evil passions: Hope, Charity, Faith, and Prayer have, in the words of Isaiah, purged the dross of his inner being, which can never more be polluted by earthly affections. Hence the grand saying of Christ quoted

by Saint Matthew, ' Lay up for yourselves treasures
in Heaven where neither moth nor rust doth corrupt,'
and those still grander words : ' If ye were of this
world the world would love you, but I have chosen you
out of the world ; be ye therefore perfect as your Father
in heaven is perfect.' "

" The second transformation of man is to Wisdom.
Wisdom is the understanding of celestial things to
which the spirit is brought by Love. The Spirit of
Love has acquired strength, the result of all vanquished
terrestrial passions ; it loves God blindly. But the
Spirit of Wisdom has risen to understanding and knows
why it loves. The wings of the one are spread and
bear the spirit to God ; the wings of the other are held
down by the awe that comes of understanding : the
spirit knows God. The one longs incessantly to see
God and to fly to Him ; the other attains to Him and
trembles. The union effected between the Spirit of
Love and the Spirit of Wisdom carries the human
being into a Divine state during which time his soul
is Woman and his body Man, the last human manifestation in which the Spirit conquers Form, or Form
still struggles against the Spirit, — for Form, that is,
the flesh, is ignorant, rebels, and desires to continue
gross. This supreme trial creates untold sufferings
seen by Heaven alone, — the agony of Christ in the
Garden of Olives.

" After death the first heaven opens to this dual and
purified human nature. Therefore it is that man dies
in despair while the Spirit dies in ecstasy. Thus, the

NATURAL., the state of beings not yet regenerated; the
SPIRITUAL, the state of those who have become Angelic
Spirits; and the DIVINE, the state in which the Angel
exists before he breaks from his covering of flesh, are
the three degrees of existence through which man enters heaven.   One of Swedenborg's thoughts expressed
in his own words will explain to you with wonderful
clearness the difference between the NATURAL and the
SPIRITUAL.   'To the minds of men,' he says, ' the
Natural passes into the Spiritual; they regard the world
under its visible aspects, they perceive it only as it can
be realized by their senses.   But to the apprehension of
Angelic Spirits, the Spiritual passes into the Natural;
they regard the world in its inward essence, and not in
its form.'   Thus human sciences are but analyses of
form.   The man of science as the world goes is purely
external like his knowledge; his inner being is only
used to preserve his aptitude for the perception of external truths.   The Angelic Spirit goes far beyond that;
his knowledge is the thought of which human science is
but the utterance; he derives that knowledge from the
Logos, and learns the law of CORRESPONDENCES by
which the world is placed in unison with heaven.   The
WORD OF GOD was wholly written by pure Correspondences, and covers an esoteric or spiritual meaning,
which according to the science of Correspondences,
cannot be understood.   ' There exist,' says Swedenborg ('Celestial Doctrine' 26), ' innumerable Arcana
within the hidden meaning of the Correspondences.
Thus the men who scoff at the books of the Prophets

where the Word is enshrined are as densely ignorant
as those other men who know nothing of a science and
yet ridicule its truths. To know the Correspondences
of the Word with Heaven ; to know the Correspondences which exist between the things visible and ponderable in the terrestrial world and the things invisible
and imponderable in the spiritual world, is to hold heaven
within our comprehension. All the objects of the manifold creations having emanated from God necessarily en-
fold a hidden meaning ; according, indeed, to the grand
thought of Isaiah, 'The earth is a garment.'

" This mysterious link between Heaven and the smallest atoms of created matter constitutes what Swedenborg calls a Celestial Arcanum, and his treatise on
the Celestial Arcana' in which he explains the correspondences or significances of the Natural with, and
to, the Spiritual, giving, to use the words of Jacob
Boehm, the sign and seal of all things, occupies not
less than sixteen volumes containing thirty thousand
propositions. 'This marvellous knowledge of Correspondences which the goodness of God granted to
Swedenborg,' says one of his disciples, ' is the secret
of the interest which draws men to his works. According to him, all things are derived from heaven, all
things lead back to heaven. His writings are sublime
and clear ; he speaks in heaven, and earth hears him.
Take one of his sentences by itself and a volume could
be made of it ; ' and the disciple quotes the following
passages taken from a thousand others that would
answer the same purpose.

" ' The kingdom of heaven,' says Swedenborg ('Celestial Arcana'), ' is the kingdom of motives. ACTION is born in heaven, thence into the world, and, by degrees, to the infinitely remote parts of earth. Terrestrial effects being thus linked to celestial causes, all things are CORRESPONDENT and SIGNIFICANT. Man is the means of union between the Natural and the Spiritual.'

" The Angelic Spirits therefore know the very nature of the Correspondences which link to heaven all earthly things; they know, too, the inner meaning of the prophetic words which foretell their evolutions. Thus to these Spirits everything here below has its significance; the tiniest flower is a thought, — a life which corresponds to certain lineaments of the Great Whole, of which they have a constant intuition. To them Adultery and the excesses spoken of in Scripture and by the Prophets, often garbled by self-styled scholars, mean the state of those souls which in this world persist in tainting themselves with earthly affections, thus compelling their divorce from Heaven. Clouds signify the veil of the Most High. Torches, shew-bread, horses and horsemen, harlots, precious stones, in short, everything named in Scripture, has to them a clearcut meaning, and reveals the future of terrestrial facts in their relation to Heaven. They penetrate the truths contained in the Revelation of Saint John the divine, which human science has subsequently demonstrated and proved materially; such, for instance, as the following (' big,' said Swedenborg, ' with many human sciences') : ' I saw a new heaven and a new earth, for the first heaven and the first earth were passed away ' (Revelation xxi. 1). These Spirits know the supper at which the flesh of kings and the flesh of all men, free and bond, is eaten, to which an Angel standing in the sun has bidden them. They see the wingèd woman, clothed with the sun, and the mailèd man. ' The horse of the Apocalyse,' says Swedenborg ' is the visible image of human intellect ridden by Death, for it bears within itself the elements of its own destruction.' Moreover, they can distinguish beings concealed under forms which to ignorant eyes would seem fantastic. When a man is disposed to receive the prophetic afflation of Correspondences, it rouses within him a perception of the Word; he comprehends that the creations are transformations only; his intellect is sharpened, a burning thirst takes possession of him which only Heaven can quench. He conceives, according to the greater or lesser perfection of his inner being, the power of the Angelic Spirits; and he advances, led by Desire (the least imperfect state of unregenerated man) towards Hope, the gateway to the world of Spirits, whence he reaches Prayer, which gives him the Key of Heaven.

" What being here below would not desire to render himself worthy of entrance into the sphere of those who live in secret by Love and Wisdom? Here on earth, during their lifetime, such spirits remain pure; they neither see, nor think, nor speak like other men. There are two ways by which perception comes, — one internal, the other external. Man is wholly external, the

Angelic Spirit wholly internal. The Spirit goes to the depth of Numbers, possesses a full sense of them, knows their significances. It controls Motion, and by reason of its ubiquity it shares in all things. 'An Angel,' says Swedenborg, 'is ever present to a man when desired' ('Angelic Wisdom') ; for the Angel has the gift of detaching himself from his body, and he sees into heaven as the prophets and as Swedenborg himself saw into it. 'In this state,' writes Swedenborg ('True Religion,' 136), 'the spirit of a man may move from one place to another, his body remaining where it is, — a condition in which I lived for over twenty-six years.' It is thus that we should interpret all Biblical statements which begin, 'The Spirit led me.' Angelic Wisdom is to human wisdom what the innumerable forces of nature are to its action, which is one. All things live again, and move and have their being in the Spirit, which is in God. Saint Paul expresses this truth when he says, *In Deo sumus, movemur, et vivimus,* — we live, we act, we are in God.

"Earth offers no hindrance to the Angelic Spirit, just as the Word offers him no obscurity. His approaching divinity enables him to see the thought of God veiled in the Logos, just as, living by his inner being, the Spirit is in communication with the hidden meaning of all things on this earth. Science is the language of the Temporal world, Love is that of the Spiritual world. Thus man takes note of more than he is able to explain, while the Angelic Spirit sees and comprehends. Science depresses man ; Love exalts the

Angel. Science is still seeking, Love has found. Man judges Nature according to his own relations to her; the Angelic Spirit judges it in its relation to Heaven. In short, all things have a voice for the Spirit. Spirits are in the secret of the harmony of all creations with each other; they comprehend the spirit of sound, the spirit of color, the spirit of vegetable life; they can question the mineral, and the mineral makes answer to their thoughts. What to them are sciences and the treasures of the earth when they grasp all things by the eye at all moments, when the worlds which absorb the minds of so many men are to them but the last step from which they spring to God? Love of heaven, or the Wisdom of heaven, is made manifest in them by a circle of light which surrounds them, and is visible to the Élect. Their innocence, of which that of children is a symbol, possesses, nevertheless, a knowledge which children have not; they are both innocent and learned. ' And,' says Swedenborg, 'the innocence of Heaven makes such an impression upon the soul that those whom it affects keep a rapturous memory of it which lasts them all their lives, as I myself have experienced. It is perhaps sufficient,' he goes on, ' to have only a minimum perception of it to be forever changed, to long to enter Heaven and the sphere of Hope.'

" His doctrine of Marriage can be reduced to the following words : ' The Lord has taken the beauty and the grace of the life of man and bestowed them upon woman. When man is not reunited to this beauty and

this grace of his life, he is harsh, sad, and sullen ; when
he is reunited to them he is joyful and complete.' The
Angels are ever at the perfect point of beauty. Marriages are celebrated by wondrous ceremonies. In these
unions, which produce no children, man contributes the
Understanding, woman the *Will;* they become one
being, one Flesh here below, and pass to heaven clothed
in the celestial form. On this earth, the natural attraction of the sexes towards enjoyment is an Effect which
allures, fatigues and disgusts ; but in the form celestial
the pair, now *one* in Spirit find within theirself a ceaseless source of joy. Swedenborg was led to see these
nuptials of the Spirits, which in the words of Saint Luke
(**xx.** 35) are neither marrying nor giving in marriage,
and which inspire none but spiritual pleasures. An
Angel offered to make him witness of such a marriage
and bore him thither on his wings (the wings are a
symbol and not a reality). The Angel clothed him in
a wedding garment and when Swedenborg, finding himself thus robed in light, asked why, the answer was :
' For these events, our garments are illuminated ; they
shine ; they are made nuptial.' ('Conjugial Love,' 19,
20, 21.) Then he saw two Angels, one coming from
the South, the other from the East ; the Angel of the
South was in a chariot drawn by two white horses, with
reins of the color and brilliance of the dawn ; but lo,
when they were near him in the sky, chariot and horses
vanished. The Angel of the East, clothed in crimson,
and the Angel of the South, in purple, drew together,
like breaths, and mingled : one was the Angel of Love,

the other the Angel of Wisdom. Swedenborg's guide told him that the two Angels had been linked together on earth by an inward friendship and ever united though separated in life by great distances. Consent, the essence of all good marriage upon earth, is the habitual state of Angels in Heaven. Love is the light of their world. The eternal rapture of Angels comes from the faculty that God communicates to them to render back to Him the joy they feel through Him. This reciprocity of infinitude forms their life. They become infinite by participating of the essence of God, who generates Him-self by Himself.

"The immensity of the Heavens where the Angels dwell is such that if man were endowed with sight as rapid as the darting of light from the sun to the earth, and if he gazed throughout eternity, his eyes could not reach the horizon, nor find an end. Light alone can give an idea of the joys of heaven. ' It is,' says Swedenborg ('Angelic Wisdom,' 7, 25, 26, 27), ' a vapor of the virtue of God, a pure emanation of His splendor, beside which our greatest brilliance is obscurity. It can compass all ; i' can renew all, and is never absorbed : it environs the Angel and unites him to God by infinite joys which multiply infinitely of themselves. This Light destroys whosoever is not prepared to receive it. No one here below, nor yet in Heaven can see God and live. This is the meaning of the saying (Exodus xix. 12, 13, 21–23) " Take heed to your-selves that ye go not up into the mount — lest ye break through unto the Lord to gaze, and many perish."

And again (Exodus xxxiv. 29–35), "When Moses came down from Mount Sinai with the two Tables of testimony in his hand, his face shone, so that he put a veil upon it when he spake with the people, lest any of them die." The Transfiguration of Jesus Christ likewise revealed the light surrounding the Messengers from on high and the ineffable joys of the Angels who are forever imbued with it. "His face," says Saint Matthew (xvii. 1–5), "did shine as the sun and his raiment was white as the light — and a bright cloud overshadowed them." '

"When a planet contains only those beings who reject the Lord, when his word is ignored, then the Angelic Spirits are gathered together by the four winds, and God sends forth an Exterminating Angel to change the face of the refractory earth, which in the immensity of this universe is to Him what an unfruitful seed is to Nature. Approaching the globe, this Exterminating Angel, borne by a comet, causes the planet to turn upon its axis, and the lands lately covered by the seas reappear, adorned in freshness and obedient to the laws proclaimed in Genesis; the Word of God is once more powerful on this new earth, which everywhere exhibits the effects of terrestrial waters and celestial flames. The light brought by the Angel from On High, causes the sun to pale. 'Then,' says Isaiah, (xix. 20) 'men will hide in the clefts of the rock and roll themselves in the dust of the earth.' 'They will cry to the mountains (Revelation), Fall on us! and to the seas, Swallow us up! Hide us from the face of Him

that sitteth on the throne, and from the wrath of the
Lamb!' The Lamb is the great figure and hope of the
Angels misjudged and persecuted here below. Christ
himself has said, 'Blessed are those who mourn!
Blessed are the simple-hearted! Blessed are they that
love!' — All Swedenborg is there! Suffer, Believe,
Love. To love truly must we not suffer? must we
not believe? Love begets Strength, Strength bestows
Wisdom, thence Intelligence; for Strength and Wisdom demand Will. To be intelligent, is not that to
Know, to Wish, and to Will, — the three attributes
of the Angelic Spirit? 'If the universe has a meaning,' Monsieur Saint-Martin said to me when I met
him during a journey which he made in Sweden, 'surely
this is the one most worthy of God.'

"But, Monsieur," continued the pastor after a thoughtful pause, "of what avail to you are these shreds of
thoughts taken here and there from the vast extent of
a work of which no true idea can be given except by
comparing it to a river of light, to billows of flame?
When a man plunges into it he is carried away as by
an awful current. Dante's poem seems but a speck
to the reader submerged in the almost Biblical verses
with which Swedenborg renders palpable the Celestial
Worlds, as Beethoven built his palaces of harmony
with thousands of notes, as architects have reared
cathedrals with millions of stones. We roll in sound-
less depths, where our minds will not always sustain us.
Ah, surely a great and powerful intellect is needed to
bring us back, safe and sound, to our own social beliefs.

" Swedenborg," resumed the pastor, " was particularly attached to the Baron de Seraphitz, whose name, according to an old Swedish custom, had taken from time immemorial the Latin termination of *us*. The baron was an ardent disciple of the Swedish prophet, who had opened the eyes of his Inner-Man and brought him to a life in conformity with the decrees from On-High. He sought for an Angelic Spirit among women; Swedenborg found her for him in a vision. His bride was the daughter of a London shoemaker, in whom, said Swedenborg, the life of Heaven shone, she having passed through all anterior trials. After the death, that is, the transformation of the prophet, the baron came to Jarvis to accomplish his celestial nuptials with the observances of Prayer. As for me, who am not a Seer, I have only known the terrestrial works of this couple. Their lives were those of saints whose virtues are the glory of the Roman Church. They ameliorated the condition of our people; they supplied them all with means in return for work, — little, perhaps, but enough for all their wants. Those who lived with them in constant intercourse never saw them show a sign of anger or impatience; they were constantly beneficent and gentle, full of courtesy and loving-kindness; their marriage was the harmony of two souls indissolubly united. Two eiders winging the same flight, the sound in the echo, the thought in the word, — these, perhaps, are true images of their union. Every one here in Jarvis loved them with an affection which I can compare only to the love of a plant for the

sun. The wife was simple in her manners, beautiful
in form, lovely in face, with a dignity of bearing like
that of august personages. In 1783, being then twenty-
six years old, she conceived a child; her pregnancy
was to the pair a solemn joy. They prepared to bid
the earth farewell; for they told me they should be
transformed when their child had passed the state of
infancy which needed their fostering care until the
strength to exist alone should be given to her.

"Their child was born, — the Seraphita we are now
concerned with. From the moment of her conception
father and mother lived a still more solitary life than in
the past, lifting themselves to heaven by Prayer. They
hoped to see Swedenborg, and faith realized their hope.
The day on which Seraphita came into the world Swedenborg appeared in Jarvis, and filled the room of the
new-born child with light. I was told that he said,
'The work is accomplished; the Heavens rejoice!'
Sounds of unknown melodies were heard throughout
the house, seeming to come from the four points of
heaven on the wings of the wind. The spirit of
Swedenborg led the father forth to the shores of the
fiord and there quitted him. Certain inhabitants of
Jarvis, having approached Monsieur Seraphitus as he
stood on the shore, heard him repeat those blissful
words of Scripture: ' How beautiful on the mountains
are the feet of Him who is sent of God!'

" I had left the parsonage on my way to baptize the
infant and name it, and perform the other duties required by law, when I met the baron returning to the

house. ' Your ministrations are superfluous,' he said ; ' our child is to be without name on this earth. You must not baptize in the waters of an earthly Church one who has just been immersed in the fires of Heaven. This child will remain a blossom, it will not grow old ; you will see it pass away. You exist, but our child has life ; you have outward senses, the child has none, its being is all inward.' These words were uttered in so strange and supernatural a voice that I was more affected by them than by the shining of his face, from which light appeared to exude. His appearance realized the phantasmal ideas which we form of inspired beings as we read the prophesies of the Bible. But such effects are not rare among our mountains, where the nitre of perpetual snows produces extraordinary phenomena in the human organization.

" I asked him the cause of his emotion. ' Swedenborg came to us ; he has just left me ; I have breathed the air of heaven,' he replied. ' Under what form did he appear?' I said. ' Under his earthly form ; dressed as he was the last time I saw him in London, at the house of Richard Shearsmith, Coldbath-fields, in July, 1771. He wore his brown frieze coat with steel buttons, his waistcoat buttoned to the throat, a white cravat, and the same magisterial wig rolled and powdered at the sides and raised high in front, showing his vast and luminous brow, in keeping with the noble square face, where all is power and tranquillity. I recognized the large nose with its fiery nostril, the mouth that ever smiled, — angelic mouth from which these words, the pledge of my happiness, have just issued, " We shall meet soon." '

" The conviction that shone on the baron's face forbade all discussion ; I listened in silence. His voice had a contagious heat which made my bosom burn within me ; his fanaticism stirred my heart as the anger of another makes our nerves vibrate. I followed him in silence to his house, where I saw the nameless child lying mysteriously folded to its mother's breast. The babe heard my step and turned its head toward me ; its eyes were not those of an ordinary child. To give you an idea of the impression I received, I must say that already they saw and thought. The childhood of this predestined being was attended by circumstances quite extraordinary in our climate. For nine years our winters were milder and our summers longer than usual. This phenomenon gave rise to several discussions among scientific men ; but none of their explanations seemed sufficient to academicians, and the baron smiled when I told him of them. The child was never seen in its nudity as other children are ; it was never touched by man or woman, but lived a sacred thing upon the mother's breast, and it never cried. If you question old David he will confirm these facts about his mistress, for whom he feels an adoration like that of Louis IX. for the saint whose name he bore.

" At nine years of age the child began to pray ; prayer is her life. You saw her in the church at Christmas, the only day on which she comes there ; she is separated from the other worshippers by a visible space.

If that space does not exist between herself and men she suffers. That is why she passes nearly all her time alone in the château. The events of her life are unknown; she is seldom seen; her days are spent in the state of mystical contemplation which was, so Catholic writers tell us, habitual with the early Christian solitaries, in whom the oral tradition of Christ's own words still remained. Her mind, her soul, her body, all within her is virgin as the snow on those mountains. At ten years of age she was just what you see her now. When she was nine her father and mother expired together, without pain or visible malady, after naming the day and hour at which they would cease to be. Standing at their feet she looked at them with a calm eye, not showing either sadness, or grief, or joy, or curiosity. When we approached to remove the two bodies she said, 'Carry them away!' 'Seraphita,' I said, for so we called her, 'are you not affected by the death of your father and your mother who loved you so much?' 'Dead?' she answered, 'no, they live in me forever — That is nothing,' she added, pointing without a trace of emotion to the bodies they were bearing away. I then saw her for the third time only since her birth. In church it is difficult to distinguish her; she stands near a column which, seen from the pulpit, is in shadow, so that I cannot observe her features.

" Of all the servants of the household there remained after the death of the master and mistress only old David, who, in spite of his eighty-two years, suffices to wait on his mistress. Some of our Jarvis people tell

wonderful tales about her. These have a certain weight
in a land so essentially conducive to mystery as ours;
and I am now studying the treatise on Incantations by
Jean Wier and other works relating to demonology,
where pretended supernatural events are recorded,
hoping to find facts analogous to those which are attributed to her."

"Then you do not believe in her?" said Wilfred.

"Oh yes, I do," said the pastor, genially, "I think
her a very capricious girl; a little spoilt by her parents,
who turned her head with the religious ideas I have just
revealed to you."

Minna shook her head in a way that gently expressed
contradiction.

"Poor girl!" continued the old man, "her parents
bequeathed to her that fatal exaltation of soul which
misleads mystics and renders them all more or less
mad. She subjects herself to fasts which horrify poor
David. The good old man is like a sensitive plant
which quivers at the slightest breeze, and glows under
the first sun-ray. His mistress, whose incomprehensible language has become his, is the breeze and the
sun-ray to him; in his eyes her feet are diamonds and
her brow is strewn with stars; she walks environed
with a white and luminous atmosphere; her voice is
accompanied by music; she has the gift of rendering
herself invisible. If you ask to see her, he will tell you
she has gone to the ASTRAL REGIONS. It is difficult to
believe such a story, is it not? You know all miracles
bear more or less resemblance to the story of the

Golden Tooth. We have our golden tooth in Jarvis,
that is all.   Duncker the fisherman asserts that he has
seen her plunge into the fiord and come up in the shape
of an eider-duck, at other times walking on the billows
in a storm.   Fergus, who leads the flocks to the sæters,
says that in rainy weather a circle of clear sky can be
seen over the Swedish castle ; and that the heavens are
always blue above Seraphita's head when she is on the
mountain.   Many women hear the tones of a mighty
organ when Seraphita enters the church, and ask their
neighbors earnestly if they too do not hear them.   But
my daughter, for whom during the last two years Seraphita has shown much affection, has never heard this
music, and has never perceived the heavenly perfumes
which, they say, make the air fragrant about her when
she moves.   Minna, to be sure, has often on returning
from their walks together expressed to me the delight
of a young girl in the beauties of our spring-time, in
the spicy odors of budding larches and pines and the
earliest flowers ; but after our long winters what can
be more natural than such pleasure?   The companion-
ship of this so-called spirit has nothing so very extraordinary in it, has it, my child?"

"The secrets of that spirit are not mine," said
Minna.   "Near it I know all, away from it I know
nothing ; near that exquisite life I am no longer myself, far from it I forget all.   The time we pass together is a dream which my memory scarcely retains.
I may have heard yet not remember the music which the
women tell of ; in that presence, I may have breathed

celestial perfumes, seen the glory of the heavens, and yet be unable to recollect them here."

"What astonishes me most," resumed the pastor, addressing Wilfrid, " is to notice that you suffer from being near her."

"Near her!" exclaimed the stranger, "she has never so much as let me touch her hand. When she saw me for the first time her glance intimidated me; she said: ' You are welcome here, for you were to come.' I fancied that she knew me. I trembled. It is fear that forces me to believe in her."

"With me it is love," said Minna, without a blush.

"Are you making fun of me?" said Monsieur Becker, laughing good-humoredly; "you my daughter, in calling yourself a Spirit of Love, and you, Monsieur Wilfrid, in pretending to be a Spirit of Wisdom?"

He drank a glass of beer and so did not see the singular look which Wilfrid cast upon Minna.

"Jesting apart," resumed the old gentleman, "I have been much astonished to hear that these two mad-caps ascended to the summit of the Falberg; it must be a girlish exaggeration; they probably went to the crest of a ledge. It is impossible to reach the peaks of the Falberg."

"If so, father," said Minna, in an agitated voice, "I must have been under the power of a spirit; for indeed we reached the summit of the Ice-Cap."

"This is really serious," said Monsieur Becker. "Minna is always truthful."

"Monsieur Becker," said Wilfrid, "I swear to you

that Seraphita exercises such extraordinary power over
me that I know no language in which I can give you
the least idea of it. She has revealed to me things
known to myself alone."

" Somnambulism ! " said the old man. " A great
many such effects are related by Jean Wier as phenomena easily explained and formerly observed in
Egypt."

" Lend me Swedenborg's theosophical works," said
Wilfrid, " and let me plunge into those gulfs of
light, — you have given me a thirst for them."

Monsieur Becker took down a volume and gave it
to his guest, who instantly began to read it. It was
about nine o'clock in the evening. The serving-woman
brought in the supper. Minna made tea. The repast
over, each returned silently to his or her occupation ;
the pastor read the Incantations ; Wilfrid pursued the
spirit of Swedenborg ; and the young girl continued to
sew, her mind absorbed in recollections. It was a true
Norwegian evening — peaceful, studious, and domestic ;
full of thoughts, flowers blooming beneath the snow.
Wilfrid, as he devoured the pages of the prophet, lived
by his inner senses only ; the pastor, looking up at
times from his book, called Minna's attention to the
absorption of their guest with an air that was half-
serious, half-jesting. To Minna's thoughts the face
of Seraphitus smiled upon her as it hovered above the
clouds of smoke which enveloped them. The clock
struck twelve. Suddenly the outer door was opened
violently. Heavy but hurried steps, the steps of a

terrified old man, were heard in the narrow vestibule between the two doors ; then David burst into the parlor.

" Danger! danger!" he cried. "Come! come, all! The evil spirits are unchained! Fiery mitres are on their heads! Demons, Vertumni, Sirens! they tempt her as Jesus was tempted on the mountain! Come, come! and drive them away."

" Do you not recognize the language of Swedenborg?" said the pastor, laughing, to Wilfrid. "Here it is ; pure from the source."

But Wilfrid and Minna were gazing in terror at old David, who, with hair erect, and eyes distraught, his legs trembling and covered with snow, for he had come without snow-shoes, stood swaying from side to side, as if some boisterous wind were shaking him.

" Is he harmed?" cried Minna.

" The devils hope and try to conquer her," replied the old man.

The words made Wilfrid's pulses throb.

" For the last five hours she has stood erect, her eyes raised to heaven and her arms extended ; she suffers, she cries to God. I cannot cross the barrier ; Hell has posted the Vertumni as sentinels. They have set up an iron wall between her and her old David. She wants me, but what can I do? Oh, help me! help me! Come and pray!"

The old man's despair was terrible to see.

" The Light of God is defending her," he went on, with infectious faith, "but oh! she might yield to violence."

" Silence, David! you are raving. This is a matter

to be verified. We will go with you," said the pastor,
" and you shall see that there are no Vertumni, nor
Satans, nor Sirens, in that house."

" Your father is blind," whispered David to Minna.

Wilfrid, on whom the reading of Swedenborg's first
treatise, which he had rapidly gone through, had produced a powerful effect, was already in the corridor
putting on his skees; Minna was ready in a few moments, and both left the old men far behind as they
darted forward to the Swedish castle.

" Do you hear that cracking sound?" said Wilfrid.

" The ice of the fiord stirs," answered Minna; " the
spring is coming."

Wilfrid was silent. When the two reached the courtyard they were conscious that they had neither the
faculty nor the strength to enter the house.

" What think you of her?" asked Wilfrid.

" See that radiance!" cried Minna, going towards
the window of the salon. " He is there! How beautiful! O my Seraphitus, take me!"

The exclamation was uttered inwardly. She saw
Seraphitus standing erect, lightly swathed in an opal-
tinted mist that disappeared at a little distance from
the body, which seemed almost phosphorescent.

" How beautiful she is!" cried Wilfrid, mentally.

Just then Monsieur Becker arrived, followed by
David; he saw his daughter and guest standing before
the window; going up to them, he looked into the
salon and said quietly, " Well, my good David, she is
only saying her prayers."

" Ah, but try to enter, Monsieur."

" Why disturb those who pray?" answered the pastor.

At this instant the moon, rising above the Falberg, cast its rays upon the window. All three turned round, attracted by this natural effect which made them quiver ; when they turned back to again look at Seraphita she had disappeared.

" How strange !" exclaimed Wilfrid.

" I hear delightful sounds," said Minna.

" Well," said the pastor, " it is all plain enough ; she is going to bed."

David had entered the house. The others took their way back in silence ; none of them interpreted the vision in the same manner, — Monsieur Becker doubted, Minna adored, Wilfrid longed.

Wilfrid was a man about thirty-six years of age. His figure, though broadly developed, was not wanting in symmetry. Like most men who distinguish themselves above their fellows, he was of medium height ; his chest and shoulders were broad, and his neck short, — a characteristic of those whose hearts are near their heads ; his hair was black, thick, and fine ; his eyes, of a yellow brown, had, as it were, a solar brilliancy, which proclaimed with what avidity his nature aspired to Light. Though these strong and virile features were defective through the absence of an inward peace, — granted only to a life without storms or conflicts, — they plainly showed the inexhaustible resources of impetuous senses and the appetites of instinct ; just as every motion revealed the perfection of the man's physical apparatus, the

7

flexibility of his senses, and their fidelity when brought
into play. This man might contend with savages, and
hear, as they do, the tread of enemies in distant forests; he could follow a scent in the air, a trail on the
ground, or see on the horizon the signal of a friend.
His sleep was light, like that of all creatures who will
not allow themselves to be surprised. His body came
quickly into harmony with the climate of any country
where his tempestuous life conducted him. Art and
science would have admired his organization in the
light of a human model. Everything about him was
symmetrical and well-balanced, — action and heart, intelligence and will. At first sight he might be classed
among purely instinctive beings, who give themselves
blindly up to the material wants of life; but in the very
morning of his days he had flung himself into a higher
social world, with which his feelings harmonized; study
had widened his mind, reflection had sharpened his
power of thought, and the sciences had enlarged his
understanding. He had studied human laws, — the
working of self-interests brought into conflict by the
passions, and he seemed to have early familiarized
himself with the abstractions on which societies rest.
He had pored over books, — those deeds of dead humanity; he had spent whole nights of pleasure in every
European capital; he had slept on fields of battle the
night before the combat and the night that followed
victory. His stormy youth may have flung him on the
deck of some corsair and sent him among the contrasting regions of the globe; thus it was that he knew the

actions of a living humanity. He knew the present
and the past, — a double history ; that of to-day, that of
other days. Many men have been, like Wilfrid, equally
powerful by the Hand, by the Heart, by the Head ;
like him, the majority have abused their triple power.
But though this man still held by certain outward liens
to the slimy side of humanity, he belonged also and
positively to the sphere where force is intelligent. In
spite of the many veils which enveloped his soul, there
were certain ineffable symptoms of this fact which were
visible to pure spirits, to the eyes of the child whose
innocence has known no breath of evil passions, to the
eyes of the old man who has lived to regain his purity.

These signs revealed a Cain for whom there was still
hope, — one who seemed as though he were seeking
absolution from the ends of the earth. Minna suspected the galley-slave of glory in the man ; Seraphita
recognized him. Both admired and both pitied him.
Whence came their prescience? Nothing could be
more simple nor yet more extraordinary. As soon
as we seek to penetrate the secrets of Nature, where
nothing is secret, and where it is only necessary to have
the eyes to see, we perceive that the simple produces
the marvellous.

"Seraphitus," said Minna one evening a few days
after Wilfrid's arrival in Jarvis, "you read the soul of
this stranger while I have only vague impressions of it.
He chills me or else he excites me ; but you seem to
know the cause of this cold and of this heat; tell me
what it means, for you know all about him."

"Yes, I have seen the causes," said Seraphitus, lowering his large eyelids.

"By what power?" asked the curious Minna.

"I have the gift of Specialism," he answered. "Specialism is an inward sight which can penetrate all things; you will only understand its full meaning through a comparison. In the great cities of Europe where works are produced by which the human Hand seeks to represent the effects of the moral nature as well as those of the physical nature, there are glorious men who express ideas in marble. The sculptor acts on the stone; he fashions it; he puts a realm of ideas into it. There are statues which the hand of man has endowed with the faculty of representing the whole noble side of humanity, or the whole evil side; most men see in such marbles a human figure and nothing more; a few other men, a little higher in the scale of being, perceive a fraction of the thoughts expressed in the statue; but the Initiates in the secrets of art are of the same intellect as the sculptor; they see in his work the whole universe of his thought. Such persons are in themselves the principles of art; they bear within them a mirror which reflects nature in her slightest manifestations. Well! so it is with me; I have within me a mirror before which the moral nature, with its causes and its effects, appears and is reflected. Entering thus into the consciousness of others I am able to divine both the future and the past. How? do you still ask how? Imagine that the marble statue is the body of a man, a piece of statuary in which we see the emotion, sentiment, passion, vice

or crime, virtue or repentance which the creating hand
has put into it, and you will then comprehend how it
is that I read the soul of this foreigner — though what
I have said does not explain the gift of Specialism;
for to conceive the nature of that gift we must
possess it."

Though Wilfrid belonged to the two first divisions of
humanity, the men of force and the men of thought, yet
his excesses, his tumultuous life, and his misdeeds had
often turned him towards Faith; for doubt has two
sides; a side to the light and a side to the darkness.
Wilfrid had too closely clasped the world under its
forms of Matter and of Mind not to have acquired that
thirst for the unknown, that longing to *go beyond* which
lay their grasp upon the men who know, and wish, and
will. But neither his knowledge, nor his actions, nor
his will, had found direction. He had fled from social
life from necessity; as a great criminal seeks the cloister. Remorse, that virtue of weak beings, did not
touch him. Remorse is impotence, impotence which
sins again. Repentance alone is powerful; it ends all.
But in traversing the world, which he made his cloister,
Wilfrid had found no balm for his wounds; he saw
nothing in nature to which he could attach himself. In
him, despair had dried the sources of desire. He was
one of those beings who, having gone through all
passions and come out victorious, have nothing more to
raise in their hot-beds, and who, lacking opportunity to
put themselves at the head of their fellow-men to trample
under iron heel entire populations, buy, at the price of

a horrible martyrdom, the faculty of ruining themselves in some belief, — rocks sublime, which await the touch of a wand that comes not to bring the waters gushing from their far-off springs.

Led by a scheme of his restless, inquiring life to the shores of Norway, the sudden arrival of winter had detained the wanderer at Jarvis. The day on which, for the first time, he saw Seraphita, the whole past of his life faded from his mind. The young girl excited emotions which he had thought could never be revived. The ashes gave forth a lingering flame at the first murmurings of that voice. Who has ever felt himself return to youth and purity after growing cold and numb with age and soiled with impurity? Suddenly, Wilfrid loved as he had never loved; he loved secretly, with faith, with fear, with inward madness. His life was stirred to the very source of being at the mere thought of seeing Seraphita. As he listened to her he was transported into unknown worlds; he was mute before her, she magnetized him. There, beneath the snows, among the glaciers, bloomed the celestial flower to which his hopes, so long betrayed, aspired; the sight of which awakened ideas of freshness, purity, and faith which grouped about his soul and lifted it to higher regions, — as Angels bear to heaven the Elect in those symbolic pictures inspired by the guardian spirit of a great master. Celestial perfumes softened the granite hardness of the rocky scene; light endowed with speech shed its divine melodies on the path of him who looked to heaven. After emptying the cup of terrestrial love which his

teeth had bitten as he drank it, he saw before him the
chalice of salvation where the limpid waters sparkled,
making thirsty for ineffable delights whoever dare apply
his lips burning with a faith so strong that the crystal
shall not be shattered.

But Wilfrid now encountered the wall of brass for
which he had been seeking up and down the earth.
He went impetuously to Seraphita, meaning to express
the whole force and bearing of a passion under which
he bounded like the fabled horse beneath the iron
horseman, firm in his saddle, whom nothing moves
while the efforts of the fiery animal only made the
rider heavier and more solid. He sought her to relate his life, — to prove the grandeur of his soul by
the grandeur of his faults, to show the ruins of his
desert. But no sooner had he crossed her threshold,
and found himself within the zone of those eyes of
scintillating azure, that met no limits forward and left
none behind, than he grew calm and submissive, as a
lion, springing on his prey in the plains of Africa, receives from the wings of the wind a message of love,
and stops his bound. A gulf opened before him, into
which his frenzied words fell and disappeared, and from
which uprose a voice which changed his being; he became as a child, a child of sixteen, timid and frightened before this maiden with serene brow, this white
figure whose inalterable calm was like the cruel im-
passibility of human justice. The combat between them
had never ceased until this evening, when with a glance
she brought him down, as a falcon making his dizzy

spirals in the air around his prey causes it to fall stupefied to earth, before carrying it to his eyrie.

We may note within ourselves many a long struggle the end of which is one of our own actions, — struggles which are, as it were, the reverse side of humanity. This reverse side belongs to God; the obverse side to men. More than once Seraphita had proved to Wilfrid that she knew this hidden and ever varied side, which is to the majority of men a second being. Often she said to him in her dove-like voice: "Why all this vehemence?" when on his way to her he had sworn she should be his. Wilfrid was, however, strong enough to raise the cry of revolt to which he had given utterance in Monsieur Becker's study. The narrative of the old pastor had calmed him. Sceptical and derisive as he was, he saw belief like a sidereal brilliance dawning on his life. He asked himself if Seraphita were not an exile from the higher spheres seeking the homeward way. The fanciful deifications of all ordinary lovers he could not give to this lily of Norway in whose divinity he believed. Why lived she here beside this fiord? What did she? Questions that received no answer filled his mind. Above all, what was about to happen between them? What fate had brought him there? To him, Seraphita was the motionless marble, light nevertheless as a vapor, which Minna had seen that day poised above the precipices of the Falberg. Could she thus stand on the edge of all gulfs without danger, without a tremor of the arching eyebrows, or a quiver of the light of the eye? If his love was to be without hope, it was not without curiosity.

From the moment when Wilfrid suspected the ethereal nature of the enchantress who had told him the secrets of his life in melodious utterance, he had longed to try to subject her, to keep her to himself, to tear her from the heaven where, perhaps, she was awaited. Earth and Humanity seized their prey ; he would imitate them. His pride, the only sentiment through which man can long be exalted, would make him happy in this triumph for the rest of his life. The idea sent the blood boiling through his veins, and his heart swelled. If he did not succeed, he would destroy her, — it is so natural to destroy that which we cannot possess, to deny what we cannot comprehend, to insult that which we envy.

On the morrow, Wilfrid, filled with ideas which the extraordinary events of the previous night naturally awakened in his mind, resolved to question David, and went to find him on pretext of asking after Seraphita's health. Though Monsieur Becker spoke of the old servant as falling into dotage, Wilfrid relied on his own perspicacity to discover scraps of truth in the torrent of the old man's rambling talk.

David had the immovable, undecided, physiognomy of an octogenarian. Under his white hair lay a forehead lined with wrinkles like the stone courses of a ruined wall ; and his face was furrowed like the bed of a dried-up torrent. His life seemed to have retreated wholly to the eyes, where light still shone, though its gleams were obscured by a mistiness which seemed to indicate either an active mental alienation or the stupid stare of drunkenness. His slow and heavy movements betrayed the glacial weight of age, and communicated an icy influence to whoever allowed themselves to look long at him, — for he possessed the magnetic force of torpor. His limited intelligence was only roused by the sight, the hearing, or the recollection of his mistress. She was the soul of this wholly material fragment of an existence. Any one seeing David alone by himself would have thought him a corpse; let Seraphita enter, let her voice be heard, or a mention of her be made, and the dead came forth from his grave and recovered speech and motion. The dry bones were not more truly awakened by the divine breath in the valley of Jehoshaphat, and never was that apocalyptic vison better realized than in this Lazarus issuing from the sepulchre into life at the voice of a young girl. His language, which was always figurative and often incomprehensible, prevented the inhabitants of the village from talking with him; but they respected a mind that deviated so utterly from common ways, — a thing which the masses instinctively admire.

Wilfrid found him in the antechamber, apparently asleep beside the stove. Like a dog who recognizes a friend of the family, the old man raised his eyes, saw the foreigner, and did not stir.

"Where is she?" inquired Wilfrid, sitting down beside him.

David fluttered his fingers in the air as if to express the flight of a bird.

" Does she still suffer?" asked Wilfrid.

" Beings vowed to Heaven are able so to suffer that suffering does not lessen their love ; this is the mark of the true faith," answered the old man, solemnly, like an instrument which, on being touched, gives forth an accidental note.

" Who taught you those words? "

" The Spirit."

" What happened to her last night? Did you force your way past the Vertumni standing sentinel? did you evade the Mammons?"

" Yes ; " answered David, as though awaking from a dream.

The misty gleam of his eyes melted into a ray that came direct from the soul and made it by degrees brilliant as that of an eagle, as intelligent as that of a poet.

" What did you see?" asked Wilfrid, astonished at this sudden change.

" I saw Species and Shapes ; I heard the Spirit of all things ; I beheld the revolt of the Evil Ones ; I listened to the words of the Good. Seven devils came, and seven archangels descended from on high. The archangels stood apart and looked on through veils. The devils were close by ; they shone, they acted. Mammon came on his pearly shell in the shape of a beautiful naked woman ; her snowy body dazzled the eye, no human form ever equalled it ; and he said, ' I am

Pleasure; thou shalt possess me!' Lucifer, prince of
serpents, was there in sovereign robes; his Manhood
was glorious as the beauty of an angel, and he said,
' Humanity shall be at thy feet!' The Queen of
misers, — she who gives back naught that she has ever
received, — the Sea, came wrapped in her virent mantle; she opened her bosom, she showed her gems, she
brought forth her treasures and offered them; waves of
sapphire and of emerald came at her bidding; her
hidden wonders stirred, they rose to the surface of her
breast, they spoke; the rarest pearl of Ocean spread
its irridescent wings and gave voice to its marine
melodies, saying, ' Twin daughter of suffering, we are
sisters! await me; let us go together; all I need
is to become a Woman.' The Bird with the wings of
an eagle and the paws of a lion, the head of a woman
and the body of a horse, the Animal, fell down before
her and licked her feet, and promised seven hundred
years of plenty to her best-beloved daughter. Then
came the most formidable of all, the Child, weeping
at her knees, and saying, ' Wilt thou leave me, feeble
and suffering as I am? oh, my mother, stay!' and he
played with her, and shed languor on the air, and the
Heavens themselves had pity for his wail. The Virgin
of pure song brought forth her choirs to relax the soul.
The Kings of the East came with their slaves, their
armies, and their women; the Wounded asked her for
succor, the Sorrowful stretched forth their hands: ' Do
not leave us! do not leave us!' they cried. I, too, I
cried, ' Do not leave us! we adore thee! stay!'

Flowers, bursting from the seed, bathed her in their fragrance which uttered, 'Stay!' The giant Enakim came forth from Jupiter, leading Gold and its friends and all the Spirits of the Astral Regions which are joined with him, and they said, 'We are thine for seven hundred years.' At last came Death on his pale horse, crying, 'I will obey thee!' One and all fell prostrate before her. Could you but have seen them! They covered as it were a vast plain, and they cried aloud to her, 'We have nurtured thee, thou art our child; do not abandon us!' At length Life issued from her Ruby Waters, and said, 'I will not leave thee!' then, finding Seraphita silent, she flamed upon her as the sun, crying out, 'I am light!' 'THE LIGHT is there!' cried Seraphita, pointing to the clouds where stood the archangels; but she was wearied out; Desire had wrung her nerves, she could only cry, 'My God! my God!' Ah! many an Angelic Spirit, scaling the mountain and nigh to the summit, has set his foot upon a rolling stone which plunged him back into the abyss! All these lost Spirits adored her constancy; they stood around her, — a choir without a song, — weeping and whispering, 'Courage!' At last she conquered; Desire — let loose upon her in every Shape and every Species — was vanquished. She stood in prayer, and when at last her eyes were lifted she saw the feet of Angels circling in the Heavens."

" She saw the feet of Angels?" repeated Wilfrid.

" Yes," said the old man.

" Was it a dream that she told you?" asked Wilfrid.

" A dream as real as your life," answered David ; " I was there."

The calm assurance of the old servant affected Wilfrid powerfully.   He went away asking himself whether these visions were any less extraordinary than those he had read of in Swedenborg the night before.

" If Spirits exist, they must act," he was saying to himself as he entered the parsonage, where he found Monsieur Becker alone.

" Dear pastor," he said, " Seraphita is connected with us in form only, and even that form is inexplicable.   Do not think me a madman or a lover ; a profound conviction cannot be argued with.   Convert my belief into scientific theories, and let us try to enlighten each other.   To-morrow evening we shall both be with her."

" What then ? " said Monsieur Becker.

" If her eye ignores space," replied Wilfrid, " if her thought is an intelligent sight which enables her to perceive all things in their essence, and to connect them with the general evolution of the universe, if, in a word, she sees and knows all, let us seat the Pythoness on her tripod, let us force this pitiless eagle by threats to spread its wings !   Help me !   I breathe a fire which burns my vitals ; I must quench it or it will consume me.   I have found a prey at last, and it shall be mine ! "

" The conquest will be difficult," said the pastor, " because this girl is — "

" Is what ? " cried Wilfrid.

" Mad," said the old man.

" I will not dispute her madness, but neither must you dispute her wonderful powers. Dear Monsieur Becker, she has often confounded me with her learning. Has she travelled? "

" From her house to the fiord, no further."

" Never left this place! " exclaimed Wilfrid. "Then she must have read immensely."

" Not a page, not one iota! I am the only person who possesses any books in Jarvis. The works of Swedenborg — the only books that were in the château — you see before you. She has never looked into a single one of them."

" Have you tried to talk with her? "

" What good would that do? "

" Does no one live with her in that house? "

" She has no friends but you and Minna, nor any servant except old David."

" It cannot be that she knows nothing of science nor of art."

" Who should teach her? " said the pastor.

" But if she can discuss such matters pertinently, as she has often done with me, what do you make of it? "

" The girl may have acquired through years of silence the faculties enjoyed by Apollonius of Tyana and other pretended sorcerers burned by the Inquisition, which did not choose to admit the fact of second-sight.

" If she can speak Arabic, what would you say to that? "

" The history of medical science gives many authentic instances of girls who have spoken languages entirely unknown to them."

" What can I do?" exclaimed Wilfrid. " She knows of secrets in my past life known only to me."

" I shall be curious to see if she can tell me thoughts that I have confided to no living person," said Monsieur Becker.

Minna entered the room.

" Well, my daughter, and how is your familiar spirit?"

" He suffers, father," she answered, bowing to Wilfrid. " Human passions, clothed in their false riches, surrounded him all night, and showed him all the glories of the world. But you think these things mere tales."

" Tales as beautiful to those who read them in their brains as the ' Arabian Nights ' to common minds," said the pastor, smiling.

" Did not Satan carry our Saviour to the pinnacle of the Temple, and show him all the kingdoms of the world?" she said.

" The Evangelists," replied her father, " did not correct their copies very carefully, and several versions are in existence."

" You believe in the reality of these visions?" said Wilfrid to Minna.

" Who can doubt when he relates them."

" He?" demanded Wilfrid. " Who?"

" He who is there," replied Minna, motioning towards the château.

" Are you speaking of Seraphita? " he said.

The young girl bent her head, and looked at him with an expression of gentle mischief.

" You too ! " exclaimed Wilfrid, " you take pleasure in confounding me. Who and what is she? What do you think of her? "

" What I feel is inexplicable," said Minna, blushing.

" You are all crazy ! " cried the pastor.

" Farewell, until to-morrow evening," said Wilfrid.

IV.

THE CLOUDS OF THE SANCTUARY.

THERE are pageants in which all the material splendors that man arrays co-operate. Nations of slaves and divers have searched the sands of ocean and the bowels of earth for the pearls and diamonds which adorn the spectators. Transmitted as heirlooms from generation to generation, these treasures have shone on consecrated brows and could be the most faithful of historians had they speech. They know the joys and sorrows of the great and those of the small. Everywhere do they go; they are worn with pride at festivals, carried in despair to usurers, borne off in triumph amid blood and pillage, enshrined in masterpieces conceived by art for their protection. None, except the pearl of Cleopatra, has been lost. The Great and the Fortunate assemble to witness the coronation of some king, whose trappings are the work of men's hands, but the purple of whose raiment is less glorious than that of the flowers of the field. These festivals, splendid in light, bathed in music which the hand of man creates, aye, all the triumphs of that hand are subdued by a thought, crushed by a sentiment. The Mind can illumine in a man and round a man a light more vivid, can open his ear to more melodious harmonies, can seat him on clouds of shining constellations and teach him to question them. The Heart can do still greater things. Man may come into the presence of one sole being and find in a single word, a single look, an influence so weighty to bear, of so luminous a light, so penetrating a sound, that he succumbs and kneels before it. The most real of all splendors are not in outward things, they are within us. A single secret of science is a realm of wonders to the man of learning. Do the trumpets of Power, the jewels of Wealth, the music of Joy, or a vast concourse of people attend his mental festival? No, he finds his glory in some dim retreat where, perchance, a pallid suffering man whispers a single word into his ear; that word, like a torch lighted in a mine, reveals to him a Science. All human ideas, arrayed in every attractive form which Mystery can invent surrounded a blind man seated in a wayside ditch. Three worlds, the Natural, the Spiritual, the Divine, with all their spheres, opened their portals to a Florentine exile; he walked attended by the Happy and the Unhappy; by those who prayed and those who moaned; by angels and by souls in hell. When the Sent of God, who knew and could accomplish all things, appeared to three of his disciples it was at eventide, at the common table of the humblest of inns; and then and there the Light broke forth, shattering Material Forms, illuminating the Spiritual Faculties, so that they saw him in his glory, and the earth lay at their feet like a cast-off sandal.

Monsieur Becker, Wilfrid, and Minna were all under

the influence of fear as they took their way to meet the extraordinary being whom each desired to question. To them, in their several ways, the Swedish castle had grown to mean some gigantic representation, some spectacle like those whose colors and masses are skilfully and harmoniously marshalled by the poets, and whose personages, imaginary actors to men, are real to those who begin to penetrate the Spiritual World. On the tiers of this Coliseum Monsieur Becker seated the gray legions of Doubt, the stern ideas, the specious formulas of Dispute. He convoked the various antagonistic worlds of philosophy and religion, and they all appeared, in the guise of a fleshless shape, like that in which art embodies Time, — an old man bearing in one hand a scythe, in the other a broken globe, the human universe.

Wilfrid had bidden to the scene his earliest illusions and his latest hopes, human destiny and its conflicts, religion and its conquering powers.

Minna saw heaven confusedly by glimpses ; love raised a curtain wrought with mysterious images, and the melodious sounds which met her ear redoubled her curiosity.

To all three, therefore, this evening was to be what that other evening had been for the pilgrims to Emmaüs, what a vision was to Dante, an inspiration to Homer, — to them, three aspects of the world revealed, veils rent away, doubts dissipated, darkness illumined. Humanity in all its moods expecting light could not be better represented than here by this young girl, this man in the vigor of his age, and these old men, of whom one was learned enough to doubt, the other ignorant enough to believe. Never was any scene more simple in appearance, nor more portentous in reality.

When they entered the room, ushered in by old David, they found Seraphita standing by a table on which were served the various dishes which compose a " tea ; " a form of collation which in the North takes the place of wine and its pleasures, — reserved more exclusively for Southern climes. Certainly nothing proclaimed in her, or in him, a being with the strange power of appearing under two distinct forms ; nothing about her betrayed the manifold powers which she wielded. Like a careful housewife attending to the comfort of her guests, she ordered David to put more wood into the stove.

" Good evening, my neighbors," she said. " Dear Monsieur Becker, you do right to come ; you see me living for the last time, perhaps. This winter has killed me. Will you sit there ? " she said to Wilfrid. " And you, Minna, here ? " pointing to a chair beside her. " I see you have brought your embroidery. Did you invent that stitch ? the design is very pretty. For whom is it, — your father, or monsieur ? " she added, turning to Wilfrid. " Surely we ought to give him, before we part, a remembrance of the daughters of Norway."

" Did you suffer much yesterday ? " asked Wilfrid.

" It was nothing," she answered ; " the suffering gladdened me ; it was necessary, to enable me to leave this life."

"Then death does not alarm you?" said Monsieur Becker, smiling, for he did not think her ill.

"No, dear pastor; there are two ways of dying: to some, death is victory, to others, defeat."

"Do you think that you have conquered?" asked Minna.

"I do not know," she said, "perhaps I have only taken a step in the path."

The lustrous splendor of her brow grew dim, her eyes were veiled beneath slow-dropping lids; a simple movement which affected the prying guests and kept them silent. Monsieur Becker was the first to recover courage.

"Dear child," he said, "you are truth itself, and you are ever kind. I would ask of you to-night something other than the dainties of your tea-table. If we may believe certain persons, you know amazing things; if this be true, would it not be charitable in you to solve a few of our doubts?"

"Ah!" she said smiling, "I walk on the clouds. I visit the depths of the fiord; the sea is my steed and I bridle it; I know where the singing flower grows, and the talking light descends, and fragrant colors shine! I wear the seal of Solomon; I am a fairy; I cast my orders to the wind which, like an abject slave, fulfils them; my eyes can pierce the earth and behold its treasures; for lo! am I not the virgin to whom the pearls dart from their ocean depths and — "

" — who led me safely to the summit of the Falberg?" said Minna, interrupting her.

"Thou! thou too!" exclaimed the strange being, with a luminous glance at the young girl which filled her soul with trouble. "Had I not the faculty of reading through your foreheads the desires which have brought you here, should I be what you think I am?" she said, encircling all three with her controlling glance, to David's great satisfaction. The old man rubbed his hands with pleasure as he left the room.

"Ah!" she resumed after a pause, "you have come, all of you, with the curiosity of children. You, my poor Monsieur Becker, have asked yourself how it was possible that a girl of seventeen should know even a single one of those secrets which men of science seek with their noses to the earth, — instead of raising their eyes to heaven. Were I to tell you how and at what point the plant merges into the animal you would begin to doubt your doubts. You have plotted to question me; you will admit that?"

"Yes, dear Seraphita," answered Wilfrid; "but the desire is a natural one to men, is it not?"

"You will bore this dear child with such topics," she said, passing her hand lightly over Minna's hair with a caressing gesture.

The young girl raised her eyes and seemed as though she longed to lose herself in him.

"Speech is the endowment of us all," resumed the mysterious creature, gravely. "Woe to him who keeps silence, even in a desert, believing that no one hears him; all voices speak and all ears listen here below. Speech moves the universe. Monsieur Becker,

I desire to say nothing unnecessarily. I know the difficulties that beset your mind; would you not think it a miracle if I were now to lay bare the past history of your consciousness? Well, the miracle shall be accomplished. You have never admitted to yourself the full extent of your doubts. I alone, immovable in my faith, I can show it to you; I can terrify you with yourself.

" You stand on the darkest side of Doubt. You do not believe in God, — although you know it not, — and all things here below are secondary to him who rejects the first principle of things. Let us leave aside the fruitless discussions of false philosophy. The spiritualist generations made as many and as vain efforts to deny Matter as the materialist generations have made to deny Spirit. Why such discussions? Does not man himself offer irrefragable proof of both systems? Do we not find in him material things and spiritual things? None but a madman can refuse to see in the human body a fragment of Matter; your natural sciences, when they decompose it, find little difference between its elements and those of other animals. On the other hand, the idea produced in man by the comparison of many objects has never seemed to any one to belong to the domain of Matter. As to this, I offer no opinion. I am now concerned with your doubts, not with my certainties. To you, as to the majority of thinkers, the relations between things, the reality of which is proved to you by your sensations and which you possess the faculty to discover, do not seem Material. The Natural universe of things and beings ends, in man, with the Spiritual universe of similarities or differences which he perceives among the innumerable forms of Nature, — relations so multiplied as to seem infinite ; for if, up to the present time, no one has been able to enumerate the separate terrestrial creations, who can reckon their correlations? Is not the fraction which you know, in relation to their totality, what a single number is to infinity? Here, then, you fall into a perception of the infinite which undoubtedly obliges you to conceive of a purely Spiritual world.

" Thus man himself offers sufficient proof of the two orders, — Matter and Spirit. In him culminates a visible finite universe ; in him begins a universe invisible and infinite, — two worlds unknown to each other. Have the pebbles of the fiord a perception of their combined being? have they a consciousness of the colors they present to the eye of man? do they hear the music of the waves that lap them? Let us therefore spring over and not attempt to sound the abysmal depths presented to our minds in the union of a Material universe and a Spiritual universe, — a creation visible, ponderable, tangible, terminating in a creation invisible, imponderable, intangible ; completely dissimilar, separated by the void, yet united by indisputable bonds and meeting in a being who derives equally from the one and from the other ! Let us mingle in one world these two worlds, absolutely irreconcilable to your philosophies, but conjoined by fact. However abstract man may suppose the relation which

binds two things together, the line of junction is perceptible. How? Where? We are not now in search of
the vanishing point where Matter subtilizes. If such
were the question, I cannot see why He who has, by
physical relations, studded with stars at immeasurable
distances the heavens which veil Him, may not have
created solid substances, nor why you deny Him the
faculty of giving a body to thought.

" Thus your invisible moral universe and your visible
physical universe are one and the same matter. We
will not separate properties from substances, nor objects from effects. All that exists, all that presses upon
us and overwhelms us from above or from below, before
us or in us, all that which our eyes and our minds perceive, all these named and unnamed things compose —
in order to fit the problem of Creation to the measure
of your logic — a block of finite Matter; but were it
infinite, God would still not be its master. Now,
reasoning with your views, dear pastor, no matter in
what way God the infinite is concerned with this block
of finite Matter, He cannot exist and retain the attributes with which man invests Him. Seek Him in facts,
and He is not; ask reason to reveal Him, and again
He is not, spiritually and materially, you have made
God impossible. Listen to the Word of human Reason
forced to its ultimate conclusions.

" In bringing God face to face with the Great Whole,
we see that only two states are possible between them,
— either God and Matter are contemporaneous, or God
existed alone before Matter. Were Reason — the light

that has guided the human race from the dawn of its existence — accumulated in one brain, even that mighty brain could not invent a third mode of being without suppressing both Matter and God. Let human philosophies pile mountain upon mountain of words and of ideas, let religions accumulate images and beliefs, revelations and mysteries, you must face at last this terrible dilemma and choose between the two propositions which compose it; you have no option, and one as much as the other leads human reason to Doubt.

" The problem thus established, what signifies Spirit or Matter? Why trouble about the march of the worlds in one direction or in another, since the Being who guides them is shown to be an absurdity? Why continue to ask whether man is approaching heaven or receding from it, whether creation is rising towards Spirit or descending towards Matter, if the questioned universe gives no reply? What signifies theogonies and their armies, theologies and their dogmas, since whichever side of the problem is man's choice, his God exists not? Let us for a moment take up the first proposition, and suppose God contemporaneous with Matter. Is subjection to the action or the co-existence of an alien substance consistent with being God at all? In such a system, would not God become a secondary agent compelled to organize Matter? If so, who compelled Him? Between His material gross companion and Himself, who was the arbiter? Who paid the wages of the six days' labor imputed to the great Designer? Has any determining force been found which was neither

God nor Matter? God being regarded as the manu-
facturer of the machinery of the worlds, is it not as
ridiculous to call Him God as to call the slave who
turned a grindstone a Roman citizen? Besides, another difficulty, as insoluble to this supreme human
reason as it is to God, presents itself.

"If we carry the problem higher, shall we not be like
the Hindus, who put the world upon a tortoise, the
tortoise on an elephant, and do not know on what the
feet of their elephant may rest? This supreme will,
issuing from the contest between God and Matter,
this God, this more than God, can He have existed
throughout eternity without willing what He afterwards
willed, — admitting that Eternity can be divided into
two eras. No matter where God is, what becomes of
His intuitive intelligence if He did not know His ultimate thought? Which, then, is the true Eternity, —
the created Eternity or the uncreated? But if God
throughout all time did will the world such as it is,
this new necessity, which harmonizes with the idea
of sovereign intelligence, implies the co-eternity of
Matter. Whether Matter be co-eternal by a divine
will necessarily accordant with itself from the beginning, or whether Matter be co-eternal of its own being,
the power of God, which must be absolute, perishes if
His will is circumscribed; for in that case God would
find within Him a determining force which would control Him. Can He be God if He can no more separate
Himself from His creation in a past eternity than in the
coming eternity?

" This face of the problem is insoluble in its cause. Let us now inquire into its effects. If a God compelled to have created the world from all eternity seems inexplicable, He is quite as unintelligible in perpetual cohesion with His work. God, constrained to live eternally united to His creation is held down to His first position as workman. Can you conceive of a God who shall be neither independent of nor dependent on His work? Could He destroy that work without challenging Himself? Ask yourself, and decide! Whether He destroys it some day, or whether He never destroys it, either way is fatal to the attributes without which God cannot exist. Is the world an experiment? is it a perishable form to which destruction must come? If it is, is not God inconsistent and impotent? inconsistent, because He ought to have seen the result before the attempt, — moreover why should He delay to destroy that which He is to destroy? — impotent, for how else could He have created an imperfect man?

" If an imperfect creation contradicts the faculties which man attributes to God we are forced back upon the question, Is creation perfect? The idea is in harmony with that of a God supremely intelligent who could make no mistakes; but then, what means the degradation of His work, and its regeneration? Moreover, a perfect world is, necessarily, indestructible; its forms would not perish, it could neither advance nor recede, it would revolve in the everlasting circumference from which it would never issue. In that case God would be dependent on His work; it would be co-eternal with Him; and so we fall back into one of the propositions most antagonistic to God. If the world is imperfect, it can progress; if perfect, it is stationary. On the other hand, if it be impossible to admit of a progressive God ignorant through a past eternity of the results of His creative work, can there be a stationary God? would not that imply the triumph of Matter? would it not be the greatest of all negations? Under the first hypothesis God perishes through weakness; under the second through the force of His inertia.

"Therefore, to all sincere minds the supposition that Matter, in the conception and execution of the worlds, is contemporaneous with God, is to deny God. Forced to choose, in order to govern the nations, between the two alternatives of the problem, whole generations have preferred this solution of it. Hence the doctrine of the two principles of Magianism, brought from Asia and adopted in Europe under the form of Satan warring with the Eternal Father. But this religious formula and the innumerable aspects of divinity that have sprung from it are surely crimes against the Majesty Divine. What other term can we apply to the belief which sets up as a rival to God a personification of Evil, striving eternally against the Omnipotent Mind without the possibility of ultimate triumph? Your statics declare that two Forces thus pitted against each other are reciprocally rendered null.

"Do you turn back, therefore, to the other side of the problem, and say that God pre-existed, original, alone?

" I will not go over the preceding arguments (which here return in full force) as to the severance of Eternity into two parts; nor the questions raised by the progression or the immobility of the worlds; let us look only at the difficulties inherent to this second theory. If God pre-existed alone, the world must have emanated from Him; Matter was therefore drawn from His essence; consequently Matter in itself is non-existent; all forms are veils to cover the Divine Spirit. If this be so, the World is Eternal, and also it must be God. Is not this proposition even more fatal than the former to the attributes conferred on God by human reason? How can the actual condition of Matter be explained if we suppose it to issue from the bosom of God and to be ever united with Him? Is it possible to believe that the All-Powerful, supremely good in His essence and in His faculties, has engendered things dissimilar to Himself. Must He not in all things and through all things be like unto Himself? Can there be in God certain evil parts of which at some future day he may rid Himself? — a conjecture less offensive and absurd than terrible, for the reason that it drags back into Him the two principles which the preceding theory proved to be inadmissible. God must be ONE; He cannot be divided without renouncing the most important condition of His existence. It is therefore impossible to admit of a fraction of God which yet is not God. This hypothesis seemed so criminal to the Roman Church that she has made the omnipresence of God in the least particles of the Eucharist an article of faith.

" But how then can we imagine an omnipotent mind which does not triumph? How associate it unless in triumph with Nature? But Nature is not triumphant; she seeks, combines, remodels, dies, and is born again; she is even more convulsed when creating than when all was fusion; Nature suffers, groans, is ignorant, degenerates, does evil; deceives herself, annihilates herself, disappears, and begins again. If God is associated with Nature, how can we explain the inoperative indifference of the divine principle? Wherefore death? How came it that Evil, king of the earth, was born of a God supremely good in His essence and in His faculties, who can produce nothing that is not made in His own image?

" But if, from this relentless conclusion which leads at once to absurdity, we pass to details, what end are we to assign to the world? If all is God, all is reciprocally cause and effect; all is ONE as God is ONE, and we can perceive neither points of likeness nor points of difference. Can the real end be a rotation of Matter which subtilizes and disappears? In whatever sense it were done, would not this mechanical trick of Matter issuing from God and returning to God seem a sort of child's play? Why should God make himself gross with Matter? Under which form is he most God? Which has the ascendant, Matter or Spirit, when neither can in any way do wrong? Who can comprehend the Deity engaged in this perpetual business, by which he divides Himself into two Natures, one of which knows nothing, while the other knows all? Can you

conceive of God amusing Himself in the form of man,
laughing at His own efforts, dying Friday, to be born
again Sunday, and continuing this play from age to
age, knowing the end from all eternity, and telling
nothing to Himself, the Creature, of what He the
Creator, does? The God of the preceding hypothesis,
a God so nugatory by the very power of His inertia,
seems the more possible of the two if we are compelled
to choose between the impossibilities with which this
God, so dull a jester, fusillades Himself when two sections of humanity argue face to face, weapons in hand.

"However absurd this outcome of the second problem
may seem, it was adopted by half the human race in
the sunny lands where smiling mythologies were created. Those amorous nations were consistent; with
them all was God, even Fear and its dastardy, even
crime and its bacchanals. If we accept pantheism, —
the religion of many a great human genius, — who shall
say where the greater reason lies? Is it with the savage,
free in the desert, clothed in his nudity, listening to the
sun, talking to the sea, sublime and always true in his
deeds whatever they may be ; or shall we find it in civilized man, who derives his chief enjoyments through
lies ; who wrings Nature and all her resources to put a
musket on his shoulder ; who employs his intellect to
hasten the hour of his death and to create diseases out
of pleasures? When the rake of pestilence and the
ploughshare of war and the demon of desolation have
passed over a corner of the globe and obliterated all
things, who will be found to have the greater reason, —

the Nubian savage or the patrician of Thebes? Your doubts descend the scale, they go from heights to depths, they embrace all, the end as well as the means.

" But if the physical world seems inexplicable, the moral world presents still stronger arguments against God. Where, then, is progress? If all things are indeed moving toward perfection why do we die young? why do not nations perpetuate themselves? The world having issued from God and being contained in God can it be stationary? Do we live once, or do we live always? If we live once, hurried onward by the march of the Great-Whole, a knowledge of which has not been given to us, let us act as we please. If we are eternal, let things take their course. Is the created being guilty if he exists at the instant of the transitions? If he sins at the moment of a great transformation will he be punished for it after being its victim? What becomes of the Divine goodness if we are not transferred to the regions of the blest — should any such exist? What becomes of God's prescience if He is ignorant of the results of the trials to which He subjects us? What is this alternative offered to man by all religions, — either to boil in some eternal cauldron or to walk in white robes, a palm in his hand and a halo round his head? Can it be that this pagan invention is the final word of God? Where is the generous soul who does not feel that the calculating virtue which seeks the eternity of pleasure offered by all religions to whoever fulfils at stray moments certain fanciful and often unnatural conditions, is unworthy of man and of God? Is it not a mockery to give to man impetuous senses and forbid him to satisfy them? Besides, what mean these ascetic objections if Good and Evil are equally abolished? Does Evil exist? If substance in all its forms is God, then Evil is God. The faculty of reasoning as well as the faculty of feeling having been given to man to use, nothing can be more excusable in him than to seek to know the meaning of human suffering and the prospects of the future.

" If these rigid and rigorous arguments lead to such conclusions confusion must reign. The world would have no fixedness; nothing would advance, nothing would pause, all would change, nothing would be destroyed, all would reappear after self-renovation; for if your mind does not clearly demonstrate to you an end, it is equally impossible to demonstrate the destruction of the smallest particle of Matter; Matter can transform but not annihilate itself.

" Though blind force may provide arguments for the atheist, intelligent force is inexplicable; for if it emanates from God, why should it meet with obstacles? ought not its triumph to be immediate? Where is God? If the living cannot perceive Him, can the dead find Him? Crumble, ye idolatries and ye religions! Fall, feeble keystones of all social arches, powerless to retard the decay, the death, the oblivion that have overtaken all nations however firmly founded! Fall, morality and justice! our crimes are purely relative : they are divine effects whose causes we are not allowed

to know.　All is God.　Either we are God or God is
not! — Child of a century whose every year has laid
upon your brow, old man, the ice of its unbelief, here,
here is the summing up of your lifetime of thought,
of your science and your reflections! Dear Monsieur
Becker, you have laid your head on the pillow of
Doubt, because it is the easiest of solutions; acting
in this respect with the majority of mankind, who
say in their hearts: ' Let us think no more of these
problems, since God has not vouchsafed to grant us
the algebraic demonstrations that could solve them,
while He has given us so many other ways to get from
earth to heaven.'

"Tell me, dear pastor, are not these your secret
thoughts?　Have I evaded the point of any? nay,
rather, have I not clearly stated all?　First, in the
dogma of two principles, — an antagonism in which
God perishes for the reason that being All-Powerful
He chose to combat.　Secondly, in the absurd pantheism where, all being God, God exists no longer.　These
two sources, from which have flowed all the religions
for whose triumph Earth has toiled and prayed, are
equally pernicious.　Behold in them the double-bladed
axe with which you decapitate the white old man whom
you enthrone among your painted clouds!　And now,
to me the axe　I wield it!"

Monsieur Becker and Wilfrid gazed at the young girl
with something like terror.

"To believe," continued Seraphita, in her Woman's
voice, for the Man had finished speaking, "to believe

is a gift. To believe is to feel. To believe in God we must feel God. This feeling is a possession slowly acquired by the human being, just as other astonishing powers which you admire in great men, warriors, artists, scholars, those who know and those who act, are acquired. Thought, that budget of the relations which you perceive among created things, is an intellectual language which can be learned, is it not? Belief, the budget of celestial truths, is also a language as superior to thought as thought is to instinct. This language also can be learned. The Believer answers with a single cry, a single gesture; Faith puts within his hand a flaming sword with which he pierces and illumines all. The Seer attains to heaven and descends not. But there are beings who believe and see, who know and will, who love and pray and wait. Submissive, yet aspiring to the kingdom of light, they have neither the aloofness of the Believer nor the silence of the Seer; they listen and reply. To them the doubt of the twilight ages is not a murderous weapon, but a divining rod; they accept the contest under every form; they train their tongues to every language; they are never angered, though they groan; the acrimony of the aggressor is not in them, but rather the softness and tenuity of light, which penetrates and warms and illumines. To their eyes Doubt is neither an impiety, nor a blasphemy, nor a crime, but a transition through which men return upon their steps in the Darkness, or advance into the Light. This being so, dear pastor, let us reason together.

" You do not believe in God? Why? God, to your thinking, is incomprehensible, inexplicable. Agreed. I will not reply that to comprehend God in His entirety would be to be God; nor will I tell you that you deny what seems to you inexplicable so as to give me the right to affirm that which to me is believable. There is, for you, one evident fact, which lies within yourself. In you, Matter has ended in intelligence; can you therefore think that human intelligence will end in darkness, doubt, and nothingness? God may seem to you incomprehensible and inexplicable, but you must admit Him to be, in all things purely physical, a splendid and consistent workman. Why should His craft stop short at man, His most finished creation?

" If that question is not convincing, at least it compels meditation. Happily, although you deny God, you are obliged, in order to establish your doubts, to admit those double-bladed facts, which kill your arguments as much as your arguments kill God. We have also admitted that Matter and Spirit are two creations which do not comprehend each other; that the spiritual world is formed of infinite relations to which the finite material world has given rise; that if no one on earth is able to identify himself by the power of his spirit with the great-whole of terrestrial creations, still less is he able to rise to the knowledge of the relations which the spirit perceives between these creations.

" We might end the argument here in one word, by denying you the faculty of comprehending God, just as you deny to the pebbles of the fiord the faculties

of counting and of seeing each other. How do you
know that the stones themselves do not deny the existence of man, though man makes use of them to build
his houses? There is one fact that appals you, — the
Infinite; if you feel it within you, why will you not
admit its consequences? Can the finite have a perfect
knowledge of the infinite? If you cannot perceive
those relations which, according to your own admis-
sion, are infinite, how can you grasp a sense of the far-
off end to which they are converging? Order, the
revelation of which is one of your needs, being infinite,
can your limited reason apprehend it? Do not ask
why man does not comprehend that which he is able
to perceive, for he is equally able to perceive that which
he does not comprehend. If I prove to you that your
mind ignores that which lies within its compass, will
you grant that it is impossible for it to conceive whatever is beyond it? This being so, am I not justified in
saying to you: 'One of the two propositions under
which God is annihilated before the tribunal of our
reason must be true, the other is false. Inasmuch as
creation exists, you feel the necessity of an end, and
that end should be good, should it not? Now, if Matter terminates in man by intelligence, why are you not
satisfied to believe that the end of human intelligence
is the Light of the higher spheres, where alone an intuition of that God who seems to you so insoluble a
problem is obtained? The species which are beneath
you have no conception of the universe, and you have;
why should there not be other species above you more

intelligent than your own? Man ought to be better informed than he is about himself before he spends his strength in measuring God. Before attacking the stars that light us, and the higher certainties, ought he not to understand the certainties which are actually about him?'

" But no! to the negations of doubt I ought rather to reply by negations. Therefore I ask you whether there is anything here below so evident that I can put faith in it? I will show you in a moment that you believe firmly in things which act, and yet are not beings; in things which engender thought, and yet are not spirits; in living abstractions which the understanding cannot grasp in any shape, which are in fact nowhere, but which you perceive everywhere; which have, and can have, no name, but which, nevertheless, you have named; and which, like the God of flesh whom you figure to yourself, remain inexplicable, incomprehensible, and absurd. I shall also ask you why, after admitting the existence of these incomprehensible things, you reserve your doubts for God?

" You believe, for instance, in Number, — a base on which you have built the edifice of sciences which you call ' exact.' Without Number, what would become of mathematics? Well, what mysterious being endowed with the faculty of living forever could utter, and what language would he compact to word the Number which contains the infinite numbers whose existence is revealed to you by thought? Ask it of the loftiest human genius; he might ponder it for a thousand

years and what would be his answer? You know
neither where Number begins, nor where it pauses,
nor where it ends. Here you call it Time, there you
call it Space. Nothing exists except by Number.
Without it, all would be one and the same substance;
for Number alone differentiates and qualifies substance.
Number is to your Spirit what it is to Matter, an incomprehensible agent. Will you make a Deity of it?
Is it a being? Is it a breath emanating from God to
organize the material universe where nothing obtains
form except by the Divinity which is an effect of Number? The least as well as the greatest of creations are
distinguishable from each other by quantities, qualities,
dimensions, forces, — all attributes created by Number.
The infinitude of Numbers is a fact proved to your soul,
but of which no material proof can be given. The
mathematician himself tells you that the infinite of
numbers exists, but cannot be proved.

"God, dear pastor, is a Number endowed with motion, — felt, but not seen, the Believer will tell you.
Like the Unit, He begins Numbers, with which He has
nothing in common. The existence of Number depends on the Unit, which without being a number engenders Number. God, dear pastor, is a glorious
Unit who has nothing in common with His creations
but who, nevertheless, engenders them. Will you not
therefore agree with me that you are just as ignorant
of where Number begins and ends as you are of where
created Eternity begins and ends?

"Why, then, if you believe in Number, do you deny

God? Is not Creation interposed between the Infinite
of unorganized substances and the Infinite of the divine
spheres, just as the Unit stands between the Cipher of
the fractions you have lately named Decimals, and the
Infinite of Numbers which you call Wholes? Man
alone on earth comprehends Number, that first step of
the peristyle which leads to God, and yet his reason
stumbles on it! What! you can neither measure nor
grasp the first abstraction which God delivers to you,
and yet you try to subject His ends to your own tape-
line! Suppose that I plunge you into the abyss of
Motion, the force that organizes Number. If I tell
you that the Universe is naught else than Number
and Motion, you would see at once that we speak two
different languages. I understand them both; you
understand neither.

" Suppose I add that Motion and Number are engendered by the Word, namely the supreme Reason of
Seers and Prophets who in the olden time heard the
Breath of God beneath which Saul fell to the earth.
That Word, you scoff at it, you men, although you
well know that all visible works, societies, monuments,
deeds, passions, proceed from the breath of your own
feeble word, and that without that word you would
resemble the African gorilla, the nearest approach to
man, the negro. You believe firmly in Number and in
Motion, a force and a result both inexplicable, incomprehensible, to the existence of which I may apply the
logical dilemma which, as we have seen, prevents you
from believing in God. Powerful reasoner that you

are, you do not need that I should prove to you that
the Infinite must everywhere be like unto Itself, and
that, necessarily, it is One. God alone is Infinite, for
surely there cannot be two Infinites, two Ones. If,
to make use of human terms, anything demonstrated
to you here below seems to you infinite, be sure that
within it you will find some one aspect of God. But to
continue.

" You have appropriated to yourself a place in the
Infinite of Number; you have fitted it to your own
proportions by creating (if indeed you did create)
arithmetic, the basis on which all things rest, even
your societies. Just as Number — the only thing in
which your self-styled atheists believe — organized
physical creations, so arithmetic, in the employ of
Number, organized the moral world. This numeration
must be absolute, like all else that is true in itself; but
it is purely relative, it does not exist absolutely, and no
proof can be given of its reality. In the first place,
though Numeration is able to take account of organized
substances, it is powerless in relation to unorganized
forces, the ones being finite and the others infinite. The
man who can conceive the Infinite by his intelligence
cannot deal with it in its entirety ; if he could, he would
be God. Your Numeration, applying to things finite
and not to the Infinite, is therefore true in relation to
the details which you are able to perceive, and false in
relation to the Whole, which you are unable to perceive.
Though Nature is like unto herself in the organizing
forces or in her principles which are infinite, she is not

so in her finite effects. Thus you will never find in Nature two objects identically alike. In the Natural Order two and two never make four; to do so, four exactly similar units must be had, and you know how impossible it is to find two leaves alike on the same tree, or two trees alike of the same species. This axiom of your numeration, false in visible nature, is equally false in the invisible universe of your abstractions, where the same variance takes place in your ideas, which are the things of the visible world extended by means of their relations; so that the variations here are even more marked than elsewhere. In fact, all being relative to the temperament, strength, habits, and customs of individuals, who never resemble each other, the smallest objects take the color of personal feelings. For instance, man has been able to create units and to give an equal weight and value to bits of gold. Well, take the ducat of the rich man and the ducat of the poor man to a money-changer and they are rated exactly equal, but to the mind of the thinker one is of greater importance than the other; one represents a month of comfort, the other an ephemeral caprice. Two and two, therefore, only make four through a false conception.

" Again : fraction does not exist in Nature, where what you call a fragment is a finished whole. Does it not often happen (have you not many proofs of it?) that the hundredth part of a substance is stronger than what you term the whole of it? If fraction does not exist in the Natural Order, still less shall we find it in the Moral Order, where ideas and sentiments may be

as varied as the species of the Vegetable kingdom and
yet be always whole. The theory of fractions is therefore another signal instance of the servility of your
mind.

" Thus Number, with its infinite minuteness and its
infinite expansion, is a power whose weakest side is
known to you, but whose real import escapes your perception. You have built yourself a hut in the Infinite of
numbers, you have adorned it with hieroglyphics sci-
entifically arranged and painted, and you cry out, ' All
is here ! '

" Let us pass from pure, unmingled Number to cor-
porate Number. Your geometry establishes that a
straight line is the shortest way from one point to another, but your astronomy proves that God has proceeded by curves. Here, then, we find two truths
equally proved by the same science, — one by the testimony of your senses reinforced by the telescope, the
other by the testimony of your mind ; and yet the one
contradicts the other. Man, liable to err, affirms one,
and the Maker of the worlds, whom, so far, you have
not detected in error, contradicts it. Who shall decide
between rectilinear and curvilinear geometry ? between
the theory of the straight line and that of the curve ?
If, in His vast work, the mysterious Artificer, who knows
how to reach His ends miraculously fast, never employs
a straight line except to cut off an angle and so obtain
a curve, neither does man himself always rely upon it.
The bullet which he aims direct proceeds by a curve,
and when you wish to strike a certain point in space,

you impel your bombshell along its cruel parabola.
None of your men of science have drawn from this fact
the simple deduction that the Curve is the law of the
material worlds and the Straight line that of the Spiritual
worlds ; one is the theory of finite creations, the other
the theory of the infinite.   Man, who alone in this
world has a knowledge of the Infinite, can alone know
the straight line ; he alone has the sense of verticality
placed in a special organ.   A fondness for the creations
of the curve would seem to be in certain men an indication of the impurity of their nature still conjoined to
the material substances which engender us ; and the
love of great souls for the straight line seems to show
in them an intuition of heaven.   Between these two
lines there is a gulf fixed like that between the finite
and the infinite, between matter and spirit, between
man and the idea, between motion and the object
moved, between the creature and God.   Ask Love the
Divine to grant you his wings and you can cross that
gulf.   Beyond it begins the revelation of the Word.

" No part of those things which you call material is
without its own meaning ; lines are the boundaries of
solid parts and imply a force of action which you sup-
press in your formulas, — thus rendering those formulas
false in relation to substances taken as a whole.   Hence
the constant destruction of the monuments of human
labor, which you supply, unknown to yourselves, with
acting properties.   Nature has substances ; your science combines only their appearances.   At every step
Nature gives the lie to all your laws.   Can you find

a single one that is not disproved by a fact? Your
Static laws are at the mercy of a thousand accidents;
a fluid can overthrow a solid mountain and prove that
the heaviest substances may be lifted by one that is
imponderable.

" Your laws on Acoustics and Optics are defied by
the sounds which you hear within yourselves in sleep,
and by the light of an electric sun whose rays often
overcome you. You know no more how light makes
itself seen within you, than you know the simple and
natural process which changes it on the throats of
tropic birds to rubies, sapphires, emeralds, and opals,
or keeps it gray and brown on the breasts of the same
birds under the cloudy skies of Europe, or whitens it
here in the bosom of our polar Nature. You know
not how to decide whether color is a faculty with which
all substances are endowed, or an effect produced by an
effluence of light. You admit the saltness of the sea
without being able to prove that the water is salt at
its greatest depth. You recognize the existence of
various substances which span what you think to be
the void, — substances which are not tangible under any
of the forms assumed by Matter, although they put
themselves in harmony with Matter in spite of every
obstacle.

" All this being so, you believe in the results of
Chemistry, although that science still knows no way
of gauging the changes produced by the flux and reflux
of substances which come and go across your crystals
and your instruments on the impalpable filaments of

heat or light conducted and projected by the affinities
of metal or vitrified flint. You obtain none but dead
substances, from which you have driven the unknown
force that holds in check the decomposition of all
things here below, and of which cohesion, attraction,
vibration, and polarity are but phenomena. Life is
the thought of substances; bodies are only the means
of fixing life and holding it to its way. If bodies were
beings living of themselves they would be Cause itself,
and could not die.

"When a man discovers the results of the general
movement, which is shared by all creations according to
their faculty of absorption, you proclaim him mighty in
science, as though genius consisted in explaining a thing
that is! Genius ought to cast its eyes beyond effects.
Your men of science would laugh if you said to them:
'There exist such positive relations between two human beings, one of whom may be here, and the other
in Java, that they can at the same instant feel the same
sensation, and be conscious of so doing; they can question each other and reply without mistake;' and yet
there are mineral substances which exhibit sympathies
as far off from each other as those of which I speak.
You believe in the power of the electricity which you
find in the magnet and you deny that which emanates
from the soul! According to you, the moon, whose
influence upon the tides you think fixed, has none
whatever upon the winds, nor upon navigation, nor
upon men; she moves the sea, but she must not affect
the sick folk; she has undeniable relations with one

half of humanity, and nothing at all to do with the other half. These are your vaunted certainties!

" Let us go a step further. You believe in physics. But your physics begin, like the Catholic religion, with an *act of faith*. Do they not pre-suppose some external force distinct from substance to which it communicates motion? You see its effects, but what is it? where is it? what is the essence of its nature, its life? has it any limits? — and yet, you deny God!

" Thus, the majority of your scientific axioms, true in their relation to man, are false in relation to the Great Whole. Science is One, but you have divided it. To know the real meaning of the laws of phenomena must we not know the correlations which exist between phenomena and the law of the Whole? There is, in all things, an appearance which strikes your senses ; under that appearance stirs a soul ; a body is there and a faculty is there. Where do you teach the study of the relations which bind things to each other? Nowhere. Consequently you have nothing positive. Your strongest certainties rest upon the analysis of material forms whose essence you persistently ignore.

" There is a Higher Knowledge of which, too late, some men obtain a glimpse, though they dare not avow it. Such men comprehend the necessity of considering substances not merely in their mathematical properties but also in their entirety, in their occult relations and affinities. The greatest man among you divined, in his latter days, that all was reciprocally cause and effect ;

10

that the visible worlds were co-ordinated among themselves and subject to worlds invisible. He groaned at
the recollection of having tried to establish fixed pre-
cepts. Counting up his worlds, like grape-seeds scattered through ether, he had explained their coherence by
the laws of planetary and molecular attraction. You
bowed before that man of science — well! I tell you that
he died in despair. By supposing that the centrifugal
and centripetal forces, which he had invented to explain
to himself the universe, were equal, he stopped the
universe; yet he admitted motion in an indeterminate
sense; but supposing those forces unequal, then utter
confusion of the planetary system ensued. His laws
therefore were not absolute; some higher problem existed than the principle on which his false glory rested.
The connection of the stars with one another and the
centripetal action of their internal motion did not deter
him from seeking the parent stalk on which his clusters
hung. Alas, poor man! the more he widened space the
heavier his burden grew. He told you how there came
to be equilibrium among the parts, but whither went the
whole? His mind contemplated the vast extent, illimitable to human eyes, filled with those groups of worlds
a mere fraction of which is all our telescopes can reach,
but whose immensity is revealed by the rapidity of
light. This sublime contemplation enabled him to perceive myriads of worlds, planted in space like flowers
in a field, which are born like infants, grow like men,
die as the aged die, and live by assimilating from their
atmosphere the substances suitable for their nourish-

ment, — having a centre and a principal of life, guaranteeing to each other their circuits, absorbed and absorbing like plants, and forming a vast Whole endowed with life and possessing a destiny.

"At that sight your man of science trembled! He knew that life is produced by the union of the thing and its principle, that death or inertia or gravity is produced by a rupture between a thing and the movement which appertains to it. Then it was that he foresaw the crumbling of the worlds and their destruction if God should withdraw the Breath of his Word. He searched the Apocalypse for the traces of that Word. You thought him mad. Understand him better! He was seeking pardon for the work of his genius.

"Wilfrid, you have come here hoping to make me solve equations, or rise upon a rain-cloud, or plunge into the fiord and reappear a swan. If science or miracles were the end and object of humanity, Moses would have bequeathed to you the law of fluxions; Jesus Christ would have lightened the darkness of your sciences; his apostles would have told you whence come those vast trains of gas and melted metals, attached to cores which revolve and solidify as they dart through ether, or violently enter some system and combine with a star, jostling and displacing it by the shock, or destroying it by the infiltration of their deadly gases; Saint Paul, instead of telling you to live in God, would have explained why food is the secret bond among all creations and the evident tie between all living Species. In these days the greatest miracle of all would be the discovery

of the squaring of the circle, — a problem which you
hold to be insoluble, but which is doubtless solved in
the march of worlds by the intersection of some mathematical lines whose course is visible to the eye of spirits
who have reached the higher spheres. Believe me,
miracles are in us, not without us. Here natural facts
occur which men call supernatural. God would have
been strangely unjust had he confined the testimony of
his power to certain generations and peoples and denied
them to others. The brazen rod belongs to all. Neither
Moses, nor Jacob, nor Zoroaster, nor Paul, nor Pythagoras, nor Swedenborg, not the humblest Messenger
nor the loftiest Prophet of the Most High are greater
than you are capable of being. Only, there come to
nations as to men certain periods when Faith is theirs.

" If material science be the end and object of human
effort, tell me, both of you, would societies, — those
great centres where men congregate, — would they perpetually be dispersed? If civilization were the object
of our Species, would intelligence perish? would it continue purely individual? The grandeur of all nations
that were truly great was based on exceptions; when
the exception ceased their power died. If such were
the End-all, Prophets, Seers, and Messengers of God
would have lent their hand to Science rather than have
given it to Belief. Surely they would have quickened
your brains sooner than have touched your hearts!
But no; one and all they came to lead the nations back
to God; they proclaimed the sacred Path in simple
words that showed the way to heaven; all were wrapped

in love and faith, all were inspired by that WORD which
hovers above the inhabitants of earth, enfolding them,
inspiriting them, uplifting them; none were prompted
by any human interest. Your great geniuses, your
poets, your kings, your learned men are engulfed with
their cities; while the names of these good pastors of
humanity, ever blessed, have survived all cataclysms.

"Alas! we cannot understand each other on any
point. We are separated by an abyss. You are on
the side of darkness, while I — I live in the light, the
true Light! Is this the word that you ask of me? I
say it with joy; it may change you. Know this: there
are sciences of matter and sciences of spirit. There,
where you see substances, I see forces that stretch one
toward another with generating power. To me, the
character of bodies is the indication of their principles
and the sign of their properties. Those principles be-
get affinities which escape your knowledge, and which
are linked to centres. The different species among
which life is distributed are unfailing streams which
correspond unfailingly among themselves. Each has
his own vocation. Man is effect and cause. He is fed,
but he feeds in his turn. When you call God a Creator,
you dwarf Him. He did not create, as you think He
did, plants or animals or stars. Could He proceed by
a variety of means? Must He not act by unity of composition? Moreover, He gave forth principles to be
developed, according to His universal law, at the will
of the surroundings in which they were placed. Hence
a single substance and motion, a single plant, a single

animal, but correlations everywhere.   In fact, all affinities are linked together by contiguous similitudes; the
life of the worlds is drawn toward the centres by fam-
ished aspiration, as you are drawn by hunger to seek
food.

" To give you an example of affinities linked to similitudes (a secondary law on which the creations of your
thought are based), music, that celestial art, is the
working out of this principle; for is it not a comple-
ment of sounds harmonized by number?   Is not sound
a modification of air, compressed, dilated, echoed?
You know the composition of air, — oxygen, nitrogen,
and carbon.   As you cannot obtain sound from the
void, it is plain that music and the human voice are the
result of organized chemical substances, which put
themselves in unison with the same substances prepared within you by your thought, co-ordinated by
means of light, the great nourisher of your globe.
Have you ever meditated on the masses of nitre de-
posited by the snow, have you ever observed a thunder-
storm and seen the plants breathing in from the air
about them the metal it contains, without concluding
that the sun has fused and distributed the subtle essence
which nourishes all things here below?   Swedenborg
has said, ' The earth is a man.'

" Your Science, which makes you great in your own
eyes, is paltry indeed beside the light which bathes a
Seer.   Cease, cease to question me; our languages are
different.   For a moment I have used yours to cast, if
it be possible, a ray of faith into your soul; to give

you, as it were, the hem of my garment and draw you
up into the regions of Prayer. Can God abase Himself
to you? Is it not for you to rise to Him? If human
reason finds the ladder of its own strength too weak
to bring God down to it, is it not evident that you must
find some other path to reach Him? That Path is in
ourselves. The Seer and the Believer find eyes within
their souls more piercing far than eyes that probe the
things of earth, — they see the Dawn. Hear this truth:
Your science, let it be never so exact, your meditations, however bold, your noblest lights are Clouds.
Above, above is the Sanctuary whence the true Light
flows."

She sat down and remained silent; her calm face
bore no sign of the agitation which orators betray after
their least fervid improvisations.

Wilfrid bent toward Monsieur Becker and said in a
low voice, " Who taught her that? "

" I do not know," he answered.

" He was gentler on the Falberg," Minna whispered
to herself.

Seraphita passed her hand across her eyes and then
said, smiling : —

" You are very thoughtful to-night, gentlemen. You
treat Minna and me as though we were men to whom
you must talk politics or commerce; whereas we are
young girls, and you ought to tell us tales while you
drink your tea. That is what we do, Monsieur Wilfrid,
in our long Norwegian evenings. Come, dear pastor,
tell me some Saga that I have not heard, — that of

Frithiof, the chronicle that you believe and have so often promised me. Tell us the story of the peasant lad who owned the ship that talked and had a soul. Come! I dream of the frigate Ellida, the fairy with the sails young girls should navigate!"

"Since we have returned to the regions of Jarvis," said Wilfrid, whose eyes were fastened on Seráphita as those of a robber, lurking in the darkness, fasten on the spot where he knows the jewels lie, "tell me why you do not marry?"

"You are all born widows and widowers," she replied; "but my marriage was arranged at my birth. I am betrothed."

"To whom?" they cried.

"Ask not my secret," she said; "I will promise, if our father permits it, to invite you to these mysterious nuptials."

"Will they be soon?"

"I think so."

A long silence followed these words.

"The spring has come!" said Seraphita, suddenly. "The noise of the waters and the breaking of the ice begins. Come, let us welome the first spring of the new century."

She rose, followed by Wilfrid, and together they went to a window which David had opened. After the long silence of winter, the waters stirred beneath the ice and resounded through the fiord like music, — for there are sounds which space refines, so that they reach the ear in waves of light and freshness.

" Wilfrid, cease to nourish evil thoughts whose triumph would be hard to bear. Your desires are easily
read in the fire of your eyes. Be kind ; take one step
forward in well-doing. Advance beyond the love of
man and sacrifice yourself completely to the happiness
of her you love. Obey me ; I will lead you in a path
where you shall obtain the distinctions which you crave,
and where Love is infinite indeed."

She left him thoughtful.

" That soft creature ! " he said within himself; " is
she indeed the prophetess whose eyes have just flashed
lightnings, whose voice has rung through worlds, whose
hand has wielded the axe of doubt against our sciences ?
Have we been dreaming? Am I awake ? "

" Minna," said Seraphitus, returning to the young
girl, " the eagle swoops where the carrion lies, but the
dove seeks the mountain spring beneath the peaceful
greenery of the glades. The eagle soars to heaven,
the dove descends from it. Cease to venture into
regions where thou canst find no spring of waters, no
umbrageous shade. If on the Falberg thou couldst not
gaze into the abyss and live, keep all thy strength for
him who will love thee. Go, poor girl ; thou knowest,
I am betrothed."

Minna rose and followed Seraphitus to the window
where Wilfrid stood. All three listened to the Sieg
bounding under the rush of the upper waters, which
brought down trees uprooted by the ice ; the fiord had
regained its voice ; all illusions were dispelled ! They
rejoiced in Nature as she burst her bonds and seemed

to answer with sublime accord to the Spirit whose breath had wakened her.

When the three guests of this mysterious being left the house, they were filled with the vague sensation which is neither sleep, nor torpor, nor astonishment, but partakes of the nature of each, — a state that is neither dusk nor dawn, but which creates a thirst for light. All three were thinking.

"I begin to believe that she is indeed a Spirit hidden in human form," said Monsieur Becker.

Wilfrid, re-entering his own apartments, calm and convinced, was unable to struggle against that influence so divinely majestic.

Minna said in her heart, "Why will he not let me love him!"

V.

FAREWELL.

THERE is in man an almost hopeless phenomenon for thoughtful minds who seek a meaning in the march of civilization, and who endeavor to give laws of progression to the movement of intelligence. However portentous a fact may be, or even supernatural, — if such facts exist, — however solemnly a miracle may be done in sight of all, the lightning of that fact, the thunderbolt of that miracle is quickly swallowed up in the ocean of life, whose surface, scarcely stirred by the brief convulsion, returns to the level of its habitual flow.

A Voice is heard from the jaws of an Animal; a Hand writes on the wall before a feasting Court; an Eye gleams in the slumber of a king, and a Prophet explains the dream; Death, evoked, rises on the confines of the luminous sphere where faculties revive; Spirit annihilates Matter at the foot of that mystic ladder of the Seven Spiritual Worlds, one resting upon another in space and revealing themselves in shining waves that break in light upon the steps of the celestial Tabernacle. But however solemn the inward Revelation, however clear the visible outward Sign, be sure that on the morrow Balaam doubts both him-

self and his ass, Belshazzar and Pharoah call Moses
and Daniel to qualify the Word. The Spirit, descending, bears man above this earth, opens the seas
and lets him see their depths, shows him lost species,
wakens dry bones whose dust is the soil of valleys;
the Apostle writes the Apocalypse, and twenty centuries later human science ratifies his words and turns
his visions into maxims. And what comes of it all?
Why this, — that the peoples live as they have ever
lived, as they lived in the first Olympiad, as they lived
on the morrow of Creation, and on the eve of the great
cataclysm. The waves of Doubt have covered all
things. The same floods surge with the same measured motion on the human granite which serves as
a boundary to the ocean of intelligence. When man
has inquired of himself whether he has seen that which
he has seen, whether he has heard the words that
entered his ears, whether the facts were facts and the
idea is indeed an idea, then he resumes his wonted
bearing, thinks of his worldly interests, obeys some
envoy of death and of oblivion whose dusky mantle
covers like a pall an ancient Humanity of which the
moderns retain no memory. Man never pauses; he
goes his round, he vegetates until the appointed day
when his Axe falls. If this wave force, this pressure
of bitter waters prevents all progress, no doubt it also
warns of death. Spirits prepared by faith among the
higher souls of earth can alone perceive the mystic
ladder of Jacob.

After listening to Seraphita's answer in which (being

earnestly questioned) she unrolled before their eyes a
Divine Perspective, — as an organ fills a church with
sonorous sound and reveals a musical universe, its
solemn tones rising to the loftiest arches and playing,
like light, upon their foliated capitals, — Wilfrid returned to his own room, awed by the sight of a world in
ruins, and on those ruins the brilliance of mysterious
lights poured forth in torrents by the hand of a young
girl. On the morrow he still thought of these things,
but his awe was gone; he felt he was neither destroyed
nor changed; his passions, his ideas awoke in full
force, fresh and vigorous. He went to breakfast with
Monsieur Becker and found the old man absorbed in
the "Treatise on Incantations," which he had searched
since early morning to convince his guest that there
was nothing unprecedented in all that they had seen
and heard at the Swedish castle. With the childlike
trustfulness of a true scholar he had folded down the
pages in which Jean Wier related authentic facts which
proved the possibility of the events that had happened
the night before, — for to learned men an idea is an
event, just as the greatest events often present no idea
at all to them. By the time they had swallowed their
fifth cup of tea, these philosophers had come to think
the mysterious scene of the preceding evening wholly
natural. The celestial truths to which they had listened
were arguments susceptible of examination; Seraphita
was a girl, more or less eloquent; allowance must be
made for the charms of her voice, her seductive beauty,
her fascinating motions, in short, for all those oratorical

arts by which an actor puts a world of sentiment and thought into phrases which are often commonplace.

" Bah ! " said the worthy pastor, making a philosophical grimace as he spread a layer of salt butter on his slice of bread, " the final word of all these fine enigmas is six feet under ground."

" But," said Wilfrid, sugaring his tea, " I cannot imagine how a young girl of seventeen can know so much ; what she said was certainly a compact argument."

" Read the account of that Italian woman," said Monsieur Becker, " who at the age of twelve spoke forty-two languages, ancient and modern ; also the history of that monk who could guess thought by smell. I can give you a thousand such cases from Jean Wier and other writers."

" I admit all that, dear pastor ; but to my thinking, Seraphita would make a perfect wife."

" She is all mind," said Monsieur Becker, dubiously.

Several days went by, during which the snow in the valleys melted gradually away ; the green of the forests and of the grass began to show ; Norwegian Nature made ready her wedding garments for her brief bridal of a day. During this period, when the softened air invited every one to leave the house, Seraphita remained at home in solitude. When at last she admitted Minna, the latter saw at once the ravages of inward fever ; Seraphita's voice was hollow, her skin pallid ; hitherto a poet might have compared her lustre to that of diamonds, — now it was that of a topaz.

" Have you seen her? " asked Wilfrid, who had wandered around the Swedish dwelling waiting for Minna's return.

" Yes," answered the young girl, weeping ; " We must lose him !"

" Mademoiselle," cried Wilfrid, endeavoring to repress the loud tones of his angry voice, " do not jest with me. You can love Seraphita only as one young girl can love another, and not with the love which she inspires in me. You do not know your danger if my jealousy were really aroused. Why can I not go to her? Is it you who stand in my way?"

" I do not know by what right you probe my heart," said Minna, calm in appearance, but inwardly terrified. " Yes, I love him," she said recovering the courage of her convictions, that she might, for once, confess the religion of her heart. " But my jealousy, natural as it is in love, fears no one here below. Alas! I am jealous of a secret feeling which absorbs him. Between him and me there is a great gulf fixed which I cannot cross. Would that I knew who loves him best, the stars or I ! which of us would sacrifice our being most eagerly for his happiness! Why should I not be free to avow my love? In the presence of death we may declare our feelings, — and Seraphitus is about to die."

" Minna, you are mistaken ; the siren I so love and long for, she, whom I have seen, feeble and languid, on her couch of furs, is not a young man."

" Monsieur," answered Minna, distressfully, " the being whose powerful hand guided me on the Falberg, who led me to the sæter sheltered beneath the Ice-Cap, there — " she said, pointing to the peak, " is not a feeble girl. Ah, had you but heard him prophesying! His poem was the music of thought. A young girl never uttered those solemn tones of a voice which stirred my soul."

" What certainty have you? " said Wilfrid.

" None but that of the heart," answered Minna.

" And I," cried Wilfrid, casting on his companion the terrible glance of the earthly desire that kills, " I, too, know how powerful is her empire over me, and I will undeceive you."

At this moment, while the words were rushing from Wilfrid's lips as rapidly as the thoughts surged in his brain, they saw Seraphita coming towards them from the house, followed by David. The apparition calmed the man's excitement.

" Look," he said, " could any but a woman move with that grace and languor? "

" He suffers; he comes forth for the last time," said Minna.

David went back at a sign from his mistress, who advanced towards Wilfrid and Minna.

" Let us go to the falls of the Sieg," she said, expressing one of those desires which suddenly possess the sick and which the well hasten to obey.

A thin white mist covered the valleys around the fiord and the sides of the mountains, whose icy summits, sparkling like stars, pierced the vapor and gave it the appearance of a moving milky way. The sun was visible through the haze like a globe of red fire. Though winter still lingered, puffs of warm air laden with the scent of the birch-trees, already adorned with their rosy efflorescence, and of the larches, whose silken tassels were beginning to appear, — breezes tempered by the incense and the sighs of earth, — gave token of the glorious Northern spring, the rapid, fleeting joy of that most melancholy of Natures. The wind was beginning to lift the veil of mist which half-obscured the gulf. The birds sang. The bark of the trees where the sun had not yet dried the clinging hoar-frost shone gayly to the eye in its fantastic wreathings which trickled away in murmuring rivulets as the warmth reached them. The three friends walked in silence along the shore. Wilfrid and Minna alone noticed the magic transformation that was taking place in the monotonous picture of the winter landscape. Their companion walked in thought, as though a voice were sounding to her ears in this concert of Nature.

Presently they reached the ledge of rocks through which the Sieg had forced its way, after escaping from the long avenue cut by its waters in an undulating line through the forest, — a fluvial pathway flanked by aged firs and roofed with strong-ribbed arches like those of a cathedral. Looking back from that vantage-ground, the whole extent of the fiord could be seen at a glance, with the open sea sparkling on the horizon beyond it like a burnished blade.

At this moment the mist, rolling away, left the sky blue and clear. Among the valleys and around the

trees flitted the shining fragments, — a diamond dust
swept by the freshening breeze. The torrent rolled
on toward them ; along its length a vapor rose, tinted
by the sun with every color of his light ; the decompos-
ing rays flashing prismatic fires along the many-tinted
scarf of waters. The rugged ledge on which they stood
was carpeted by several kinds of lichen, forming a noble
mat variegated by moisture and lustrous like the sheen
of a silken fabric. Shrubs, already in bloom, crowned
the rocks with garlands. Their waving foliage, eager
for the freshness of the water, drooped its tresses above
the stream ; the larches shook their light fringes and
played with the pines, stiff and motionless as aged men.
This luxuriant beauty was foiled by the solemn colonnades of the forest-trees, rising in terraces upon the
mountains, and by the calm sheet of the fiord, lying
below, where the torrent buried its fury and was still.
Beyond, the sea hemmed in this page of Nature, written
by the greatest of poets, Chance ; to whom the wild
luxuriance of creation when apparently abandoned to
itself is owing.

The village of Jarvis was a lost point in the landscape,
in this immensity of Nature, sublime at this moment like
all things else of ephemeral life which present a fleeting
image of perfection ; for, by a law fatal to no eyes but
our own, creations which appear complete — the love
of our heart and the desire of our eyes — have but one
spring-tide here below. Standing on this breast-work
of rock these three persons might well suppose themselves alone in the universe.

" What beauty ! " cried Wilfrid.

" Nature sings hymns," said Seraphita. " Is not her music exquisite? Tell me, Wilfrid, could any of the women you once knew create such a glorious retreat for herself as this? I am conscious here of a feeling seldom inspired by the sight of cities, a longing to lie down amid this quickening verdure. Here, with eyes to heaven and an open heart, lost in the bosom of immensity, I could hear the sighing of the flower, scarce budded, which longs for wings, or the cry of the eider grieving that it can only fly, and remember the desires of man who, issuing from all, is none the less ever longing. But that, Wilfrid, is only a woman's thought. You find seductive fancies in the wreathing mists, the light embroidered veils which Nature dons like a coy maiden, in this atmosphere where she perfumes for her spousals the greenery of her tresses. You seek the naiad's form amid the gauzy vapors, and to your thinking my ears should listen only to the virile voice of the Torrent."

" But Love is there, like the bee in the calyx of the flower," replied Wilfrid, perceiving for the first time a trace of earthly sentiment in her words, and fancying the moment favorable for an expression of his passionate tenderness.

" Always there? " said Seraphita, smiling. Minna had left them for a moment to gather the blue saxifrages growing on a rock above.

" Always," repeated Wilfrid. " Hear me," he said, with a masterful glance which was foiled as by a dia-

mond breast-plate. "You know not what I am, nor
what I can be, nor what I will. Do not reject my last
entreaty. Be mine for the good of that world whose
happiness you bear upon your heart. Be mine that my
conscience may be pure ; that a voice divine may sound
in my ears and infuse Good into the great enterprise I
have undertaken prompted by my hatred to the nations,
but which I swear to accomplish for their benefit if you
will walk beside me. What higher mission can you ask
for love? what nobler part can woman aspire to? I
came to Norway to meditate a great design."

"And you will sacrifice its grandeur," she said, " to
an innocent girl who loves you, and who will lead you
in the paths of peace."

"What matters sacrifice," he cried, "if I have you?
Hear my secret. I have gone from end to end of the
North, — that great smithy from whose anvils new races
have spread over the earth, like human tides appointed
to refresh the wornout civilizations. I wished to begin
my work at some Northern point, to win the empire
which force and intellect must ever give over a primitive people ; to form that people for battle, to drive
them to wars which should ravage Europe like a conflagration, crying liberty to some, pillage to others,
glory here, pleasure there ! — I, myself, remaining an
image of Destiny, cruel, implacable, advancing like
the whirlwind, which sucks from the atmosphere the
particles that make the thunderbolt, and falls like a
devouring scourge upon the nations. Europe is at an
epoch when she awaits the new Messiah who shall de-

stroy society and remake it. She can no longer believe
except in him who crushes her under foot. The day is
at hand when poets and historians will justify me, exalt
me, and borrow my ideas, mine! And all the while
my triumph will be a jest, written in blood, the jest of
my vengeance! But not here, Seraphita; what I see
of the North disgusts me. Hers is a mere blind force;
I thirst for the Indies! I would rather fight a selfish,
cowardly, mercantile government. Besides, it is easier
to stir the imagination of the peoples at the feet of the
Caucasus than to argue with the intellect of the icy
lands which here surround me. Therefore am I tempted
to cross the Russian steppes and pour my triumphant
human tide through Asia to the Ganges, and overthrow
the British rule. Seven men have done this thing before me in other epochs of the world. I will emulate
them. I will spread Art like the Saracens, hurled by
Mohammed upon Europe. Mine shall be no paltry
sovereignty like those that govern to-day tho ancient
provinces of the Roman empire, disputing with their
subjects about a customs right! No, nothing can bar
my way! Like Genghis Khan, my feet shall tread a
third of the globe, my hand shall grasp the throat of
Asia like Aurung-Zeb. Be my companion! Let me
seat thee, beautiful and noble being, on a throne! I
do not doubt success, but live within my heart and I
am sure of it."

" I have already reigned," said Seraphita, coldly.

The words fell as the axe of a skilful woodman falls
at the root of a young tree and brings it down at a

single blow.   Men alone can comprehend the rage that
a woman excites in the soul of a man when, after showing her his strength, his power, his wisdom, his superiority, the capricious creature bends her head and
says, " All that is nothing ; " when, unmoved, she
smiles and says, " Such things are known to me," as
though his power were nought.

" What ! " cried Wilfrid, in despair, " can the riches
of art, the riches of worlds, the splendors of a court — "

She stopped him by a single inflexion of her lips, and
said, " Beings more powerful than you have offered me
far more."

" Thou hast no soul," he cried, — " no soul, if thou
art not persuaded by the thought of comforting a great
man, who is willing now to sacrifice all things to live
beside thee in a little house on the shores of a lake,"

" But," she said, " I am loved with a boundless love."

" By whom ? " cried Wilfrid, approaching Seraphita
with a frenzied movement, as if to fling her into the
foaming basin of the Sieg.

She looked at him and slowly extended her arm, pointing to Minna, who now sprang towards her, fair and
glowing and lovely as the flowers she held in her hand.

" Child ! " said Seraphitus, advancing to meet her.

Wilfrid remained where she left him, motionless as
the rock on which he stood, lost in thought, longing to
let himself go into the torrent of the Sieg, like the fallen
trees which hurried past his eyes and disappeared in the
bosom of the gulf.

" I gathered them for you," said Minna, offering the

bunch of saxifrages to the being she adored. "One of them, see, this one," she added, selecting a flower, "is like that you found on the Falberg."

Seraphitus looked alternately at the flower and at Minna.

"Why question me? Dost thou doubt me?"

"No," said the young girl, "my trust in you is infinite. You are more beautiful to look upon than this glorious nature, but your mind surpasses in intellect that of all humanity. When I have been with you I seem to have prayed to God. I long — "

"For what?" said Seraphitus, with a glance that revealed to the young girl the vast distance which separated them.

"To suffer in your stead."

"Ah, dangerous being!" cried Seraphitus in his heart. "Is it wrong, oh my God! to desire to offer her to Thee? Dost thou remember, Minna, what I said to thee up there?" he added, pointing to the summit of the Ice-Cap.

"He is terrible again," thought Minna, trembling with fear.

The voice of the Sieg accompanied the thoughts of the three beings united on this platform of projecting rock, but separated in soul by the abysses of the Spiritual World.

"Seraphitus! teach me," said Minna in a silvery voice, soft as the motion of a sensitive plant, "teach me how to cease to love you. Who could fail to admire you; love is an admiration that never wearies."

" Poor child ! " said Seraphitus, turning pale ; " there is but one whom thou canst love in that way."

" Who ? " asked Minna.

" Thou shalt know hereafter," he said, in the feeble voice of a man who lies down to die.

" Help, help ! he is dying ! " cried Minna.

Wilfrid ran towards them. Seeing Seraphita as she lay on a fragment of gneiss, where time had cast its velvet mantle of lustrous lichen and tawny mosses now burnished in the sunlight, he whispered softly, " How beautiful she is ! "

" One other look ! the last that I shall ever cast upon this nature in travail," said Seraphita, rallying her strength and rising to her feet.

She advanced to the edge of the rocky platform, whence her eyes took in the scenery of that grand and glorious landscape, so verdant, flowery, and animated, yet so lately buried in its winding-sheet of snow.

" Farewell," she said, " farewell, home of Earth, warmed by the fires of Love ; where all things press with ardent force from the centre to the extremities ; where the extremities are gathered up, like a woman's hair, to weave the mysterious braid which binds us in that invisible ether to the Thought Divine !

" Behold the man bending above that furrow moistened with his tears, who lifts his head for an instant to question Heaven ; behold the woman gathering her children that she may feed them with her milk ; see him who lashes the ropes in the height of the gale ; see her who sits in the hollow of the rocks, awaiting the father! Behold all they who stretch their hands in want after a lifetime spent in thankless toil. To all peace and courage, and to all farewell!

" Hear you the cry of the soldier, dying nameless and unknown? the wail of the man deceived who weeps in the desert? To them peace and courage; to all farewell!

" Farewell, you who die for the kings of the earth! Farewell, ye people without a country and ye countries without a people, each with a mutual want. Above all, farewell to Thee who knew not where to lay Thy head, Exile divine! Farewell, mothers beside your dying sons! Farewell, ye Little Ones, ye Feeble, ye Suffering, you whose sorrows I have so often borne! Farewell, all ye who have descended into the sphere of Instinct that you may suffer there for others!

" Farewell, ye mariners who seek the Orient through the thick darkness of your abstractions, vast as principles! Farewell, martyrs of thought, led by thought into the presence of the True Light. Farewell, regions of study where mine ears can hear the plaint of genius neglected and insulted, the sigh of the patient scholar to whom enlightenment comes too late!

" I see the angelic choir, the wafting of perfumes, the incense of the heart of those who go their way consoling, praying, imparting celestial balm and living light to suffering souls! Courage, ye choir of Love! you to whom the peoples cry, ' Comfort us, comfort us, defend us!' To you courage! and farewell!

" Farewell, ye granite rocks that shall bloom a flower;

farewell, flower that becomes a dove ; farewell, dove that shalt be woman ; farewell, woman, who art Suffering, man, who art Belief! Farewell, you who shall be all love, all prayer ! "

Broken with fatigue, this inexplicable being leaned for the first time on Wilfrid and on Minna to be taken home. Wilfrid and Minna felt the shock of a mysterious contact in and through the being who thus connected them. They had scarcely advanced a few steps when David met them, weeping. " She will die," he said, " why have you brought her hither? "

The old man raised her in his arms with the vigor of youth and bore her to the gate of the Swedish castle like an eagle bearing a white lamb to his mountain eyrie.

VI.

THE PATH TO HEAVEN.

THE day succeeding that on which Seraphita foresaw her death and bade farewell to Earth, as a prisoner looks round his dungeon before leaving it forever, she suffered pains which obliged her to remain in the helpless immobility of those whose pangs are great. Wilfrid and Minna went to see her, and found her lying on her couch of furs. Still veiled in flesh, her soul shone through that veil, which grew more and more transparent day by day. The progress of the Spirit, piercing the last obstacle between itself and the Infinite, was called an illness, the hour of Life went by the name of death. David wept as he watched her sufferings; unreasonable as a child, he would not listen to his mistress's consolations. Monsieur Becker wished Seraphita to try remedies; but all were useless.

One morning she sent for the two beings whom she loved, telling them that this would be the last of her bad days. Wilfrid and Minna came in terror, knowing well that they were about to lose her. Seraphita smiled to them as one departing to a better world; her head drooped like a flower heavy with dew, which opens its calyx for the last time to waft its fragrance on the breeze. She looked at these friends with a sadness that was for them, not for herself; she thought no longer of herself, and they felt this with a grief mingled with gratitude which they were unable to express. Wilfrid stood silent and motionless, lost in thoughts excited by events whose vast bearings enabled him to conceive of some illimitable immensity.

Emboldened by the weakness of the being lately so powerful, or perhaps by the fear of losing him forever, Minna bent down over the couch and said, " Seraphitus, let me follow thee ! "

" Can I forbid thee ? "

" Why will thou not love me enough to stay with me ? "

" I can love nothing here."

" What canst thou love ? "

" Heaven."

" Is it worthy of heaven to despise the creatures of God ? "

" Minna, can we love two beings at once ? Would our beloved be indeed our beloved if he did not fill our hearts ? Must he not be the first, the last, the only one ? She who is all love, must she not leave the world for her beloved ? Human ties are but a memory, she has no ties except to him ! Her soul is hers no longer ; it is his. If she keeps within her soul anything that is not his, does she love ? No, she loves not. To love feebly, is that to love at all ? The voice of her beloved makes her joyful ; it flows through her veins in a crimson tide more glowing far than blood ; his glance is the light that penetrates her ; her being

melts into his being. He is warm to her soul. He
is the light that lightens; near to him there is neither
cold nor darkness. He is never absent, he is always
with us; we think in him, to him, by him! Minna,
that is how I love him."

"Love whom?" said Minna, tortured with sudden
jealousy.

" God," replied Seraphitus, his voice glowing in their
souls like fires of liberty lighted from peak to peak upon
the mountains, — " God, who does not betray us! God,
who will never abandon us! who crowns our wishes;
who satisfies His creatures with joy — joy unalloyed
and infinite! God, who never wearies but ever smiles!
God, who pours into the soul fresh treasures day by
day; who purifies and leaves no bitterness; who is all
harmony, all flame! God, who has placed Himself
within our hearts to blossom there; who hearkens to
our prayers; who does not stand aloof when we are His,
but gives His presence absolutely! He who revives
us, magnifies us, and multiplies us in Himself; GOD!
Minna, I love thee because thou mayst be His! I love
thee because if thou come to Him thou wilt be mine."

" Lead me to Him," cried Minna, kneeling down;
" take me by the hand; I will not leave thee!"

" Lead us, Seraphita!" cried Wilfrid, coming to
Minna's side with an impetuous movement. " Yes,
thou hast given me a thirst for Light, a thirst for the
Word. I am parched with the Love thou hast put into
my heart; I desire to keep thy soul in mine; thy will is
mine; I will do whatsoever thou biddest me. Since I

cannot obtain thee, I will keep thy will and all the thoughts that thou hast given me. If I may not unite myself with thee except by the power of my spirit, I will cling to thee in soul as the flame to what it laps. Speak!"

" Angel!" exclaimed the mysterious being, enfolding them both in one glance, as it were with an azure mantle, " Heaven shall be thine heritage!"

Silence fell among them after these words, which sounded in the souls of the man and of the woman like the first notes of some celestial harmony.

" If you would teach your feet to tread the Path to heaven, know that the way is hard at first," said the weary sufferer; " God wills that you shall seek Him for Himself. In that sense, He is jealous; He demands your whole self. But when you have given Him yourself, never, never will He abandon you. I leave with you the keys of the kingdom of His Light, where evermore you shall dwell in the bosom of the Father, in the heart of the Bridegroom. No sentinels guard the approaches; you may enter where you will; His palaces, His treasures, His sceptre, all are free. 'Take them!' He says. But—you must *will* to go there. Like one preparing for a journey, a man must leave his home, renounce his projects, bid farewell to friends, to father, mother, sister, even to the helpless brother who cries after him, — yes, farewell to them eternally; you will no more return than did the martyrs on their way to the stake. You must strip yourself of every sentiment, of everything to which man clings. Unless you do this you are but half-hearted in your enterprise.

" Do for God what you do for your ambitious projects, what you do in consecrating yourself to Art, what
you have done when you loved a human creature or
sought some secret of human science. Is not God the
whole of science, the all of love, the source of poetry?
Surely His riches are worthy of being coveted! His
treasure is inexhaustible, His poem infinite, His love
immutable, His science sure and darkened by no mysteries. Be anxious for nothing, He will give you all.
Yes, in His heart are treasures with which the petty
joys you lose on earth are not to be compared. What
I tell you is true ; you shall possess His power ; you
may use it as you would use the gifts of lover or mistress. Alas ! men doubt, they lack faith, and will, and
persistence. If some set their feet in the path, they
look behind them and presently turn back. Few decide between the two extremes, — to go or stay, heaven
or the mire. All hesitate. Weakness leads astray,
passion allures into dangerous paths, vice becomes
habitual, man flounders in the mud and makes no
progress towards a better state.

" All human beings go through a previous life in the
sphere of Instinct, where they are brought to see the
worthlessness of earthly treasures, to amass which they
gave themselves such untold pains ! Who can tell how
many times the human being lives in the sphere of
Instinct before he is prepared to enter the sphere of
Abstractions, where thought expends itself on erring
science, where mind wearies at last of human language? for, when Matter is exhausted, Spirit enters.

Who knows how many fleshly forms the heir of
heaven occupies before he can be brought to understand the value of that silence and solitude whose
starry plains are but the vestibule of Spiritual Worlds?
He feels his way amid the void, makes trial of nothingness, and then at last his eyes revert upon the Path.
Then follow other existences, — all to be lived to reach
the place where Light effulgent shines. Death is the
post-house of the journey. A lifetime may be needed
merely to gain the virtues which annul the errors of
man's preceding life. First comes the life of suffering,
whose tortures create a thirst for love. Next the life
of love and devotion to the creature, teaching devotion to the Creator, — a life where the virtues of love,
its martyrdoms, its joys followed by sorrows, its angelic
hopes, its patience, its resignation, excite an appetite
for things divine. Then follows the life which seeks
in silence the traces of the Word; in which the soul
grows humble and charitable. Next the life of longing; and lastly, the life of prayer. In that is the noon-
day sun; there are the flowers, there the harvest!

"The virtues we acquire, which develop slowly within
us, are the invisible links that bind each one of our existences to the others, — existences which the spirit
alone remembers, for Matter has no memory for spiritual things. Thought alone holds the tradition of the
bygone life. The endless legacy of the past to the
present is the secret source of human genius. Some
receive the gift of form, some the gift of numbers,
others the gift of harmony. All these gifts are steps of

progress in the Path of Light. Yes, he who possesses a single one of them touches at that point the Infinite. Earth has divided the Word — of which I here reveal some syllables — into particles, she has reduced it to dust and has scattered it through her works, her dogmas, her poems. If some impalpable grain shines like a diamond in a human work, men cry: 'How grand! how true! how glorious!' That fragment vibrates in their souls and wakes a presentiment of heaven: to some, a melody that weans from earth; to others, the solitude that draws to God. To all, whatsoever sends us back upon ourselves, whatsoever strikes us down and crushes us, lifts or abases us, — *that* is but a syllable of the Divine Word.

" When a human soul draws its first furrow straight, the rest will follow surely. One thought borne inward, one prayer uplifted, one suffering endured, one echo of the Word within us, and our souls are forever changed. All ends in God; and many are the ways to find Him by walking straight before us. When the happy day arrives in which you set your feet upon the Path and begin your pilgrimage, the world will know nothing of it; earth no longer understands you; you no longer understand each other. Men who attain to a knowledge of these things, who lisp a few syllables of the Word, often have not where to lay their head; hunted like beasts they perish on the scaffold, to the joy of assembled peoples, while Angels open to them the gates of heaven. Therefore, your destiny is a secret between yourself and God, just as love is a secret between two hearts. You may be the buried treasure, trodden under the feet of men thirsting for gold yet all-unknowing that you are there beneath them.

" Henceforth your existence becomes a thing of ceaseless activity; each act has a meaning which connects you with God, just as in love your actions and your thoughts are filled with the loved one. But love and its joys, love and its pleasures limited by the senses, are but the imperfect image of the love which unites you to your celestial Spouse. All earthly joy is mixed with anguish, with discontent. If love ought not to pall then death should end it while its flame is high, so that we see no ashes. But in God our wretchedness becomes delight, joy lives upon itself and multiplies, and grows, and has no limit. In the Earthly life our fleeting love is ended by tribulation; in the Spiritual life the tribulations of a day end in joys unending. The soul is ceaselessly joyful. We feel God with us, in us; He gives a sacred savour to all things; He shines in the soul; He imparts to us His sweetness; He stills our interest in the world viewed for ourselves; He quickens our interest in it viewed for His sake, and grants us the exercise of His power upon it. In His name we do the works which He inspires, we act for Him, we have no self except in Him, we love His creatures with undying love, we dry their tears and long to bring them unto Him, as a loving woman longs to see the inhabitants of earth obey her well-beloved.

" The final life, the fruition of all other lives, to which the powers of the soul have tended, and whose

merits open the Sacred Portals to perfected man, is the
life of Prayer. Who can make you comprehend the
grandeur, the majesty, the might of Prayer? May my
voice, these words of mine, ring in your hearts and
change them. Be now, here, what you may be after
cruel trial! There are privileged beings, Prophets,
Seers, Messengers, and Martyrs, all those who suffer
for the Word and who proclaim it; such souls spring
at a bound across the human sphere and rise at once to
Prayer. So, too, with those whose souls receive the
fire of Faith. Be one of those brave souls! God
welcomes boldness. He loves to be taken by violence; He will never reject those who force their way
to Him. Know this! desire, the torrent of your will,
is so all-powerful that a single emission of it, made
with force, can obtain all; a single cry, uttered under
the pressure of Faith, suffices. Be one of such beings,
full of force, of will, of love! Be conquerors on the
earth! Let the hunger and thirst of God possess you.
Fly to Him as the hart panting for the water-brooks.
Desire shall lend you its wings; tears, those blossoms
of repentance, shall be the celestial baptism from which
your nature will issue purified. Cast yourself on the
breast of the stream in Prayer! Silence and meditation are the means of following the Way. God reveals Himself, unfailingly, to the solitary, thoughtful
seeker.

" It is thus that the separation takes place between
Matter, which so long has wrapped its darkness round
you, and Spirit, which was in you from the beginning,

the light which lighted you and now brings noon-day
to your soul.   Yes, your broken heart shall receive the
light; the light shall bathe it.   Then you will no longer
feel convictions, they will have changed to certainties.
The Poet utters; the Thinker meditates; the Righteous
acts; but he who stands upon the borders of the Divine World prays; and his prayer is word, thought,
action, in one!   Yes, prayer includes all, contains all;
it completes nature, for it reveals to you the mind
within it and its progression.   White and shining virgin
of all human virtues, ark of the covenant between earth
and heaven, tender and strong companion partaking of
the lion and of the lamb, Prayer!   Prayer will give
you the key of heaven!   Bold and pure as innocence,
strong, like all that is single and simple, this glorious,
invincible Queen rests, nevertheless, on the material
world; she takes possession of it; like the sun, she
clasps it in a circle of light.   The universe belongs to
him who wills, who knows, who prays; but he must
will, he must know, he must pray; in a word, he must
possess force, wisdom, and faith.

"Therefore Prayer, issuing from so many trials, is
the consummation of all truths, all powers, all feelings.
Fruit of the laborious, progressive, continued development of natural properties and faculties vitalized anew
by the divine breath of the Word, Prayer has occult activity; it is the final worship — not the material worship of images, nor the spiritual worship of
formulas, but the worship of the Divine World.   We
say no prayers, — prayer forms within us; it is a

faculty which acts of itself; it has attained a way
of action which lifts it outside of forms; it links
the soul to God, with whom we unite as the root of the
tree unites with the soil; our veins draw life from the
principle of life, and we live by the life of the universe.
Prayer bestows external conviction by making us penetrate the Material World through the cohesion of all
our faculties with the elementary substances; it bestows internal conviction by developing our essence
and mingling it with that of the Spiritual Worlds. To
be able to pray thus, you must attain to an utter aban-
donment of flesh; you must acquire through the fires
of the furnace the purity of the diamond; for this complete communion with the Divine is obtained only in
absolute repose, where storms and conflicts are at rest.

" Yes, Prayer — the aspiration of the soul freed absolutely from the body — bears all forces within it, and
applies them to the constant and perseverant union of
the Visible and the Invisible. When you possess the
faculty of praying without weariness, with love, with
force, with certainty, with intelligence, your spiritual-
ized nature will presently be invested with power.
Like a rushing wind, like a thunderbolt, it cuts its
way through all things and shares the power of God.
The quickness of the Spirit becomes yours; in an
instant you may pass from region to region; like the
Word itself, you are transported from the ends of the
world to other worlds. Harmony exists, and you are
part of it! Light is there and your eyes possess it!
Melody is heard and you echo it! Under such con-

ditions, you feel your perceptions developing, widening; the eyes of your mind reach to vast distances. There is, in truth, neither time nor place to the Spirit; space and duration are proportions created for Matter; spirit and matter have naught in common.

"Though these things take place in stillness, in silence, without agitation, without external movement, yet Prayer is all action; but it is spiritual action, stripped of substantiality, and reduced, like the motion of the worlds, to an invisible pure force. It penetrates everywhere like light; it gives vitality to souls that come beneath its rays, as Nature beneath the sun. It resuscitates virtue, purifies and sanctifies all actions, peoples solitude, and gives a foretaste of eternal joys. When you have once felt the delights of the divine intoxication which comes of this internal travail, then all is yours! once take the lute on which we sing to God within your hands, and you will never part with it. Hence the solitude in which Angelic Spirits live; hence their disdain of human joys. They are withdrawn from those who must die to live; they hear the language of such beings, but they no longer understand their ideas; they wonder at their movements, at what the world terms policies, material laws, societies. For them all mysteries are over; truth, and truth alone, is theirs. They who have reached the point where their eyes discern the Sacred Portals, who, not looking back, not uttering one regret, contemplate worlds and comprehend their destinies, such as they keep silence, wait, and bear their final struggles. The worst of all

those struggles is the last ; at the zenith of all virtue
is Resignation, — to be an exile and not lament, no
longer to delight in earthly things and yet to smile, to
belong to God and yet to stay with men ! You hear
the voice that cries to you, ' Advance ! ' Often celestial
visions of descending Angels compass you about with
songs of praise ; then, tearless, uncomplaining, must
you watch them as they reascend the skies ! To murmur is to forfeit all. Resignation is a fruit that ripens
at the gates of heaven. How powerful, how glorious
the calm smile, the pure brow of the resigned human
creature. Radiant is the light of that brow. They who
live in its atmosphere grow purer. That calm glance
penetrates and softens. More eloquent by silence than
the prophet by speech, such beings triumph by their
simple presence. Their ears are quick to hear as a
faithful dog listening for his master. Brighter than
hope, stronger than love, higher than faith, that creature of resignation is the virgin standing on the earth,
who holds for a moment the conquered palm, then,
rising heavenward, leaves behind her the imprint of her
white, pure feet. When she has passed away men flock
around and cry, ' See ! See ! ' Sometimes God holds
her still in sight, — a figure to whose feet creep Forms
and Species of Animality to be shown their way. She
wafts the light exhaling from her hair, and they see ;
she speaks, and they hear. ' A miracle ! ' they cry.
Often she triumphs in the name of God ; frightened
men deny her and put her to death ; smiling, she lays
down her sword and goes to the stake, having saved the

Peoples. How many a pardoned Angel has passed from martyrdom to heaven! Sinai, Golgotha are not in this place nor in that; Angels are crucified in every place, in every sphere. Sighs pierce to God from the whole universe. This earth on which we live is but a single sheaf of the great harvest; humanity is but a species in the vast garden where the flowers of heaven are cultivated. Everywhere God is like unto Himself, and everywhere, by prayer, it is easy to reach Him."

With these words, which fell from the lips of another Hagar in the wilderness, burning the souls of the hearers as the live coal of the word inflamed Isaiah, this mysterious being paused as though to gather some remaining strength. Wilfrid and Minna dared not speak. Suddenly HE lifted himself up to die : —

" Soul of all things, oh my God, thou whom I love for Thyself! Thou, Judge and Father, receive a love which has no limit. Give me of thine essence and thy faculties that I be wholly thine! Take me, that I no longer be myself! Am I not purified? then cast me back into the furnace! If I be not yet proved in the fire, make me some nurturing ploughshare, or the Sword of victory! Grant me a glorious martyrdom in which to proclaim thy Word! Rejected, I will bless thy justice. But if excess of love may win in a moment that which hard and patient labor cannot attain, then bear me upward in thy chariot of fire! Grant me triumph, or further trial, still will I bless thee! To suffer for thee, is not that to triumph? Take me, seize me, bear me away! nay, if thou wilt, reject me! Thou art He who can do no evil. Ah!" he cried, after a pause, " the bonds are breaking."

"Spirits of the pure, ye sacred flock, come forth from the hidden places, come on the surface of the luminous waves! The hour now is; come, assemble! Let us sing at the gates of the Sanctuary; our songs shall drive away the final clouds. With one accord let us hail the Dawn of the Eternal Day. Behold the rising of the one True Light! Ah, why may I not take with me these my friends! Farewell, poor earth, Farewell!"

VII.

THE ASSUMPTION.

THE last psalm was uttered neither by word, look,
nor gesture, nor by any of those signs which men employ to communicate their thoughts, but as the soul
speaks to itself; for at the moment when Seraphita
revealed herself in her true nature, her thoughts were
no longer enslaved by human words. The violence of
that last prayer had burst her bonds. Her soul, like a
white dove, remained for an instant poised above the
body whose exhausted substances were about to be
annihilated.

The aspiration of the Soul toward heaven was so
contagious that Wilfrid and Minna, beholding those
radiant scintillations of Life, perceived not Death.

They had fallen on their knees when *he* had turned
toward his Orient, and they shared his ecstasy.

The fear of the Lord, which creates man a second
time, purging away his dross, mastered their hearts.

Their eyes, veiled to the things of Earth, were opened
to the Brightness of Heaven.

Though, like the Seers of old called Prophets by men,
they were filled with the terror of the Most High, yet
like them they continued firm when they found themselves within the radiance where the Glory of the
Spirit shone.

The veil of flesh, which, until now, had hidden that glory from their eyes, dissolved imperceptibly away, and left them free to behold the Divine substance.

They stood in the twilight of the Coming Dawn, whose feeble rays prepared them to look upon the True Light, to hear the Living Word, and yet not die.

In this state they began to perceive the immeasurable differences which separate the things of earth from the things of Heaven.

LIFE, on the borders of which they stood, leaning upon each other, trembling and illuminated, like two children standing under shelter in presence of a conflagration, That Life offered no lodgment to the senses.

The ideas they used to interpret their vision to themselves were to the things seen what the visible senses of a man are to his soul, the material covering of a divine essence.

The departing SPIRIT was above them, shedding incense without odor, melody without sound. About them, where they stood, were neither surfaces, nor angles, nor atmosphere.

They dared neither question him nor contemplate him; they stood in the shadow of that Presence as beneath the burning rays of a tropical sun, fearing to raise their eyes lest the light should blast them.

They knew they were beside him, without being able to perceive how it was that they stood, as in a dream, on the confines of the Visible and the Invisible, nor how they had lost sight of the Visible and how they beheld the Invisible.

To each other they said : " If he touch us, we can die ! " But the SPIRIT was now within the Infinite, and they knew not that neither time, nor space, nor death, existed there, and that a great gulf lay between them, although they thought themselves beside him.

Their souls were not prepared to receive in its fulness a knowledge of the faculties of that Life; they could have only faint and confused perceptions of it, suited to their weakness.

Were it not so, the thunder of the LIVING WORD, whose far-off tones now reached their ears, and whose meaning entered their souls as life unites with body, — one echo of that Word would have consumed their being as a whirlwind of fire laps up a fragile straw.

Therefore they saw only that which their nature, sustained by the strength of the SPIRIT, permitted them to see; they heard that only which they were able to hear.

And yet, though thus protected, they shuddered when the Voice of the anguished soul broke forth above them — the prayer of the SPIRIT awaiting Life and imploring it with a cry.

That cry froze them to the very marrow of their bones.

The SPIRIT knocked at the SACRED PORTAL. " What wilt thou ? " answered a CHOIR, whose question echoed among the worlds. " To go to God." " Hast thou conquered ? " " I have conquered the flesh through abstinence, I have conquered false knowledge by humility, I have conquered pride by charity, I have conquered the earth by love; I have paid my dues by suffering, I am purified in the fires of faith, I have longed for Life by prayer: I wait in adoration, and I am resigned."

No answer came.

"God's will be done!" answered the SPIRIT, believ- ing that he was about to be rejected.

His tears flowed and fell like dew upon the heads of the two kneeling witnesses, who trembled before the justice of God.

Suddenly the trumpets sounded, — the trumpets of Victory won by the ANGEL in this last trial. The re- verberation passed through space as sound through its echo, filling it, and shaking the universe which Wilfrid and Minna felt like an atom beneath their feet. They trembled under an anguish caused by the dread of the mystery about to be accomplished.

A great movement took place, as though the Eternal Legions, putting themselves in motion, were passing upward in spiral columns. The worlds revolved like clouds driven by a furious wind. It was all rapid.

Suddenly the veils were rent away. They saw on high as it were a star, incomparably more lustrous than the most luminous of material stars, which detached it- self, and fell like a thunderbolt, dazzling as lightning. Its passage paled the faces of the pair, who thought it to be THE LIGHT Itself.

It was the Messenger of good tidings, the plume of whose helmet was a flame of Life.

Behind him lay the swath of his way gleaming with a flood of the lights through which he passed.

He bore a palm and a sword. He touched the SPIRIT
with the palm, and the SPIRIT was transfigured. Its
white wings noiselessly unfolded.

This communication of THE LIGHT, changing the
SPIRIT into a SERAPH and clothing it with a glorious
form, a celestial armor, poured down such effulgent
rays that the two Seers were paralyzed.

Like the three apostles to whom Jesus showed himself, they felt the dead weight of their bodies which
denied them a complete and cloudless intuition of THE
WORD and THE TRUE LIFE.

They comprehended the nakedness of their souls;
they were able to measure the poverty of their light by
comparing it — a humbling task — with the halo of the
SERAPH.

A passionate desire to plunge back into the mire of
earth and suffer trial took possession of them, — trial
through which they might victoriously utter at the
SACRED GATES the words of that radiant Seraph.

The Seraph knelt before the SANCTUARY, beholding
it, at last, face to face; and he said, raising his hands
thitherward, "Grant that these two may have further
sight; they will love the Lord and proclaim His word."

At this prayer a veil fell. Whether it were that the
hidden force which held the Seers had momentarily
annihilated their physical bodies, or that it raised their
spirits above those bodies, certain it is that they felt
within them a rending of the pure from the impure.

The tears of the Seraph rose about them like a vapor,
which hid the lower worlds from their knowledge, held

them in its folds, bore them upward, gave them forgetfulness of earthly meanings and the power of comprehending the meanings of things divine.

The True Light shone; it illumined the Creations,
which seemed to them barren when they saw the source
from which all worlds — Terrestrial, Spiritual, and
Divine — derived their Motion.

Each world possessed a centre to which converged all
points of its circumference. These worlds were themselves the points which moved toward the centre of
their system. Each system had its centre in great
celestial regions which communicated with the flaming
and quenchless *Motor of all that is.*

Thus, from the greatest to the smallest of the worlds,
and from the smallest of the worlds to the smallest
portion of the beings who compose it, all was individual,
and all was, nevertheless, One and indivisible.

What was the design of the Being, fixed in His essence and in His faculties, who transmitted that essence
and those faculties without losing them? who manifested them outside of Himself without separating them
from Himself? who rendered his creations outside of
Himself fixed in their essence and mutable in their
form? The pair thus called to the celestial festival
could only see the order and arrangement of created
beings and admire the immediate result. The Angels
alone see more. They know the means; they comprehend the final end.

But what the two Elect were granted power to contemplate, what they were able to bring back as a testi-

mony which enlightened their minds forever after, was the proof of the action of the Worlds and of Beings; the consciousness of the effort with which they all converge to the Result.

They heard the divers parts of the Infinite forming one living melody; and each time that the accord made itself felt like a mighty respiration, the Worlds drawn by the concordant movement inclined themselves toward the Supreme Being who, from His impenetrable centre, issued all things and recalled all things to Himself.

This ceaseless alternation of voices and silence seemed the rhythm of the sacred hymn which resounds and prolongs its sound from age to age.

Wilfrid and Minna were enabled to understand some of the mysterious sayings of Him who had appeared on earth in the form which to each of them had rendered him comprehensible, — to one Seraphitus, to the other Seraphita, — for they saw that all was homogeneous in the sphere where he now was.

Light gave birth to melody, melody gave birth to light; colors were light and melody; motion was a Number endowed with Utterance; all things were at once sonorous, diaphanous, and mobile; so that each interpenetrated the other, the whole vast area was unobstructed and the Angels could survey it from the depths of the Infinite.

They perceived the puerility of human sciences, of which he had spoken to them.

The scene was to them a prospect without horizon, a boundless space into which an all-consuming desire prompted them to plunge. But, fastened to their miserable bodies, they had the desire without the power to fulfil it.

The SERAPH, preparing for his flight, no longer looked towards them; he had nothing now in common with Earth.

Upward he rose; the shadow of his luminous presence covered the two Seers like a merciful veil, enabling them to raise their eyes and see him, rising in his glory to Heaven in company with the glad Archangel.

He rose as the sun from the bosom of the Eastern waves; but, more majestic than the orb and vowed to higher destinies, he could not be enchained like inferior creations in the spiral movement of the worlds; he followed the line of the Infinite, pointing without deviation to the One Centre, there to enter his eternal life, — to receive there, in his faculties and in his essence, the power to enjoy through Love, and the gift of comprehending through Wisdom.

The scene which suddenly unveiled itself to the eyes of the two Seers crushed them with a sense of its vastness; they felt like atoms, whose minuteness was not to be compared even to the smallest particle which the infinite of divisibility enabled the mind of man to imagine, brought into the presence of the infinite of Numbers, which God alone can comprehend as He alone can comprehend Himself.

Strength and Love! what heights, what depths in those two entities, whom the Seraph's first prayer placed like two links, as it were, to unite the immensities of the lower worlds with the immensity of the higher universe!

They comprehended the invisible ties by which the material worlds are bound to the spiritual worlds. Remembering the sublime efforts of human genius, they were able to perceive the principle of all melody in the songs of heaven which gave sensations of color, of perfume, of thought, which recalled the innumerable details of all creations, as the songs of earth revive the infinite memories of love.

Brought by the exaltation of their faculties to a point that cannot be described in any language, they were able to cast their eyes for an instant into the Divine World. There all was Rejoicing.

Myriads of angels were flocking together, without confusion; all alike yet all dissimilar, simple as the flower of the fields, majestic as the universe.

Wilfrid and Minna saw neither their coming nor their going; they appeared suddenly in the Infinite and filled it with their presence, as the stars shine in the invisible ether.

The scintillations of their united diadems illumined space like the fires of the sky at dawn upon the mountains. Waves of light flowed from their hair, and their movements created tremulous undulations in space like the billows of a phosphorescent sea.

The two Seers beheld the SERAPH dimly in the midst of the immortal legions. Suddenly, as though all the arrows of a quiver had darted together, the Spirits swept away with a breath the last vestiges of the human form ; as the SERAPH rose he became yet purer ; soon he seemed to them but a faint outline of what he had been at the moment of his transfiguration, — lines of fire without shadow.

Higher he rose, receiving from circle to circle some new gift, while the sign of his election was transmitted to each sphere into which, more and more purified, he entered.

No voice was silent ; the hymn diffused and multiplied itself in all its modulations : —

" Hail to him who enters living ! Come, flower of the Worlds ! diamond from the fires of suffering ! pearl without spot, desire without flesh, new link of earth and heaven, be Light ! Conquering spirit, Queen of the world, come for thy crown ! Victor of earth, receive thy diadem ! Thou art of us ! "

The virtues of the SERAPH shone forth in all their beauty.

His earliest desire for heaven re-appeared, tender as childhood. The deeds of his life, like constellations, adorned him with their brightness. His acts of faith shone like the Jacinth of heaven, the color of sidereal fires. The pearls of Charity were upon him, — a chaplet of garnered tears ! Love divine surrounded him with roses ; and the whiteness of his Resignation obliterated all earthly trace.

Soon, to the eyes of the Seers, he was but a point of flame, growing brighter and brighter as its motion was lost in the melodious acclamations which welcomed his entrance into heaven.

The celestial accents made the two exiles weep.

Suddenly a silence as of death spread like a mourning veil from the first to the highest sphere, throwing Wilfrid and Minna into a state of intolerable expectation.

At this moment the SERAPH was lost to sight within the SANCTUARY, receiving there the gift of Life Eternal.

A movement of adoration made by the Host of heaven filled the two Seers with ecstasy mingled with terror. They felt that all were prostrate before the Throne, in all the spheres, in the Spheres Divine, in the Spiritual Spheres, and in the Worlds of Darkness.

The Angels bent the knee to celebrate the SERAPH's glory; the Spirits bent the knee in token of their impatience; others bent the knee in the dark abysses, shuddering with awe.

A mighty cry of joy gushed forth, as the spring gushes forth to its millions of flowering herbs sparkling with diamond dew-drops in the sunlight; at that instant the SERAPH reappeared, effulgent, crying, " ETERNAL ! ETERNAL ! ETERNAL ! "

The universe heard the cry and understood it; it penetrated the spheres as God penetrates them; it took possession of the infinite; the Seven Divine Worlds heard the Voice and answered.

A mighty movement was perceptible, as though whole planets, purified, were rising in dazzling light to become Eternal.

Had the SERAPH obtained, as a first mission, the work of calling to God the creations permeated by His Word?

But already the sublime HALLELUJAH was sounding in the ear of the desolate ones as the distant undulations of an ended melody. Already the celestial lights were fading like the gold and crimson tints of a setting sun. Death and Impurity recovered their prey.

As the two mortals re-entered the prison of flesh, from which their spirit had momentarily been delivered by some priceless sleep, they felt like those who wake after a night of brilliant dreams, the memory of which still lingers in their soul, though their body retains no consciousness of them, and human language is unable to give utterance to them.

The deep darkness of the sphere that was now about them was that of the sun of the visible worlds.

" Let us descend to those lower regions," said Wilfrid.

" Let us do what he told us to do," answered Minna. " We have seen the worlds on their march to God; we know the Path. Our diadem of stars is There."

Floating downward through the abysses, they re-entered the dust of the lesser worlds, and saw the Earth, like a subterranean cavern, suddenly illuminated to their eyes by the light which their souls brought with them, and which still environed them in a cloud of the paling harmonies of heaven. The sight was that which of old struck the inner eyes of Seers and Prophets. Ministers of all religions, Preachers of all pretended truths, Kings consecrated by Force and Terror, Warriors and Mighty men apportioning the Peoples among them, the Learned and the Rich standing above the suffering, noisy crowd, and noisily grinding them beneath their feet, — all were there, accompanied by their wives and servants ; all were robed in stuffs of gold and silver and azure studded with pearls and gems torn from the bowels of Earth, stolen from the depths of Ocean, for which Humanity had toiled throughout the centuries, sweating and blaspheming. But these treasures, these splendors, constructed of blood, seemed worn-out rags to the eyes of the two Exiles. "What do you there, in motionless ranks?" cried Wilfrid. They answered not. "What do you there, motionless?" They answered not. Wilfrid waved his hands over them, crying in a loud voice, "What do you there, in motionless ranks?" All, with unanimous action, opened their garments and gave to sight their withered bodies, eaten with worms, putrified, crumbling to dust, rotten with horrible diseases.

"You lead the nations to Death," Wilfrid said to them. "You have depraved the earth, perverted the Word, prostituted justice. After devouring the grass of the fields you have killed the lambs of the fold. Do you think yourself justified because of your sores? I will warn my brethren who have ears to hear the Voice, and they will come and drink of the spring of Living Waters which you have hidden."

"Let us save our strength for Prayer," said Minna. "Wilfred, thy mission is not that of the Prophets or the Avenger or the Messenger; we are still on the confines of the lowest sphere; let us endeavor to rise through space on the wings of Prayer."

"Thou shalt be all my love!"

" Thou shalt be all my strength ! "

" We have seen the Mysteries ; we are, each to the other, the only being here below to whom Joy and Sadness are comprehensible ; let us pray, therefore : we know the Path, let us walk in it."

" Give me thy hand," said the Young Girl, " if we walk together, the way will be to me less hard and long."

" With thee, with thee alone," replied the Man, " can I cross the awful solitude without complaint."

" Together we will go to Heaven," she said.

The clouds gathered and formed a darksome dais. Suddenly the pair found themselves kneeling beside a body which old David was guarding from curious eyes, resolved to bury it himself.

Beyond those walls the first summer of the nineteenth century shone forth in all its glory. The two lovers believed they heard a Voice in the sun-rays. They breathed a celestial essence from the new-born flowers. Holding each other by the hand, they said, " That illimitable ocean which shines below us is but an image of what we saw above."

" Where are you going ? " asked Monsieur Becker.

" To God," they answered. " Come with us, father."

JESUS CHRIST IN FLANDERS.

PHILOSOPHICAL STUDIES.

JESUS CHRIST IN FLANDERS.

To Marceline Desbordes-Valmore.

To you, daughter of Flanders, and one of her modern
glories, I offer this naïve tradition of your native land.

De Balzac.

At a somewhat uncertain period in Brabantian history communication between the island of Walcheren
and the coast of Flanders was carried on by means of a
small vessel for the conveyance of passengers. Middel-
burg, the capital of the island, so celebrated in after
days in the annals of Protestantism, had scarcely more
than two or three hundred houses at the time of which
we write. Ostend, now so wealthy, was then an unknown port, flanked by a straggling hamlet thinly
populated by fishermen, petty traders, and unmolested
buccaneers. Nevertheless the little town, though it
contained only a score of houses and some three hundred huts, cottages, and hovels built of the remains
of wrecked ships, boasted of a governor, a militia, a
gibbet, a convent, a burgomaster, — in short, of all the
evidences of an advanced civilization.

Who reigned in Brabant, Flanders, and Belgium at
this period? As to that, tradition is silent. Let us

admit at once that the following history is full of the
vague indefiniteness and mystery of the marvellous
which the favorite orators of Flemish festivals delighted
in imparting to their native legends, as diverse in poetry
as they were contradictory in details.   Told from age
to age, repeated day and night from hearth to hearth by
grandsires and narrators, this chronicle has received a
different coloring from each century through which it
has been handed down.   Like buildings whose construction reflects the caprices of the architecture of
their day, but whose blackened, time-worn masses are
the delight of poets, such legends are the despair of com-
mentators, — sifters of words and facts and dates.   The
narrator believes in them, as all the superstitious minds
of Flanders have believed, without becoming either
firmer or weaker in the faith.   Finding it impossible to
harmonize the various versions, we here give the tale,
stripped, perhaps, of its romantic simplicity (difficult,
indeed, to reproduce), but with its bold assertions which
history disavows, its morality which religion sanctions,
its mystical blossom of imagination and its esoteric
meaning, which the wise may gather.   To each his
own nutriment and the duty of sifting the wheat from
the chaff.

The vessel which carried passengers from the island
of Walcheren to Ostend was about to start.   Before
casting off the iron chain which held the boat to a stone
post of the little jetty from which the passengers em-
barked, the captain of the craft blew his horn at intervals to hasten late-comers, this being his last trip for

the day. Night was coming on ; the rays of the setting
sun scarcely enabled him to distinguish the distant coast
of Flanders, or to see belated passengers, if any were
hurrying along the embankments that surrounded the
fields or making their way among the tall reeds of the
marsh. The vessel was full, and a cry arose: " Why
do you wait? let us start."

Just then a man appeared a few steps away from the
jetty. The captain, who had neither seen him nor
heard his step, was surprised. The passenger seemed
to have suddenly risen from the ground, as though he
were a peasant asleep in the fields, roused by the blow-
ing of the horn. Was he a robber? perhaps a custom-
house officer, or a constable? When he reached the
jetty to which the boat was moored, the seven persons
who were sitting in the after-part of the little vessel
hastened to take their seats on the benches, so as to
keep by themselves and not allow the stranger to join
them. This was done from a quick, instinctive impulse,
— one of those aristocratic thoughts which come into
the minds of the rich. Four of these personages belonged to the higher nobility of Flanders. One was
a young man, accompanied by two handsome hounds,
wearing a cap adorned with jewels on his floating hair ;
he clanked his gilded spurs and twirled his moustachios
insolently from time to time, casting contemptuous
glances on the other passengers. A haughty young
lady bore a falcon on her wrist and spoke only to her
mother or to an ecclesiastic of high rank — a relation,
no doubt — who accompanied them. These persons

made much noise and conversed together as if they alone were on the vessel. Beside them, however, was a man of great importance in the country, a stout burgher of Bruges, wrapped in a large cloak. His servant, armed to the teeth, was in charge of two bags filled with coin. There was also near them a man of science, — a professor of the University of Louvain, — attended by his secretary. These personages, who were all contemptuous of each other, were separated from the forward part of the boat by the thwarts of the rowers.

When the belated passenger stepped into the boat he threw a rapid glance at the stern, saw no place, and turned to seek one among the passengers who were sitting in the bows. The latter were poor people. On the appearance of this man with bare head, coat and breeches of brown camlet, an open collar and smock of heavy linen without ornament, holding neither hat nor cap in his hand and without purse or sword at his belt, every one took him to be a burgomaster sure of his authority, — a kindly, worthy man, like many of the old Flemish burgomasters whose ingenuous characters and nature have been so admirably preserved by the painters of their native land. The poor people in the bows received the stranger with demonstrations of respect which excited satirical whisperings among the group at the stern. An old soldier, a man of toil and hardships, gave up his place on a bench to the stranger and seated himself on the gunwale of the boat, maintaining his equilibrium by bracing his feet against the wooden cross-pieces, like the spine bones of a fish, which served to bind the boat-planks together. A young woman, mother of a little child, belonging apparently to the working-women of Ostend, drew aside to make room for the new-comer. The movement showed neither servility nor contempt. It was one of those proofs of kind-heartedness by which poor people, who know the value of a service and the pleasures of brotherhood, reveal the nature and the sincerity of their souls, always so candid in exhibiting both their good qualities and their defects. The stranger thanked them both with a gesture full of noble feeling. Then he sat down between the young mother and the old soldier. Behind him was a peasant and his son about ten years of age. A beggar-woman, with a basket that was almost empty, old and wrinkled and ragged, — a type of misery and listless indifference, — lay huddled in the bows, crouching on a coil of rope. One of the rowers, an old sailor, having known her handsome and prosperous, had given her a passage (in the admirable language of the poorer classes) " for the love of God."

" Thank you, Thomas," said the old creature ; " I 'll say a *Pater* and two *Aves* for you to-night in my prayers."

The captain blew his horn again, looked round the silent shore, flung the chain into the boat, ran to the tiller, took the bar in his hand and stood looking before him ; then, after watching the sky for awhile, he called out to the rowers in a loud voice, the boat being now well out to sea, " Row hard, row hard ! make haste ! the sea looks ugly, the hag! I feel the swell at the rudder and the storm in my joints!"

These words, said in the hoarse tones of an old sailor, and almost unintelligible to ears not accustomed to the noise of the waves, caused a precipitate, though always measured movement of the oars, — a unanimous movement, as different from that which had preceded it as the trot of a horse is different from its gallop. The distinguished company sitting in the stern took pleasure in watching the vigorous arms of the rowers, the brown faces with their fiery eyes, the strained muscles and diverse human forms, all acting in concert to put them across the straits for a trifling toll. Far from deploring the hardships of such labor, they pointed out to each other, laughing, the grotesque expression which the labor brought into each toil-worn face. Forward, the soldier, the peasant, and the old woman were looking at the sailors with a compassion natural to persons who, living by the sweat of their brow, understand the harsh pains and the feverish fatigues of labor. Besides, accustomed as they were to life in the open air, they understood from the signs in the sky the danger that threatened them, and were grave and anxious. The young mother was rocking her child in her arms and singing him to sleep with an ancient hymn.

"If we get safely over," said the soldier to one of the peasants, "it will be because God has set His mind on our living."

"Ah! He is the master," said the old woman; "I think it is His good pleasure to call us to Himself. Do

you see that light over there?" With a nod of her head
she motioned to westward, where lines of fire were cut-
ting sharply through a heavy cloud-bank tinged with
crimson, which seemed about to unchain a furious wind.
The sea gave forth a muttered sound, an inward roar,
like the noise of a dog when he only growls. After all,
Ostend was not so far off. At this moment the sea and
the sky presented one of those sights to which neither
painting nor language can give a longer duration than
that they actually have. Human creations require
powerful contrasts. Therefore it is that artists ordi-
narily seize the most vivid phenomena of Nature, despairing, no doubt, of being able to render the grand
and glorious poetry of her daily charm, — though the
human soul is often as deeply stirred by tranquillity as
by movement, by silence as by storm.

There came a moment when every one in the boat
kept silence and gazed at the sea and sky, either from
apprehension or in obedience to that religious melancholy which takes possession of all of us at the decline
of day, at the hour of prayer, the moment when Nature
is silent and the bells speak. The sea cast up a wan,
white gleam, changing into the colors of steel. The
sky was chiefly gray. To the west stretched narrow
spaces like streams of blood, while to the eastward
dazzling lines, drawn as if with the finest brush, were
separated by clouds ridged like the wrinkles on an old
man's brow. On all sides the sea and the sky showed
a dull, dead ground of neutral tints which threw into
strong relief the sinister fires of the setting sun. This

aspect of nature inspired terror. If it is allowable to put the bold figures of the common people into written language, we might say with the soldier that the weather was sounding the retreat, or, with the peasant who answered him, that the sky had the look of an execu, tioner. The wind suddenly rose, coming from the westward, and the captain, who had never ceased to watch the sea, noticing the swell on the horizon, called out, "Hau! hau!" At this cry the sailors stopped rowing and let their oars float on the surface of the water.

"The captain is right," said Thomas, stolidly, when the boat, borne on the crest of an enormous wave, plunged downwards as if into the open jaws of the sea.

At that violent movement, that sudden rage of Ocean, the passengers in the stern grew livid, and cried out in terror, "We shall perish!"

"Oh, not yet!" answered the captain, quietly.

The clouds at this instant were torn apart by the wind exactly above the boat. The gray masses rolled with threatening rapidity to the east and to the west; a twilight gleam fell full upon the passengers through the rent made by the blast, and they saw each other's faces. One and all, nobles and wealthy men, mariners and beggars, were held for a moment in surprise at the aspect of the last-comer. His golden hair, parted in the centre of his calm, serene brow, fell in heavy locks upon his shoulders, outlining upon the iron-gray atmos- phere a head sublime in gentleness, from which the Divine Love shone. He did not despise death, for he was certain of not perishing. But although the persons in the stern forgot for an instant at the sight of this man the storm whose implacable fury threatened them, they soon returned to their selfish feelings and to the habits of their life.

" How lucky for that stupid man that he does not see the danger we are all in," said the University professor ; " he is like a dog who dies without a struggle."

The learned man had hardly uttered this judicial sentence when the tempest unchained its legions. The winds blew from all quarters ; the boat was whirled round like a top, and the sea broke over her.

" Oh, my poor child ! my child ! Who will save my child ? " cried the mother in a heartrending voice.

" You, yourself," replied the stranger.

The ring of that voice entered the soul of the young woman, and with it hope ; she heard the tuneful words above the hissings of the storm, above the cries of the passengers.

" Holy Virgin of Succor ! thou of Antwerp ! I promise a thousand wax candles and a statue if you will bring me out of this," cried the burgher, kneeling on his bags of gold.

" The Virgin is not at Antwerp any more than she is here," declared the professor.

" She is in heaven," said a voice that seemed to come from the sea.

" Who spoke ? "

" It was the devil, for he mocked at the Virgin of Antwerp," said the servant.

" Let alone your Virgin," cried the captain to the passengers, " take those buckets and bale the boat. And you," he added to the sailors, " row steady! we have a moment's respite ; in the name of the devil who leaves you a little longer in this world, let us be our own providence. The straits are frightfully dangerous, as everybody knows, but I have been crossing them these thirty years. Is this the first time, think you, I've battled with a storm?"

Then, standing beside the tiller, the captain continued to watch, alternately, the sea, the boat, and the sky.

" He scoffs at everything, the skipper," said Thomas, in a low voice.

" Will God let us die with those poor wretches?" said the proud young girl to the handsome cavalier.

" No, no, my noble demoiselle. Listen," he said, putting his arm round her and whispering in her ear. " I can swim, but do not tell it. I will take you by that beautiful hair and draw you gently ashore. But I can save only you."

The daughter glanced at her mother. The lady was on her knees asking absolution of the bishop, who was not listening to her. The cavalier read a feeble sentiment of filial pity in the eyes of his beautiful mistress, and he said in muffled tones : " Submit to the will of God ! If he chooses to call your mother to himself it is doubtless for her happiness — in another world," he added in a still lower voice. " And for ours in this," thought he. The lady of Rupelmonde possessed seven fiefs, beside the barony of Gâvres. The daughter lis-

tened to the voice of her. own life; the self-interests of
her love spoke by the mouth of the handsome adven-
turer, — a young miscreant, who haunted churches in
search of prey, a girl to marry, or a round sum of money
in hand. The bishop blessed the waves and ordered
them to be still, though despairing of it; he thought of
his concubine, awaiting him with some delicate repast,
perhaps at this moment taking her bath, perfuming and
robing herself in velvet, clasping her necklace and putting
on her jewels. Far from remembering the powers of
holy Church and consoling the people around him by ex-
horting them to trust in God, the worldly bishop mingled
earthly regrets and thoughts of love with the words of
his breviary. The gleam from above which lighted these
pale faces gave to view their diverse expressions, when
suddenly the boat, lifted into the air by a wave, then
plunged into the trough of the sea and shaken like a
withered leaf whirled by the autumn winds, cracked
loudly in its hull and seemed about to go to pieces
Horrible cries arose followed by dreadful silence.

The conduct of the persons sitting in the forward part
of the boat contrasted strangely with that of the rich
and powerful in the stern. The young mother strained
her babe to her breast each time that the waves threatened to engulf the frail vessel; but she relied on the
hope which the stranger had put into her heart; at each
new peril she turned her eyes upon the man and gathered from his face renewed faith, — the faith of a feeble
woman, the faith of a mother. Living by the divine
word, by the word of love that man had uttered, the

simple creature awaited with confidence the fulfilment
of what seemed a promise, and scarcely dreaded danger.
The soldier, holding fast to the gunwale of the boat,
never took his eyes off the singular being on whose
composure he modelled the expression of his own rough
and sunburnt face; thus calling into play his intelligence and his will, whose powerful springs were but
little weakened or vitiated by the course of a passive
and mechanical existence. Emulous of being calm
and tranquil like that higher courage before him, he
ended by identifying himself, perhaps unconsciously,
with the hidden principle of that interior power.
His admiration became an instinctive fanaticism, a
boundless love, a belief in that man like the enthusiasm
that soldiers feel for their leader when he is a man of
power, surrounded with the halo of victory, and march-
ing amid the dazzling light of genius. The old beggar-
woman kept saying in a low voice, " Ah, wicked sinner
that I am! Have I not suffered enough to expiate the
joys of my youth? Ah, why, poor wretch! did I lead
that life of pleasure? why did I squander the things
of God with the servants of the Church, the money of
the poor with usurers and extortioners? Ah! I have
sinned! My God! my God! let me finish my hell in
this world of misery! Or else, — Holy Virgin, mother
of God, have pity on me!"

"Take comfort, mother," said the soldier, "the good
God is not a usurer. Though I've killed people right
and left, the bad and the good together, I am not afraid
of the resurrection."

" Ah! corporal, but how lucky they are, those fine
ladies, to have a bishop with them, the saintly man!"
said the old creature. " They will get absolution for
their sins. If I could only hear the voice of a priest
saying to me, 'Your sins are forgiven,' I could believe it."

The stranger turned to her, and his merciful look
made her quiver.

" Have faith," he said, " and you will be saved."

"May God reward you, my good gentleman," she
said. " If you say true, I will make a pilgrimage with
bare feet for you and for me to our Lady of Lorette."

The two peasants, father and son, were silent, resigned, and submissive to the will of God, like men
accustomed to follow instinctively, as an animal does,
the propulsion of nature.

So here on one side were riches, knowledge, pride,
debauchery, crime, — the whole of human society, such
as thought, education, arts, and the laws of man have
made it; here also, and on this side only, were cries,
terrors, a thousand feelings struggling with frightful
doubts, here alone the agony of dread. Above them
stood a man of power, — the captain of the boat, — believing and doubting nothing; the king, the fatalist,
making himself his own providence, crying out, " Bale
her! bale her!" defying the storm and struggling hand
to hand against the sea. At the other end of the little
bark behold the weak·ones! The mother holding to
her bosom the babe smiling at the storm, an old
woman, once jovial, now the victim of remorse; a

soldier, crippled with wounds, obtaining no other compensation for his indefatigable devotion than a mutilated life. With barely a crust moistened by sweat to keep life in him, he laughed at all things, went his way without anxiety, happy if he could drown his glory in a pot of beer, or recount it to the children who followed and admired him. Gayly he committed to God the care of his future. Finally, the two peasants, creatures of toil and exhaustion, toil incarnate, the labor by which the whole world lives. These simple beings, unknowing of thought and its treasures and ready to engulf them all for a belief, possessed a faith the more robust because they had never discussed nor analyzed it, — virgin natures in which the conscience continued pure and the feelings powerful. Remorse, misfortune, love, and labor had exercised, purified, concentrated, and increased their will, — the only thing in man which resembles what learned men have called a soul.

When the boat, guided by the marvellous skill of her captain, came in sight of Ostend and was only fifty feet from the shore, she was driven back by a sudden revulsion of the tempest and began to sink. The stranger with the luminous countenance spoke to that little world of anguish, and said, "Those who have faith will be saved; follow me."

Then he arose and walked with a firm step upon the sea. The young mother clasped her child in her arms and walked beside him. The soldier stood up, saying in his untutored way, "Ha! by my pipe! I'll follow

thee to the devil," and without seeming to be surprised,
he trod the waves. The old woman, the sinner, believing in the power of God, followed the man, and
she too walked upon the water. The two peasants
said to each other, " If they can walk upon the sea,
why cannot we?" and they rose and hurried after them.
Thomas wished to do likewise, but his faith failed him ;
he fell several times into the water, but rose again ;
then, after three attempts, he, too, walked upon the
sea. The bold captain clung like a barnacle to the
planks of his boat. The burgher had faith and was
about to step upon the sea, but he wished to carry
away his gold and the gold carried him to the bottom
of the ocean. The man of science, ridiculing the
charlatan and the fools who heeded him, laughed as
he heard the stranger proposing to the passengers to
walk upon water, and the sea swallowed him up. The
young girl was dragged to the bottom by her lover.
The bishop and the old lady went down, heavy perhaps
with crime, but heavier still with unbelief and confidence in graven images, heavy with cant, light of
charity and true religion.

The faithful flock, treading with firm feet and dry
the plain of angry waters, heard around them the horrible tumult of the storm. Enormous waves broke
before them ; an unseen force rent the Ocean. In
the distance the faithful beheld through the mist a
feeble light glimmering from the hut of some fisherman. All, walking courageously toward that light,
fancied they heard above the roaring of the sea the

voice of their companions crying, "Courage!" And
yet, watchful of their own danger, no one spoke a
word. Thus they reached the shore. When all were
seated by the fisherman's hearth, they looked about
them for their shining guide, but in vain. From the
top of a rock against whose base the tempest had flung
the captain, still clinging to his plank with the strength
displayed by sailors in their struggles with death, THE
MAN stepped down and drew in the drowning one,
whose force was well-nigh spent, to whom he said, laying the helping hand upon his head, "Safe now, but
do it not again; the example is an evil one."

He took the sailor on his shoulders and bore him to
the hut. Then, knocking on the door that the hapless
man might be admitted to that humble refuge, the
Saviour disappeared. Later a Convent of Mercy for
the benefit of mariners was built on that spot, where
the print on the sand left by the feet of Jesus Christ
was long, they say, visible. In 1793, at the time of
the entrance of the French into Belgium, the monks
carried away this precious relic, the visible sign of the
last visit made by Jesus to this Earth.

There it was that, weary of life, I found myself not
long after the revolution of 1830. If you had asked
the reasons of my despair it would have been impossible
for me to tell them to you, so nerveless and fluid had
my soul become. The springs of my mind were relaxed
by the current of a west wind. The sky was cold and
black; the dark clouds passing above my head gave

a sinister expression to Nature. The immensity of the
sea — everything said to me : " Death to-day, death
to-morrow, death must come at last, and then — "
I wandered on, thinking of the uncertain future, of my
lost hopes. A prey to many funereal thoughts, I
mechanically entered the convent church, whose gray
towers looked to me just then like phantoms looming
through the sea-mists. I gazed without interest at the
forest of columns whose foliated capitals supported the
light arches of a labyrinth of aisles. I walked unheed-
ing through the lateral naves which spread before me
like those porticoes that double back upon themselves.
The dim light of an autumn evening scarcely enabled
me to see, above the sculptured key-stones of the
arches, the delicate ribs which defined so cleanly the
graceful spring of the vaulted roof. The organs were
silent. My footsteps alone woke the solemn echoes
that lurked in the dark chapels. I sat down beside
one of the four pillars that sustained the dome, near
the choir. From there I could see the whole interior
of the structure, which I gazed at without attaching
a single idea to it. The mechanical use of my eyes
showed me the imposing array of columns, the tracery
of the immense rose-windows, so wonderfully hung
above the lateral doors and the great portal, the lofty
galleries and the slender shafts which divided the glass
windows, topped by arches, by trefoils, or by wreaths,
a charming filagree of stone. A dome of glass at the
farther end of the choir sparkled as though a mass of
precious stones were inserted in it. Contrasting with

the brightness of this cupola, which was partly white
and partly colored, were the black shadows of two deep
naves on the right and left, in the depths of which the
dim shafts of a hundred gray columns were indistinctly
visible.

By dint of looking fixedly at these marvellous ar-
cades, these wreaths and spirals and arabesques, these
Saracenic fantasies, interlacing with one another and
capriciously lighted, my perceptions became confused.
I was, in fact, on the confines of illusion and reality,
caught in a series of optical snares and bewildered by
the multitude of the vistas about me.   Little by little
those hewn stones faded from my sight, veiled by a
cloud of golden dust like that which dances in the sun-
rays striking athwart a room.   From the bosom of the
vaporous atmosphere, which made the outline of all
forms indistinct, the lace-work of the rose windows
shone forth resplendent.   Every line of their tracery,
the least detail of their carving was burnished.   The
sun lighted fires in the glass, whose rich colors glowed.
The columns stirred, their capitals swayed softly.   A
gentle tremor shook the edifice and its friezes nodded
with graceful precaution.   Several large pillars moved,
slowly and with dignity, like the dancing of dowagers
who courteously take part in a quadrille at the end of
a ball.   Certain slim, erect columns, adorned with their
trefoil crowns, began to laugh and skip.   Pointed arches
oscillated with the long, slim windows, which resembled
those dames of the middle-ages who wore the armorial
bearings of their families emblazoned on their robes.

The dance of the mitred arches with these elegant windows was like the scene of a tournament. Soon every stone of the church vibrated, but did not move from its place. The organs spoke, and I heard a divine harmony in which the voice of angels mingled, — a wondrous music, accompanied by the muffled bass of the bells, which told that the two colossal towers of the church were swaying on their foundations.

This singular gala seemed to me the most natural thing in the world, for what could surprise me after beholding the overthrow of Charles X.? I was myself gently swayed like a swing; and this afforded me a pleasure of the nerves of which it is quite impossible to give an idea. And yet, in the midst of this glowing bacchanalia the choir seemed cold as winter. I saw within it a multitude of women clothed in white, motionless and silent. A few censers shed their soft odors, which penetrated my soul and gladdened it. The tapers flamed ; the pulpit, gay as a bard in his cups, rolled like a Chinese image. I perceived that the cathedral itself was whirling with such rapidity that everything in it appeared to keep its place. The colossal Christ above the high altar smiled with a malicious benignity which frightened me ; I avoided looking at it, and began to admire a blue vapor gliding among the pillars and lending them an indescribable grace. A few ravishing female faces appeared in the friezes. The cherubs who supported the great columns beat their wings. I felt myself uplifted by some divine power which plunged me into an infinite joy, an ecstasy both soft and tender. I would, I think, have given my life to have prolonged this phantasmagoria, when suddenly a shrill voice sounded in my ear, " Wake up, wake up! follow me! "

A withered woman took my hand and communicated to my nerves a horrible sensation of cold. Her bones could be seen through the wrinkled skin of her livid and almost greenish face. The chilling old creature wore a black gown trailing in the dust, and on her neck some white thing which I dared not examine. Her eyes, raised to heaven, left only their whites in view. She dragged me across the church, marking her path with ashes which fell from her dress. As she walked, her bones rattled like those of a skeleton. I heard behind me the ringing of a bell, whose sharp tones smote my ears like those of an harmonica.

" Men must suffer, men must suffer," she said to me.

We left the church and passed through the filthiest streets of the town; then she brought me to a dingy house and made me enter, crying out in a voice as discordant as a cracked bell: " Defend me! defend me! "

We mounted a winding staircase. She rapped on a dimly lighted door, and a man resembling the familiars of the Inquisition silently opened it. We entered a room hung with ragged tapestries, filled with old rags, old linen, faded muslins, gilded copper.

" Here are the eternal riches," she said.

I shuddered with horror as I now saw distinctly by the light of a tall torch and two wax tapers that this woman must have issued recently from a cemetery. She had no hair. I tried to escape; she moved her fleshless arm and circled me in an iron band armed with spikes. At her movement a cry broke forth from millions of voices, the hurrah of the dead, and it echoed round us.

"I will make thee everlastingly happy," she said. "Thou art my son."

We were now seated by a hearth on which the ashes were cold. The old creature held my hand so tightly that I was forced to remain. I looked at her fixedly, and tried to guess the history of her life by examining the habiliments in which she was huddled. But was she actually living? It was a mystery. I saw that she must once have been young and beautiful and adorned with the graces of simplicity, a Grecian statue with the virginal brow.

"Ha! ha!" I cried, "now I recognize you. Miserable woman, why did you prostitute yourself to men? You grew rich in the heyday of your passions, and you forgot your pure and fragrant youth, your sublime devotions, your innocent principles, your fruitful beliefs. You abdicated your primitive power, your supremacy wholly intellectual, to gain the powers of the flesh. Abandoning your linen vestments, your mossy couch, your grottoes illumined with divine lights, you have sparkled in diamonds, in luxury, and in lust. Proud, insolent, desiring all things, obtaining all things, overthrowing all things that were in your way, like a prostitute in vogue who pursues her pleasure, you have been

sanguinary as a queen besotted by will.   Do you not
recall how stupid you have been at times; then, suddenly, miraculously intelligent, like Art issuing from an
orgy?   Poet, painter, singer, lover of all splendid ceremonies, your protection of the arts was, perhaps, no
more than a caprice, the delight of sleeping beneath the
treasures of its magnificence.   There came a day when
you, fantastic and insolent — you who were born to be
chaste and modest! — you subjected all things to your
feet and flung your slipper on the head of sovereigns
possessed of power, and money, and the genius of this
world!   Insulting man, you found pleasure in seeing
how far human folly could go; you made your lovers
crawl on all fours, give you their possessions, their
wealth, their wives even — if they were worth anything!
You have destroyed without motive millions of men;
you have scattered them like sand-clouds before the
whirlwind from West to East.   You descended from the
heights of thought to sit by the side of kings.   Woman!
instead of consoling men you have tormented them,
afflicted them.   Sure of obtaining it, you demanded
blood!   And yet you could have been happy on a
handful of flour, brought up as you were to eat bread
and mingle water with your wine.   Original in all
things, you forbade your exhausted lovers to eat food,
and they did not eat.   Why did you push your madness
to excess and desire the impossible?   Why did you dote
on folly like some courtesan spoiled by adorers? why did
you not undeceive those who explained or justified
your errors?   The final day came, and you reached your

last passions. Terrible as the love of a woman of forty,
you blushed! you sought to strangle the whole universe
in a last embrace, but the universe, which was yours,
has escaped you! After the young men, the old men
and the impotent fell at your feet, and they have made
you hideous. Nevertheless, a few with eagle eyes
have known you and said to you with a look : ' Thou
shalt perish without glory because thou deceivedst, and
because thou hast broken the promises of thy youth.
Instead of being an angel with a brow of peace, instead of spreading light and happiness along thy way,
thou hast been a Messalina, loving the games and
debaucheries, and abusing thy power. Thou canst
not again be virgin ; a master is needful to thee. Thy
time has come. Death is upon thee. Thine heirs
think thee rich ; they will kill thee, but they will get
nothing. Fling aside those old garments that are out
of date, and become once more what thou once wert.
But no! thou hast committed suicide ! ' — Is not that
the truth? " I said ; " does it not tell your history?
old, decrepit, toothless, cold, and now forgotten so that
men pass you without a look ! Why do you live on?
Why seek to entice when no one desires to follow you?
What have you? Where is your wealth? did you waste
it? Where are your treasures? What have you done
that is glorious?

At this question the old woman rose on her skeleton
legs, flung off her rags, grew taller, full of light, smiled,
and came out of her black chrysalis. Then, like a new-
born butterfly, a tropical creature issuing from the

palms, she stood before me young and beautiful, robed in a linen garment. Her golden hair floated on her shoulders, her eyes sparkled, a luminous cloud was about her, a golden halo hovered above her head. She made a gesture toward space, waving a fiery sword. " See and believe ! " she said.

Suddenly I saw in the distance thousands of cathedrals like the one I had just quitted ; all were adorned with pictures and frescos. I heard delightful music. Around the structures millions of men were swarming like ants on an anthill. Some were endeavoring to save books and to copy manuscripts ; others were succoring the poor ; all were studying. Among these innumerable crowds were colossal statues erected by them. A peculiar light, projected by some luminary as mighty as the sun, enabled me to read on the pedestals of these statues the words : SCIENCES ; HISTORY ; LITERATURES.

The light went out. I found myself before the young girl, who gradually sank into her chilly frame, her mortuary tatters, and became once more an aged creature. Her familiar brought a little peat with which to renew the ashes of her foot-warmer, for the weather was cold ; then he lighted — for her who once had thousands of wax tapers in her palaces — a little oil-lamp, that she might see to read her prayers in the night.

" There is no Belief now," she said.

Such was the situation in which I beheld the noblest, truest, fruitfullest, and most gigantic of all powers.

" Wake up, monsieur, we are going to lock the doors," said a hoarse voice.

Turning round I saw the horrid face of the giver of holy water, who had shaken me by the arm. The cathedral was buried in shadow, like a man wrapped in a cloak.

" To believe," I said to myself, " is to live! I have lately seen the obsequies of a Monarchy ; we must now defend THE CHURCH."

THE EXILES.

PHILOSOPHICAL STUDIES.

THE EXILES.

IN 1308 only a few houses stood upon the tract of ground formed by the alluvial soil and sand of the Seine above the Cité and behind the church of Notre-Dame. The man who first dared to build upon this barren spot, so liable to frequent inundations, was a police officer of Paris who had rendered certain trifling services to the clergy of the chapter of Notre-Dame, in return for which the bishop had leased to him twenty-five perches of the said land, remitting all quit-rents and fees for the privilege of building.

Seven years before the day on which this history begins, Joseph Tirechair, one of the harshest police officers in Paris, as his name perhaps indicates, had, thanks to his share in the fines collected by him for misdemeanors committed in the streets of the Cité, built his house on the bank of the Seine, at the very extremity of the rue du Port-Saint-Landry. To guarantee the safety of the merchandise landed on the wharf the town had built a sort of stone abutment, which protected the piles of the wharf from the action of the water and the ice, and may still be seen on some of the old maps of Paris. The sergeant had profited by this structure to place his house upon it, and thus it happened that he was obliged to go up several steps to reach his home.

Like all the houses of that day, the little dwelling was surmounted by a pointed roof which overhung the façade, giving the upper part the shape of a lozenge. To the regret of archæologists, there are not more than two or three such roofs now remaining in Paris. A round opening lighted the garret in which the wife of the sergeant dried the linen of the Chapter; for she had the honor to wash for Notre-Dame, certainly no slight affair. On the first floor were two chambers, each of which was let, year-by year, to strangers for forty sous parisis (an ancient coin), — a great price, justified only by the luxury which Tirechair had put into their furnishing. The walls were hung with Dutch tapestries; large beds with testers of green serge, like those of the peasantry, were liberally supplied with mattresses and good sheets of fine linen. Each room had its heater, a sort of stove which need not be described. The floors, carefully kept in order by the laundry apprentices, shone like the wood of a shrine. Instead of mere stools to sit upon, the tenants had large arm-chairs of carved walnut, the spoil, no doubt, of some pillaged castle. Two chests inlaid with pewter and a table with twisted legs in each room completed an equipment that was thought worthy of the most eminent knights banneret whom private affairs might bring to Paris.

The windows of the two chambers looked out upon the river. From one you could only see the shores of the Seine and three desert islands, two of which have since been united and now form the Île Saint-Louis ; the third was the Île Louviers. From the other could be seen, across an opening of the Port Saint-Landry (the quarter called La Grève), the bridge of Notre-Dame with its houses, and the high towers of the Louvre, recently built by Philip-Augustus, looking down upon this poor, puny Paris, which suggests to the imagination of modern poets so many false marvels.

The lower floor of the house of Tirechair (to use the common expression of those days) contained a large room where his wife did her laundry work, and through which the lodgers had to pass to reach their rooms by a staircase as winding as that of a mill. Farther on was the kitchen and a bedroom, both of which looked to the Seine. A little garden, redeemed from the current, spread patches of onions and green cabbages at the foot of this humble abode, while several feet of rose-bushes, protected by stakes, formed a species of hedge. A shed, made of wood and mud, served as the kennel of a large dog, a necessary guardian for the lonely house. Beside this shed was an enclosed space where clucked the hens whose eggs were sold to the Chapter. Here and there on the barren ground, muddy or dry according to the caprices of Parisian weather, grew a few small trees, — constantly lashed by the wind, broken and defaced by loungers, — stunted willows, reeds, and tall grass. This tract of ground, the

Seine, the wharf, and the house, were closed in toward
the west by the enormous basilica of Notre-Dame, which
cast, at the pleasure of the sun, its cold, gray shadow
over them.   In those days, as now, Paris contained no
spot more lonely, no scene more solemn or more melancholy. The loud voice of the waters, the chanting of
the priests, the whistling of the wind, alone broke the
silence of this species of jungle, where occasionally a
few lovers landed to whisper secrets at hours when the
services kept the clergy in their church.

One evening in the month of April of the year 1308
Tirechair came home unusually out of temper.   For
three days past everything had gone on well in the
public streets.   In his quality of police officer nothing
annoyed him more than to feel himself useless.   He
flung down his halberd angrily, growled out a few dis-
jointed words as he pulled off his jerkin and put on a
shabby spencer made of camlet.   Taking a slice of
bread from the pan and spreading a layer of butter
upon it, he sat down on a bench and looked round at
his four white-washed walls, counted the joists of his
ceiling, took an inventory of his household utensils
hanging on nails, fumed at the evidences of a care that
left him nothing to complain of, and looked at his wife,
who said not a word as she ironed the albs and surplices
of the sacristy.

" By my soul ! " he said, by way of opening the con-
versation, " I don't know where you pick up your
apprentices, Jacqueline ! Look at that one," pointing
to a woman who was folding an altar cloth rather

awkwardly. "Hey! the more I look at her the more she seems to me a girl who is ready for mischief; she's not one of your good stout country wenches. Why, her hands are as white as a lady's! Day of God! if her hair does n't smell of scent! And her hose are as fine as a queen's! No, by the double horn of Mohammed, things are not going to my liking here!"

The woman colored, and looked at Jacqueline with an air that expressed both fear and dignity. The washerwoman answered the look with a smile; then she left her work and said in a sharp voice to her husband : —

"Come, don't make me angry. You need n't accuse me of any underhand dealing. Trot your pavement your own way, but don't meddle with what goes on here, except to sleep in peace and drink your wine, and eat whatever I put before you. If not, I sha'n't trouble myself any longer to keep you in health and happiness. I 'd like to know where in all this town one could find a man happier than that old monkey!" she cried, making a reproachful face at him. "He has money in his wallet, a house of his own, a trusty halberd on one side, and virtuous wife on the other, a home as clean, ay, as neat as my eye; and here he is complaining like a pilgrim burning with Saint Anthony's fire!"

"Ha!" retorted the sergeant, "do you think, Jacqueline, that I want to see my house razed to the ground, my halberd in the hands of somebody else, and my wife in the pillory!"

Jacqueline and the delicate-looking workwoman turned pale.

"Explain what you mean," said the washerwoman, "and let's see what you've got in your pouch. I have noticed for some days, my lad, that there was some nonsense in your head. Come, tell over your beads! You must be a coward to mind petty taunts when you carry the halberd of the *Parloir aux Bourgeois*, and live under the protection of the Chapter."

So saying, she marched straight to the sergeant and took him by the arm. "Come," she added, obliging him to rise and leading him out on to the steps.

When they were in the little garden and close to the edge of the water, Jacqueline looked at her husband with a sarcastic air.

"You had better know, you old vagabond, that every time that fine lady comes to the house a gold piece goes into our savings."

"Ho! ho!" said the sergeant, who became thoughtful and quiet when alone with his wife. But presently he began again, "We are lost! why does that woman come here?"

"She comes to see the pretty lad we have up there," replied Jacqueline, pointing to the chamber which overlooked the course of the Seine.

"A curse upon it!" cried the sergeant; "for a few miserable crowns you have ruined me, Jacqueline. Is that the sort of traffic the prudent and virtuous wife of a police officer should engage in? Be she countess or baroness, that lady couldn't pull us out of the scrape you will get us into sooner or later. There'll be a husband furious and powerful, for, by the Lord! she's handsome enough."

"There! there! she's a widow, you old goose! How dare you suspect your wife of wickedness and nonsense? The lady has never spoken to the young fellow; she is content to look at him and think about him. Poor boy! if it were not for her he'd be dead with hunger; she has been half a mother to him. And he, the cherub, he's as easy to deceive as a new-born babe. He thinks his poor pennies are lasting still, whereas he has eaten them up twice over in the last six months."

"Wife," said the sergeant, solemnly, pointing to the place de Grève, "do you remember the flames you saw the other day in which they roasted that Danish woman?"

"What then?" said Jacqueline, frightened.

"What then!" echoed Tirechair; "why, those two strangers we are lodging upstairs smell of fire likewise. There is no Chapter, nor countess, nor any protection at all against them. Here is Easter coming, and out of our house they go, and fast and quick, too! Do you suppose a sergeant of police can't tell a gallows-bird when he sees one. Our two lodgers kept company with that woman, that Danish heretic, — or Norwegian, I don't know which, — I mean the one you heard give her last shriek. Ha! she was a brave devil, she never quailed at those fagots; which abundantly proves her intimacy with Satan. I saw her as near as I now see

you ; she went on preaching to the crowd, telling them
she was in heaven and saw God ! I tell you that since
that day I have n't been able to sleep in peace. He
whom we 've got upstairs is more of a sorcerer than a
Christian. By my faith ! I tremble every time that old
man passes me. At night he never sleeps. If I happen
to wake up, his voice is sounding like the hum of bells ;
I hear him saying over his incantations in the language
of hell. Did-you ever see him eat an honest crust of
bread, or a roll made by the hands of a Catholic baker?
That brown skin of his has been roasted to a cinder at
the fires of hell. Day of God ! his eyes can charm you
like those of a snake ! Jacqueline, I tell you I won't
have those two men in our house any longer. I live too
near to Justice not to know that a man had better keep
out of her way. You are to turn our two lodgers out,
— the old one because I suspect him, and the young
one because he is too pretty. Neither of them seems to
have Christian friends, — they certainly don't live as we
do ; the young one is always gazing at the moon and
the stars and the clouds, like a witch watching for
midnight to mount her broom. The old sly one uses
that poor boy for some witchcraft or other, I am certain. I won't risk bringing down the fires of heaven
upon my head ; they must go. That 's my last word.
Don't flinch."

In spite of her despotism in her own home, Jacqueline
was dumfoundered by this indictment fulminated by the
sergeant against his two lodgers. Happening at the
moment to glance at the window of the room occupied

by the old man, she trembled with terror as she suddenly beheld that sombre, melancholy face and profound look, which made even the sergeant tremble, accustomed as he was to the sight of criminals.

At this epoch every one, little and great, clergy and laity, all trembled at the thought of supernatural power. The word " magic " was as potent as a leper to quench feelings, sunder social ties, and freeze the pity of all hearts, even the most generous. The sergeant's wife suddenly bethought herself that she had never seen her two lodgers do any act that proved them human creatures. Though the voice of the younger was soft and melodious as the notes of a flute, she heard it so seldom that she was now tempted to consider it a proof of sorcery. Recalling the extreme beauty of the lad's face, so pure and glowing, his blond hair and the liquid fire of his eye, she fancied she could perceive the snares of Satan. She remembered how for days together she had never heard the slightest noise from the rooms of the two strangers. Where were they during all those long hours? Suddenly other very singular circumstances crowded into her memory. She was completely terrified, and now believed she saw a proof of magic arts in the love which the rich lady bore to the lad Gottfried, — a poor orphan who had come from Flanders to Paris to study at the University. She put her hand quickly into her pocket and drew out four large silver pieces called *livres tournois*, and looked at them with a mixture of avarice and fear.

" That certainly is n't counterfeit money," she said,

showing the coins to her husband. "Besides," she added, "how can we turn them out when they have paid the rent in advance for the coming year?"

"Ask the dean of the Chapter," replied the sergeant. "It is certainly his place to tell us how to conduct ourselves with such extraordinary beings."

"Yes, yes, very extraordinary!" said Jacqueline. "See the malice of it! to come and plant themselves within the very pale of the Church! But," she continued, "before I consult the dean, had n't I better warn that noble lady of the risk she is running?"

Saying these words, Jacqueline, with the sergeant, who had certainly not missed his shot, re-entered the house. Tirechair, as became a man trained in the wiles of his business, pretended to take the unknown lady for an ordinary workwoman, — though the awe of a courtier in presence of a royal incognito was visible beneath his apparent indifference. Six o'clock was striking from the tower of Saint-Denis-du-Pas, a little church which stood between Notre-Dame and the quay Saint-Landry, the first cathedral ever built in Paris, and on the very spot, so the chronicles say, where Saint Denis was put upon his gridiron. Instantly the hour of day flew from clock to clock throughout the Cité. Then confused cries were heard coming from the left bank of the Seine behind Notre-Dame, in the region where the various schools of the University swarmed. At this signal the elder of the two lodgers began to move about his room. The sergeant, his wife, and the unknown lady heard the abrupt opening and shutting of a door, and then the

heavy step of the stranger sounding on the stairway.
The sergeant's new-born suspicions gave a deep interest
to the appearance of this personage, and his face and
his wife's assumed so startled an expression that even
the lady was influenced by it. Connecting, like all who
truly love, the alarm of the couple with the lad in whom
she was so much interested, the lady awaited with a
sort of uneasiness some approaching trouble which the
evident fear of her pretended employers indicated.

The stranger stood for a moment on the threshold of
the door to examine the three persons who were in the
room, and seemed to be looking for his companion.
The glance which he cast, indifferent as it was, troubled
the hearts of those present. It would have been impossible for any one, even a man of firm mind, not to
admit that Nature had imparted extraordinary powers
of some kind to this being, in appearance supernatural.
Though his eyes were deeply sunken beneath the great
arches outlined by the eyebrows, they were, like those of
a falcon, surrounded by such broad eyelids and bordered
by a black circle so strongly marked above the cheeks
that their balls seemed actually to project. Those magic
eyes had something unspeakably despotic and piercing
in them, which grasped the soul of a spectator with a
weighty glance that was full of thought, — a look both
brilliant and lucid, like that of snakes or birds, and
which paralyzed the recipients or crushed them under
the instantaneous communication of a great sorrow or
some superhuman power. The rest of his person was
in keeping with that leaden fiery glance, fixed yet mo-

16

bile, stern and calm. Though in that grand eagle eye
earthly tumults seemed in a measure stilled, the face,
lean and worn, bore traces of unhappy passions, and
also of great deeds accomplished. The nose descended
in a straight line so far that the nostrils seemed to hold
it back. The bones of the face were sharply defined
by the wrinkles which furrowed the withered cheeks.
Every hollow of that visage was gloomy. You might
have thought it the bed of a torrent, where the violence
of the rushing flood was proved by the depth of the
furrows that revealed some awful and eternal struggle.
Like the lines left upon the water by the oars of a boat,
broad folds of skin falling away from each side of his
nose, strongly emphasized the face, and gave to his
mouth, which was firm and without curves, a character
of bitter sadness. Above the tempest painted on that
face, the tranquil brow rose with a sort of valor, and
crowned it with a marble dome.

The stranger maintained the grave, intrepid bearing
of a man accustomed to misfortune and formed by nature to confront composedly a raging crowd, and to
look danger in the face. He seemed to move in a
sphere of his own, where he soared above humanity.
His gesture, like his glance, possessed an irresistible
power; his emaciated hands were those of a warrior;
if others must needs lower their eyes when his eyes
plunged into them, it was equally impossible not to
tremble when by speech or gesture he addressed the
soul. He walked enshrined in silent majesty, like a
despot without guards, a god without a nimbus. His

clothing added to the ideas inspired by the singularities of his countenance and demeanor. The soul, the body, and the garments harmonized in a way to impress even the coldest imagination. He wore a kind of surplice of black cloth without sleeves, which fastened in front and fell some distance below the knee, leaving the throat bare and without collar. The close-fitting tunic and the boots were black. On his head was a velvet cap like that of a priest, which encircled his forehead with a line unbroken by the escape of a single hair. It was the deepest and gloomiest mourning raiment that ever man put on. Were it not for the long sword hanging at his side from a leathern belt, whose clasp could be seen at an opening of the black surplice, an ecclesiastic might have greeted him as a brother. Though of medium height he appeared tall; looking into his face, he seemed gigantic.

"The clock has struck, the boat is ready, are you not coming?"

At these words, spoken by the old man in bad French and easily heard in the dead silence, a light movement was made in the other chamber, and the young man came down the stairs with the rapidity of a bird. When Gottfried appeared the lady's face grew crimson; she trembled, shuddered, and put up her hands as if to veil herself. Every woman would have shared her emotion at the sight of this young man, apparently about twenty years of age, whose form and figure were so slender and delicate that he seemed at first sight to be either a child or a disguised young girl. His black

cap, like a Basquebcretta, left to sight a white forehead, pure as the snow, where grace and innocence
sparkled and a divine sweetness shone, the reflection of
a soul perfect in faith.　The imagination of a poet
would have seen upon it the star which a mother in
some nursery tale, I know not which, entreats the
fairy-godmother to lay upon the brow of her infant
abandoned like Moses to the will of the stream.　Love
breathed in the golden locks which fell upon his shoulders.　His throat, a true swan's neck, was white and
charmingly round.　His blue eyes, limpid and full of
life, seemed to reflect the sky.　The features of his
face, the shape of his brow were of a delicacy, a tran-
scendence fit to enrapture a poet.　That flower of
beauty which in the faces of women fills us with such
speechless emotion, the exquisite purity of lines and a
luminous halo surrounding the adorable features, were
joined in delicious contrast with manly tints and a power
that was still adolescent.　It was, in fact, one of those
melodious faces which, though mute, speak to us and
win us ; and yet, if observed with attention, it was possible to detect a species of blight, caused by some great
thought or passion, in the fresh purity which made the
youth resemble a young leaf unfolding in the sunshine.
No contrast was ever more abrupt or more vivid than
that presented by the association of these two beings.
The sight was like that of a graceful fragile shrub growing in the hollow of an old willow stripped by time,
furrowed by lightning, gnarled, decrepit, majestic, the
admiration of painters, under shelter of whose trunk a

tender bush is growing safe from storm. The one was a God, the other an angel ; one the poet who feels, the other the poet who interprets, — a suffering prophet, and a praying Levite. The two passed by in silence.

" Did you notice how he whistled him down ? " cried the sergeant the moment the footsteps of the two strangers sounded on the gravelly shore. " Is n't that the devil and his page ? "

"Ouf!" cried Jacqueline. " I am suffocating. I never examined them so closely before. It is a great misfortune for us women that the devil can wear such a pretty face."

" Throw some holy water on him and you 'll see him change to a toad," cried Tirechair. " I shall go and state the whole thing to the authorities."

Hearing these words, the lady roused herself from the revery into which she had sunk and looked at the sergeant who was putting on his blue and red coat.

" Where are you going ? " she said.

" To inform the magistrates in self-defence that we are harboring sorcerers."

The lady smiled.

" I am the Countess Mahaut," she said, rising with a dignity which set the sergeant aghast. " Be careful not to trouble your guests in any way. Show the utmost respect to the old man especially ; I have seen him in the presence of your king, who welcomed him courteously. You will be very ill-advised if you cause him the least annoyance. As to my visits to your house, say nothing about them if you value your life."

The countess said no more and fell back into thought. Presently, however, she raised her head, made a sign to Jacqueline, and the two went upstairs to Gottfried's chamber. The beautiful countess looked at the bed, the wooden chairs, the chest, the tapestries, the table, with a joy like that of an exile who sees on his return the clustering roofs of his native town nestling at the foot of a mountain.

"If you have not deceived me," she said to Jacqueline, "I will give you a hundred gold crowns."

"See, madame," said the landlady, "the poor angel has no distrust; here are all his possessions."

So saying, Jacqueline opened the table-drawer and showed a number of parchments.

"Oh, God of Mercy!" cried the countess, seizing a deed which caught her eye, and reading on it: "Gothofredus Comes Gantiacus" — "Gottfried, Count of Ghent."

She let the parchment fall and passed her hand across her brow; then, unwilling no doubt to compromise herself by allowing Jacqueline to witness her emotion, she resumed her cold manner.

"I am satisfied," she said.

Then she went down stairs and left the house. The sergeant and his wife stood in their doorway and saw her take the path to the pier. A boat was moored close by. When the sound of her footsteps made itself heard, a man rose suddenly, helped the lady to seat herself in the skiff, and then rowed away at a pace which sent the boat skimming like a swallow down the current of the Seine.

"What a fool you are!" said Jacqueline, tapping the sergeant familiarly on the shoulder. "We have earned one hundred golden crowns this day."

"I don't like lords for lodgers any more than I do sorcerers. I don't know which of them are most likely to bring us to the gibbet," answered Tirechair, taking his halberd. "I am going on my rounds through Champfleuri," he added. "May God protect us, and send some street girl in my way with her earrings blazing in the dark like glowworms."

Jacqueline, left alone in the house, went hastily upstairs into the room of the old man to see if she could find some clue to this mysterious affair. Like men of science who take such infinite pains to complicate the simplest and most obvious facts of nature, she had already constructed a vague romance which explained to her thinking the meeting of the three personages under her poor roof. She ransacked the chest and examined everything, but failed to find anything extraordinary. There was nothing on the table except an inkstand and some sheets of parchment with writing on them; but as she could not read, the latter afforded her no information. A womanly sentiment carried her back to the chamber of the handsome young man, from the window of which she saw her two lodgers crossing the Seine in the ferryman's boat.

"They are like a pair of statues," she said to herself. "Ah! they are going to land at the rue du Fouarre. Isn't he nimble, the little darling? he skipped ashore like a bulfinch! The old one is like a stone saint in

the cathedral compared to him. They are going to the
old school of the Quatre-Nations. There! they are out
of sight. This is where he breathes, the poor cherub,"
she went on, looking round at the furniture of the room.
" Is n't he dainty and sweet? Ah! these lords, they
are made of other stuff than we."

Thereupon Jacqueline went down stairs after passing
her hand over the coverlet of the bed, dusting the chest,
and asking herself for the hundredth time, " How the
devil does he spend his blessed days? He can't
always be looking at the blue sky and the stars
God has hung up there for lanterns. The dear child
has got some grief on his mind. But why the old
master and he scarcely ever speak to each other I
can't make out." Then she lost herself in thoughts
which presently in her female brain tangled themselves
up like a skein of thread.

The old man and the young one entered one of the
schools which, at the period of which we write, rendered the rue du Fouarre famous throughout Europe.
The illustrious Sigier, the famous doctor of mystical
theology in the University of Paris, was just ascending
his rostrum as Jacqueline's lodgers reached the École
des Quatre-Nations held in a large low hall on a level
with the street. The cold stone floor was garnished
with fresh straw, on which a goodly number of students
were kneeling on one knee, the other being raised in
front of them to take down the improvisation of the
master in those short-hand characters which are the
despair of modern chirographic decipherers. The hall

was full, not with scholars only but also with the most
distinguished men among the clergy, the court, and the
justiciary. Learned foreigners, men of the sword, and
rich bourgeois, were likewise present. There could be
seen those broad faces, protuberant brows, and venerable beards which inspire us with a sort of religious
awe for our ancestors as they appear to us in the portraits
of the Middle Ages. Lean faces with brilliant sunken
eyes, surmounted by skulls yellow with the toils of a
powerless scholasticism (the favorite passion of the
period) contrasted with ardent young faces and grave,
inquiring old ones, with warlike heads, and the rubicund
cheeks of financiers. These lessons, dissertations, public arguments held by the greatest geniuses of the thir-
teenth and fourteenth centuries, excited the enthusiasm
of our forefathers and were, indeed, their bull-fights,
their opera, their drama, their ballet, in a word, their
whole theatre. The presentation of mysteries did not
come until after these brilliant mind combats, which,
perhaps, led the way to the French stage. An eloquent
improvisation which combined the attractions of the human voice cleverly managed with the subtleties of eloquence and a bold research into God's secrets, satisfied
curiosity, kindled the soul, and was in fact the theatre in
vogue. Theology not only included the sciences but it
was science itself, like grammar among the Greeks in
ancient times. It afforded a fruitful future to those who
distinguished themselves in these word duels where, like
Jacob, the orators wrestled with the Spirit of God. Am-
bassadors, umpires between sovereigns, chancellors, and

ecclesiastical dignitaries were among the men whose tongues were practised in theological controversy. The academic chair was the tribune of the age; and the system lasted until the day when Rabelais gave a death-blow to sophistry by his terrible sarcasm, just as Cervantes killed chivalry with a written comedy.

To understand that extraordinary age, and the intellect which created masterpieces unknown at the present day, and to explain it all to our own minds, it is enough to study the history and system of the University of Paris and examine the curious methods of instruction then in full vigor. Theology was divided into two Faculties: that of Theology properly so-called; and that of Decree. The Faculty of Theology had three sections: the Scholastic, the Canonical, and the Mystical. It would be irksome to explain the province of these various branches, since only one, the Mystical, is the subject of this study. Mystical Theology embraced the whole study of Divine Revelation and the explanation of Mysteries. This branch of ancient theology is still secretly held in honor among us. Jacob Boehm, Swedenborg, Martinez Pasqualis, Saint-Martin, Molinos, Mesdames Guyon, Bourignon, and Krudener, the great sect of Ecstatics, and that of the Illuminati have, at different epochs, faithfully handed down the doctrines of this science whose object has indeed something awful and gigantic in it. In these days, as in those of Doctor Sigier, it means the gift of wings to man to penetrate into the sanctuary where God conceals himself from human eyes.

This digression is necessary to the full comprehension of the scene which the old man and the young one had crossed the river to take part in. It may also serve to protect this study from the criticism of severe judges who might otherwise consider our story false or tax it with hyperbole.

Doctor Sigier was very tall and in the vigor of his age. Rescued from oblivion by the annals of the university, his face offers striking analogies to that of Mirabeau. It was stamped with the seal of eloquence, impetuous, ardent, and terrible eloquence. On his brow were the signs of a religious belief and a fervent faith, lacking, of course, to his counterpart. His voice was gifted with persuasive sweetness, a ring that was both clear and winning.

At this hour the daylight, grudgingly admitted by the leaded panes of the windows, colored the assembly with capricious tints, creating violent contrasts here and there by the mixture of light and shadow. Here, in a dark corner, sparkled eager eyes ; there, masses of black hair played upon by the light seemed actually luminous above faces which were in heavy shadow. A few discrowned heads, circled with a slender fringe of white hair, appeared in the midst of the crowd, like battlements touched by the moonlight. All faces, mute and impatient, were turned towards the doctor. The monotonous voices of the professors in the adjoining schools could be heard in the silent street like the murmuring of a distant tide. The footsteps of the two strangers as they drew near attracted general attention. Doctor Sigier, who was about to begin his address, saw the majestic old man standing at the entrance, glanced hastily about him for a seat, and seeing none, so great was the crowd, came down with an air of deep respect and placed him on the platform of the rostrum, giving him his own seat. The company greeted this attention with a murmur of approval, recognizing in the old man the hero of an admirable treatise lately discussed at the Sorbonne. The stranger cast upon the audience, above whom he was now placed, that awful look which uttered a whole poem of sorrows, and they on whom the look fell trembled with indescribable emotions. The lad, who followed the old man, seated himself on a step and leaned against the doctor's desk in a charming attitude of grace and melancholy. The silence grew intense; the doorways and even the street were crowded with students who had deserted the other classes.

Doctor Sigier was on this occasion to sum up in a final discourse the theories which he had put forth in his preceding lectures on the resurrection and on heaven and hell. His singular doctrines answered to the sympathies of his epoch, and satisfied the overweening desires for the miraculous which torture men in all ages of the world. This effort of a man to grasp an infinite which ceaselessly eluded his feeble hands, this last struggle of thought with itself, was a work worthy of an assembly made brilliant by the presence of many of the great lights of the century, among whom now shone the highest, perhaps, of all human imaginations.

The doctor began by simply recalling in a quiet tone and without emphasis the principal points which he had already established.

" No intelligence was the exact equal of another. Had man the right to arraign his Creator for the inequalities of the moral powers bestowed on each one? Without expecting to penetrate at once the designs of God, must we not consider it a fact that, by reason of their general unlikeness, intelligences should be divided into spheres. From the sphere in which the lowest intelligence works to that of the most translucent where souls perceive the path to heaven, was there not a positive gradation in spirituality? Did not spirits belonging to the same sphere comprehend each other fraternally in soul, in flesh, in thought, in feeling?"

At this point the doctor developed marvellous theories relative to the sympathies. He explained in Biblical language the phenomena of love, the instinctive repulsions, the keen attractions which disregard all laws of space, the sudden cohesion of souls who seem to recognize each other. As to the different degrees of strength of which our affections are susceptible, he resolved this question by the greater or lesser distance from the centres which the beings occupy in their respective circles. He revealed, mathematically, a great thought of God in the co-ordination of the various human spheres. In man, he said, these spheres created an intermediate world between the intelligence of the brute and the intelligence of the angels. According to him, the *divine* Word nourished the *spiritual* Word,

the spiritual Word nourished the *living* Word, the
living Word nourished the *animal* Word, the animal
Word nourished the *vegetable* Word, and the vegetable
Word expressed the life of the *sterile* Word. These
successive transformations of the chrysalis which God
imposes upon our souls, and this species of infusorial
life which from one zone to another is communicated
with ever increasing life, spirituality, and perception,
explained confusedly, but perhaps marvellously enough
for his inexperienced auditors, the movement impressed by the Most High upon Nature. Supporting
himself by numerous passages from Scripture, which
he used as a commentary upon himself, to express by
actual images the abstract arguments he was unable
to produce, he waved the Spirit of God like a torch
through the depths of creation, with an eloquence that
was all his own and in accents which persuaded his
auditors to conviction. Developing this mysterious
system, with its consequences, he gave the key of all
symbols, vocations, special gifts, all genius, and human
talents. He explained the animal resemblances de-
picted on human faces by primordial analogies and by
the ascendant movement of creation. He made his
hearers follow the play of Nature, assigning a mission,
a future to minerals, plants, and animals. Bible in
hand, and after spiritualizing Matter and materializing
Spirit, after showing that the will of God entered into
all things, and impressing respect for His minutest
works, he admitted the possibility of passing at once
by Faith from one sphere to another.

This was the first part of his discourse and he applied these doctrines by adroit digressions to the feudal system. Religious and profane poetry, the abrupt and startling eloquence of the period played a large part in this great thesis, into which the philosophic systems of antiquity were fused and out of which the doctor brought them elucidated, purified, and remodelled. The false dogmas of the two principles and those of pantheism were swept away by words which proclaimed the Divine unity and left to God and his angels the knowledge of ends, the means of which were so dazzlingly magnificent to the eyes of men. Armed with demonstrations by which he explained the material world, Doctor Sigier constructed a spiritual world whose spheres, rising gradually, separated us from God just as a plant is separated from us by an infinity of gradations through which it passes. He peopled the heavens, the stars, the planets, the sun. In the name of Saint Paul he invested men with a new power ; he showed them their birthright of ascending from world to world to the sources of Life Eternal. The mystic ladder of Jacob was at once the religious formula of that divine secret and the traditional proof of the fact. He travelled through space, bearing the eager souls of his hearers on the wings of his speech ; making them feel the Infinite and plunging them in the waves of the celestial ocean. The doctor likewise explained hell logically by other circles or gradations placed inversely to the brilliant spheres which rose to God, where suffering and darkness took the place of light and spirit. Tortures were made as comprehensible as joy. Terms of comparison were found in the transitions of human life, in its diverse atmospheres of pain and of intelligence. Thus the most startling fables as to hell and purgatory were elucidated as natural realities.

He deduced in a wonderful manner the fundamental causes of our virtues. The religious man, living in poverty, proud of his conscience, at peace with himself, steadfastly resolved not to lie in his heart in spite of all spectacles of triumphant vice, was an angel, fallen and punished, who remembered his origin, foresaw his recompense, accomplished his task, and thus obeyed his glorious mission. The sublime resignations of Christianity were portrayed in all their glory. He put the martyrs at their stake and stripped them of half their merit by robbing them of their sufferings. He showed their *inward angel* in the heavens, while their outward man was seared by the irons of the executioner. He drew a picture of angels among men and made them recognizable by certain celestial signs. He searched the inmost recesses of the understanding for the meaning of the word *fall*, which is found in every language. He recalled significant traditions to demonstrate the truth of our origin. He explained with the utmost clearness the passion existing in all men to raise themselves, to rise higher and higher, an instructive ambition, the perpetual revelation within us of our destiny. He forced his hearers to embrace at a glance the whole universe, and described the substance of God

as flowing with full banks like a mighty river from the
centre to the extremities, from the extremities to the
centre. Nature, he declared, was one and homological.
In the puniest atom as in the greatest work all obeyed
this law. Each creation contained in miniature an exact reproduction of one image, be it the sap of a plant,
the blood of a man, or the course of the planets. He
piled proof on proof; ever fashioning his thought by a
melodious gift of poetry. All objections he stated and
met boldly, while he himself arraigned with eloquent
interpellation the monumental work of our sciences,
and the superadded deeds of men, to the doing of
which society called into requisition the elements of the
terrestrial world. He asked if our wars, our misfor-
tunes, our degradations, hindered the grand movement
ordained of God for all his worlds. He caused a laugh
at human impotence as he showed how human effort
was everywhere effaced. He evoked the shades of
Tyre, of Carthage, of Babylon; he commanded Babel
and Jerusalem to appear; and among them he sought,
but in vain, for the wheel-marks of the chariot of civilization. Humanity floated, he said, on the surface of
the world like a ship whose wake is lost on the placid
level of the ocean.

Such were the fundamental ideas of the discourse
pronounced by Doctor Sigier,— ideas which he wrapped
in the mystical phrases and fantastic Latin of the
period. The Scriptures, of which he had made a special
study, furnished the weapons with which he endeavored
to hurry forward the march of his century. He hid his

boldness as it were with a mantle beneath his vast learning, and covered his philosophy with the sanctity of his life. At the close of the address, after bringing his audience face to face with God, after reducing the world to a thought, and almost unveiling the thought of the world, he contemplated for a moment the silent and palpitating audience; then he turned to the stranger and questioned him with a look. Spurred, no doubt, by the presence of that singular being, he added the following words, — here disentangled from the corrupt Latin of the Middle Ages : —

" Where, think you, can God obtain his fructifying truths if not from the bosom of God himself? What am I? The feeble interpreter of a single sentence bequeathed by the first of the apostles, a single saying amid a thousand others of a light as vivid. Before our time Saint Paul hath said : *In Deo vivimus, movemur, et sumus ;* in God we live, and move, and have our being. To-day we, with less faith and more knowledge — or less informed and more skeptical — we ask of the apostle : ' What use is there in that perpetual movement? Where goes the life which moves through zones? Why that intelligence, beginning with the confused perceptions of marble and rising, sphere by sphere, to man, to the angel, and to God? Whence its source? What if life, attaining to God through the worlds, through the stars, through matter and through spirit, were to descend again toward another end?' Ha! we wish to see the universe on both sides. We are willing to adore the sovereign provided we are allowed to

sit upon his throne for a moment. Fools that we are!
we deny to intelligent animals the gift of understanding
our thoughts and the object of our actions, we are without pity for the creatures of the spheres beneath us, we
drive them from our world, we refuse them the faculty
of guessing human thought, and yet we seek to know
the loftiest of all ideas, the Idea of the Idea! Then
go, seek, rise from globe to globe! fly through space!
Thought, Love, and Faith are the keys of mystery.
Traverse the spheres, approach the throne! God is of
greater clemency than you; he opens his temple to all
created things. But forget not the example of Moses.
Take your shoes from off your feet before you enter the
sanctuary; strip yourself of all that is unclean; abandon your body, or you will be consumed, for God —
God is LIGHT."

As Doctor Sigier with ardent face and hand upraised
uttered these glorious words, a ray of sunlight entered
through an open casement and flung across the hall, as
if by magic, a brilliant fillet, a long, triangular band
of gold which wrapped the audience like a scarf. All
present accepted this effect of the setting sun as a
miracle. A unanimous cry arose, " *Vivat! vivat!*"
The sky itself seemed to applaud. Gottfried, full of
reverence, looked alternately at the old man and at
Doctor Sigier, who were speaking together in low tones.

" Glory to the Master!" said the stranger.

" A fleeting glory!" replied Sigier.

" I would I could perpetuate my gratitude!" returned the old man.

"One line from you," replied the doctor, "would give me the immortality of earth."

"Can we give that which we have not?" said the unknown.

Accompanied by the crowd, who, like courtiers around a king, followed their steps at a respectful distance, Gottfried, the old man, and Sigier walked toward the muddy shore, where, in those days, no houses had yet been built, and where the ferryman and his boat were waiting. The doctor and the stranger conversed gravely in some unknown language that was neither Latin nor Gallic. Their hands were sometimes raised to heaven, and anon they pointed to earth. More than once Sigier, to whom the windings of the shore were familiar, guided the old man carefully along the narrow planks thrown like bridges across the mud. The crowd watched them with curiosity, and a few students envied the privilege of the young lad who followed the two sovereigns of speech. The doctor bowed to the stranger as the ferryman pushed off.

At the moment when the boat reached the middle of the stream and rocked upon the current, the sun flamed through the clouds like a conflagration, poured a flood of light upon the fields, colored the various roofs of slate and thatch with its red tones and brown reflections, touched with fire the tall towers of Philip-Augustus, inundated the heavens, dyed the waters, sparkled on the herbage and awakened the insects that were still drowsing. The long flame of light kindled the clouds; it was like the last verse of an evening hymn. All hearts must have quivered in response, for Nature was sublime. The stranger watched the sight, his eyelids moistened by the semblance of a human tear. Gottfried wept! his trembling hand sought that of the old man who turned to the lad and suffered him to see his emotion; then, as if to save his dignity, compromised by that single tear, he said in a hollow voice: —

"I mourn my country; I am exiled. Young man, at this hour I left my native land. There, at this hour, the glowworms issued from their fragile dwellings and hung like diamonds on the iris reeds. At this hour, the breeze, softer than sweetest poetry, rose from a valley bathed in light and wafting flowery perfumes. There, on the horizon, I saw the golden city, like Jerusalem the blest, — the city whose name must never pass my lips. There winds a river. That city, with its wondrous buildings, that river, with its ravishing perspectives, its heaven-reflecting currents mingling, parting, interlacing in harmonious strife, rejoicing mine eyes, inspiring love, where are they? At this hour, the waters gathered from the sunset sky fantastic tints and drew capricious pictures. The stars distilled a loving light, the moon laid everywhere her graceful lures; she gave another life to trees, to colors, to forms; varying the charm of glistening waters, of those mute heights, those eloquent structures. The city spoke, she sparkled, she called me back! Columns of smoke were rising beside that glorious tower that shone with whiteness on the breast of night; the lines of the horizon were visible athwart the evening mists, all was

harmony and mystery. Nature refused to say to me
farewell; she willed to keep me. Ah! that city was all
in all to me; mother, child, wife, glory! The very bells
lamented my exile. Oh, marvellous land! beautiful as
heaven! Since that hour the universe has been my
dungeon. Dear country, why hast thou exiled me! —
But I shall triumph!" he cried, flinging forth the words
with such a tone of conviction, such a startling ring,
that the boatman trembled, fancying he heard the sound
of a trumpet.

The old man stood erect in a prophetic attitude, his
face toward the south, pointing to his native land across
the regions of the sky. The ascetic paleness of his
face was replaced by a flush of triumph, his eyes
gleamed, he was sublime, like a lion when he erects
his mane.

"And thou, poor child!" he said presently, looking
down at Gottfried, whose cheeks bore a chaplet of sparkling drops, "thou hast not studied life like me upon a
bloody page; why dost thou weep? what hast thou to
regret in thy few years?"

" Alas!" answered Gottfried, " I regret a country
more beautiful than all the kingdoms of the earth; a
country I have never seen, and yet, which I remember.
Oh! had I wings to fly through space I would go — "

" Where?" said the Exile.

" ABOVE," replied the youth.

The stranger trembled at that word; turning his
weighty glance upon the lad, he silenced him. But
their souls communicated with effusion; they heard

each other's longing in the bosom of that teeming silence, journeying naturally together like two doves winging their way on the same pinion, until the grounding of the boat upon the gravelly shore roused them from their revery. Then, still buried in their thoughts, they walked in silence to the serjeant's house.

" And so," said the great stranger to himself, " that poor lad thinks himself an angel exiled from heaven. Who among us has the right to undeceive him? Is it I? I who am so often lifted above this earth by magic power; I who belong to God; I who am to myself a mystery? Have I not seen the most beautiful of all angels living on this base earth? Is the lad either more or less beside himself than I am? Has he taken a bolder step than I into faith? He believes; his belief will doubtless lead him in some luminous path like that in which I walk. Ah! he is beautiful as an angel, but is he not too feeble to bear the cruel struggle? "

Intimidated by the presence of his companion, whose awe-inspiring voice explained to him his own thoughts as the lightning interprets the will of heaven, the youth contented his soul by gazing at the stars with the eyes of a lover. Overwhelmed by a wealth of sensibility too great for his heart to bear, he was feeble and timid, like a gnat paralyzed by the sun. Sigier's words had brought before the minds of both the mysteries of the moral world. The grand old man might clothe them with his own glory, but the youth, though he felt their presence within him, had no power to utter them

All three expressed, each in his living way, the images of Science, Poetry, and Feeling.

When they reached home the old man shut himself in his room, lit his inspirer, — his lamp, — and gave himself up to the terrible demon of toil, asking words of silence, ideas of the night. Gottfried sat by his window, looking at the moonlight reflected in the water and studying the mystery of the heavens. He yielded himself up to an ecstasy of a kind that was familiar to him; he passed from sphere to sphere, from vision to vision, listening and believing that he heard the low murmuring of the voice of angels; seeing, or believing that he saw, divine lights, in the brightness of which he lost his way ever striving to attain a farther point, — the source of all light, the principle of all harmony. Soon the great clamor of Paris, borne along the current of the river, lessened, the lights went out one by one, silence reigned throughout the vast expanse, and the great city slept like a weary giant. Midnight sounded. The slightest noise, the dropping of a leaf, or the flitting of a jackdaw from place to place upon the towers of Notre-Dame, would have recalled the spirit of the exile to earth or that of the youth from the celestial heights to which his soul had risen on the wings of ecstasy.

At this moment the old man heard with horror from the adjoining chamber a moan, followed by the fall of a heavy weight, which the experienced ear of the Exile recognized as that of a human body. He left his room hastily, and entering that of Gottfried, found the lad stretched on the floor with a long rope fastened to his neck, the other end coiling on the floor. When the old man unfastened the knot, the youth opened his eyes.

" Where am I ? " he asked, with an expression of delight.

" At home," said the old man, examining with surprise Gottfried's neck and the nail to which the rope had been fastened, which was still at the end of it.

" In heaven," said the youth in a voice of joy.

" No, on earth," replied the Exile.

Gottfried rose, walked through the band of light cast by the moon across the room, the casement of which was open, and looked at the shimmering Seine, at the willows and shrubs of the desolate shore. A misty atmosphere lay above the water like a dais of smoke. At the sight, to him so grievous, he crossed his hands upon his breast with a gesture of despair. The old man came to him with amazement on his face.

" Did you mean to kill yourself ? " he asked.

" Yes," answered Gottfried, allowing the stranger to pass his hands about his throat and examine the parts where the rope had pressed.

Except for a few abrasions, the lad had suffered little. The old man concluded that the nail had immediately given way under the weight of the body, and that the fatal attempt had simply ended in a fall of no danger.

" But why, dear child, did you wish to die ? "

" Ah ! " replied Gottfried, no longer restraining the tears that filled his eyes, " I heard the voice from

heaven. It called me by name. Never before had it
named me ; but this time it bade me enter heaven !
Oh, how sweet the voice was ! As I could not spring
upward to the skies," he added, with an artless gesture,
" I took the only way we have to go to God."

" Oh, child, sublime child ! " exclaimed the old man,
folding Gottfried in his arms and pressing him to his
heart. " Thou art a poet ; thou canst ride the storm !
Thy poesy is voiceless in thy heart ! Thine ardent
thoughts, thy keen desires, thy creations live and grow
within thy soul. Go thy way, give not thy thoughts,
thy creations to the vulgar world ; be the altar and the
victim and the priest in one ! Thou knowest heaven,
dost thou not? Hast thou not seen those myriads of
white-winged angels with the golden timbrels, moving
with steady flight toward the Throne? Hast thou not
admired the snowy plumes swaying in unison at the
voice of God, like the crests of forests before a storm?
Oh, how beautiful is that limitless expanse ! tell me,
is it not? "

The old man wrung the young man's hand con-
vulsively, and they both gazed upward at the firma-
ment, whence the stars shed rapturous poems which
they both could read.

" Oh, to see God ! " said Gottfried, softly.

" Child ! " said the stranger suddenly, in a stern
voice, " hast thou forgotten the sacred instructions of
our good master, Doctor Sigier? If we seek, — thou to
return to thy celestial home, I to behold once more my
earthly country, — must we not obey the voice of God?

Let us walk, resigned, in the rough paths his powerful
finger pointed out to us. Dost thou not shudder at the
danger to which thou hast exposed thyself? Entering
the Presence without orders, crying ' I am here ! '
before the time, must thou not perforce have fallen
back into a lower world than the one in which thy soul
to-day is fluttering? Poor wandering cherub, bless
God who has made thee to live in a sphere where
thou canst hear the heavenly harmonies! Art thou
not pure as the diamond, beautiful as a flower?
Think ! if, like me, thou knewest naught but the
city of woe ! Treading its ways, long since my heart
wore out. Ah ! groping among the tombs for their
horrible secrets ; wiping the hands crimson with blood ;
seeing, night after night, those hands stretched out to
me imploring pardon which I could not give ; studying
the convulsions of the murderer and the last cries of his
victim ; listening to hideous noises and to awful silence,
— the silence of the father devouring his sons ; ana-
lyzing that laugh of souls in hell ; seeking some human
semblance amid the discolored masses that crime has
coiled together and distorted ; hearing words that living
man cannot hear without dying ; ceaselessly evoking
the Dead only to arraign them and to judge them ;
tell me, is that to Live ? "

" Stop ! " cried Gottfried, " I cannot look at you, I
cannot listen to you longer ! My mind wanders, my
sight grows dim. You light a fire within me which will
burn me to ashes."

" But I must continue," replied the old man, waving

his hand with a peculiar motion which affected the youth as it were by a spell.

For a moment the stranger turned his sunken, woful eyes on his companion; then he pointed with his finger to the earth; you might have thought that a gulf yawned before them at his command. He stood erect, lighted by the vague, uncertain gleams of the moon, through which his forehead shone resplendent as with a solar brilliancy. At first an expression that was like disdain crossed the gloomy lines of his face, then his look returned to its habitual fixity, which seemed to indicate the presence of some object invisible to the common organs of sight. Of a certainty his eyes beheld the far-off scenes hidden from our eyes by the portals of the tomb. Never perhaps did the man appear so grand, so mighty. An awful struggle convulsed his soul and reacted upon his bodily presence. Powerful as he seemed to be, he bent like the grass of the field beneath the breath of a coming storm. Gottfried stood silent, motionless, magnetized; an unknown force chained him to the floor; and, as often happens when our attention is diverted from ourselves, in battle, for instance, or in sight of a conflagration, he no longer felt the presence of his own body.

" Wilt thou that I reveal to thee the doom toward which thou wert advancing, poor angel of love? Listen. To me it has been given to see the eternal spaces, the bottomless abysses, where all human creations are swallowed up; the shoreless sea to which this great river of men and angels flows. Journeying among the gloomy regions of eternal punishment I was saved from death by the mantle of an Immortal, that vesture of glory granted to genius, — the which whole centuries of men obtain not, — I, poor mortal! But when my way I took through fields of light where congregate the Blessed, the love of a woman, the wings of an angel supported me; borne upon Her heart I could taste the ineffable pleasures whose enjoyment is more dangerous for us mortals than all the anguish of this evil world. Pursuing my pilgrimage across the gloomy regions of the nether world, I passed from sorrow to sorrow, from crime to crime, from punishment to punishment, from cruel silence to heart-rending cries, until I reached the upper gulf which circles Hell. There I saw afar the beacon light of Paradise, shining at illimitable distance. I was in darkness, and yet upon the confines of the Light. I flew, borne onward by my guide, propelled by a power like that which in our dreams transports us into spheres invisible to the bodily eye. The halo which encircled our brows swept the shadows from our path like impalpable dust. Far off, the suns of all the worlds cast forth a light feebler than the glowworms of my native land. I was about to reach the fields of ether where, toward Paradise, masses of light accumulated; the azure depths were soft to cleave; the innumerable worlds sprang forth like flowers in a meadow.

"Turning, I saw upon the last concentric line, where dwelt the phantoms whom I left behind me (like unto griefs we fain would cast away), a Shade. Standing

erect, in eager posture, that soul devoured the spaces
with a look; his feet were fastened by the power of
God upon the outer edge of that dark circle, where
ceaselessly they strained with cruel tension to spring
upward, like birds preparing to take flight. It was a
man; he did not look at us, he did not hear us. His
muscles throbbed and quivered; he seemed to feel at
every instant, although he made no step, the weary toil
of crossing that infinitude which parted him from Paradise, from the heaven to which his eyes were strained,
believing that they saw a cherished form. On that last
gate of Hell I read, as on the first, ' All hope must be
abandoned.' The wretched soul was crushed by such
dire force, I knew not what, that his pains seized my
bones and froze me. I turned for succor to my guide,
whose presence brought me back to peace and stillness.
Like the merlin, whose piercing eye sees or divines the
falcon in the air above her, the Shade uttered a cry.
We looked where he looked, and beheld as it were a
sapphire floating above our heads in the realms of
light. The dazzling star descended, rapidly, like a
sun-ray when the orb of day rises on the horizon
and sends its first beams gliding furtively across the
earth.

"THE SPLENDOR came nearer; it increased. Soon I
beheld the glorious cloud into whose breast the Angels
rise — a brilliant vapor, emanating from their divine
substance, lambent, here and there, with tongues of
fire. A noble head — the radiance of which I never
could have borne without the help of mantle, laurel

wreath, and palm, the attributes of Power my guide possessed — appeared above that cloud, white and pure as snow. It was a light within a light. The quivering wings left dazzling oscillations in the spheres through which he passed as the glance of God passes among the worlds. I beheld the Archangel in his glory! The flower of eternal beauty which adorns the angels of the Spirit shone upon him. In one hand he held a verdant palm, in the other a flaming sword; the palm to decorate the pardoned Shade, the sword to drive Hell backward with a gesture.

" At his approach we inhaled the perfumes of the sky, which fell like dew. In the region where the Archangel dwelt the air took on the colors of opal; it throbbed with the undulations whose impulse came from him. He reached the spot, looked at the Shade, and said: ' To-morrow !' Then toward heaven he turned with graceful motion, stretched forth his wings and departed through the spheres, as a vessel, cleaving the waters, withdraws its white sails from the gaze of exiles sorrowing on a desert shore. The Shade uttered intolerable cries, to which the Damned responded, from the lowest deep of that vast cone of suffering worlds up to the more restful circle at the mouth of which I stood. The most poignant of all agonies had appealed to every other ! Their wail mingled with the roaring of a sea of fire, — the bass notes of the awful harmony of innumerable millions of suffering souls.

" Suddenly the Shade took wing and flew through the City of Woe down to the depths of hell; then rose as suddenly, returned, plunged yet again into those bottomless concentric circles ; flew round them, hither and thither, like a caged vulture exhausting itself in useless efforts. The Shade had the right to wander thus ; he might cross those zones of Hell, glacial, fetid, burning, without undergoing the sufferings there endured ; he could glide through that horrible immensity like a ray of sunshine lighting up the gloom. ' God has not inflicted punishment upon him,' said the Master, ' and yet not one of the souls whose tortures thou hast seen would change his doom for the hope beneath whose anguish that Shade succumbs.' As my Master spoke, the Shade returned to his former station near us ; brought back by the invincible force which condemned him to stand upon the brink of Hell. My divine guide, guessing my curiosity, touched the hapless being with his palm. The Shade trembled ; perhaps his thoughts were measuring the cycles of anguish which lay between that moment and the ever fugitive ' to-morrow.'

" ' Do you ask to know the meaning of my misery ? ' he said in a mournful voice. ' Oh, I am glad to tell it. I am *here*, Teresa is *there ;* that is the whole of it. On earth we were happy ; we were always together. When first I saw my dear Teresa Donati she was ten years old. We loved each other then, without knowing that it was love. Our lives were one life ; I trembled with her griefs, I was happy with her joy ; together we gave ourselves up to the delights of thinking, of feeling ; and so from one another we learned to love. We were married in Cremona. Never did we see each

other's lips without the chaplet of a smile; our eyes
glowed ever; our locks were not less blended than
our wishes; our heads were as one when reading;
always our feet kept unison when we walked. Life
was an endless kiss, our home a couch. One morning
Teresa grew pale and said to me, " I suffer." And I—
I did not suffer! She never rose again. I saw her
sweet face change, her golden locks lose color, and yet, I
did not die! She smiled, to hide her sufferings from me;
but I read them in the azure of her eyes, whose faintest
quiver I could so well interpret. " Honorino, I love
thee!" she was saying at the moment when her lips
grew white; she pressed my hand in hers as death relaxed them. I killed myself; I would not have her lie
alone in that sepulchral bed beneath the marble sheets.
She is there, above, my Teresa; and I am here! I
would not leave her, and God has parted us! why then
did he unite us on this earth? He is a jealous God.
Paradise is doubtless lovelier since Teresa went there.
Do you see her? She is sad amid her happiness, for
I am absent! Yes, Paradise must be a desert to her.'
' Master,' I said, weeping, for I thought of my own loves,
' if he desired Paradise for God's sake only would he
not be released?' The Father of Poesy gently bowed
his head, assenting. Then we passed on, cleaving the
air; yet making no more noise than birds which sometimes fly above our heads as we lie prone beneath the
shade of trees. It was in vain to try to stop the blasphemy of that most wretched man, — one misery of
those angels of darkness being that they cannot see the

light, even when it is all about them. The Shade could
not have understood us."

At this instant the hurried tramp of many horses was
heard without in the deep silence. The dog barked ;
the grumbling voice of the sergeant called to him. The
riders dismounted, and knocked on the door with a
noise that sounded like a sudden explosion. The two
exiles, the two poets, fell to earth down the vast heights
which separate mankind from heaven. The painful
crash of the fall ran like another blood throughout their
veins, hissing, and driving in sharp stinging points.
Their suffering was in some sort an electric shock.

The heavy and sonorous tramp of an armed man and
the iron clanking of his sword, cuirass, and spurs,
echoed on the stairs ; then a soldier entered the presence of the surprised Exile.

" We can return to Florence," said the man, whose
strong voice sounded gentle as he uttered the Italian
words.

" What is that thou sayest? " demanded the old
man.

" The *Bianchi* triumph."

" Art thou not mistaken? " said the poet.

" No, dear Dante," replied the soldier whose warlike
voice expressed the tumult of battle and the joys of
victory.

" To Florence! to Florence! O my Florence! " cried
DANTE ALLIGHIERI, rising to his feet. Then he looked
through air and space, fancied he saw Italy, and became
gigantic.

" And I, when shall I go to heaven?" said Gottfried,
kneeling before the immortal poet like an angel at the
gates of the Sanctuary.

"Come to Florence!" replied Dante in a pitying
voice. " My child, when thou seest that adorable landscape from the heights of Fiesole thou wilt think thyself in Paradise."

The soldier smiled. For the first, for the only time
perhaps, the sombre and terrible face of Dante gave
forth joy ; his eyes, his brow expressed the happiness he
so gloriously described in his Paradiso. Perhaps he
heard the voice of Beatrice. At this instant the light
step of a woman and the rustle of a dress was heard
through the silence. The dawn was casting upward its
first beams. The beautiful Countess Mahaut entered
the room and ran to Gottfried.

" Come, my child, my son ! at last I may acknowl-
edge thee. Thy birth is recognized ; thy rights are
protected by the King of France, and thou shalt find a
paradise in the heart of thy mother."

" I hear *the voice,* the voice from heaven !" cried the
enraptured child.

The cry aroused the POET ; he turned and saw the
youth twined in his mother's arms ; then, bidding them
farewell with a look, he left his young companion on the
maternal breast.

" Let us go !" he cried in a voice of thunder. "Death
to the Guelfs !"